CRITICAL AC⌐LAIM

The Mastermind

"The corruption and hopelessness of modern Guatemalan politics interfere in the life of a womanizing lawyer in this engaging novel… Through the lens of Guillermo's doomed relationship, Unger successfully evokes the tragedy and futility of life in a raw and unforgettable novel." *Publishers Weekly*

"This novel by Guatemalan-born Unger offers a compelling portrait of a country shattered by government corruption, civil war, mass murder, drug cartels, ordinary street crime, inequality, desperate poverty, and even the effects of globalization…The rich but tragic sense of place Unger develops in this intriguing literary thriller will appeal to lovers of international crime fiction." *Booklist*

"*The Mastermind* teems with the pulse of daily life in the tropics: the sights and sounds, the smells and tastes. Unger takes millionaires, whores, provocateurs, hit men, bankers with deep pockets and political agendas and weaves them into a dazzling tapestry. What befalls those driven by hubris—the writing on the wall, a fall from the heights to the depths—are part of the pattern, the biblical tales of warning, the consequences that cannot be avoid…Unger is the poet of his complicated homeland…How fortunate we are that when Unger speaks for them, his words soar." *Valerie St. Rossy American Book Review*

The Price of Escape

"Evoking both Kafka and Conrad, Unger's character study of a broken man in a culture broken by a ravenous corporation makes compelling reading."

—Booklist

"Unger does a great job with fish-out-of-water situations, as [protagonist] Samuel's travails—sometimes Kafkaesque, sometimes Laurel and Hardy—nicely pit his timidity against his growing desperation."

—*Publishers Weekly*

"David Unger's tale utterly seduces with its mix of the exotic and the familiar."

—*Toronto Star*

"Unger's rendering of human contradiction is masterful, for in the space of Samuel's four days of awe, Unger reveals life's slippery terms of engagement in all their complexity with a clarity that still contains compassion . . . We can be grateful for the message of this wondrous book: despite our fears, even the least heroic among us can find the will to go forward."

—*Review: Literature and Arts of the Americas*

"David Unger spins a fascinating tale of weird redemption in The Price of Escape, leading us on a tense journey from 1938 Nazi Germany all the way to Guatemala. The sinister United Fruit Company casts a giant shadow over this vividly rendered landscape, devouring everyone and everything in its path. Unger has created a compelling protagonist in the flawed and anguished Samuel Berkow, a man on the run from his own demons and the terrible forces of history."

—*Jessica Hagedorn, author of* Dream Jungle

"The Price of Escape is a supremely well-crafted emotional and historical tale of a lonely Jewish man's flight from Nazi Germany to Guatemala, a supposed tropical paradise that is also cursed, and where he must carve out a new life."

—*Francisco Goldman, author of* The Art of Political Murder

IN MY EYES, YOU ARE BEAUTIFUL

IN MY EYES, YOU ARE BEAUTIFUL

A Novel by
David Unger

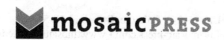

Library and Archives Canada Cataloguing in Publication

Title: In my eyes, you are beautiful / David Unger.

Names: Unger, David, 1950- author.

Identifiers: Canadiana (print) 20230221394 |
Canadiana (ebook) 20230221440 |

ISBN 9781771617161 (softcover) | ISBN 9781771617178 (PDF) |
ISBN 9781771617185 (EPUB) | ISBN 9781771617192 (Kindle)

Classification: LCC PS3621.N44 I5 2023 | DDC 813/.54—dc23

Published by Mosaic Press, Oakville, Ontario, Canada, 2023.

MOSAIC PRESS, Publishers
mosaicpress.ca
Copyright © David Unger 2023

Printed and bound in Canada.

MOSAIC PRESS
1252 Speers Road, Units 1 & 2, Oakville, Ontario, L6L 5N9
(905) 825-2130 • info@mosaic-press.com • www.mosaic-press.com

For Anne, as always...
For Fortuna, Mia, Zoe y Lisa: the strong women in my life...

To the real "Olivia."

Books by David Unger

Guatemala's Miguel Angel Asturias' National Literature Prize for Lifetime Achievement, 2014

FICTION

The Mastermind, Akashic Books (New York, 2016), translated into Spanish, Italian, Arabic, Polish, Macedonian, Armenian, Romanian and Turkish.

Vivir en el maldito trópico, translated into the Spanish by Javier Mosquera (F y G Editores, Guatemala, 2016)

El precio de la fuga, F y G Editores (Guatemala, 2013)

Para mí, eres divina, Editorial Cultura (Guatemala, 2023, 2014), Random House Mondadori (Mexico, 2011), Storytel (audiobook, 2016, Spain)

The Price of Escape, Akashic Books (New York, 2011)

Ni chicha, ni limonada, short stories in Spanish, F y G Editores (Guatemala, 2019, 2009). Recorded Books, 2010.

Life in the Damn Tropics, Syracuse: Syracuse University Press, April 2002, Paperback, 2004, Wisconsin University Press. *Vivir en el maldito trópico*, Plaza y Janes, Random House Mondadori) 2004. Audio: Recorded Books 2005; Locus Publishing, Taiwan, 2006 and Yingpan Brother, China, 2007

CHILDREN'S BOOKS

Jose Feeds the World (New York: Sourcebooks, 2023)

Sleeping With the Lights On, (Toronto: Groundwood Books, 2020; in Spanish 2023 Durmiendo con la luz puesta, (Guatemala: F y G Editores)

Topo pecoso/Moley Mole, (Miami: Green Seeds Publishing 2021)

La Casita, CIDCLI (Mexico, 2012)

BOOK TRANSLATIONS

Mr. President by Miguel Angel Asturias New York: Penguin Classics, 2022.

Folktales for Fearless Girls: Stories We Were Never Told, New York: Philomel, 2019.

Once Upon a Time: Traditional Latin American Tales by Rueben Martínez, New York: Harper Collins/Rayo, 2010.

Secret Legacy by Rigoberta Menchú, Toronto: Groundwood Books, 2008.

Old Dog by Teresa Cárdenas, Toronto: Groundwood Books, 2007.

Letters to My Mother by Teresa Cardenás, Toronto: Groundwood Press, 2006.

The Honey Jar by Rigoberta Menchú, Toronto: Groundwood Press, 2006.

The Girl from Chimel by Rigoberta Menchú, Toronto: Groundwood Press, 2005.

Me in the Middle by Ana María Machado, Toronto: Groundwood Press, 2002.

Bordes deshilachados/Frayed Edges by Anne Gilman, Matanzas, Cuba: Ediciones Vigia. 2001.

To Be What I Will Be by Silvia Molina, Madrid: Everest, 2001.

The Love You Promised Me by Silvia Molina, Willimantic, CT: Curbstone Press, 1999. Sor Juana Inés de la Cruz Prize in fiction, 1999. Finalist for Impac Prize.

The Popol Vuh version by Victor Montejo, Toronto: Groundwood Press, 1999.

First Love and Look for my Obituary by Elena Garro, Willimantic, CT: Curbstone, 1997. Sor Juana Inés de la Cruz Prize in fiction, 1996.

The Dead Leaves by Bárbara Jacobs, Willimantic, CT: Curbstone, 1993.

Antipoems: New and Selected by Nicanor Parra, New York: New Directions, 1985 (editor and co-translator).

World Alone by Vicente Aleixandre, Boston: Penmaen Press, 1981 (co-translated with Lewis Hyde).

Just Passing Through by Isaac Goldemberg, Hanover, NH: Point of Contact/Ediciones del Norte co-edition, 1981 (co-translated with author).

The Dark Room and Other Poems by Enrique Lihn, New York:
New Directions, 1978 (co-translated with Jon Cohen and John
Felstiner).

PROSE

"*Hanging from an Invisible White Hair*" in *Medium Magazine*, 2022.
"*Nicanor Parra, the Alpha Male Poet*" in the *Paris Review*, January
2018, republished in Spanish, French and German translation.
"*Gabo and Me*", *www.Guernicamag.com*, November 2007 and in
Letras Libres, Abril 2008.

(1970)

Olivia found an issue of *Vanidades* near the communal dining hall, stashed behind the box for kindling and the stinky barrel of garbage. At first, she didn't want to pick up the magazine because it was covered with cucumber peels and smelled of stale *Gallo* beer. But on the cover, surrounded by a halo of lights, a blond woman wearing a cowboy outfit and pointed leather boots smiled. She stood with her heels very close together and her left hand gripped the braided leather belt riding a half-inch above her hips. The buckle on the belt had silver and turquoise quarter moons. A blue Stetson, with Indian beads, sat securely on her head. Though six-year-old Olivia couldn't know this, the caption read: *You, Too, Can Be Beautiful.*

This woman embodied perfection, what Olivia wished she could become.

As she opened the magazine, the inside pages fell to the ground. Olivia was left holding only the cover in her hands. Then she noticed what should have stood out immediately—below the photograph, separated from all the words she couldn't read, she recognized the six letters of her name. O-L-I-V-I-A she whispered repeatedly. She realized they were *tocayas,* sharing a name, and she was sure that she and this other Olivia must have many other things in common.

Olivia bent down to pick up the fallen pages. They were not from the *Vanidades* issue, as she had at first thought, but the grainy photos of a girlie magazine. As she turned the pages, her mind focused on the cover—she tried to ignore the black-and-white newsprint cameos of women lying in bed, eyes closed or looking askance. These women had unshapely breasts, scant or oversized nipples, and opened their orifices with their fingers to the camera's eye. They were ordinary women, with faces marked by the hunger and desperation Olivia knew all too well. There was nothing noble about them. Still, she continued to turn the pages, in a kind of daze, still hoping to find more pictures of her smiling cowgirl.

Olivia looked back at the cover. That this woman had blue eyes and blond ringlets cascading from the sides of her head and Olivia herself was plump with plain features made no difference. The woman seemed to look straight at her, with soulful knowledge: and those stars flickering like sparklers above her head confirmed that Olivia Newton-John was the image of perfect beauty: Mary, the carpenter's wife, mother of Jesus, son of God.

Olivia heard footsteps approaching the dining hall. She quickly stashed the magazine back where she had found it, afraid to be caught with it and have someone tell her mother. As she hurried back to her hut, she burned the image of the cowgirl into her mind. Her feet barely touched the ground, she was almost flying.

*

Later that evening, Olivia curled up to sleep on her mat, smelling the coffee grounds in the tin pitcher and the tortilla bits on the griddle by the fire. Her three-month old brother Guayito was across the room with her mother, swaddled. Olivia was used to sleeping on the ground, with no door or glass to keep out the morning cold. Tonight she felt sure that soon she would be whisked away from this world of mud, gruel and numbing labor.

The starlet's image in her mind was real—with verifiable details, shape and weight; Olivia would one day claim it as her own. Like Princess Ixkik', the Mayan goddess of the *Popol Vuh*, Olivia had a secret. And just as the Princess had been tested, Olivia knew she would face challenges before her heroic destiny would be revealed. There would be rivers and fields to cross. Tricksters and villains to outfox.

One day she would get there.

Patience. She needed patience.

*

Hours later, she woke to the muffled sound of her mother's pacing. A stump of a candle barely gave off light.

"Mamá?"

"What is it?"

"My head hurts," Olivia said.

"Go back to sleep," her mother barked.

Olivia's mother worked in the fields with Guayito on her back or nursing at the breast; no husband to share the aches or the complaints. Only the pale memory of life in San Pedro La Laguna to sustain her.

But why was her mother annoyed? What had Olivia done wrong?

Her mother turned around and knelt next to her. Without looking into her eyes, she drew the back of her hand across her forehead. "You're fine." She rearranged the thin bed cloth over Olivia to cover her feet. She pointed to the candle and the altar behind her.

"I don't want you to get sick. Pray to *San Antonio del Monte*. I need you tomorrow in the fields."

Olivia nodded. Her mother often insisted on silent prayer. Before she could stop herself, Olivia blurted out: "Mamá, am I beautiful?"

"What a silly question." When Olivia had been born, her mother had discarded hopeful names because she had been born with olive skin and thick hair. Instead of blossoming into perfect babyhood, she seemed to grow darker and darker, more languid.

"Really, Mamá! Like the girls on magazine covers?"

Her mother couldn't understand where Olivia got her ideas. She brushed hair away from her face and looked into her daughter's anxious eyes. With a softer tone, she whispered the only words that occurred to her: "In *my* eyes, you are beautiful."

The cadence of her mother's words was pure music. This wasn't the answer Olivia had wanted, yet she was pleased. Her mother loved her, saw her beauty, even if extracting those words from her mouth required a great effort.

Olivia could sleep now. She saw her mother crossing back and forth in front of her, like a shuttlecock, with baby Guayito still asleep in the sling on her back. Below the hem of her mother's wrap-around skirt, Olivia could see her flattened feet. Her toenails were mud-covered and curled upward like tiny lamb horns.

God was cruel and capricious, delighting in the suffering of his people. Yet Olivia believed with all her heart that He, despite his unpredictability, would one day redeem her. God was like Anibal Cofinio, the coffee *patrón*, who showed no mercy to his pickers, but who could, in one beneficent gesture, give them a roast pig for *Noche Buena* or a dried fish for Easter. Cofinio was a wizard capable of chartering an old Bluebird bus so that his pickers could appreciate the carpet of colored sawdust and flowers the Antigua Indians placed on the *Quinta Avenida* to commemorate *Semana Santa*.

Olivia wiped her nose with the back of the hand and let her mind drift toward sleep. She wanted to re-enter the dream in which she rode a sun-powered oxcart like a chariot up through the sky into the vault of heaven. She would approach God's throne humbly, and her rags would be transformed into silk robes.

*

In the morning, after the 6 AM breakfast, she carried the coffee grounds and the breakfast waste to the trash barrel by the communal dining room. Of course, the magazine was gone, as she suspected it would be. She glared at the *zopilotes*—turkey vultures—grimly smiling at her from their roof perch. They had bare, elongated necks and a bib of feathers growing thickly on their chests. She was certain they knew who had taken the magazine even though they stared back at her mute and listless.

Did the God who made the blond Olivia make *zopilotes*? Was he clever enough to create creatures of such repulsiveness with the same skill as he made beauty?

Olivia bent down next to the barrel, clutching her Virgin Mary and baby Jesus medallion. The sky was lightening; she would have to hurry. In her prayers, she admitted her own worthlessness and the superior strength of He who had made her. She knew vanity was a sin—hadn't Hermano Pedro de Betancourt preached the need for selflessness and sacrifice in the face of God's glory and majesty? Prayers were for salvation: for the ill to heal; for the lost to find their way; for the humble to seek deliverance.

Olivia had visited Hermano Pedro's remains sealed in the eastern flank of the San Francisco Church in Antigua with her mother. On the wall containing his bones, there were shrines of ex-votos with crutches, drawings, photographs, and even small tin paintings depicting mishaps that had befallen his believers. The tacked-on messages thanked Brother Pedro for miracles that had saved them or their injured relatives. There were also requests for tools, a wagon or farm animals to ease the burden of living. With so many people petitioning for ways to lessen pain, how could Olivia ever ask him to make her beautiful?

If anyone could grant her wish, it would be the bearded and brown-robed monk, with arms hanging down and hands spread openly as if he had nothing to hide. He would see her need beyond vanity. Olivia had been born disadvantaged: poor where money mattered and naïve where slyness would have served her better. A good education might rescue her from despair. And as plain as Olivia knew she was, she hadn't been born crippled or disfigured. She only needed the slightest of interventions. It would really be easy for him to help her. For example, one day she could go to the banks of the *Río Pensativo* and see a colored stone mid river. Brother Pedro could make sure that when Olivia came out of the water, with the stone in hand, she would be transformed into a woman of startling beauty.

It would be recorded as the simplest of miracles.

(1972)

Olivia slipped her head out from under her cloth sash and sat down on a flat rock between the coffee bushes. Her neck ached fiercely. It wasn't only the weight of the sash hanging diagonally from her left shoulder to her right hip, but the fact that she had developed a rash on the side of her neck under the strap. The almost full sash needed to be emptied. She still had to finish her row and loop back down the next row before she could reach the hopper and weigh and empty her load. She touched her neck and felt the crusted scars. At least they weren't bleeding.

She and her mother Lucia had been picking coffee for nearly three years in the *finca* outside of *Ciudad Vieja*. Olivia no longer thought of the red berries growing in clusters under their shiny, green leaves as beautiful. In fact, she had grown to hate them. They were responsible for her stiff neck and the stems sticking out of the earth that pierced the skin between her little toes. What a source of misery.

Lucia was working ahead of her, almost at the end of a row. Her stumpy fingers twisted bunches of them quickly, in a single stroke, and then would pluck off the individual beans, discarding the stems to the sides of the path. She harvested three or four times as many beans as Olivia, dropping them cleanly into the basket she carried like a pregnancy about her waist.

Olivia was only eight and could continue to harvest beans in her sash until she turned ten. Every day she begged her mother to store the stems, not toss them on the path so that her feet wouldn't bleed.

By the time they stopped working at four, having been in the fields since six-thirty in the morning (they were given 30 minutes to eat lunch in the fields), Lucia would have met her quota. The contents of her basket were weighed and then emptied into a hopper. Later where the beans would be washed and sorted for drying the next day.

Olivia could hear her mother breathing heavily above the whistles of the *mot-mots*. They were almost done for the day.

*

That first year had been the hardest. The fields gave off a dampness that settled over the coffee fields for weeks at a time. It never seemed to disappear, even during the dry season. While sitting around the fire of their huts at night, the damp merely receded like smoke to the back of the fields. By sunup, it was once again surrounding them. Lucia often reminded Olivia of how boldly the sun rose over the mountains in the village of her birth on Lake Atitlán: how clearly the sunlight etched everything in San Pedro La Laguna.

"From the moment the sky lightened, you could see the treetops and also the boats tied to the wooden pier. The roosters crowed happily because they were grateful. Each day was a gift," she would tell her daughter wistfully.

Olivia nodded even though there was no way for her to remember.

What Olivia did remember was how hard it was working in the fields that first year. Her mother slapped her many times because she kept snapping the beans instead of twisting them off gently. They had been warned that if the shrubs were damaged, they wouldn't flower the next year and part of their compensation would be deducted—the coffee shrubs never died on their own, only from mistreatment by the pickers.

Olivia had been six years old back then. There were times she didn't care if the shrubs ever flowered again, if a storm rolled in from the sea and flattened them all. She would cheer to see the coffee beans flying away like speckled birds. How could something so beautiful cause so much pain?

The coffee shrubs were a curse.

After that first harvest, Olivia and her mother were told that they would rest for a month, let their cracked hands and feet heal. Of course, they wouldn't be paid to rest. Some of the pickers were chosen to tend to the coffee saplings growing in cans, while others were given a pair of sandals with rubber tire soles and the opportunity to go to Escuintla and Mazatenango to pick bananas. This much Olivia could be grateful for: Lucia made sure they never went there. The other pickers had warned them that the banana *fincas* were earthly hells: jungles ruled by unbearable heat, fevers and *lombrices*—worms—, a place where pickers died with their sandals still strapped to their feet.

Lucia said that no matter what, they would stay behind even if they starved. Luckily they were chosen to trim and prune the saplings so they would be big and strong and could be planted in new rows the following May.

*

Lucia told Olivia that they had come to the coffee finca because of her father. Melchior was a proud *ladino*, not an Indian, and because of him, Lucia would have to pick beans for just one harvest in the *cafetales*—coffee fields—around *Ciudad Vieja* before being promoted as a dryer. The work would become easier; that's what he had promised her. "Lucia, you will thank me for this," he had said to her, drunk with satisfaction, his eyes twinkling.

He asked her to imagine herself every morning drawing a huge wooden rake across a concrete slope above the fog line, making sure the beans were laid out flat. A few hours later, she would turn over the beans with the same rake, but mostly she'd sit on a chair in the shade of a ceiba and watch the beans dry in the cloudless October light. And when the sun was about to set, she would sweep the coffee beans underneath a canvas roof to protect them from an unexpected rainfall during the night. This was what he had promised her.

"Melchior was a cheat and a liar. And I was a fool to believe him."

That first year Melchior disappeared and Lucia was not promoted. The second year she got pregnant with a *caporal* who came into her hut and groaned. That was reason enough for her and Olivia not to have to go to the coast to pick bananas.

"Your father will never come back for us. And if he does, he won't have anything to do with me because of the bastard," she said bitterly, referring to Guayito.

Those first two years of picking nearly killed them. Olivia told her mother to have a third child. If she planned it right, she would be pregnant during the harvest and wouldn't have to work. Sleeping with the *caporales* was the only trick the women pickers could use to get out of working. What could be better than having the women fighting over them? The *caporales* were more than happy to oblige. At worse, the women pickers would have another mouth to feed.

Next year Olivia would be considered an adult and be required to fill up a 150-pound sack of her own. In another few years, when Guayito turned five, he could start picking beans with a sash. And if Lucia had another baby, he too would be a picker. It was all simple mathematics.

Though Lucia had come to the finca with no husband, that first year she didn't want to be ostracized for trying to steal one. In the small picker's village, this could bring trouble. Not that anyone cared. If the pickers quarreled with one another, they'd be less likely to come together and protest how they lived and worked. The *patrón* liked it when the pickers fought. To him, they were no better than goats.

In fact, they were goats.

On holidays, when they'd sit in the communal dining room drinking *atol de elote* and eating *tamalitos* or *chuchitos*, the older *Cakchiquel* women still wearing their *trajes* would bring the pickers together. They would tell them stories from long ago—*when the men worked their own plots and the wives stayed home weaving on back-strap looms, embroidering colorful cloth and caring for the house and the children. On Sundays, the men would put on white shirts and trousers, caites on their feet, and a Panama on their heads to go to church. Their wives would wear their fanciest* huipiles.

Heaps of copal would be burning on the church steps and in little dishes on the pine needles on the floor. The priest would complain to God on behalf of his people and the spirits of the dead would journey back from the underworld to be with their families. This would be their chance to tell their relatives whether they were comfortable in heaven and had enough to eat.

When the *Cakchiquel* women told this part, Olivia would imagine skeletons floating about the church. She couldn't figure out how the dead spoke if they were only bones and their tongues had fallen off years earlier.

And after services, all the women would stay and talk. The kids would run around the churchyard, playing tag or tormenting the stray dogs, and the men would go off to the cantina and get drunk. Sundays were the days that women would get pregnant, the elders said, giggling and covering their mouths with a piece of cloth. Sometimes—because of the alcohol—their husbands would hit them. Still they would say that it was a happy way of life.

However, those times ended. The men lost their ancestral plots and began working in the *cafetales*, alongside the women. To prove to themselves that they were still men, they would often visit the women brought in by truck on Friday nights. This was for the men still working the coffee fields.

Sometimes soldiers with rifles showed up and met with the men. Many simply vanished. Their wives suspected they had been forced to serve in the army. The *patrón* said that he would find out what had happened to their husbands, but most likely, they had volunteered to fight the guerilla bands in the mountains of Zacapa province. But the *patrón* never reported back—he was pleased that the men were gone—in this way, their wives would work harder, without distraction.

No one said it, but the women were thinking: What do Indian men know about guns and uniforms, bullets and guerillas? They never came back.

*

Olivia heard her mother working down the row next to hers and held her breath. She was entitled to sit and rest. Besides, her sash was nearly full.

Olivia couldn't remember her father's face. Lucia said that he was a truck driver from Sololá who used to make deliveries of soda pop to San Pedro La Laguna and the other villages around Lake Atitlán. He would give her a few bottles of *Fanta* and begin flirting—she was a pretty Indian woman, then, with a smile always breaking across her face. After they fooled around, the lies started. He lied about so many things that Lucia changed his name from Melchior to *Mentiroso*. "That's the perfect name for him because lies simply flowed out of his mouth," she would sneer. "For me, he's a white cross on the mountain road between Los Encuentros and Chichicastenango."

"But what did he look like, mamá?" Olivia would ask.

"Don't get me to talk about him, Olivia," her mother had said. "*Mentiroso* is dead."

"I want to see my father."

"All you need to know is that he was responsible for my leaving my family in San Pedro La Laguna. He had seductive eyes and a silk tongue." She got pregnant, brought shame to her family in the village and was forced to move to Sololá. Lucia gave birth to Olivia and they lived there for three years while he drove a truck from Puerto Barrios to the capital. He never spent more than a night at home.

"And all the time, I was less than 20 kilometers from my mother and father," she told Olivia. "Not even God, the Father, can find a way to get them to forgive me."

*

When the workday was over, the coffee in the basket and sashes were weighed on rusted scales before the beans were dumped into the hopper. The *caporales* wrote numbers down in their logbook. For some reason, the final weight always came up short. Lucia knew that she was entitled to receive three *quetzales* credit: two for her harvest and one for what Olivia picked—half a 150-pound bag.

Because the priests tell them that they must put their trust in the *patrones*, the pickers never challenge the calculations of the *caporales. You are the lambs of God and must believe you are being treated fairly*. But the older *Cakchiquel* women, those that can no longer work in the fields but are full of stories—the ones who describe how the Amazing Twins used their intelligence to defeat the wicked Lords of the Underworld--, tell the pickers that they have been cheated for years, decades, whole centuries, since life began. The *caporales* complain that the pickers pick too many beans that float and bob in the water instead of sink. These dead beans must be thrown out. They credit Lucia with 2¾ *quetzales* a day because they have to dump many of her beans even though everyone knows that this isn't true. If she were to complain, she'd be accused of inciting the workers to riot.

The pickers have learned to hold their tongues. *To speak is to accuse and to accuse is to be punished*. Father Perussina tells them that prayer, not protestations, will bring them to Kingdom Come. *If you trust in Him, then all your enemies will be turned back. After all, there is a final reckoning, the Judgment Day, when the good and the pure will be freed forever*.

"It is easier for a camel to go through the eye of a needle than for a rich man to get into heaven," he tells them gripping the huge gold cross in front of his brown cassock.

But Olivia prefers to remember the words of a song that Sister Carina once sang to her:

> *Oh, had I the wings of the dove*
> *I would fly away and join my love.*

Olivia wants to fly away.

*

Father Perussina insists that the congregation shouldn't speculate about what will happen to them today, tomorrow or the day after. Olivia likes to dream, but the priest once told her that dreams keep people from discovering the true message of God—only prayer, obedience and alms will improve their lives.

Olivia prays a lot but doesn't see any change. She thinks it's because she prays for the wrong things. Father Perussina said that *You must devote yourselves to God, for He knows better than we what will become of us. And we should not pray for silly things because it wastes His time.*

Olivia suspects that all her prayers are about silly things.

Both the priests and the *cofradías*—the Indian leaders—all agree that what will be has already been written by God. The pickers must learn to accept—they must learn to see their fate as a simple part of God's master plan. *The last chapter will be written in heaven when you are dead.*

But Olivia can't wait for death, to be a skeleton with a shriveled tongue.

"Knowledge is power," Sister Carina whispers to the young children during Sunday school, looking all around her, almost afraid that someone might hear her words. She teaches at a school in Antigua but spends Sunday mornings visiting the churches in the outlying communities.

Rather than simply telling them Bible stories, she is teaching the poor children to read. It's their only chance to escape from the fields.

*

Olivia stood up, realizing she had been sitting for nearly a quarter of an hour. Her mother must already be weighing her basket. She must hurry.

As she turned toward the final row, she remembered the dream about riding an oxcart all the way to heaven. It would have gold wheels, a painted carriage, lots of flowers and very soft pillows. She pictures herself seated in the middle like a princess.

This dream had not come true.

She remembered the time she found a magazine with a woman named Olivia on the cover. She had a special message for her, or so she had thought at the time. She could see it in her eyes. Because Olivia still trusts in her, she knows that one day she will be taken away from the *cafetal*. She can't say a word of this to Father Perussina or even to Sister Carina. Certainly not to her mother.

Olivia does not believe her father is dead. He will come back and save her. No man would abandon his wife and daughter to such a miserable fate. And he will save Guayito, too, even though he is not his son. *Through prayer, there is forgiveness*. He will forgive her mother.

One of the Indian women told her that Guayito's father was a *caporal*. She said that Lucia threw herself on him even though she knew he had a wife in Chimaltenango. The talkative old woman told Olivia that one day Guayito's father also disappeared. *Maybe he had crossed another* caporal *or cheated the* patrón. *So don't expect him to come back and take you away from here*.

Olivia's feet must be bleeding, she can feel the burning. She is walking down the final row, snapping up handfuls of coffee beans just like her mother. In an instant, she has learned how to harvest beans and toss the stems into the mud. As she hurries along she realizes that no doubt she will be saved, that this excruciating work is not her destiny.

But when?

One day she will fly away from the finca on the tail of a kite or the string of a balloon. She can't say for sure when that will happen. Perhaps if she fills her lungs with enough air, she'll rise up and float away over the mountains to a place where there are no coffee fields and garbage dumps.

Through prayer, there is salvation.

But the sun has vanished over the mountains and the shadows of the *chalum* trees shading the coffee bushes in the valley have grown longer.

The *gegene* worms that like the coolness of the late afternoon will soon come out and bite their feet.

Olivia takes a deep breath and hurries along twisting off the berries. Her wrist are sore. If it's not one thing, it's another.

She suddenly grows afraid that her Mother will beat her if she doesn't make it soon to the weighing station with her sash full.

Olivia will not disappoint her mother.

(1973)

When she was done working in the fields, before having to help her mother at home, Olivia liked to walk down the *caminito* to a creek at the bottom of a ravine. The *caminito* led from the back of the communal dining hall past a small clearing where a tin-roofed hut had been built. It was a plain pine plank shack, with braided wire for a door handle and a small-framed window. One Friday afternoon, Olivia saw a girl with small eyes and broad lips staring out the window. They looked at each other for a brief second before the girl pulled her head back into the hut's darkness.

Olivia had heard stories that there were young women, hardly more than girls, who were driven out on weekends to be with the men since the nearest brothel was in Chimaltenango 30 kilometers away. She had heard her own mother say that the *caporales* were sure to bring in a different girl each week. "We work as hard as the men, but no one thinks of our entertainment. They're allowed to drink like *bolos* and have their fun."

At first, these girls had been brought in for the unmarried workers or those who had left their families in Indian villages hundreds of kilometers away. But now all the men who picked coffee in the *cafetales* visited them. These were the same men who never had money for cheese or chicken, but always had *cincuenta centavos* for *aguardiente* or for a visit to the hut.

*

That Friday, as Olivia walked quickly past the shack holding her breath, a line of men sat on a fallen trunk, bottles in hand, waiting their turn. They wouldn't meet her eyes. She felt awkward, oddly complicit, a witness to their deception.

Once past the clearing, she took a deep breath as if the fresh air could provide her with a gentle cleansing.

Olivia found her favorite spot by the creek and sat there listening to the water passing softly over the rocks. She had brought in her *morral* the two Walt Disney picture books that Sister Carina had given her weeks earlier.

Though Olivia had never been to school, Sister Carina taught her and the other children the alphabet at the Sunday school in Ciudad Vieja. All 32 Spanish letters. To practice, Olivia spent hours repeating the letters and visualizing them in her mind. She even did this as she picked coffee beans, swept the floor of the hut or washed dishes at the *pila*. By repeating the letters under her breath and looking at the Disney books, Olivia was beginning to read by herself. Sister Carina would be surprised.

Like the *Vanidades* magazine, Olivia kept her reading a secret, especially from her mother whose reaction, she figured, would be critical.

Alone now, Olivia pulled one of the books out of *morral* and began reading aloud *El Pato Donald y su trencito—Donald Duck's Toy Train*, sounding out each syllable though she had no idea what purpose a train might serve.

Sister Carina was making her way through the woods to the small plantation church near *San Antonio Aguas Calientes*. She hated walking along this *caminito* that passed by these men who believed that paradise awaited them inside the shack. But it was the most direct path and its frequent use made it safer. The sister was mumbling her latest prayer for the souls of these men and for the poor girls forced to service them when she heard a slow dull sound ahead.

Sister Carina was surprised to see Olivia sitting cross-legged on a mahogany stump and reading aloud:

El Pato Donald tenía en el patio de su casa un trencito nuevo. Un día, Donald se ocupaba en poner nuevos tramos de rieles, cuando de pronto se encontró con un árbol muy grande.

She couldn't believe her ears. "Olivia, you can read!"

Startled, Olivia glanced at the nun and her dark eyes filled with tears. "Oh Sister Carina, please don't tell my mother," she begged.

"Why wouldn't I do that?" Sister Carina was in her sixties, gray and bespectacled, but she had the high trilling voice of a schoolgirl.

Maybe the years of teaching in the lower school had frozen her voice at a childlike pitch. Unlike the other nuns, for whom tending to the needs of the poor was a burden that distracted them from prayers of penance and devotion, Sister Carina actually enjoyed human contact. "You surprise me, *m'hija*."

Olivia looked helpless. "I'm reading one of the books you gave me."

"Child, I can see that. But who taught you? How did it happen? I don't understand." She sat on the stump, spreading her black habit over it, and pulled Olivia down on her lap.

Olivia started to cry. Her tears ran down her brown face. Sister Carina put her arms around her. Olivia was all skin and bones, except for her distended belly, which stuck out like a soccer ball. Surely, a *lombriz* or tapeworm was curled up inside there.

"I'm not angry with you, Olivia. Just surprised."

Olivia dropped the book and rubbed her eyes with both hands. "I only repeated the letters you wrote on the board. After a while, I started to see how they connected to make words."

"Give me an example," Sister Carina asked kindly.

"Like *casa*. I took the letter that sounded like "k" and joined it with the "a" and then the "s" and then the "a". I didn't mean to do anything wrong."

Sister Carina rocked Olivia in her arms—she knew that this child was used to her mother's constant reprimands. "You should be in school, *m'hija*. You're wasting your time in the fields...I'm going to speak to Lucia about this."

"Please don't," Olivia pleaded.

Sister Carina kissed her on the head. "I will discuss it with her Sunday after services. You should be studying. You're wasting away working in the fields." Sister Carina helped her up and put her books back into her *morral*. She took Olivia by the hand and they began walking back toward the coffee *finca*. Olivia couldn't stop whimpering, certain that her mother would be livid at the proposal that her daughter not work alongside her. Guayito was only three and a slow walker. How would her mother survive without Olivia's quota of coffee beans?

As they walked by the tin-roofed shack, Sister Carina picked Olivia up and folded her face into her chest. She hurried by the men who stood up and turned away from her in embarrassment.

When they reached the communal dining room, Sister Carina gave Olivia a kiss. "Child, you shouldn't worry. This is something good. I know how to talk to your mother." She put her down and again took the path back to the plantation church near *San Antonio Aguas Calientes*.

*

Two days later, after Sunday services, Sister Carina hurried over to catch Lucia as she was leaving the church. She was nearly out of breath as she told Olivia's mother her idea. She wanted to sponsor her daughter's studies at the *Colegio Parroquial* in Antigua. Olivia would attend classes and daily prayer services; she would sleep in a dormitory with the other boarders. She would be clothed and given all her meals. See a doctor regularly. There would be a future for her.

Lucia was puzzled by Sister Carina's sudden interest in her daughter. What right did she have to interfere in her life? "Yes, well, the church has its interests, but I have mine. Olivia has no need for school. Besides, I need her in the fields."

"That's a waste of time," Sister Carina said flatly. "She could be learning things that one day soon would give her a future—and permit you to stop picking coffee."

Lucia laughed. "We must appear so stupid to you. We are lied to by our *patrones* and offered silly dreams by our Church. I've made myself clear—I need my daughter with me."

"On Saturdays, after morning classes, she'll come home to you," Sister Carina explained. "She won't need to return to school until Sunday night, in time for six o'clock mass. You will see a lot of her."

"And who will help me pick?"

"Lucia, think how much easier it will be having one less mouth to feed."

"I see Olivia as two more hands to work. Besides, I need her around the house. She watches Guayito when I tend the corn patch or wash clothes. No, her leaving is out of the question."

"Perhaps you would prefer for me to take this up with Father Perussina or don Cofinio?" Sister Carina was not above using all the weapons at her disposal to deal with stubbornness. She had butted up against much stronger individuals within the church than her own congregants.

Father Perussina was a fool, but Lucia knew that if Sister Carina spoke to don Cofinio she might lose her job and her home. People with power all spoke the same language and belonged to the same private fraternity, whether they were rich landowners, Church leaders or simple Catholic practitioners. In practical terms, Lucia and her children were slaves to the fields. The fantasy that God was in the earth, air, water and sky and would respond to prayers was a lie set in motion by people who wanted the destitute to stay as they were. The poor are born poor and expected to stay poor. They will inherit the earth, but the piece parceled out to them will be dry and barren, unable to grow anything but spurs.

It was all part of a grand deception!

Lucia had left San Pedro La Laguna and gone to Sololá with her mind filled with Melchior's dreams. She had no idea that her future life would be cursed. She had been the victim of multiple seductions and had ended up with a dirt floor shack, two children and no husband to care for her. She was indentured to a coffee plantation that had been offered to her as the way to escape the hopeless life and dreams of her unambitious parents on Lake Atitlán. And it had all turned to rot.

The die had been cast long ago and Lucia knew she had no choice. Her face was one of surrender and Sister Carina could tell, to her relief, that she wouldn't be forced to appeal to the higher-ups to get her way. She disliked forcing her ideas on people with fewer resources than her, but she understood the limits of repeating the simple entreaties and mindless homilies that her own church promoted. "I will come and pick her up on Monday morning."

"But she has no clothes," Lucia protested.

"She won't need them. The school will give her blue uniforms, white blouses and black leather shoes."

"And what about me?"

Sister Carina looked at her with expressionless eyes. "Lucia, Sunday school is about to begin. I have to go back to the children."

Sister Carina pulled out a twenty-quetzal bill from her habit and gave it to Olivia's mother. "There's something else, Lucia."

"And what could that possibly be?" Lucia snarled, putting the bill in her blouse.

"Don't take your anger out on the child. I will examine her on Monday for bruises. This is a threat, not a warning." And she turned around and left without another word.

That afternoon, when Olivia came back from church, her mother wouldn't talk to her. At one point, Olivia tried to touch her mother's hand, but Lucia recoiled as if pricked by a knife.

Olivia knew that Sister Carina had spoken to her mother, and that she wasn't pleased. This was a harsh early lesson for Olivia: *to move ahead, you betray loved ones.*

Silence and betrayal is what going to school meant to Olivia.

(1973)

One hundred and twenty girls studied in the *Colegio Parroquial*, a two-story building off of *Calle del Desengaño* near La Merced Church. The Sisters of Mercy had opened the school in the early 50's during the Arbenz' regime to show their support for the president's campaign to extend educational opportunities to the poor. The nuns wanted to offer hope to people who had experienced mostly servitude. But by 1960, six years after Arbenz's overthrow, the experiment was over. As the poorer students graduated, wealthier girls replaced them. The school became a benign reformatory for middle-and upper-class girls between the ages of eight and eighteen, who couldn't, or wouldn't, attend private or parochial schools and live at home. The *Colegio Parroquial* was a mere 35 kilometers from the capital; it offered traditional and rigorous instruction, with a strong moral and religious underpinning.

Before enrolling Olivia in the school, Sister Carina took her to Doctor Elias Porrua Madrid who ran his practice out of a colonial house facing the Convento de Santa Clara. He was a kindly doctor, trained in Boston, accustomed to treating rich native families and the several dozen American and German expatriates who made Antigua their home. He knew about neurasthenia, insomnia, migraines, and variant forms of arthritis and had, on occasion, put casts on fractured bones. He was proud that no patient had ever died on him--he had conquered death and achieved a muted form of immortality by refusing to treat illnesses he felt were beyond his domain.

He abhorred the thought of surgery.

When he offered to tend to the *Colegio Parroquial* girls, it was understood that he would be treating sprains and minor infections—earaches, sore throats—that affected well-to-do girls living in a damp climate. Dr. Madrid was adept at using a flashlight to look inside ears and scour throats for signs of infection. If the girls developed something more serious, they were sent to Dr. Héctor Sánchez, a licensed surgeon.

Olivia's rags repelled Dr. Madrid. Perhaps he should've had her bathe before examining her though that would've meant having her use the tub in his own home. He was repulsed by the image of dirt filming the porcelain. He asked Sister Carina to wait in his office and he directed Olivia to undress behind a Japanese screen while he donned a pair of rubber gloves. "And put on the gown that's on the chair. Come back when you're ready and lie down here," he said, pointing to the black examination table.

Olivia did as she was told. She felt nervous to be alone with a man. Aware of her nakedness under the gown, she covered her sex with her hands.

"Face up, please. And put your hands at your sides."

Dr. Madrid stepped over to her, squeezed her arms and legs looking for fractures.

"Any pain?"

"No."

He then pressed the palm of his hand into the pit of her stomach.

Olivia let out a whelp. Tears leaked out of the corners of her eyes.

Dr. Madrid took off his gloves. He went to his desk and wrote a few words on a notepad. Then he came back to Olivia who had remained prostrate.

He moved his hands gently over her distended belly. "Is your *popo* soft and smelly?"

Olivia didn't know how to answer him. *Popo* is always smelly, she thought. And it comes out in scummy streams. How could she say this and not have her tongue trip over itself? She glanced at the doctor's photograph of lava flowing down the sides of the Pacaya Volcano. "Well, usually it comes out just like that."

Doctor Madrid smiled. "Very aptly put, my young girl." He paused. "You can get dressed now and go sit with Sister Carina in my office."

The doctor opened a huge black volume he kept on a lectern and spent several minutes turning the pages. Medicine, if practiced correctly, he mused, could be a most pleasant profession. He didn't believe in tests: if you considered symptoms, no stool sample or blood work was required.

He closed the book with a thump and walked over to his office. "As I suspected, my good Sister," Dr. Madrid crowed, "This young girl has scurvy, worms and amoebas. Fresh fruits, vegetables and vitamin C supplements will cure the scurvy. Here's a prescription to treat the intestinal worms and amoebas. You'll notice a change within a week. She will be perfectly healthy within the month."

Olivia felt embarrassed. She had never been the object of speculation. People either spoke directly to her or not at all. She couldn't look either Sister Carina or the doctor in the face. She wanted to run all the way back to the *cafetal* and resume her old life. She would be happy to simply walk down the path between the coffee shrubs placing red berries in her sack. She preferred monotony and the weight of the sack pulling on her shoulders to being scrutinized.

She had not asked for this.

*

It was mid-year. Olivia was placed in a third-floor dorm with eleven other girls. The beds had straw-filled mattresses and pillows, and a woolen San Francisco del Alto blanket on top. A pewter cross was nailed on each headboard and small runners, where the children genuflected and prayed before going off to sleep, lined the beds.

Olivia had never slept in a bed. She was used to her straw *petate* on the ground covered with a thin cotton cloth. Her first instinct was to lie down on the rug.

"When it gets very cold in January, don't expect them to give you another blanket," said Jimena Chang. She'd been pulled out of class to welcome Olivia, who was assigned the bed next to hers so that they might be friends. Olivia later learned that Jimena was the only other Antigua girl in her grade.

Jimena had nutty brown skin, like Olivia, and a flurry of dark moles on her neck and back. Some of the moles were quite large—like flattened coffee beans on her skin.

Jimena sat on Olivia's bed. She was constantly pushing up with the back of her left hand her dark framed glasses, which kept slipping from the bridge to the end of her nose as she talked. "I've complained so many times—do you know who my father is?"

Olivia shook her head. She was in a state of panic. Worse: Dr. Madrid had given her two pills for the amoebas and she felt her stomach churning and rolling over.

"Arturo Chang. Everyone calls him *Chino*. We own *Almacén La Fe* in the plaza—the one with the big green door and two yellow windows at the sides. The school buys all their sheets and blankets from my father's store. Towels, too. You must know it."

Olivia nodded.

Jimena snorted. "Do you even talk?"

"I've walked by the store many times," Olivia lied.

"My mother is Salvadora Bonilla Urrutia, daughter of one of the richest men in Los Aposentos!"

The teachers liked Jimena, with her brown eyes swimming behind her thick lenses, because she was quiet and studious in the classroom. They didn't know she was a terror to the boarders because she knew her way around Antigua and was *valiante*—cocky—despite her queer appearance. "You look Indian. From Chi Chi or Santa Cruz del Quiché!"

"No we're from—"

"Ah, Mazatenango. You're from Mazatenango," said Jimena bouncing up and down on Olivia's bed. It seemed that the whole world was her very own trampoline.

Olivia knew the limits of lying. "We live in Ciudad Vieja, but my parents are originally from San Pedro La Laguna."

Jimena sat on her bed. "Ciudad Vieja is uglier than any town on the moon, don't you think? All the buildings are made of shit-colored adobe. Why won't they paint them? *Because they're too cheap to buy limestone!* Hey, do you want to go with me to my father's store?"

"Sister Carina told me we weren't allowed to leave school."

"Not now, stupid. Later, when the nuns are praying or napping. Besides, three quarters of them are practically blind. Didn't you notice how thick their glasses are? If you want to know the truth, we boarders run the school," Jimena said defiantly.

"Where are the other girls?" Olivia asked, her voice cracking from sheer nerves and the stomach cramps. She was sure that Jimena could see how flustered she was.

"Still in class. Sister Carina asked me to come up and welcome you. Most of the girls here are creeps. I'll introduce you to the good ones. Stick with me and I'll make sure you join *Las Valentinas*. It's our secret club." Jimena drew closer and whispered into her ear though there was no one else in the dorm. "We drink and smoke--and steal. Just stay away from Meme. She's the class freak. Sold into prostitution at the age of nine by her very own mother. Both she and her mother are whores."

Olivia felt sharp spasms in her stomach. The doctor had warned her about the sudden need to empty her bowels. This could go on for a week. She would do well not to stray too far from a toilet. At the time, she had had no idea what the doctor had been talking about—now she knew!

"I need to make popo!" she finally cried.

Jimena grabbed Oliva's hand. "Come with me."

She led her to the bathrooms, which were stationed between the dorms. Each had three toilets and two private showers. Jimena pointed to one of the stalls.

Olivia didn't know what to do. She was sure that her ignorance showed on her face. "Jimena, where do I go?" she asked, in a sweat.

Jimena knew that Olivia was one step above an Indian. She was certain that she had never even seen a toilet in her life. She opened one of the stall doors.

"You sit on the black seat and do your business. When you're done, wipe yourself with this paper—use as much of it as you want. It's also from my father's store!" She tore about a dozen sheets of tissue from the roll and dropped it in the bowl. "And when you are done, you pull on this string like this—." Jimena pulled on the chain next to the bowl and water rushed down along the pipe from the tank above them. The paper disappeared.

Olivia heard fresh water filling the bowl. "Take your time. I'll wait outside," said Jimena, closing the bathroom door behind her.

*

When Olivia had finished, Jimena led her up the black cast-iron staircase flanking the side of the building from the ground to the roof terrace where bed sheets and school uniforms were drying on laundry lines. Olivia had never been up so high. She saw the sun glinting off of the tin roofs of the Antigua houses and, off to the east, looming over the valley, the *Volcán de Agua* with a bib of clouds around its lip.

She was about to say that she lived in a *cafetal* not far from the foot of the volcano, when she caught herself. "This is so pretty."

"That's right. We come up here to smoke after lights are out," Jimena said. She lifted her right arm into the air and pointed. "See that big water tank on the right side of the square?"

Olivia's eyes scanned the horizon. Since she had never seen such a wide landscape all at once, she had a difficult time focusing.

"The square is where you see all those trees. Now look to the right. Do you see that big thing that looks like a teapot?"

"I see something red," Olivia said nervously.

"Red for China. It holds enough water for all the stores and homes on the block," Jimena boasted. "It's above my father's store. A red storage tank for water!"

*

The Colegio Parroquial was a complex world of alliances, friendships and deceptions. During her first week at school Olivia stayed close to Jimena who was happy to parade her around like some odd circus animal, bestowing small gifts--cigarettes and *canillas de leche*--upon her.

Jimena was a true leader. She spearheaded nightly escapades to the roof, the theft of money and jewelry from the younger girls, the pilfering of candy and trinkets from the stores around the school. Olivia cried herself to sleep, wracked by the pain of the medicine killing the microbes in her belly and the fear that the girls would discover she was an imposter—a girl without a father and a barefoot Indian for a mother—someone who hadn't even known what a toilet was until she had come into the school. She lived in constant panic—doodling during the compulsory Wednesday letter writing hour and having no stories to tell when the girls returned Sunday night from having spent the weekend with their parents.

On weekends, she slept on the floor of her mother's hut and washed clothes in a stream—is this what she would tell her classmates during the half-hour Monday show-and-tell?

*

Mercedes—Meme—was Jimena's enemy. She had brown wavy hair to her shoulders, which she brushed forty times each morning, and lush green cat's eyes. Her vaulted forehead was smoothly polished. Her ten-year-old hips had rounded out and her breasts pressed proudly against her uniform. She was beautiful and voluptuous—everything Jimena was not. No wonder she was jealous of Meme—Jimena's chest and buttocks were absolutely flat—compared to her, she was a walking stick figure.

Meme's bed was at the other end of the room, next to the linen closet where sheets and towels were stored. The first time she and Olivia were alone together she said:

"I know you're Jimena's best friend."

"I'm not," Olivia countered.

"Uh, uh, uh."

"She just thinks I am."

Meme nodded and brightened her eyes. "You can be honest with me. I won't hurt you. I promise."

Olivia didn't know what to say.

"Would you like me to teach you how to kiss?"

Olivia remembered the shack in the woods, where the men pulled down their pants to couple with strange women. And she remembered the time a man had shared her mother's *petate* and nine month's later, Guayito had been born. Olivia had tried to block out the shuffling and grunting—especially the end, when her mother whimpered softly.

Olivia had often puckered her lips and kissed the back of her hand, as an experiment. On the whole, she was really quite innocent.

Meme leaned over and kissed her. Olivia felt the easy softness of her lips and she tensed up. Meme simply pressed her mouth harder until Olivia could taste her fruity sweetness. After what seemed an eternity—three seconds at most—of locking lips, Meme pulled away and clutched Olivia's hand in hers.

"What do you think?" she asked, softly rubbing her wrist.

"You're a great kisser," Olivia said thirstily, not sure what had just happened.

Meme sprung happily up and down on her bed. "Thank you, oh thank you," she beamed. "I do think I am good. Next time I'll teach you to tongue kiss. It's a completely different experience. It makes you feel warm inside."

*

Unlike Jimena, Meme was pure. Olivia loved her self-assuredness, the direct way in which she did things, without ever wanting or needing applause. That she had chosen Olivia with whom to share her most intimate secrets, away from the other girls, made her realize how lucky she was to have Meme's friendship.

"No one here knows this, but my father has five wives. Well, really not five since he never married even one of them. He was born in Poland but ended up in Zacapa. I saw him once. He's short and ugly and doesn't close his mouth when he chews. Like a toad. I don't know what my mother saw in him. Maybe he had money or simply told her that. I have a sister in Jutiapa and another one in Chiquimula. My oldest sister Rosita lives in Guatemala City—she takes care of me."

"You have such a big family," Olivia said.

"My brother Felipe is in San Francisco and Eduardo's in a military school in Cobán. I've never seen either one. I don't really need my father."

"Where's he now?"

"No one knows…"

"Please tell me."

"Okay. He's dead. He died in Zacapa. In another woman's bed. He was fifty-three."

"What if I told Jimena?" Olivia was also affected by the meanness in the school.

"You wouldn't. I trust you."

Olivia felt atop a mountain, surrounded by flowers and sweeps of air. Not to be blown off, she had to sit still, extremely still. Meme had said that she trusted her.

"To be honest, I never even saw my father either. He's also dead," Olivia confessed.

Meme looked at her. "Oh you poor thing, you poor, poor thing. We are so much alike, you know that? Both of us are bastards in a school of prim and proper rich girls."

Then Meme's face was serious. Quite unexpectedly, she burst out laughing and pulled Olivia over to her. "We are bastards sworn to secrecy. If Jimena ever knew, we would be her slaves. I don't want to be anyone's slave. Do you?"

Olivia shook her head. She now took Meme's arm and held it tight. "We're bastards sworn to secrecy," she repeated, not sure what a bastard really was, but sensing that it was better than being beholden to Jimena.

(1974)

The *Colegio Parroquial* offered Olivia entree into worlds she hadn't even imagined existed—a bed in a dorm, toilets and showers with running water (hot water at that!), her own sheets and towels! How could Olivia explain to her mother that three times a day she could walk down a line in the cafeteria and have women dressed in white serving food onto her plate, as much food as she wanted, when all her mother knew was the communal dining room with its dirt floor, damp air and meager portions? When she first walked through the school library aisles and saw floor-to-ceiling bookcases, Olivia had wanted to blurt out how much it felt like walking through the coffee fields, only here there were thousands of books instead of thousands of coffee beans all around her!

Jimena would have merely laughed at her.

Olivia loved spending time in the library, surrounded by cloth-covered books on religion, history and geography. There were shelves of Spanish classics--*Don Quixote*, *La Celestina*, *El Libro del Buen Amor*—that the older girls warned her she would one day *have to read*. And there were translations of thick novels by French writers such as Alexander Dumas, Balzac and Stendhal and by English writers like Brönte and Austen.

What other new worlds awaited her? There were books about space travel, microscopic life, tunnels that went under rivers—things she didn't know even existed. One book was filled with pictures of a rocket ship that had taken three men to the moon, her white moon, which usually hung lifelessly in the sky like some abandoned ornament. Olivia couldn't read any of these books, yet she felt reverential pleasure sitting among them, grateful for her hard wooden chair and the musty air that held so much silence. After all, it was a book about Donald Duck's train that had led to her new life at the *Colegio Parroquial*.

In the classroom Olivia learned to add, subtract, multiply and divide. These skills would've made her popular among her fellow coffee pickers who were swindled by the counters and the *caporales* in so many ways! With her newly acquired expertise, Olivia could've intervened on their behalf and put an end to all the cheating. But the last thing she wanted was to return to a place where drudgery and sameness determined each day, where hope was defined by the rumored happiness of others. Here she could measure what she had simply by looking around her. She realized that the *Vanidades* issue with Olivia Newton-John had sparked the dream of entering a world of beauty and imagination. The *caminito* toward the stream had been another path and now the *Colegio* was that new world.

She would never go back to the fields. Never. Ever. She would rather die.

*

Olivia could've become the best student in her grade, but she wasn't willing to stand out. She felt like an interloper, someone who had been admitted illegally to the school, only through Sister Carina's intervention. If she stayed in the middle of the pack, perhaps she could poke along without stirring up too much attention--this was the lesson she had learned from her years of picking coffee. Questions were asked that she could've answered; she remained silent when presented with math problems that were no challenge to her. Her strategy was to be a follower—this would ensure her safety in the classroom and in the dorms as well.

The *Colegio* was a comfortable, but confusing, place. In the coffee fields, Olivia knew that the *caporales* were the enemy and you had to be vigilant should they turn against you. But one wrong step at school could expose her to social quarantine, to unremitting ridicule from the other girls. Personality divided them, but they were also split between rich and poor, those of pure Spanish ancestry and mestizo blood, the day students and those interned for the week. The nuns tried everything—group sessions, prayer retreats, field trips, individual counseling—to try to engender unity and camaraderie among the girls. Just as they seemed to solve one problem—the nasty retorts in the classroom, the scornful laughter at wrong answers—there would be sadistic episodes in the dorms: rotten sausages in *mochilas*, dead bugs under the pillows, urine in the mouthwash.

The nuns refused to regard these episodes as simple childish pranks, the immaturity of girls vying for attention. Instead of merely accepting the sneers and the practical jokes as a phase, they viewed their conduct as proof that they had failed to teach the girls the most rudimentary lessons of moral and civil behavior. They insisted on discussing these issues openly after prayers, but the nuns were no match for girls bored by the idea of discovering the roots to their actions. Whatever palliatives were considered proved ineffective, since the girls refused to even cooperate.

The nuns were bound to fail. The parents of the girls had placed their daughters in the *Colegio* at the very moment they most needed them. The girls lacked love and received instruction instead--they found themselves caught in the backwash of contradictory feelings and the nuns were simply clueless. These sheathed women knew virtually nothing about indulging a fantasy or catering to a whim; they were no more affectionate than the starched cotton sheets that the girls slept on.

What made matters worse, the *Colegio Parroquial* girls were at the dawn of their own sexual awakening, overwhelmed by erotic dreams that made them desire and hate one another—all at the same time. And the nuns, with their severe vows and denials, survived within the school and convent by adhering to rigorous schedules and relentless prayer. They would have been hopelessly lost in the carnal world. Most of them barely recalled how zealously they had prayed as teenagers and they would never admit that they had joined their monastic order for reasons other than faith—to counter their sexual urges. They were frightened of Satan's temptations.

Sister Carina was the only nun who had an inkling of what was going on.

While ministering in the plantation churches in the nearby countryside, she had been awakened to the many emotional and physical hurdles her congregants faced. She became familiar with the issues of survival, housing, and malnutrition that overwhelmed them. Certainly Sister Carina would not ever face down Anibal Cofinio over these issues, but she acknowledged the suffering of her parishioners, even if she counseled patience or would dismiss their complaints as being part of a larger divine plan.

This insight allowed Sister Carina to offer advice on ways to soften the blows of their hardscrabble lives. She encouraged the women to join together and air their grievances. At the same time, she warned the plantation foremen that they would do well to respond to their complaints before dissension escalated.

"If you don't listen to them now, you will be sorry later," she'd warn them.

When the women saw results, Sister Carina felt confident to discuss issues of childrearing so that the abuse visited upon them by the *caporales* or their husbands wasn't transferred down to their children during fits of frustration. She tried to get them to pause before disciplining, to use words rather than corporal punishment. She taught them to count to ten before reacting.

With no running water and few commodities, personal cleanliness in the fields was also a challenge. Sister Carina discussed hygiene and menstruation and challenged the women to be more open about these issues with their daughters. She knew that many of the women had been abused first by the *caporales* and then by their husbands, and she urged them not to be silent or complicit. She talked to them about the house in the woods and how what went on inside the pine planks was an offense that was destroying the very fabric of their homes.

"You must find a way to do something," she exhorted them.

She was not surprised to learn that one Sunday the shack burned down.

*

The situation at the *Colegio* was far different. Sister Carina felt as self-conscious as the other nuns in discussing sex with the girls, but at least she tried. She suggested that sanitary napkin dispensers and aspirins be placed in all the bathrooms, but the other nuns were unsure and confused, thinking that any acknowledgment of their menstruation would encourage exploration.

She did manage to convince her colleagues to at least broach the subject of sex as part of their classroom instruction. The younger nuns did so rather timidly in biology, discussing animal reproduction in the most general of terms or in insisting on personal hygiene in their weekly health class. When the girls hooted and sneered, mostly out of embarrassment, the nuns gladly enforced silence in the classroom, which, for them, was the true path for meditation and reflection upon God and all his wonders. The nuns were even further relieved that most of the girls who boarded went home on weekends and extended holidays. *Let their parents deal with them!*

But this was a miscalculation on their part since the parents had no desire to embark on parenting when weekends were the only reprieve from the week's labor. Saturday and Sundays were for socializing with friends and going to parties to comment upon their gowns, discussing fine wines and liqueurs or bragging about where their husbands would be taking them for the Semana Santa or Navidad vacations. They yearned to be featured and photographed for the society pages of *La Prensa Libre, El Imparcial* or *La Prensa Gráfica.* Or else they retreated to the exclusive tennis and golf clubs that had opened along the shores of nearby Lake Amatitlán.

Their daughters were simple annoying appendages to the weekend activities, expected to take part in the social events without creating a fuss or demanding too much attention. And by 6 PM on Sunday, the family chauffeurs would drive the girls back to Antigua and their dorm routines and their mothers would collapse in bed, liberated and exhilarated. The parents were grateful to the *Colegio Parroquial* for helping them raise their children in a safe, cloistered environment where boys—the source of sexual misery—were nowhere to be seen. The nuns would make sure to restrict contact between the girls and the community in which they lived. They were never allowed off school grounds on their own, period, Jimena's escapades notwithstanding.

But the mothers never even suspected that their daughters had developed the skills to feed and nourish their own curiosity.

A hidden, sexualized world operated in the dorms upstairs— there were stashes of *Teen Screen* magazine; folded posters of shirtless American heartthrobs like George Harrison and Robert Redford; transistor radios that played Motown and disco tunes over and over; sex toys. The girls were swept into uncontrollable, frenzied raptures by the slightest thing. With breasts firming, they felt the first rush of adolescence outpacing them.

Without boys, the girls had no choice but to explore sexuality with one another. Their parents would have been appalled, since they imagined their eleven-and twelve-year-old's sleeping safely alone in their cold starched sheets, under wood and pewter crucifixes. They would've been horrified to learn that waves of girls slipped out of their beds when the lights were turned off and went up to the roof. Hidden by laundry flapping gently in the cross breezes, these renegades found warmth rebelling with one another—cursing and smoking--and, later even in each other's beds.

This confused Olivia. After Jimena and her friends returned to bed at eleven, she could hear other girls slipping out of their beds, even the occasional muffled moans and purrs once they had returned from the roof an hour later. She knew Jimena was not involved since their beds were next to each other and she could hear her snoring from the moment her head hit the pillow. Olivia wondered if Meme joined the second renegade group or if perhaps she was the ringleader—she could still feel Meme's lips against her own and she had mentioned the possibility of tongue kissing.

If Meme did not invite her to the roof, it was because she didn't find her attractive. Olivia had no illusions about her looks. She felt ugly and growing plumper each day. Few girls would want to have a fat, dark girl wrapping her arms around them. Certainly not Meme-- a girl with brown, silk hair and green eyes.

What Olivia didn't know is that what went on up on the roof had nothing to do with love or intimacy, but rather with control. And Meme wanted Olivia to have no part of it—she was protecting her.

*

Olivia was forced to navigate alone through the shoals of her own sexuality. Her mother had discussed menstruation with her and given her a few cloths. She told her to wash them out every day and to chew eucalyptus leaves to stanch the cramps. Olivia's classmates used the sanitary napkins their parents provided for them: none of the girls— ever—had to wash out cloths. She would wash them in secret before lunch or after dinner, before study hall, and dry them on pins clipped to the springs under her bed.

Meme once complained to Olivia that menstruation was proof that God did not exist. "This is the suffering we women must endure for the honor to propagate the race," she said, imitating the voice and words of their biology teacher Sister Alfreda.

"What bullshit."

"I agree, Meme."

"When I turn fourteen, my sister Rosita is going to put me on the pill."

"A pill to get rid of cramps?"

Meme burst out laughing. "My dear, birth control pills. You take them and you stop having periods. No more pads. You can even have sex all the time and never get pregnant. Don't tell me you like getting your period."

Olivia flushed and said: "There are times I can barely walk."

"Exactly," Meme answered. She gave Olivia some yellow pills, which did ease the pain and made her periods shorter. How could Olivia ever go back to living in the fields? Chewing on eucalyptus leaves! How embarrassing!

In addition to the yellow pills, Meme gave Olivia aspirins and some of her own sanitary napkins.

"I have my own," Olivia said.

Meme shook her head. "I've seen you washing your cloths at the sink. You've got to stop living in the Dark Ages, Olivia. And please don't lie to me. I can't stand lies."

"Meme, I..."

"Not another word, hear?" her friend shushed her up. "We're bastards sworn to secrecy," remember.

Olivia could do nothing but nod.

*

Whenever Olivia was cross, Meme would simply say: "It must be that time of the month again!"

"How do you know?" Olivia would say, astonished.

"I've been menstruating since I was nine. I know all about it. It won't ever get better, but you'll get used to it," she would tell her.

One Sunday night, while the other girls were studying in the library, Meme signaled to Olivia to follow her up to the roof. The sky above them was broad, rimless, and seemed festooned with hundreds of pulsing stars. To the south was the dark outline of the Volcán de Agua, which seemed to resemble a triangle cylinder. Meme lit a cigarette. After inhaling, she passed it to Olivia.

"No thanks."

Meme shrugged. "Sometimes I wish I were dead, simply dead."

Olivia looked at her. "What an awful thing to say."

"I just don't know what is real anymore."

Olivia knew what her friend meant. "I feel that way, too. Is this world real or the one I came from? If you saw my home, if you met my mother and brother—"

Meme held the cigarette between thumb and forefinger. She inhaled deeply and blew out perfect circles of smoke. When she had finished, she said: "Why don't I go home with you next Saturday?"

"I would never let you do that. You're my best friend, but I would die of embarrassment."

"It can't be so bad."

"Have you ever slept on the ground? Do you know what it's like to have the wind blow into your house all the time because it has no windows? To go to bed hungry and wake up knowing that hour after hour of walking down a row twisting and turning coffee beans and dropping them into your basket awaits you? There are girls in this school who have never seen a coffee shrub, never had to squat in an open field."

Silence followed. Meme moved the bangs off Olivia's forehead.

"And I thought I had it bad. The sooner you forget that world, the better. You don't live there anymore."

"I'm there every weekend."

"Well it's true that each time you go back there, you return to school miserable."

Olivia nodded.

*

Home was misery: Guayo and her mother hated her. Saturday afternoon and evening and all day Sunday felt like a return to servitude. She tried to do as many chores as possible—washing clothes, sweeping the floor of the hut, mending torn garments. Olivia thought that if she worked nonstop for the 30 hours she was home, that her mother would be grateful, recognize how hard Olivia wanted to please her. What she couldn't understand was that nothing she did could ever thwart her mother's anger.

"I look at you," her mother would say, "and I'm reminded of your father. You knit your brow just like him. You are the ghost of Melchior—only darker."

"Mami," Olivia would plead. "I'm your daughter."

Lucia would shake her head. "You've become skilled at fooling me."

"Please don't say that."

Lucia glared at her with pure hate. "See how you act all innocent? I don't know what mistakes I made for you to turn out to be just like him."

Olivia closed her eyes and repeated over and over "This isn't true, this isn't true." She opened her eyes and looked at Guayito for support.

He was sitting on his mother's *petate* playing with his *capirucho*. He looked expressionless at his sister. His four-year old face was as frozen as his heart.

*

Meme felt she and Olivia were spiritual sisters united by fate. She wanted to protect Olivia—as her own mother, with her many husbands, had never protected her. Poor Olivia. No father, and an uncaring, selfish mother. An orphan child caught between the coffee farm and a new school. Meme knew exactly what she had experienced and for this reason she had to look out for her.

Meme couldn't confess to Olivia that she did go up to the roof of the school after the smokers went to bed. She enjoyed the kissing, especially with Zoilita, who never said no to her. Meme could order her to move her brittle hands over her breasts and nipples and Zoilita would obey. As she felt her body surging, she would tell Zoilita to bring her hands down to the curve between her legs. Meme would squeeze her thighs together and rub herself softly until her body slipped into deep spasms.

She never thought to include Olivia in these escapades—she had no idea if she would even want to take part in them. Besides, Meme wanted to keep Olivia all to her own, pure and separate. At the same time, she realized that all her pressings with Zoilita had a coarse, automatic feel to them, like playing with sex toys.

It was true that within days of Olivia's arrival at the *Colegio Parroquial*, Meme had welcomed her by teaching her how to kiss.

Unlike Zoilita's thin cold lips, Olivia's had felt thick and welcoming, absolutely natural. What a difference.

But from one day to the next, Meme decided that she no longer wanted to go up to the roof. She was happy knowing that her friend was sleeping snugly across the room.

She could enjoy sleeping alone in her bed, too.

(1976)

On the first Saturday of February, after years of putting her off, Olivia relented and decided to bring Meme home with her. Her friend offered to make sandwiches at school so that Lucia could not block her from staying overnight by saying that she didn't have enough food, but Olivia said that her mother would be insulted by that polite gesture just the same.

Olivia agreed that Meme could bring Lucia a kilo of black beans as a gift.

As for bedding, Meme brought her own sleeping bag, one that she had received from her big brother Eduardo who had pilfered it from his military school in Cobán. The air to breathe, the water to drink, was all for free; Lucia could not fabricate an excuse for Meme not being allowed to stay.

Most of the girls had either been picked up by their chauffeurs or had taken car services to their homes in Guatemala City when Meme and Olivia left the *Colegio Parroquial* after the noon lunch. They walked south along Alameda de Santa Lucía, a cobblestone street skirting the market and the *Terminal de Buses*.

It was a crisp day, cool and cloudless. The sun was high on the horizon and the aromatic odor of eucalyptus and pine trees competed with the slightly fetid smell of pork boiling in pots behind walls. Since it was market day in Antigua, there was an explosion of movement as traders made their way back and forth to the buses pulling in and out of the bus terminal. A group of men carried clay jugs and other ceramics in net bags on their backs, held by the leather straps pressing into their foreheads. Many women walked briskly along, balancing baskets of fruit and vegetables on their heads.

All around there was screaming and shouting, and Mexican *rancheras* blaring from so many portable radios. The streets were crowded as well with Indians cooking corn, tamales and taquitos from their portable braziers, while their children played, ran and hooted on the sidewalks.

The girls walked out of Antigua along the main road that traversed the Almolonga Valley toward Ciudad Vieja. Once in the sun, Meme took off her pink sweatshirt and tied it around her waist. At a point just beyond Finca Brockmann, a plantation that catered to tourists who wanted to visit coffee fields and bring back homegrown, roasted coffee, Olivia stopped, faced her friend, and flicked her head to the right. She was beginning to feel tension in her head.

Meme stopped, out of breath, not used to so much walking. She aped the gesture of her friend. "Which means what, Olivia?"

Olivia shook her head, unable to feign her disgust. She grabbed Meme's hand and pulled her toward an opening between two fenced-in coffee fields almost invisible from the road. Olivia was feeling that this overnight visit would be a disaster—she dropped Meme's hand and, leaning against a post, took off her shoes and dropped them into her *morral*.

"You should do the same."

Meme refused, wiggling her toes in her sneakers. She was not about to expose herself to worms that transported all kinds of diseases—scurvy, beriberi, huge tapeworms. She could be with her friend overnight, but not get sick.

Feeling chilled, she put her sweatshirt back on. Besides, they would be walking through the woods full of mosquitoes and black and white spiders with poisonous drools. "I'll keep them on, just the same."

"Whatever."

"Is something bothering you, Olivia? I can't stand this silent mood of yours!"

Without stopping, Olivia waved her right hand in the air and pointed down the dirt track. They made their way slowly through the coffee fields, pushing back the giant ferns and elephant ears that grew against the barbed wiring. Meme was used to urban sounds—clattering traffic, voices, scratchy music—and the trill of warblers and mockingbirds was deafening to her.

After walking for ten minutes, the girls reached a clearing where spikes of sunlight lit up the curled brown earth like giant spotlights. In the center, under one of the sun spikes, was a rubber tree spreading its broad branches in the air and its thick roots in the mud. Behind the clearing, under a web of lianas and fallen branches was Lucia's *new* adobe home, looking shabbier than ever. The mud bricks had been whitewashed just a year earlier, but most of the paint had been scrubbed out by rain or bored through by beetles and other insects. It looked like a chewed and spit-out chunk of beef.

And the new door barely hung on its hinges.

Guayito, all of six now, was playing marbles off to the side of the front door, near a rusting punctured barrel of garbage. His pale head had been shaved. He glanced up to see his sister and Meme, but his eyes were vacant. He lowered them to the ground and flicked a large blue marble toward six or seven yellow balls sitting in a plateau surround by thick ruts, like the inside crater of a volcano.

"Guayito, what happened to your hair?"

"Lice." he said, without inflection. The big marble couldn't ford the groove and it rolled back to his lap. Once more he snapped his thumb against the marble, only harder; this time the large glass ball went over the ruts but failed to hit any of the smaller marbles. It landed at the foot of an orange tree, which despite its flush of leaves, had not borne fruit for years. Guayito humpfed.

"Again?" Olivia asked bounding toward her brother and extending a hand to touch his face.

Before his sister could touch him, Guayo spun away from her and stood up. "Who's that?"

"My friend Meme."

"Hi, Guayo." Meme said cheerily.

"You know that mamá doesn't like visitors."

"Where is she?" Olivia's neck was hot. She felt the way she had when Sister Carina had caught her reading and said she would discuss with Lucia the idea of sending her to school. Having her friend visit was all wrong; she should never have given in to Meme's petition.

"The *patrón* called a meeting."

"On a Saturday afternoon?"

Guayo nodded. "There's some problem. All the men are leaving."

"Why?"

Her brother shrugged. He resembled a fungus on a stone. "You should ask Mamá. Someone important has been killed and everyone's scared."

"And where are they meeting?"

"In the communal dining room."

Olivia couldn't decide if it would be better to wait for Lucia to come home or bring Meme to the meeting where there would be less of a chance of her mother making a scene. She brought Meme inside the shack. "Leave your sleeping bag there. Let's go look for my mamá." By the time they got to the meeting, it had broken up. Lucia was walking back with several women. When she saw Olivia with Meme, she said something to her friends and broke away from the group. The women, some of whom Olivia had known since childhood, hurried away down the path to their own huts without even greeting her.

When they were out of ear range, Lucia asked through her teeth: "Who's this?"

"Meme. My best friend. I've told you all about her," Olivia answered.

"I thought she was Chinese."

"Jimena? I hate her," Olivia said sharply. She went over to try and hug her mother.

Lucia turned away. "We barely have room for you, Olivia. We certainly have no room for your friend. This is a very, very bad moment!"

"Mamá, what's wrong?"

"The world is crashing down."

"Why, Mamá?"

"A big coffee finquero has been killed in Ixil. They call him the *Tiger of Ixcán*. And we will all have to pay for it."

"But that's hundreds and hundreds of kilometers away. What does that killing have to do with us?"

"The *patrón* says that he was killed by the Guerrilla Army of the Poor. But we suspect his employees clubbed him to death--in his own finca. Chopped up and burned—and it was on payday. Our men heard about it and got scared. They turned into jackrabbits and monkeys and have fled into the forest. They don't want to be dragged away or shot. Or forced to join the army and beat up their own people."

"Is that what would happen?" Meme asked. Everything she knew about life was skewed with humor and absurdity. What Lucia said seemed all too real. Almost vile. Lucia screwed up her small brown face. She had wrinkles forming on top of wrinkles from so much frowning. She couldn't relax her baboon-like face even when she slept. "In which world do you live?"

Meme pulled on her sweatshirt.

"Mamá! She's my friend."

Her mother spat on the ground. "Now I have two idiots spending Saturday night with me." Lucia glanced upward through the web of tree leaves. "What kind of God are you?" she asked the blue sky. And she turned to trudge home.

*

Lucia's mood barely lightened when Meme handed her the kilo of beans. She emptied the bag in a tin colander and went over to the back of the shack where the rainwater sliding off from the corrugated roof fell into a barrel. Since it hadn't rained for a month, the water was scummy, with webs of dead leaves and twigs. She ladled two spoonful's of water from the barrel into the colander and began picking out pebbles from the beans. Then she put the beans in a wooden bowl on the floor and covered them with water.

"We are having a simple dinner," Lucia warned.

Meme nodded.

The sun disappeared rapidly. With the coming darkness the only light in the hut was from a fat candle Lucia lit and which she placed on a shelf between the picture of *San Antonio del Monte* and a wooden crucifix.

Lucia struck a match; the kindling and paper lit rapidly. She put a blackened pot of old beans on the fire and then made a *refresco* of water and peppermint leaves, measuring out the crystals of sugar as if they were gold filings. Then Lucia pulled out a brick of soggy rice wrapped in newspaper, which she reheated, once the beans were warm. Finally she threw a few old tortillas on a griddle for just a minute.

When the meal was ready, they sat together on flat stones around the fire and ate on tin plates, using the tortillas to push the rice and beans into their mouths. Their bodies threw out large shapeless shadows on the brown walls.

There was no conversation over dinner—how could there be? Lucia cared nothing about Olivia's week at the *Colegio Parroquial*. And what interest did she have in Meme, her daughter's friend?

Who cared where this green-eyed girl lived and what her parents did? Lucia was into the sixth year of punishing her daughter with silence, the same silence that had greeted her every weekend since she had left home. Olivia's attempts to touch her mother and Guayo were rebuffed as if she had some terminal disease.

To counter their "revulsion," Olivia immersed herself in household chores: sweeping the hut, washing dishes and clothes, mending and darning. Anything to keep busy, to shield her from her mother's pinprick eyes, which reduced her to dust or from the silence that slowly abraded the little confidence she had. *Olivia, the betrayer.* She knew her mother's attitude would not change even if she decided to leave school, come back home to work in the fields. No, nothing would change her. That Lucia had revealed the murder of the *finquero* in the communal dining room was conversation enough. Her mother didn't have to explain her silence to a bunch of twelve-year-old's.

Guayo, too, was equally distant. While Lucia's eyes wore Olivia down, his were listless, like dead stars, matches that had burnt out and turned to dust. Nothing could change his inscrutable expression. As soon as he had been old enough, he had replaced Olivia in the fields. He did his work quietly, like a prisoner condemned to a lifetime of servitude, burrowing like a miner into the earth's core, away from sunlight and fresh air. He could survive on dust and ash, even though most days, birdsong and seas of green surrounded him.

Olivia's weekend visits meant nothing to him.

*

After dinner, Meme opened her sleeping bag and placed it on the ground next to Olivia's *petate*. They would sleep together back-to-back, while her brother shared the cot with his mother. Seconds after they had lain down for the night, Meme heard Olivia sniffling—little tears streaming down her friend's face into a little pool on her straw mat. As soon as Lucia and Guayo were asleep, Meme turned over, unzipped her bag and snuggled into her friend's back. She tugged on Olivia's shoulder until she turned over. Meme ran the back of her forefinger down her friend's cheek in the half-light and then kissed her softly on the lips, as they had kissed years earlier. Olivia sobbed and Meme buried her friend's head between her breasts, pulling her tight into her sleeping bag. Olivia felt Meme's nipples hardening. She was afraid to move and stayed absolutely still.

Olivia stayed awake, her head gently bobbed by Meme's breasts. She hated this world, not because of its poverty but because she couldn't understand the bitterness of people like her mother. She thought of her simple cot at the *Colegio Parroquial*, the thin blanket, and the straw mattress whose needles sometimes dug into her skin. What pleasure! She wished she were back there. Olivia knew she had made a mistake in bringing Meme into a world of misery—her home.

Already Olivia knew she would never come back to live here. She had come out of her mother's womb, drunk from her milk breasts, been cleaned, swaddled and tickled by her, but she was now the focus of her mother's misery. Maybe it had started at her birth, when she had been born ugly, with layers of hair on her face, and her father had left her mother...

Olivia knew that Melchior was still alive, somewhere. It wasn't true what her mother said. *Lucia had abandoned her, not her father.*

She saw Melchior sitting inside the cab of his truck, with a crucifix on the dashboard and several blue and white Guatemalan flags glued to the windshield. He had gold teeth, a crooked mouth, he hadn't shaved for several days, but he was smiling, listening to rancheras, thinking of his only daughter. He was a nice, jolly man, who knew how to squeeze pleasure out of life.

With this image, Olivia fell asleep.

*

In the middle of the night, after the fire had gone out and the horned owls had stopped hooting, the ground began to shake. It started out as a slight rumble, like a gentle drum roll, but as the stirring intensified, objects started dancing on the shelves—the little altar, the drink cups, the few ceramic dishes, the fat stump of a candle—before they tumbled down to the shack's dirt floor. Everything danced like water droplets on a hot griddle. Guayo, barely on the lip of his mother's bed, fell to the ground, crying: "Someone is shaking the house."

Olivia woke up, so did Meme. The forest sounds ceased and the night turned absolutely quiet.

Lucia, who had also woken up, pulled her blanket up to her chin.

A roiling started again and the mot-mots, woodpeckers and warblers, birds that normally were asleep, began chattering. The sound of pebbles falling, sand shifting, could be heard and bits of adobe started to spill from the walls. It was a soft sound, like hands gently rubbing paper or salt being poured. Then the corrugated sheets of the tin roof clanged as if being shaken against each other.

"*Dios de mi alma*, we are going to die," Lucia said, jumping out of bed in her linen nightgown. "The house is collapsing."

There was nothing of value to save in the shack: not the radio that had stopped working, not the clothes full of holes, certainly not the iron that sat like a sentinel in the corner hungrily awaiting a morsel of coal. She ran to the door and began pulling on the twined rope that served as the door handle.

The bricks of the shack had shifted so quickly that the door, usually barely clinging to its hinges, could not be sprung open. On the contrary, it seemed lodged into the bricks like a soldered bank vault door.

Lucia pulled and pulled, but she could not open it. She went over to where Guayo sat on the floor, clinging to his blanket and held him tightly.

"The Lord is punishing us for our sins," she began to cry.

"It's an earthquake. We have to get out before the walls crash down on us," said Meme. Without a second thought, she grabbed a wooden bench and dumped on the ground Lucia's assortment of blackened, hardly flattened pans, which had been on top. She put the bench below the shack's one window and tore off the cloth curtain. Blue light entered the room; daybreak was beginning. She took Guayo into her arms, climbed onto the bench and hoisted him through the opening. "Run to the clearing, run to the clearing," she ordered him.

"Lucia, Olivia come here!"

By now Olivia was up. She went over to help Meme lift Lucia, whose body was completely slack as if she had determined that she would not be moved.

"It's the end, it's the end," she kept repeating.

As Meme and Olivia lifted her up, a wall collapsed on Lucia's bed, sending up sprays of orange dust. The ground shook some more and the ceiling collapsed over the bricks of adobe on the bed, closing down the wall. There was little time before the entire shack would flatten.

The girls pushed Lucia feet first through the window though she
kept trying to crawl back in. Meme gave her body a violent push.
When Lucia's feet touched the ground, Meme shouted "Olivia's
coming through next. Help her down."

But Lucia simply lay inert on the ground.

Meme helped Olivia through the window and followed her down.
When they were outside the shack, it collapsed inward. Olivia and
Meme dragged Lucia to the clearing, which, because of the falling
trees, was more like a corral. Guayo sat there quietly in the center,
eyes spookily opened.

By the time they reached him, Lucia's shack was a heap of broken
bricks and billowing dust.

*

The earth shook for 53 seconds, but it was followed by dozens
of aftershocks. Meme, wearing only her nightgown, said she
was walking back to school to call her family in Guatemala City.
When Olivia offered to go with her, Meme told her she should stay
with her mother.

"Though she won't admit it," Meme said, "Lucia needs you."

Olivia hugged her friend. She knew that if it hadn't been for
Meme, none of them would have survived.

*

Twenty-seven thousand Guatemalans died. The dead, mostly Indians,
lived in cramped adobe homes in the nearby city of Chimaltenango
and in dozens of adobe villages that were no more than outcroppings
on the furry green mountains of central Guatemala. Bodies of babies,
the old and the infirm, were found weeks later among the rubble.
Millions of dollars were raised in donations. Before the first reports of
destruction were broadcast on the radio, the government of General
Kjell Laugerud had invented elaborate schemes for stealing money
from the aid agencies that came to their help. Many Guatemalans
became millionaires overnight, by stealing donations earmarked for
earthquake relief efforts. Even the boxes of canned foods and drinks
flown in cargo planes to the Aurora Airport somehow ended up in

the houses of officers and soldiers who resold them to the *tiendas* at inflated prices.

The *Colegio Parroquial* suffered little—the octagonal pink fountain that graced the center of the first-floor courtyard had split in half and the naked Artemis statue that sprayed water from its nipples had tipped over and cracked the walls so that water and goldfish seeped out. Statues and vases had fallen in the chapel, but the building, with its meter-thick walls had survived intact. The beds had skittered along the ground, and the Bibles on the night tables and the prayer books in the chapels had cascaded down to the floor.

Antigua also suffered little. Many of the already ruined churches were ruined some more, but no deaths were reported. Walls had cracked, trees had fallen, cobblestone streets had buckled and wavered. And there was a sudden influx, almost a plague, of *zopilotes* as if all the buzzards in Guatemala had decided to vacation or migrate to this region at this specified time. The Indian families were terrified to leave their young children alone for fear they would be scooped up alive, but the buzzards kept their distance from the survivors, having more than enough offal from the farm animals crushed by falling bricks, trees and debris.

For weeks to come the sky was blackened by buzzards turning and wheeling in the air.

*

Lucia was deeply shaken by the earthquake. It was as if she had seen a ghost, the ghost of the Walking Skeleton, and she had lost her will to fight.

"I'm leaving," she said, as the coffee pickers in their nightgowns gathered together at the communal dining room later that morning. The dining room had survived because it had been built of concrete blocks by the patrón. In fact, the drying field was intact as was all the equipment needed for the coffee production. Not only here, but also in Finca Brockmann and Finca Cofinio, and all the other important fincas in the Almolonga Valley. Everything survived, except for a dozen pickers or so and many of their adobe shacks. The *patrón* told them not to worry, that soon their houses would be rebuilt, with electricity this time, and wells—and he promised it before the

May rains. In the meantime, they would live in army tents wherever there was a clearing.

"I'm leaving," Lucia kept repeating, under her breath. "I'm going back to San Pedro La Laguna."

Guayito, wearing just a thin shirt on his back, was crying. Olivia went over to hug her brother, and this time, he let her embrace her.

"What about me?" he asked.

"She'll take you, too. Don't worry," Olivia calmed him down. She didn't think that her mother would just go off and leave Guayito by himself. "Or else I will leave school and come and take care of you."

That afternoon, Olivia walked back to school barefoot and in her nightgown. The Colegio Parroquial would provide her with new uniforms and another pile of used, ill-fitting garments. As she walked through Antigua's quiet streets, without lights and radios, the people huddled on the streets and murmured softly to one another. Nothing much had happened, but everyone was afraid of the aftershocks.

Weeks went by, and things returned to normal. Lucia never made good on her threat to leave. She accepted the charity of the *patrón* and lived for weeks in a tent. He later made good on his pledge to rebuild their houses out of adobe, not concrete as he had promised. When the rains began, Guayo and Lucia moved into a new gray plank home— the *patrón* had purchased the wood cheaply from a lumberyard in Huehuetenango because it had large, ugly knots.

But everyone had a home.

(1978)

Bonifacia, the kind Sister superior who peppered her talk with quotes from *Romans*, could not understand how girls living in a school requiring devotions in the chapel before classes, evening prayers before sleep, and Mass on Wednesday and Sunday nights, could talk to one another with such venom. The girls should address each other with the quiet deference and gentle voices with which they were instructed.

After one Wednesday evening Mass, she asked the girls of the first year of high school to remain in the chapel. With Juana Quiroga at her side, she announced that the following afternoon they would hike to the top of the *Volcán de Agua*. They would sleep inside the cone of the inactive volcano, meditating on how nature is a manifestation of God's perfection and how prayer can dispel petty thoughts. *"Be not overcome with evil, but overcome evil with good,"* she sang out. The following morning they would go back down the volcano, changed.

"Olivia will never make it," Angelina said, elbowing Jimena sitting next to her. "The nuns will have to hire Indians to carry her to the top!"

"What about you, Angelina?" Olivia countered, almost laughing. "How will you ever sleep on the volcano floor without your precious comforter?" Angelina always complained about the narrow cots and the lumpiness of the straw mattresses, even though her friend Jimena's father had supplied both to the school.

Olivia, accustomed to dirt floors, thought her bed was regal.

Angelina glared back at Olivia while Jimena asked Sister Bonifacia: "But where will we sleep? And what will we eat?"

"Just have your cook meet you at the top with chop suey!" answered Meme.

Sister Bonifacia was too deaf to hear the chorus of laughter, hisses and shrieks that followed. Juana Quiroga walked over to the pulpit and whispered something in the old woman's ear.

Sister Bonifacia nodded and raised her cane to speak. "This is why this retreat is necessary. You girls have strayed from righteousness. *'Be kindly affectioned one to another with brotherly love.'*"

The shrieks turned to whoops and some of the girls started drumming their shoes on the chapel floor. "Brotherly love, brotherly love," they chanted.

Juana Quiroga craned her neck to see who was stirring up the ruckus. As she was short and the chairs had high backs, she saw nothing. She then walked up and down the aisle, her face a frozen glare, while Sister Bonifacia rapped her wooden cane again and again against the pulpit.

The girls finally quieted down. "*A soft answer turneth away wrath, but grievous words stir up anger.*" she said, almost at a whisper. "I wish for you to be gentler in the way that you speak to one another."

A chorus of girls woodenly answered her: "*Verily, we have sinned and beseech your forgiveness.*"

Sister Bonifacia beamed through wet eyes. "Girls, I know your hearts are pure. A night in the wilderness will focus your attention on the good that you can do—"

"But Sister, the volcano is miles away. We'll die before we even get there—" Jimena faked a cry.

"Girls, my sweet girls. We will take a van to the village of Santa María de Jesús and then climb to the top from there—"

"You'll be climbing with us, Sister Bonifacia?" asked Zoilita, not so innocently.

The girls all laughed. Sister Bonifacia was seventy if a day. Her gnarled cane was her third leg—without it she could not walk down the halls of the school. Her back was curved like a clothes hanger.

"*Salvajes,*" interrupted Juana Quiroga. "Of course Sister Bonifacia won't be going with us. We'll bring sleeping bags, clothes and incidentals. Sisters Carolina and Tabitha will help me—"

"Why can't the school hire mules or horses to carry our things up?" asked wispy Loretta, who barely nibbled during meals. Having attended the *Colegio Inglés* for the first six years of her education, she spoke Spanish with an exaggerated British accent, puffing out the words as if they were bubbles. Her eyes were usually focused on her nails, which she constantly filed and painted.

"You needn't worry about mules, my dear," answered Jimena. "We'll simply helicopter you to the top!"

"Or have you dropped down. You're so skinny your dress will be like a parachute—" added Angelina, rolling her body against Jimena.

Sister Bonifacia only heard taunting voices, not what the girls were saying. Her face was a map of disappoint and frustration. "Jimena and Angelina, I would simply advise you to 'Love your enemies, bless them that curse you.'" She widened her eyes and tried to look kindly upon Loretta. "We are going on this retreat to meditate on the idea of 'Kindness of Thought, Gentleness of Gesture.' I want all of you to pledge to me now to stop seeing the world, as the Apostle Paul warns us, through a glass darkly. I know you can do it."

Once again, most of the girls answered in a falsely repentant chorus: "Verily, verily we have sinned and beseech your forgiveness."

Frustrated by this fake absolution, the Sister Superior simply closed her eyes.

*

To prepare for the climb, Meme and Olivia spent the afternoon running up and down the stairs from their dorm floor to the roof with book-filled mochilas on their backs. They did this ten times, hoping that they'd be able to trot up, billy-goat style, to the top of the volcano. They imagined collapsing on a cushiony surface up there, in a state of total euphoria.

But Thursday morning they both woke up in a bad mood. All the exercise had simply made them stiff and sore. Olivia, in particular, felt that she wouldn't be able to make the climb and went to see Sister Tabitha before breakfast.

But the nun would have none of this: "Take the morning off and rest if you'd like. But everyone must go, Olivia. Even you."

*

The van picked the girls up at the front of the school after lunch. The clouds were low on the horizon, like a bulldog's jowl, and it had begun drizzling. Still, the girls were happy to go on an adventure: if nothing else, they could wear jeans and pullovers instead of the starched blue and white uniforms, which branded them as schoolgirls.

Olivia, of course, wore hand-me-downs. As a scholarship student, every stitch of her clothing had been donated. This was true of her uniform, identical so no one could know, in theory, who the poor girls were. But every Monday at noon, a box of washed and pressed outfits were delivered to the school and the scholarship students were invited during lunch to look through them. Initially, Olivia had been grateful for the donations because she had no other clothes to speak of for weekends and holidays. But she resented asking to be excused from the lunchroom.

On the drive up to Santa María de Jesús, the girls fought the boredom of the van ride and the nausea of the dozen hairpin turns on the muddy roads by singing:

Panameña, Panameña, Panameña hija mia
Yo quiero que tú me lleves al tambor de la alegría

Al tambor, al tambor, al tambor de la alegría
Yo quiero que tú me lleves al tambor de la alegría.

Olivia was sure she was getting the flu. Her legs ached, and no amount of rubbing or stretching could help. Her boots were too small, cramping her toes, and her one-size-fits-all green poncho made her resemble a huge amphibious creature.

Meme slouched against her and dozed, burrowing her head deep into Olivia's right shoulder. She was angry at her for this, and because Meme didn't understand why she got so upset at the other girls' taunts. "What do you care what they say? Do you think any of them is any better? They're just a bunch of ugly *gueguechas!*" Meme had said, referring to their classmates as goitered girls.

This was easy for Meme to do, Olivia thought. Despite the disruptions in her household and her scattered siblings, Meme had the same confidence that the other girls in the *Colegio* had. She was not interested in being accepted or popular, but her defiance was rooted in the belief that she was privileged and had a unique *destiny*. Meme had seen the way Olivia and her family lived and never said a word. This is what made Olivia's poverty worse: to her friend, it was almost invisible. And Meme was rapturous.

Gueguechas or not, Olivia was at a disadvantage, always on the verge of being found out. Everyone knew she was from the Antigua area, but who her parents were and where they lived remained a mystery. Jimena teased her by saying that her mother probably made *huipiles* in San Antonio Aguas Calientes and her father picked corn.

"Where do you go Saturday afternoons?" she would question. And then before Olivia could answer Jimena would say that anyone could identify her own parents by simply going to the *Almacén La Fe*. "You can see my parents there every day of the week. I'll bet Olivia's father is a barefoot corn picker."

And all this because after Olivia's first week at the *Colegio Parroquial*, she had chosen to be Meme's friend instead of hers.

*

The van drove through Santa María del Jesús and stopped at a muddy clearing just beyond the village.

"I need to use the bathroom," Angelina said, stepping out of the van. She looked around. The clearing was full of rutted puddles and all she could see was a small shack with a tin Coca Cola sign nailed to its front under a huge amate tree.

"Wait for me here by the bus," Juana Quiroga said, and she went into the shack. A few seconds later, she came out with several rolls of toilet paper: "Girls, you'll have to do your business in the woods."

"Sister Juana (she was not a nun but the girls still referred to her as one), I can't pee out here," said Angelina, almost in tears. "What if there are snakes?"

"I'd be more worried about the *zompopos*. When the fire ants see your flimsy little white behind, they'll have a biting party," said Jimena.

The girls mewled in tears, on the verge of mutiny. Olivia joined in their protest, but there was no alternative. Sister Carolina and Tabitha handed them balls of paper and sent them two at a time into the brush. Olivia was inwardly pleased, having seen a toilet for the first time in Dr. Madrid's office and later that same day in the dorms of the

Colegio Parroquial. Now her schoolmates would experience what she already knew.

*

Two gnarled Indians, wearing mud-streaked white shirts, knee pants and *caites*, seemed to appear as if from nowhere. Both held walking sticks. Like old cars, they seemed reliable as long as something unusual didn't occur. One went over to unlock a gate whose path would lead them up the volcano while the other spoke to Juana Quiroga and her two assistants.

When the girls were altogether, the lead guide said in broken Spanish: "We have to hurry, before the sun sets. *Listas*?"

Juana Quiroga put her arms around the girls nearest to her. "We're ready!"

They started through the gate. In total, there were fifteen trekkers, including the guides. Each girl had to carry her own food, a change of clothes, a plastic sheet and sleeping bag. Juana Quiroga went to the front to accompany the lead guide; Sister Tabitha stayed in the middle; and Sister Carolina pulled up the rear with the second guide.

Because of the rain, the path was slippery. Worse, the girls were forced to clasp nearby vines to continue the climb when the dirt turned into solid rock. Without these anchoring supports, they would never have made it to the first plateau, which was at the end of a short, but steep jaunt.

It took them half an hour of steady climbing to reach this first plateau. Here they stopped to drink water from their thermoses. From this elevated clearing, they looked out toward the west. Several fires smoldered in the cornfields on the outskirts of Santa María del Jesús and the gray smoke from the fireplaces in the village rose up to the clouds in curled ropes. From here, the vegetation clung to the nearby slopes like balls of wool. Beyond these fields and the village, everything was wrapped in gray film and nothing could be distinguished.

And in this unprotected lookout, a cold mist started falling.

Before the girls had barely caught their breath, the lead guide had taken off again. Within five minutes they rose above the tree line and the path was overtaken by fog. The girls could barely see or be seen. Every few seconds, the wind swirled, shifting directions, and in the

various clearings stunted bushes with hard blue berries appeared—
the only remaining vegetation.

The girls were scared, but before anyone could say a thing, Juana
Quiroga urged them on. "Hurry along, it's getting late." She, too, was
nervous and much preferred being back at school serving as Sister
Bonifacia's enforcer.

She was not only afraid of the impending darkness, but also of
bandits who were rumored to suddenly surprise climbers and steal
whatever money and jewelry they carried. She wondered if Sister
Bonifacia had been prudent to require this retreat. She would question
her about it later—if they survived.

The lead guide walked spiritedly, hardly glancing back or to his
sides. It was as if he were a mute boatman ferrying the girls from
shore to a distant island. He hadn't been hired to talk, assist, explain
or lessen, in any way, the severity of the journey.

The track to the entrance into the cone angled around the
southern flank of the volcano. It was here where the rain clouds hit a
wall of mountain and dropped their moisture.

Olivia and Meme walked together, at times in single file and at
other times holding hands when the path permitted it. Olivia couldn't
stop her teeth from chattering as the cold rain fell in wide swaths and
the sparse vegetation offered little protection. Unlike the other girls,
she thought she should know how to suffer the elements—wasn't
she the peasant here?—but this climate was much too harsh for her.
When they reached the second plateau, she too joined the other girls in
pleading with Juana Quiroga that they turn back while it was still light.

Sister Quiroga questioned the guide who simply shook his head.
He insisted that they had to continue. In a mixture of Cakchiquel and
Spanish, he indicated that they had passed the worst part and that
soon the course would straighten and offer a moderate incline. "As if
you were walking up the steps to church," he said, smiling, showing a
few gold teeth and lots of gaps. Having taken it hundreds of times, the
old man knew the path by instinct. Still, it was obvious that he hadn't
counted on the wet ash from the nearby Volcán de Pacaya blowing
into their faces and obscuring this final ascent.

"We're almost there," he mumbled. He raised his cane and pointed
to a spot in the fog where there was nothing to see. "We have to get to
the other side of the volcano. Ten, twenty minutes," he growled.

Juana Quiroga noticed that he didn't have a watch, probably never had had one, didn't even know how to tell time. Twenty minutes! Had Sister Bonifacia been thinking: that facing death builds character?

Worse than the wet ash was the roiling wind and fog that blew right into their faces and through their clothes. Olivia and Meme now held hands—all the girls did—for fear of being blown off the path and being lost forever. If they could see two feet in front of them they could see a mile.

The Volcán de Fuego was depositing ash in their track. The girls were forced to let go of each other and to trudge on hands and knees to make any headway. Juana Quiroga also was crawling, afraid of simply being blown off the volcano. She could hear many of the girls openly weeping and Sister Tabitha calling from the middle that they had to stop.

Who knew if Sister Carolina and the rear guard had been blown off the volcano?

"It's not safe to continue," Juana Quiroga proclaimed. She felt there was nothing to accomplish by continuing further. It had been a difficult climb—the girls had learned a lesson. The end.

But the guide would not give in. "We can't go back now. With all the rain, the path down would be a river of mud and we could drown. If we stay here we will die. See?" he said, punching his walking stick into the ground. "We'll soon be on the other side of the volcano, away from the ash. In five minutes we'll be at the cone entrance."

And he trudged off, about to disappear into the fog again.

"I can't get through this," cried Angelina, sitting down, black ash in her mouth.

Jimena held her in her arms with eyes closed. When she opened them again she blinked several times: "I see a monster out there!"

The guide came back to where the girls had stopped.

The fog suddenly swept down and the girls looked up toward a bald patch bathed in sunlight. On a distant ridge, some twenty feet away, they saw a gray horse with short hair. It seemed to be watching them. His unblinking eyes were open and there seemed to be half a smile on his face.

"That's the gate to the barn," the guide laughed. "We're almost there."

He gave a high-pitched whistle trying to spook the horse, but it stood its ground and continued watching them with level brown eyes.

Then another wave of fog, mist and ash blew in, obscuring their view. They heard thumping, braying, and when the air cleared again, the horse had disappeared.

"Wild horses, here," mumbled the guide. "And sometimes you see a *quetzal*," he added, referring to the nearly extinct national bird that was a symbol of liberty.

"We have just a short way to go," he said, softly now.

Juana Quiroga shook her head. She looked back at the girls and signaled with her head that they had to continue.

The girls crawled out of the ash and stood up. They started walking again, in pairs, arms around each other. Within minutes the path dipped down and the fog blew away from them. The vegetation seemed to thicken and grass and lichen had replaced the ash. They walked another two hundred meters and all of a sudden they were in a clearing, clothed in a thin veneer of mist that sparkled in the sunlight.

As the guide had predicted, they had curved around the northern edge of the Volcán de Agua and now found themselves at the third plateau. Below them was a sweeping valley and beyond it, bathed in the yellow western light, was the tranquil town of Antigua. The roof tiles were bright orange in the sunlight and here and there, above the canopy of trees and buildings, the first twinkling of streetlights could be seen. Night was sweeping into the Almolonga Valley and the evening star was beginning to brighten.

Though the girls could not see the *Colegio Parroquial*, the fountain in the town central square was clearly visible flanked by a crown of trees and eight streetlamps.

The trekkers stood in a flat spot at the edge of the fractured cone. It was as if they had walked out of a gray ashen planet and now faced the celestial light of creation. The guides came together and sat down on a flat stone that extended over the cliff. They calmly rolled cigarettes for themselves, as if what they had just experienced were all in a day's work. The rear guard lit the cigarettes and the men smoked puff after puff, unaware that there were any other people around them.

"Girls, girls," whispered Sister Tabitha. "Come sit around me."

Juana Quiroga and Sister Carolina helped the girls take off their backpacks and sleeping bags.

Sister Tabitha unrolled a large piece of brown plastic and pointed to the middle. "I want you all to sit here in a half circle and hold hands," she said. "Angelina and Olivia, Olivia and Jimena, Jimena and Meme, Meme and Leticia—all of you—come sit around me."

The girls, drained of resistance, sat down as instructed. Squinting, they looked across the sloped fields at the town that was their home, the huge cross on the *Cerro de la Cruz*. The sun was bathing the cross in golden filigree. Above it all, against the rising dark blue sky, they saw Venus sparkling like a pearl teardrop.

"*God is light, and in him there is no darkness...If we walk in the light, as He is in the light, we have fellowship one with another*. Girls, it's so important that you remember this moment and realize what you have all gone through together. There is a lesson here. I hope you now can recognize that together you are so much more powerful, infinitely more powerful, than each of you is alone....Let us pray in the Name of the Father, the Son and the Holy Ghost."

The girls sat silently and with half-closed eyes—they had never, ever been so frightened. They had never realized how close death could be. None of them, Olivia included, had ever experienced true religious feelings or felt their own insignificance within the larger scope of things. But here they were, praying quietly, in a soundlessness that no one would ever have thought possible.

*

There were two little adobe huts and a large *rancho*-style house inside the cone. It wasn't a cone as much as a protected little rain forest: a plateau with a semi-circular wall of very lush trees. Five lit lanterns provided light inside. Two soldiers slept in one of the huts, while the other served as both office and supply depot.

The ranch house had been built out of mahogany and had a large porch and a slated roof. Colonel Ydigoras Fuentes, Guatemala's president, had built it ten years earlier when he had wanted to prove to his countrymen that Guatemala was safe from guerillas, bandits, and thieves. With great fanfare, he had the *rancho* built with an outhouse and even a rooftop *tinaca* to catch rainwater. There was no electricity. One October afternoon during the dry season, he and a staff of ten well-armed soldiers rode horses up to the cone. They were trailed by a large army transport helicopter outfitted with gas generators and enough provisions for the President to spend a week inside the cone, had he wanted to. Four reporters and photographers were invited to mark the event. The president spent a single night in the cone and the following morning he took the army helicopter back to the Campo Marte base, a few short blocks from his presidential home.

One of the soldiers led Juana Quiroga, Sisters Tabitha and Carolina, and the schoolgirls into the *rancho* where they would spend the night.

Though it was just after sunset, the girls were exhausted. They ate their sandwiches and drank water under gas lamps. By eight o'clock, they had placed their sleeping bags like the spokes of a cartwheel on the wooden floor and got ready to go to sleep.

Tonight there would be no teasing, no talk of spiders, ants, or scorpions. No belittling of one another: who hated whom and who was afraid of what…

Olivia was also bone tired. She was grateful that her classmates had felt such terror because it saved her and others from being the butt of jokes.

Sister Bonifacia would have felt vindicated. Her schoolgirls had survived the dangerous climb and had learned to be decent to one another—at least for one night in their lives.

(1979)

Olivia claimed to be sick so she wouldn't have to go on the school trip to visit the *Finca Brockmann*, a coffee plantation near her mother's home. The field trip would include a visit to the nursery and seedling farm as well as a tour of the fields, the cleaning and drying facilities and the *beneficio*—the processing plant. They would even witness the roasting process and end up drinking a cup of coffee from beans grown and freshly ground in the *Finca*.

The coffee plantation where her mother worked was across the highway and a kilometer by foot down a dirt road. Still, Olivia feared that if she went along, she could run into someone—a checker, a *caporal*, a dryer or another picker—who knew her or her mother. Olivia would die of embarrassment right then and there, in front of everyone, if she were to be recognized. She would simply die.

She visualized her classmates passing the homes of the finca workers: staring at the piglets running free, the *chompipes*—turkeys—gobbling and scurrying about. They would realize that this is how Olivia lived. They would all know she slept on a *petate* on the floor when she went home and that her mother cooked meals over an open fire. They would see her hut with the broken spring on the new wooden door and learn that Lucia was still waiting for glass to be put in the windows. No running water, no toilet. Insects, bugs and worms inching along the dirt floor.

Olivia said she had cramps, awful cramps, the worst cramps imaginable and that she couldn't get out of bed. Standing up was a challenge, walking around was absolutely impossible. She could barely move.

"Should we send for Dr. Madrid?" asked Juana Quiroga. Since the expedition up the Volcán de Agua, she had been named the school administrator to deal with personal and disciplinary problems. Like the nuns, she hadn't married and was "wedded" to the Church though she hadn't taken any vows and certainly didn't spend her free time in prayer. She was answerable to God, but no differently than other humans were. The interpretation of God's message to His lambs was not her responsibility. Still she walked through the school wearing a black outfit, often holding the huge iron cross that hung from her neck for support. If she were to release it, the girls thought, she would surely collapse on the floor.

"I don't need a doctor. I need rest. Can't Meme stay with me?"

"I'm sorry, my dear, but she has to come with us. This is not an optional excursion. The coffee plantation is considered among our most important educational field trips for the older students. This is a firsthand opportunity to understand the role coffee has played historically and its present significance in our society. You can understand that."

"Yes, I know how important coffee cultivation is," Olivia said ill-temperedly.

"It would be better if you were to come. You know so much—"

"What? To provide firsthand experience working in a cafetal?"

Juana Quiroga brushed back the coarse black hair that fell over Olivia's face. "You know that I didn't mean that. You can tell us so much about life in the fields--"

"But I'm too sick to go," Olivia said, falling back in her bed and turning her back to Juana Quiroga. "And I don't need to see Dr. Madrid!"

All month long they had been studying the arrival of the German coffee barons to Guatemala from Costa Rica at the turn of the 20th century. They had studied how the large *fincas* operated and how American entrepreneurs had tried to dominate the coffee industry in the early twenties by mechanizing the production process. They learned about how President Ubico, despite his pro-Fascist sympathies, had used World War II as a pretext to steal the *fincas* from the few remaining German coffee growers. One book spoke about how men like Anibal Cofinio had managed to enlarge their holdings during this period by urging the agriculture minister in the Ubico government to seize plantations not owned by natural-born Guatemalans.

In art they had studied and drawn coffee shrubs: white flowers giving way to green beans and finally the red clusters begging to be harvested.

The girls in biology debated whether banana, *gravileas* or *chalum* trees provided the best shade for the shrubs, and which tree was less apt to draw nutrients away from the soil over time. There were reports prepared comparing the future of coffee, banana and nickel production and which commodity offered Guatemala the largest economic reward in the world markets. Olivia had sunk down in her seat during these discussions, feigning ignorance and indifference or both.

"Sister Carina says that I should let you be. Well, if you want to stay back, pout and pretend you are sick, that is your business. I won't have Meme stay here and sulk with you. I must go now." And Juana Quiroga walked out of the dorm room.

Olivia stayed in bed, pretending to sleep. As soon as her classmates had left on the excursion, Olivia got dressed and sneaked out of the *Colegio Parroquial*. It was barely nine o'clock and they wouldn't be back till well after noon. She doubted that Juana Quiroga, with so many managerial responsibilities, would have the time to look in on her, but nonetheless, she stuffed her pillow and sweaters under her blanket. Nobody would bother her if they thought she were sleeping.

Olivia wanted to be alone, away from the *Colegio*. She walked north, toward the outskirts of Antigua and took the steep road that wound through the foothills and led up to the cross on the *Cerro de la Cruz*.

*

It was a beautiful October day. The sun was shining brightly and the *cenzontles* were singing contrapuntally from their hideouts in the trees to a marimba that was clearly being tuned. The air was crisp—it was the beginning of the dry season. A dragonfly dashed in front of her and stopped in midair, beating its silky, blue-tipped wings before darting off across a burning *milpa*—the charred smell of corn stalks was as fragrant as any perfume! This reminded Olivia of holidays on the finca, when the coffee workers would roast *cerdos* on spits for their Sunday afternoon *almuerzo* in the communal dining room. Had she actually experienced happiness back then? She only had to recall her mother's scowl and the frequent scoldings to remember that most of the time she had been miserable. Again, she promised herself that she would never ever go back and live at home with her mother.

The *Cerro* road traversed rutted dirt streets lined with adobe huts and laminated tin roof shanties. She passed *cargadores* jogging toward the center of Antigua with sacks filled with corn and kindling and Indian women walking briskly, pulling along their children. At one point, near the top of the bluff, she passed an open field with goal posts; she was reminded of when their finca's soccer team, *The Niguas* beat *The Zompopos* for the Almolonga Valley Championship! She was six years old and had been sitting alone on a bench watching the teenagers playing while the women gossiped and the fathers got drunk. Guayito was with the nursemaid and the other three-month-old's. Their team had won, and she remembered that a girl she knew had kicked the winning goal!

Back then Olivia couldn't wait to grow up and play as well. Maybe soccer would be her escape!

She passed a rancho with a hand-drawn sign on a jacaranda tree advertising fresh *tamales*. Olivia had not eaten a *tamale* or a *chuchito* in Antigua since arriving at the Colegio Parroquial seven years earlier. *Had it already been seven years?*

The old woman selling them sat on the shack porch next to a small cloth-covered hamper. She said something in a language that Olivia didn't understand—Cakchiquel?— and motioned for her to come closer. The smell of damp cornmeal and chicken made her hungry. She could almost taste the red pepper and the green olive inside.

"*Buenos,*" said Olivia in Spanish. "How much are the tamales?"

The woman's face was a web of creases. She smiled and her two front teeth flapped over her bottom lip like tusks. She put her hand into the basket, not taking her eyes off Olivia, but not really seeing her either. Her eyes seemed to focus on a spot meters away from her. The old woman was blind.

In very broken Spanish she said: "*Pollito. Cuántos? Diez len o tres por un macaco,*" she said, using the Indian word for twenty-five cents.

Olivia took out her change purse and counted out a few coins. "*Solamente uno, nada más.*" She put money in the old woman's moist, wrinkled, hand.

The woman felt the coins and dropped them into a pouch inside her blouse. She fished out a couple of tamales wrapped in dark banana leaves. "*Dos para la niña bonita,*" she said in Spanish. She then felt around on the dirt floor till she found a plastic bag. She put the tamales in and added a paper napkin.

"*Solamente uno.*"

"*Dos para la niña bonita,*" the old woman repeated, stretching the bag into the air. "*Algo de beber? Coca grande 8 len y la pequeña 6. Fría muy fría.*"

"*La grande.*"

The old woman pointed to the cold chest in her shack next to a cabinet that had chiclets, cigarettes, *canillas the leche* and glazed fruit under glass. The opener was on a string. Olivia took out a coke and wedged open the cap.

"*Adónde vas?*" the old woman asked, perhaps wondering if she should charge a bottle deposit.

"Al *Cerro de la Cruz.*"

The woman smiled. "*Dios la bendiga*"—God bless you. She crossed herself and kissed the silver *chachal* around her neck. "*Que el más santísimo dios nos bendiga a todos.*"

Olivia took the tamales and went on her way.

The climb to the top took another ten minutes. Once there, Olivia sat on a flat rock under the stone cross that rose high over Antigua and the whole surrounding valley. Directly in front of her, ten kilometers, away, was the *Volcán de Agua*, inert and placid. Buzzards, mere specks against the blue sky, circled around the cone. Olivia looked around her as if to find someone to whom she could say *I slept there once. We almost died getting to the top. I was there.* But there was no one to tell.

The smell of the tamales began to make Olivia's mouth water. She took one out of the bag and started to unwrap it. Warm water trickled out of the banana leaves and down her hands and arms. She licked the water. Corn sweet.

Olivia took a bite. The tamale was dense and the red pepper and olive gave it a slightly tangy taste. As she took a second bite, her throat tightened, her eyes swelled, and she began crying.

Why was she crying? The view was breathless, the tamale was delicious, few days were as beautiful as this one. Was she happy or sad? Olivia couldn't figure it out. But there were tears leaking out of her eyes.

She was thinking of her mother. When Olivia had entered the *Colegio Parroquial* it would have been nice to have had her mother give her a hug and a kiss goodbye. Something to remember her by. Or when Olivia came home, it would have been nice if her mother had welcomed her back with a smile or a special meal like *fiambre* or a chicken *pepian*. Olivia had once offered to bring beef or chicken home and her mother had simply laughed at her. Was it because she hadn't believed she could get it or because the very idea of eating meat made her laugh?

Meme had offered to give her the money to buy the ingredients.

Why couldn't Lucia prepare *mosh*—oatmeal—for her Sunday breakfast? Anything to make her feel special or loved. Is this why she was crying?

Olivia felt alone. As if she had stepped off a bluff to find herself floating in mid-air. Her classmates ridiculed their own home lives, but Olivia would have been happy to go to any of their homes, to put her head on any mother's lap and feel a gentle, warm hand on her face. She wanted a mother who would worry about makeup, about acne or age lines, and about her husband possibly having an affair as she drew up a list of what the maid should buy for the evening's dinner party.

She would have given anything to put her head on a pillow and lie on the floor of a big modern house, with a plush rug cushioning her, in front of a fireplace that was mostly ornamental, not used for cooking. Or to do what Meme said her aunt liked to do: drive her car to the *Hipódromo* in the *Zona Dos*, where there was a huge blue and green relief map of Guatemala that extended half a block on the ground, where you could climb a tower and see Tikal, the Petén, Cobán, the Cuchumatanes, Quiché Province, the Atlantic and Pacific Ocean all from the same spot. And Mexico.

Was it so wrong to dream?

Olivia suddenly felt nauseous. Maybe the old woman had given her pork instead of chicken tamales. The pork was often old and rancid, and there was always the fear of picking up trichinosis or some mysterious disease. The bits of corn meal still in her mouth were no longer sweet but seemed to excrete a bitter liquid. Olivia flipped off the cap of her Coke and took a huge sip.

The Coke was warm and sour, hardly curative. Olivia pushed away the rest of the tamale and lay down on one arm against the flat stone, shutting her eyes. She could feel her stomach rumbling and tried to distract herself by reciting the names of animal groups that are part of the different seawater phyla: coelenterates, mollusks, echinoderms…

But reciting made her even more nauseous. And she felt cold.

Once Jimena had told her that her Antigua home had many fireplaces. The one in her bedroom had a large grate, a poker and a rake, and a triangular woodpile nearby; whenever it got cold, one of her three maids would light it. And when she went home on weekends in January, a maid would get up at five in the morning to set fire to the kindling so that when Jimena woke up to go to Sunday Mass at the San Francisco Church, her room would be warm and toasty.

"My parents adore me, "Jimena would say, hugging herself with her thin arms. Olivia would be jealous at the same time that she wondered if they loved her so much, why had they put her in a parochial boarding school when her home was less than a mile away? The truth was that her parents probably couldn't bear to have her at home. When Olivia had first met Jimena, she had been nice: hadn't she helped her to use a bathroom? Maybe Olivia had made a tactical mistake: she should have shunned Meme and joined up with Jimena and *Las Valentinas*. She would've received many special favors.

Olivia heard a cough and opened her eyes.

In front of her stood a *Santa María del Jesús* Indian. He had a red wool shoulder bag and carried bundled kindling on his back in a net bag. A leather *mecapal* creased his brow, leaving all the weight on his neck and his hands free.

His hair stood straight up on his head like black straw partly because of the *mecapal* and partly because he had a blue *cinta* just below the hairline.

"*Está bien*?" he asked in decent, but broken, Spanish.

Olivia pushed herself up. "My stomach hurts."

"It's better if you vomit."

Olivia nodded. Before she could stop herself, her throat tightened, salt invade her gullet and she vomited in two systematic volleys. The food spread over the edge of the stone where she had been sitting, but none landed on her uniform.

She pulled her white sleeve along her mouth.

"Now drink the Coke. All of it." The Indian got down on one knee, keeping distance between them. He made no effort to drop his load.

Olivia did as she was told. The warm, gurgly liquid didn't taste sour now and seemed to settle her stomach. Within moments, she no longer felt weak and nauseous.

The man continued to watch her without saying anything. Finally, when he saw that Olivia was doing better, he said: "You shouldn't be here alone. *Vámonos!* The Cerro is full of thieves and people looking for trouble. There are also too many *cantiles*," he said, referring to the poisonous snakes that live in the Petén jungles.

Olivia had to smile. "*Cantiles* live hundreds of kilometer from here."

The man smiled back, pulling down on the corners of his mouth, and shrugged. It was a fact that the old Indian seemed to know. He gave Olivia his free arm and pulled her up.

"Would you like a *chiclet*?" the man asked her, pulling a yellow box out of his pants pocket. Without waiting for an answer he shook out two white rectangles in her palm and put two others in his own mouth even though he barely had teeth.

He smiled a gummy smile.

"Thank you," she said.

He merely bowed.

They walked down the hill together, arm in arm, toward the center of Antigua—he carrying the load on his back and she walking with only a paper bag in her hand. If someone had looked at them, he might have assumed that father and daughter were walking into town together, they seemed so at ease with one another.

And if anyone who had known her before had looked at Olivia straight from the front, in her blue and white school uniform, he would have said that she was no longer a chubby, slightly misshapen girl, but an adolescent well on her way to becoming a woman. Her body was gaining shape and her legs lengthening. The hem of her skirt now fell above her knees, which were no longer knobby and dark but smooth like *zapote* seeds.

Olivia's dark eyes, always so nondescript against her olive skin, had taken on a certain degree of deepening and had a spark of their own, teasingly so, even now when she wasn't feeling tiptop.

Her lips, too, seemed for the first time to be inviting.

This change might have happened almost overnight.

The sky had grown overcast and a cool breeze blew steadily from the north, signaling rain. It was nearly noon, Olivia knew she should hurry. The field trip might have been cut short, Juana Quiroga might have stopped to look in on her in bed. Still, Olivia felt unhurried, comforted by the wizened man's deliberate pace and lulled by the sound of his *caites* shuffling on the cobblestones as they walked.

Olivia enjoyed chewing on the sweet peppermint gum. She didn't know why, but she felt free enough to breathe.

(1980)

In January, when Olivia turned sixteen, Guatemala experienced an increase in violence. Army forces firebombed the Spanish Embassy in the capital, killing thirty-nine Indian *campesinos* who had taken it over to protest army repression in *Quiché* province. More strikes and protests followed and, in the ensuing months, trade union activists, student leaders, journalists and social workers were killed by the dozen. One day several armed men went to the campus of the *Universidad de San Carlos*, a hotbed of anti-government activity, and simply started shooting students as they disembarked from public buses on their way to classes. In total, over 50 students were killed and many more were kidnapped.

Changes were also taking place at the *Colegio Parroquial*. It all started when Jimena went to see Sister Bonifacia in her office in early February and told her that Angelina was pregnant. Normally a serene individual never at a loss for words, the nun was in a state of panic. What was she to do? She thanked Jimena somewhat icily for having ratted out her supposed good friend. Sister Bonifacia suddenly felt lightheaded— she was too old and frail to be dealing with these kinds of crises.

She called Angelina into her office.

"Is it true that you are with child?" Sister Bonifacia asked.

Angelina responded by fainting on the floor.

Sister Bonifacia had Angelina taken to her dorm room. She immediately called Dr. Madrid and asked him to come to the school.

Amid tears, Angelina refused to let the doctor examine her. To some degree, the doctor was relieved—he took no pleasure in internal examinations. He looked at the girl sobbing in bed, saw the lump around her midriff, and issued his medical assessment--though she had successfully hidden it, Angelina was at least seven months pregnant.

It hardly mattered that Dr. Madrid's estimate was two months off—Angelina was entering her fifth month—but Sister Bonifacia did not hesitate in deciding: "Pack your things, my dear, you are leaving the school this very afternoon." And without consulting Juana Quiroga, Sister Carina or the other nuns, she called Angelina's parents and told them that their daughter was being immediately expelled from school. The *Colegio Parroquial* was not about to tolerate promiscuity.

Meme, no great friend of Angelina's, felt that a grave injustice had been done to her. As Angelina packed her clothes, she rallied the students to her support—it was decided that she and Olivia would go see Sister Bonifacia, first to insist, and that failing, to beg her to reconsider her decision.

What kind of school was the *Colegio Parroquial* if the director could simply expel one of the students without so much as a hearing?

Sister Bonifacia ushered the two girls into her office, which boasted a collection of iron and wood crucifixes on one wall and a bookcase with all kinds of miniature porcelain frogs, of varying sizes and colors, along the other. The two windows in the room were curtained in brown burlap material and the desk lamp, at 35 watts, barely illuminated the cavernous room. The girls were directed to sit on a wooden slatted sofa before her desk. Sister Bonifacia faced them sitting stiffly in a high back chair, regaled in her thickest black habit.

Meme spoke in rapid-fire, giving several reasons for why Angelina must stay: she had been at the school for 10 years; her parents were monsters, maybe even child abusers; she was one of the school's best students, with high grades in history and religion. Angelina was a school leader. She tutored the younger girls. She was the library monitor two nights a week. Sister Bonifacia listened silently to Meme's arguments, at most turning down the corners of her mouth each time Meme gave a reason for why she should rethink her decision.

When she had finished, Sister Bonifacia waited a few seconds. She took a deep breath and replied: "*The body is not for fornication, but for the Lord; and the Lord for the Body.* What Angelina has done is against everything we have taught you. We cannot offer her sanctuary within our walls."

Meme was almost in tears, as if mounting her own defense, which in fact she was. Since the beginning of the year she had been sneaking out to meet Isidro Fonseca, and they were far beyond simple kissing.

But because her sister gave her birth control pills, Meme was fairly sure she would avoid Angelina's fate and not get pregnant. Still she was nervous. She tried a different tack, couching her argument in the Biblical language that Sister Bonifacia so much admired: "But by throwing her out you've judged her. You're always telling us: "*Judge not, that ye be not judged*—isn't that so, Olivia?"

Since Olivia was on scholarship, she felt she had no right to speak—she was more a trespasser at the school than a fully qualified student. But if anyone knew, about sin, it was she—hadn't she witnessed the young girls forced into sex so near her mother's hut in the coffee fields? Wouldn't she know that housekeepers were sexually exploited in the homes of the wealthy? Still she felt too vulnerable and uncertain to come out openly in Angelina's defense.

"It's not her fault," was all she could say.

Sister Bonifacia shook her head—she was not in the mood to debate because she knew that her own position was weak. What did she know of sex? She had barely touched herself, never even considered sinning with the body of another. Her thoughts were pure. "My girls, I feel perfectly confident that if needed, I could cast the first stone. This is not to say that I am without sin—on the contrary, I spend hours asking the Lord for forgiveness. But let's be clear: I'm not judging that poor, unfortunate girl—this will happen at the Gates of Heaven. She simply cannot remain with us. My decision is final."

"But you can't just cast her out. She's one of us. Like Mary Magdalene. Jesús forgave her—you know that Angelina will never sin again," Meme countered.

Sister Bonifacia looked at the two girls. She raised her right eyebrow as if to ask: "What else?"

When Olivia saw that the nun was standing firm, she said: "Why can't she just have the baby here? We can help her take care of it!"

Sister Bonifacia stood up, flattening out her habit. She was about to say to Olivia something about the Indians being child factories, having one baby right after the other, but she held back. "I think it's best for her family to deal with this situation. I have already called her parents and they will be here soon to take her home."

"Sister Bonifacia you're always telling us that we're a community. Olivia's right. We are Angelina's family," said Meme, wiping tears from her eyes.

"We can take care of the baby," Olivia repeated, thinking of how she had cared for her brother Guayito when he had been born so long ago—she had kept him clean, tickled him, fed him when her mother was working in the fields.

Sister Bonifacia walked over to the girls and motioned for them to stand up. The girls looked at one another and rose. The nun was not so glacial that she lacked feelings. She took Meme and Olivia's heads and pulled them against her bony chest. She searched her memory for words that could possibly serve as guidance. "Girls, girls, you are so full of sweet thoughts. But there is a lesson here, one that will, hopefully, properly serve all of you: *Walk in the Spirit, and ye shall not fulfill the lust of the flesh.* I know you are good girls. You want to help someone who you care for very much. But Angelina has committed one of the worst carnal sins. She has forsaken her sacred duty to keep her body pure. Let this be a warning to all of you. We are surrounded by temptation, but I ask you to walk in the paths of righteousness. Remember how Satan tried to tempt Our Savior with gifts of worldly power? He would not give in. Remember this verse from the Epistle of James: *Blessed is the man that endureth temptation; for when he is tried, he will receive the crown of life.* I think you girls should go back to your room now and think about how you can free yourselves from sin."

*

That afternoon, after Angelina had been taken away, several nuns came to see Sister Bonifacia for a more detailed explanation of her decision. She told them to schedule a full staff meeting for tomorrow in the chapel while the girls would be having lunch.

The rest of the afternoon Sister Bonifacia deflected curt replies, whispering and frowns as she walked the halls of the *Colegio Parroquial*—she sensed that her fellow sisters were conspiring against her. The morning of the meeting she waited in her office for either Sister Carina or Tabitha to come and speak to her, to help her strategize, but neither did. She felt isolated—about to be reprimanded or censured by the very school she had found. It was not fair.

She looked around the chapel and saw a sea of unfriendly faces. She started the meeting by announcing that she was resigning, effective immediately.

Though she and Sister Carina had been rivals for many years, often sparring at meetings, Sister Bonifacia recognized that in these difficult times, the school needed someone younger, less rigid, a person who could bend like a willow in the wind. This was Sister Carina.

Sister Bonifacia had done what she could to direct the girls, to equip them with the moral and ethical tools to survive in a world increasingly given over to sin and venal habits. She could sense it in the magazines the girls read and the music they listened to, in the sassy way that they spoke to one another and even to the teaching staff. In the way they moved and hiked up their skirts.

Events were rushing by her, and she did not know how to deal with them. She was nearly seventy-five years old. She would be better off dedicating the remaining years of her life to her frog collection and to prayer and devotion.

*

With Angelina gone, the girls were somber and dogged. Sister Carina determined that what the girls needed was some levity: to be away from the school, out of classes, in different surroundings, away from their usual routine. Distraction.

She suggested that Sisters Tabitha and Carolina take the girls on a one-week excursion to visit the many fine churches in Huehuetenango, Quetzaltenango and Chichicastenango, the principal cities of the Guatemalan highlands. And as a nod to Guatemala's Mayan past, they could also explore the pre-Columbian ruins in Zacaleu and Utatlán, near Santa Cruz del Quiché, where Pedro de Alvarado defeated the Maya.

The trip was planned to the final details—where they would sleep, who would bunk with whom, where they might eat. But it all came to naught when a Spanish priest was murdered in Quiché province after having witnessed the shooting and killing of eighteen women who had gone to the Nebaj army garrison to inquire about their disappeared husbands. To risk the lives of the girls for the sake of a religious retreat was regarded by Sister Carina as sheer lunacy.

*

All in all, 1980 had been a hard school year for the girls in Olivia's grade, ranging in age from sixteen to eighteen. To their teachers, they seemed distracted in the classroom, sullen and tight-lipped, happier doing rote exercises and being lectured to than in taking part in discussions. Where before they had competed to be in the chorus or to help in the Wednesday night services, now the girls grudgingly did so, preferring to stay in their rooms and talk or hideout in the library. They no longer resisted going to bed at ten o'clock either.

The mood cast a pall over the school. There was no spirit or excitement, at least none that the nuns could perceive. The girls that returned to their homes in Guatemala City for the weekend seemed obsessed with organizing their weekend parties, so much in vogue, with drinking, smoking and God knew what else. This was all part of the whispered rumors that coiled through the dorms. And there was talk that some of these things went on in the *Colegio Parroquial* after the nuns retired to prayers in their rooms. What were they to do? Hire dorm guards and turn the *Colegio Parroquial* into a prison? The older girls would simply rebel and their resistance would filter down and be most damaging to the younger girls who were still community-minded and easily disciplined. The nuns refused to turn the school into an armed camp.

Olivia was in her own funk, spending so many of her waking hours wondering what would happen once she graduated from school. Though she wouldn't admit that she was totally happy at the *Colegio*, it had been a godsend that had saved her from a life of servitude. She would never go back to being the girl who followed her mother in the *cafetales*. It was almost as if her past before the *Colegio Parroquial* was something she had read about in one of her textbooks, not something she had experienced. Even when she went home now, to spend a day with her mother and brother, she would try to arrive as late as she could Saturday afternoon. She would dream up an excuse that she had to leave early on Sunday to go to the library to research a paper due Monday in school or that she had been asked by Sister Carina to help straighten out the prayer missals in the chapel.

Lucia, in time, stopped battling Olivia—it was as if she had simply written her daughter out of her life. She now found solace in lighting candles and taking part in Saturday afternoon services in the Assembly of God, the new evangelical church that had been built in the clearing near the shack where the young girls had provided services for the men had once stood. Lucia hated the Catholic Church for emphasizing the need to live in a Christian manner at the same time that it amassed obscene wealth and insisted on unquestioning respect of their established hierarchy. She would never again take orders from a priest who answered to a pope living in gilded splendor in the Vatican. The Protestant missionary leaders--despite their blond hair, white shirts and thin black ties--built simple churches out of wood and spoke about how each person could talk directly to Christ. They stressed the importance of personal salvation, good deeds on this earth, and the singing of Gospel prayers until their bodies shook with fervency.

Lucia felt that the evangelical ministers showed little pretension and certainly no attitude of superiority—everyone was a lamb of God.

Guayo, too, fell under the spell of the new missionaries and became a committed young catechist. He devoted his free hours to helping find new converts for the church in the streets of Ciudad Vieja and Antigua.

At almost age twelve, he was tall and strapping, with brown muscles that flexed and rippled when he walked. He now spoke quietly and with authority, as if he had been imbued with the quiet serenity of a true believer. He hardly smiled, and his eyes focused intently and without blinking on whoever was speaking. They were not exactly vacant eyes, but rather expressionless as if holding a secret. And as part of his church duties, he had been asked to be part of a sacred mission to get the few remaining males in the *cafetales* to join the *kaibiles*—Civil Defense patrols made up of Indians to protect villagers from the guerillas. He carried around a machete and though he did not own a gun, he had been taught to shoot Galils by a rifle instructor—a fellow evangelical assigned to the Antigua garrison encamped near Ciudad Vieja.

His long, sharp ears were keenly perked to hear the footsteps of guerillas should they decide to attack coffee plantations in the night and force the workers to take up arms against the landowners. His conversations became sprinkled with a mixture of religion and army fervor, and he felt he was a soldier in the Army of God.

All this made Olivia uncomfortable—she soon felt that the moon might be a more hospitable place than the home that her mother and Guayo shared.

*

The clock was ticking for the girls. In another year they would be gone their separate ways. They would be leaving the refuge that had allowed them to act out brazenly and without care—yet for most of them, the future seemed full of hope. With their parents' money and connections, they would either go to college in the U.S. or be sent to finishing schools in Paris, Geneva or London. At worst, a few of the girls would be obliged to stay home, attend classes at the Marroquín or del Valle colleges until they received propositions of marriage from the offspring of their parent's wealthy friends.

Olivia had no idea what she would do after graduation. She had decent grades, good enough to take courses at the *Universidad de San Carlos*. But who would pay for her studies and who would cover the costs of her living arrangements? She saw graduation day in the future like a storm brewing in the not so far off distance. The world as she knew it would disappear, and she had no idea what course or direction her life would take. She would never go back to her mother's shack with her head hanging down, defeated by events beyond her control. There was nothing there for her. Where could she go?

Meme, the one person who Olivia had consistently depended upon, was of little help to her. She seemed more remote each day, and more deeply involved with Isidro, her boyfriend. Two or three nights a week she would meet him behind *La Merced* or mid-block on *Calle Desengaño*, where the streetlamps had burned out. She would slip back into the school a good bit after midnight.

Meme seemed casting around for her own future, more confused than committed. One night, when Antigua was under a deluge of rainwater and there was no way she could meet Isidro, she came and sat on Olivia's bed. The other girls were asleep but Olivia still had her night lamp on.

Meme was wearing a light blue silk nightgown, with a pattern of faint yellow stars. She crossed one leg under the other and leaned her back against the wall. "You know, Olivia, I might just marry Isidoro," she whispered.

Everyone recognized that Meme was beautiful, with mahogany skin and opal eyes. She exuded confidence, a kind of womanly voluptuousness that made people shudder in her presence. When Meme walked through the school, in her white blouse and swaying blue skirt hugging her thighs, even the elderly nuns would turn around automatically to stare at her calves and shapely behind.

"What do you know about him?" Olivia asked, in her own cloud of ignorance.

"Well, he says he's in love with me, but I don't really believe him. He says the most impudent things. He likes my breasts and says that I am *tetona pero muy sabrosona*."

Olivia found herself staring at Meme's breasts, with their straight long nipples pushing against her nightgown. She understood Isidro's desire for she, too, at this moment, wished she could put them in her mouth. She felt heat rising to her face.

"Oh Meme, don't forget what happened to Angelina. It could happen to any of us," was all Olivia could say.

Meme laughed loudly. "Angelina was careless. She didn't use protection with Raúl—"

"You don't mean Jimena's brother?" Olivia gasped.

Meme pulled her hair back with both hands and shook her head. "Don't tell me you didn't know?"

"Well—"

"That's why Jimena ratted Angelina out. She found love notes in her brother's room, and other things, too--"

"Like what?"

Meme leaned closer to Olivia and whispered in her ear. "Packs of condoms. Boys put them on their penises—"

"Stop!" Olivia covered her ears. "I don't want to hear any more." She felt dryness in her mouth and a blurring in her eyes—she didn't know if she was about to vomit or cry. She took deep breaths, full breaths, even though she felt her mouth was a salty cesspool.

"We're not young girls anymore," Meme said.

Olivia swallowed hard, trying to move the saltiness in her throat back down into her stomach. The breathing had helped, maybe she should start humming. Humming calmed her down.

Meme could never talk about things straightforwardly. She made every situation seem so dramatic—surely she should pursue a career in theater. It had been years since they had spoken intimately, and Olivia had almost forgotten that she never could anticipate what would be coming out of Meme's mouth next. She met her eyes, which were fiery and defiant, like a wild animal's.

"That scares me," Olivia said, the lump rolling out of her throat. There were tears in her eyes.

"I can't tell you what it feels like when Isidro starts fiddling with the buttons of my blouse. It's not as if he knows what to do on his own. I have to tell him what to do, step by step. But I start feeling so hot that I'm about to burst, and then I do burst." Meme pointed toward the space between her legs. "I get all wet, and all I want to do is get him inside of me."

Olivia barely could get her words out. "He's so much older than you."

Meme leaned forward. "I know. And he's ugly. Very, very ugly. He wears thick-framed glasses that pinch his nose. His lips droop down—you can see how crooked his front teeth are. And he puts too much grease in his hair."

"Why are you with him?"

Meme shrugged. "I guess I really don't know why. Well, I do know why—I think I am using him sexually. He is my instrument. And I also like how his mind works. He's constantly talking to me about a man named Marx who might be the world's greatest thinker. I really can't understand what Isidro is talking about. All I know is that he pays attention to me."

Meme was talking about feelings that Olivia had yet to experience. In fact, she had no desire to experience these things and this made her wonder if there was something wrong with her. Olivia remembered what she had felt when Meme had kissed her so many years ago, that first year she had been in the school. She had felt warmth down there. Meme had promised to teach her to tongue kiss—is that how the warmth turned to wetness?

Without realizing it, Olivia had closed her eyes and seemed to be in a state of narcotic sleep where her mind was exploring areas of her body that she had never dared to touch in that way.

"Are you okay?" Meme had touched Olivia's arm.

Olivia smiled, a bit embarrassed. "I was remembering when you first kissed me."

Meme seemed to have forgotten. "We must have been kids."

"It's when our dorm was on the second floor. My bed was next to Jimena's and yours was all the way back by the linen closet."

Meme smiled, her eyes lighting up again. "That was the year you arrived at the school. I had never seen anyone so scared. You were so nervous. I was afraid that if anyone spoke loudly to you, you'd break into tears. I thought that maybe here was someone who didn't have one mean bone in her body."

"It was all so new to me," Olivia said.

"You were from another world."

"I had never been out of the fields."

Meme smiled. "And you had never been kissed on the lips."

*

The two girls chatted some more, but it was more Meme's monologue. One minute she was talking about marrying Isidro and the both of them joining the guerrillas in Santa Cruz del Quiché province. The next minute she talked of accepting her older sister's offer to pay for her schooling in a junior college in Orlando, Florida. And finally she mentioned the possibility of joining a theater troupe in Guatemala City that staged political farces.

"You have so many choices," Olivia said, somewhat resentfully.

Meme looked deeply into her friend's eyes. "So do you, Olivia."

"Please don't tease me."

"Olivia, you are silly. You have so much more going for you than any of us. And you have nothing to tie you down. Certainly, you aren't ever going back to that hideous shack where your mother lives. That's out of the question."

"I know that. So how can you say I have so much? I have no money, no rich relatives, no one to watch over me. Sister Carina is always reminding me of that. She's become just like Sister Bonifacia, always quoting from the Bible to prove her point. Just yesterday she said to me "*Put on charity, which is the bond of perfectness.*" What does she think I will live on, bread and water?"

Meme smiled. "Olivia, you should live on what you have always lived on."

"And that means?" Olivia questioned.

"You are such a silly creature. You are pure goodness. It's what you've always had. Do you know how rare that is?"

Olivia was confused. "And how will that help me?"

Meme yawned. "Most people are wicked. They walk around as if they know everything. One day your innocence will serve you. Believe me."

And with that Meme kissed her cheek and went to bed.

(1981)

Meme was not the only *Colegio Parroquial* girl interested in boys—most of Olivia's classmates ached for sex and didn't care if it masqueraded as true love. The school roof, which had offered them sufficient privacy to smoke, kiss and tell jokes when they were younger, was too dangerous for the courting of boys and was left to the younger girls to follow in their footsteps. Since Jimena knew Antigua's hidden corners best, it fell upon her to find the girls an isolated retreat.

For years Jimena had ridiculed and excluded any girl who failed to swear a binding allegiance to her. She had unleashed so much trouble around her not only at school, but also at home because of her betrayal of Angelina and her brother, which had cost her several friendships. She realized that she would be graduating in less than a year and didn't want her classmates to remember her as the school terror. She became friendly, in a neutral sort of way, and accepted her new role as facilitator with great humility. Gone were the days when, with her merciless tone, she led the charge to denigrate her classmates.

Even her father Arturo Chang was convinced that though Raúl had gotten Angelina pregnant, it wouldn't have happened had Jimena served as a model to her younger brother. Jimena had spent many hours devising hideous tortures: frogs in his shoes, nails in his bicycle tires, anything to make her shine brighter in the eyes of her parents and reduce her brother to dirt. So when Raúl was implicated in Angelina's pregnancy, Arturo Chang—instead of showering Jimena with gratitude for having revealed his son's duplicity—decided to punish her by announcing that she would not be going to college. Jimena was expected to stay at home and use all her newly acquired bookkeeping skills to make sure *Almacén La Fe* retained its position as the most important dry goods store in Antigua. She protested his decision with tears and rants, but her father would not be moved. In the end, she was forced to accept his decision.

Jimena thought long and hard about finding a nearby refuge, away from public scrutiny. The *Parque Central*—the social as well as the geographical center of Antigua—was too exposed. The town's elders would gather there on evenings to gossip and converse while the young people talked and flirted with one another. The boys would circle in pairs clockwise around the park while the girls went counterclockwise—this was the accepted courtship ritual. Couples looking for privacy would huddle on benches as far as possible from the fountain, at the park center, and away from the bandshell where sometimes marimba music played. The park was the focal point to see and be seen, not what the *Colegio Parroquial* girls wanted.

Churches were Antigua's lifeblood--they were beacons for religious prayer, community and instruction; sites whose large courtyards and patios permitted visitors an escape for reading, writing poetry and quiet contemplation. Half a dozen powerful earthquakes had reduced most of them to rubble, rendered them roofless, leaving only vestiges of their Baroque finery to rot alongside the truncated towers and belfries. Except for the Santiago Cathedral, the San Francisco Church and the new evangelist chapels that had been refitted out of abandoned warehouses, most were in ruins. Many like *Santa Clara* and *La Recolección* functioned as museums or simply served as homes for raccoons, crows and field mice.

The logical place for a rendezvous was in one of Antigua's abandoned churches, many dating back to the mid-seventeenth century. At night they offered the privacy that couldn't be found elsewhere in town. Jimena found the ideal spot in the convent ruins behind *La Merced*. To get there, the girls had to clamber down a rickety ladder into an abandoned building behind the school. They would walk together, arm in arm, down the middle of *Callejón Campo Seco* because this alleyway was avoided by all—it had no streetlights and was piled high with garbage and reeked of human excrement. The girls walked quickly, clasping each other tightly, though in truth they had nothing to fear: they never encountered anyone other than a muttering drunk, a mangy dog or two or three *limosneros* who had bedded down on cardboard next to the side of a building.

At the end of the *Callejón* stood *La Merced*, a massive yellow structure with thick filigreed walls and saint-filled niches. The girls circled around the darkened church and entered the convent ruins through a gate with a broken lock. Here they'd meet secretly with boys who they had met during weekends home or who simply knew that several nights a week girls from the *Colegio* would be there to drink and smoke. Of course the nuns knew nothing about these night-time escapades.

As was the custom in Guatemala, the boys were older than the girls. They drove their pickups into Antigua from the capital or from their *fincas* in the country dressed in jeans, boots and cowboy hats. On most nights, five or six girls would be there, drifting in and out of the shadows, with the moon casting only the palest of light. Kissing and fondling was the order of the day though the more experienced girls, like Meme, paired off with their dates in cloistered recesses on the first and second floor.

Jimena not only found this site for these trysts, but she also even invited three or four local boys with whom she had grown up. Jimena introduced them to her classmates—Olivia among them—and they would congregate near the huge dry orange fountain situated in the convent's first patio. Shy and polite, they came to the convent like clockwork every Thursday night, almost as if attending a church meeting or a *tertulia* at a café. Jimena planted herself at the center of this group and tried to offer topics of conversation, which allowed her to decry anecdotes or exploits. But after being indulged during the first two or three of these gatherings, she was ignored by her friends who had moved on to her classmates. In the end, Jimena simply stopped coming.

Of all these local Antigua boys, Olivia especially liked Jesús, who everyone referred to by his nickname *Chucho*, because he had a kind of hangdog expression—his cheeks drooped like saddlebags and he had sad, listless eyes. He seemed to have no expectations in life— he would take whatever was dealt to him and seemed to enjoy life without ambition. His father was a manager of the *Pan Lido* bakery in Antigua and his mother stayed home caring for his six brothers and sisters: they were religious children, all well-dressed, extremely obedient, never challenging. Serene, bookish, almost complacent, this was Chucho--and though at times his quiet ways exasperated Olivia, she really had no experience with boys.

He was happy to hold hands with her, look down at his shoes and talk about his plans to study biology at the Universidad del Valle in Guatemala City or tell her about his growing collection of forest butterflies. She wished that he would look at her when he talked and, even if he didn't find her pretty, would at least say so. When she squeezed his hand, he would look across at the water lily blossoms carved into the fountain stone or simply survey the church, with its crumbling pillars and pilasters. He would then start to talk about his latest catch and how he would like to invite Olivia to his house to see his collection, never quite meeting her eyes.

"Most people collect field butterflies, but I collect rarer ones that live deep in the forests. I have them set in glass and wooden boxes in my bedroom."

"I would like to see them," she said to him, arching her eyebrows.

"Maybe next Sunday. You could come for lunch. I'd like you to meet my parents and my brothers and sisters."

Very often, Olivia and Chucho would be the only couple left by the fountain and this bored her. It wasn't that she was tiring of his words, but she wished he were more declarative in his actions and feelings.

"Wouldn't they be meeting *me*?" It's not that she expected Chucho to take her into his arms, but why couldn't he have said *I want my parents to meet you*? Said that way meant that she was worth having his parents meet *her*, not the other way around.

"Well, yes," he answered. "You would be meeting each other."

One night after the other couples had drifted away, she led him by the hand up the stone steps in the rear of the patio to the second floor, a maze of stone rooms without roofs. She gripped his hand hard and felt wetness—the palm of his hand was sweating. Was he nervous or was he excited as she was?

It was a moonless night. Scorpio was etched broadly in the sky above them and the twinkling of its three pincer stars seemed to crackle. Olivia heard other voices nearby and dragged Jesús to a small chamber with a grassy, overgrown floor.

"I don't think we should be here, Olivia," Chucho said.

"Are you frightened?"

"I want to preserve your reputation."

Olivia felt emboldened to say: "I don't care what others say."

"Well, you should care." Jesús turned his head away and looked toward the lintel doorway they had just crossed. His shoes were stamping on the ground.

"Chucho, will you look at me?" Olivia insisted.

Jesús raised his eyes. He was shorter than Olivia, seemed to be a life-size marionette, stiff with fear, beside her. He blinked several times, almost as if he could not focus his eyes, and ended up lowering them.

Olivia pushed him into a corner and pressed herself against him. He stumbled backward a foot or two until his shoulders were against the wall. She had no idea what she was doing, but she placed his hands on her full and fiery breasts. She closed her eyes in pleasure.

But Chucho simply left them there, as if his hands were glued to spigots. Was he expected to do something?

Olivia locked her arms behind his back and pressed her mouth against his. She tried opening his lips with her tongue, as Meme had once taught her, but he seemed inert, unable to react, almost as if disgusted by her efforts. She moved his hands from her breasts down her sides and forced them to raise up her skirt just a little and touch her buttocks.

She was not wearing underwear.

"Please, Olivia, we shouldn't be doing this," Jesús said, turning his face away. "It's wrong." His face scrunched up like a paper bag, his forehead had furrowed.

Olivia pretended she hadn't heard him. She felt the heat of her blood, like sap running up a tree, throughout the tips of her body. She began trembling, almost out of control. She pushed harder against him until she had raised herself up against his body, pushing her pelvis against his hipbone. Olivia could not stop.

Jesús kept saying "We better go back down—". He moved his hands away from her buttocks and tried feebly to push her hips away from him. She dug her head into one of his shoulders, which remained pressed against the stone wall and rocked into his hipbone, back and forth, back and forth, unable and unwilling to stop.

"You're hurting me," she heard him say, but she was already surging. When she felt the first spasm of pleasure, she let out a cry like a baby's whimper. It rose up through her body, making her nipples harden and her tongue dry. She felt a vise releasing her throat and the words "I love you" spurted out of her lips.

Olivia had the sensation she was floating through the air on large wooden wings, letting the wind currents direct her movements. She saw an oxcart, a sailing ship, and a pool of water far below her. With a flick of her wings she could rise or fall.

Olivia opened her eyes. Jesús was whimpering.

"I want to go home. I want to go home now," he kept repeating. Jesús was twenty. He had never been with a woman. And though no sin had occurred, how would he explain this away to the priest at confession?

I let a girl use my body for her pleasure. No, not like that. It's hard to explain. No, I don't think--

Olivia moved away from Jesús, feeling grateful. She let her blue schoolgirl's skirt back down over her hips. Then she shifted back toward him and began kissing his face.

He pushed her away. "I hate you. I hate you," he said aloud, turning away from her. He began walking out of the roofless room.

"Jesús," she called after him. "Chucho."

He didn't answer.

"Please don't be angry with me."

Olivia allowed her body to fall against the stone wall. She thought it odd that she had said she loved him, but actually she hadn't cared that Chucho had left. It was the first time she had not cared what another person thought or felt. She experienced no regret. Meme would be proud of her, pleased that she had acted through her desires.

She had lost her innocence, in a way, but wouldn't have been able to describe it.

Olivia suddenly felt cold and realized she should go back to the school. She listened for other sounds of her classmates, as she went down the stairs, but heard nothing.

When she got back to the *Colegio Parroquial*, Olivia undressed and lay quietly in bed. She wanted to wait up for Meme who had broken up with Isidro weeks earlier and already had a new boyfriend, Francisco "Paquito" Obregón. But after waiting an hour, Olivia drifted away to sleep.

*

Meme now seemed completely enthralled by this new boyfriend, whose father owned the service station outside Antigua, on the road to Guatemala City. "Paquito" was considered a "bad" boy—he was twenty-four to Meme's seventeen and had been accused of killing a friend a year earlier, thus earning the nickname "*El Fusil.*" The shooting had happened at his father's finca in San Lucas Sacatepéquez. He and his friends had gone there, drunk a bottle of Ron Botrán and spent the night three sheets to the wind riding horses bareback and shooting beer bottles off wooden fences with his father's many guns and rifles.

Paquito had shot Mario Tejada pointblank from six feet away and he had died from a single gunshot wound to the head. His friends said it was an accident, an unfortunate accident—Paquito had simply tried to shoot off Mario's hat but the horse had suddenly reared up and his friend's head entered the line of fire.

Some of the boys grumbled about how Paquito and Mario had always disliked each other—grudges extending back from the time they were in their teens—but Edgar Obregón, Paquito's father, was a rich man and his *quetzales* bought heaps of silence. And who would dispute the police claim that the killing was just an unfortunate accident?

A week in jail was punishment enough. Paquito's father was a sly one, his son even slyer. Tejada was not the first person *El Fusil* had killed, but certainly the first one to have a name. Paquito was part of a conservative faction at the *Universidad de San Carlos* that believed the university had come under the control of Marxist revolutionaries. Paquito's group had confronted the Marxists on the steps of the *Paraninfo Universitario* near the National Palace. Several of the leftist students had been killed.

But Meme, accustomed to chaos, was in love with Paquito, in love with the danger he represented. Her green eyes turned insatiably sultry the second that Paquito's slim, mustached face appeared.

*

When Meme came in later that night around two in the morning, Olivia stirred. She roused herself up when she heard footfalls and went over to Meme's bed.

"You won't believe what happened to me tonight," she whispered.

Meme looked at her friend, smiling as she stretched fully dressed on her bed. "It better be good because I'm very tired this evening, Olivia."

"I did something I've never done before."

"You made love," Meme answered.

"Yes," Olivia said, pulling her shoulders up and wrapping her arms around her own body as if she were dancing with herself.

Meme pushed herself up and spun her legs around the side of the cot.

"Come here you, fool!" She stood up. "Let me give you a hug."

Olivia allowed herself to be embraced.

"In the morning you can tell me all about it. Was it with Jesús? Did you go all the way? Did he put it into you?"

"I can't say," Olivia giggled.

Meme had drunk too much Ron Botrán to play guessing games. She held Olivia, in her arms as a mother would hold a child. "You've crossed to the other side," was all that she could say. And she gave her friend a kiss in the forehead.

"I'm sure you used protection. Let's go to sleep. I'm dead tired."

"Me too," smiled Olivia, letting a wide yawn escape. She walked quietly back to her cot. She felt peaceful. *Crossed to the other side,* she repeated. She had rubbed hard against Jesús's hip and lost her virginity. She had had no need for protection.

(1982)

Olivia was awaiting some kind of sign. She really didn't know what she was going to do, with the formal graduation just weeks away. Her friend Meme only talked about how much she was in love with Paquito and the other girls were going on and on about their graduation trips and their colleges.

Meme had said to Olivia to keep her eyes open—that she would receive a sign for what she must do when she least expected it.

All the girls were giddily nervous, but at least they had plans. What were Olivia's? To go back to the finca and pick coffee alongside her mother?

Never!

Guayito had disappeared two months earlier when he turned thirteen. Lucia thought that the army had kidnapped him, but she knew as well as Olivia that he had joined the *kaibiles*. Guayito certainly liked singing prayers and songs with the Pentecostals, but he preferred guns and uniforms more—it was just a matter of time before he would leave home on his own.

Olivia remembered seeing Guayito in the Assembly of God Church with his wooden rifle on one side and Lucia on the other. He would close his eyes and sit entranced as the blond-haired man from Provo, Utah sermonized in his broken Spanish, beseeching the congregation to do battle with the devil—the one preaching socialism and the other gnawing at their hearts.

Guayito was probably serving in an army outpost in *Quiché* province which, according to the government, was seething with guerillas.

"I want to be a Lion of God," she heard him say one Sunday after services as they walked back to the shack together. Lucia, who had grown to love the Pentecostals almost as much as she hated the Catholic Church, nodded her approval. "We wasted all those years listening to priests and nuns telling us to be patient and forgiving—so that they could continue to steal our money."

Olivia had wanted to protest, to say that if it weren't for the Church, for Sister Carina, she would still be picking coffee in the fields, but she knew she would only receive back their glaring looks of hostility. It was as if she weren't even there.

With Guayito gone, Lucia began mumbling to herself under her breath or spending hours in silence. She had aged tremendously in three months, too—her head resembling a small coconut shell and her scraggily hair went from black to gray. When she cooked or cleaned, no words come out. Guayito was her support, and she seemed miserable navigating alone in her world as if on only one leg.

Olivia, on the other hand, was relieved that Guayito was gone. There was no future for him in Ciudad Vieja. She tried to convince Lucia years ago that she should talk to Sister Carina about Guayito joining the Jesuit school for boys, but her mother insisted that three years of primary school was plenty and she needed him working at her side. Picking coffee in the fall and sending him down to Escuintla to cut bananas in the winter, hoping that don Anibal Cofinio would notice that he worked harder than a mule and would make a dependable foreman. But working on the coast made Guayito sick—he was only ten when he began there, and it was a miracle he didn't die. Trudging through muddy fields and then sleeping on the wet ground. The worms, the mosquitoes, the crushing heat and all that disease.

When Ríos Montt seized power, he proclaimed that all Guatemalans were soldiers in the service of the Assembly of God and that through prayer and devotion, the citizenry would triumph over the devil. The blond minister of the Assembly of God who came to their wooden church insisted one Saturday that the entire congregation had to accompany him to the new fundamentalist church that had been built in *Ciudad Vieja* across from the market. There a Pastor Amílcar preached a scientific sermon on evil—that the devil had escaped, split into a thousand atoms and taken different forms to enter the human heart. Satan had managed to infiltrate and infect families, social institutions, political parties and even sister religions that were under the protection of Jesús and God the Father in much the same way that electrons fly through the air. This was the moment for all believers to take up arms and embark on the crusade against the devil and his followers. All the parishioners in that enormous church were so frightened that they started looking around wondering whom among them had been corrupted by Satan.

Father Amílcar's words sickened Olivia. Even though she was a devout Catholic, she didn't believe that she was any closer to God than anyone else. She believed that her faith was her own and her beliefs had been guided by the pastorals of the nuns and priests that served her school. Whenever she truly needed to have her prayers answered, she would beseech *San Antonio del Monte*. Even though the little plastic statue of him was covered with candle wax and ignored by Lucia, Olivia still felt that he and Brother Pedro were the only saints who listened to her. Hadn't they saved the family from the earthquake?

Olivia began accompanying her mother to the new Assembly of God church on Sundays just to keep peace between them.

As for Guayito, the die had been cast a long time ago. He grudgingly accepted his fate though he waited for any kind of signal that would justify his leaving. Olivia suspected that it was only a matter of time before he would climb up on the back of an army truck and leave.

Guayito was not the only one to go. Except on market day, Ciudad Vieja seemed nearly deserted—a ghostly town of lonely women, old men, mangy dogs, and chickens too skinny to be eaten. Most of the Indian and ladino young men were happy to get away from there. The fundamentalist preachers had filled them with the fear that any moment the guerillas would sweep down from the nearby mountains and either force them to join them or simply shoot them in the head. Father Amílcar related accounts of the favorite forms of guerilla torture—pulling of nails, burning the soles of feet. He challenged the youngsters to be ready to do combat—why would anyone want to stay in the fields? Since only the army could protect the people, they were obliged to join in as soon as they could.

Sister Carina had once said at the Wednesday night mass at the *Colegio Parroquial* that the government forces were the ones employing the cruelest forms of torture. Sister Bonifacia, who continued living on the school grounds even after retiring, told her to shush. It wasn't safe to say what was on your mind in Guatemala, even in the sanctity of the Church. There were spies everywhere, and Catholics were pretty much on the defensive, on account of President Ríos Montt's weekly sermons and attacks.

Sister Carina had once mentioned in senior theology class that Father Perussina and Pastor Amílcar were locked in a fierce struggle to win over the souls of the Almolonga Valley parishioners. They both claimed greater allegiance to God and the personal support of Anibal Cofinio who, Olivia was sure, enjoyed having two servants of God battling for his endorsement. Don Anibal wasn't happy enough just owning the bodies of the coffee pickers—why shouldn't he also possess their souls?

By the time Olivia was graduating from the Colegio Parroquial, mostly women worked in the coffee fields—they and the few privileged men who directed them. How was it that the *caporales* escaped from serving in the army? As Sister Carina had hinted several times, there was always a special dispensation for those who were appointed by the oligarchs to rule over other people and had been sanctioned by men of the cloth from the Assembly of God.

Especially when a little bribe was involved.

Olivia wished that she could say that Guayito's imminent departure would grieve her. But from the start, it was as if they had been born not only of two different fathers, but also different mothers. After Sister Carina had taken Olivia away from home when she had been eight and Guayito three, he seemed to have decided that she was not his blood sister—but someone who had intentionally left him and Lucia behind. How could Olivia explain it to him? She was sure that Lucia told him that she had left by choice. The simple truth was that Olivia had not wanted to go, had been scared to death when Sister Carina had taken her away.

The first time Olivia had come back to the shack, wearing her school uniform, his eyes had displayed no warmth. She wasn't able to break through to him—his eyes were like wax seals on the back of letters. She had taken off her uniform and put on one of her old outfits, the brown pants that came up to her knees and the shirt with the torn pockets, and asked Guayito if he had wanted to play marbles. He had shaken his head and gone out to play alone with his *capirucho* under a *chalum* tree.

Olivia had wanted to cry, her heart was broken. She did cry a lot that first year in the *Colegio Parroquial*, thinking of her Mamá and Guayito. She wanted so much to fit in with the other girls at the school, but also to feel that her mother and brother were proud of her for having survived away from them and actually learned some skills that would be valuable to them all when the time came for her to go home. The truth was that Lucia felt betrayed by Olivia's departure—as if she had had a choice in her decision to leave home. If Guayito had wax covering his eyes, Lucia had lead—and she was clearly the one that had turned Guayito against her.

Whenever Olivia felt the urge to cry back then, she would repeat the verses of the song that Sister Carina used to sing to her:

Oh, had I the wings of the dove
I would fly away and join my love.

*

If Olivia had picked the one word that described how she felt at the cusp of her graduation, she would have said *anxious*. She was also in a *state of panic*. It's as if she looked inside a crystal ball and all she saw was a swirl of gray smoke—she had no idea what would become of her once she left school even though Meme felt that her future was about to unfold in front of her. "Innocence will serve you," she had said, but Olivia know that her friend was such a crazy dreamer!

And Sister Carina, who had plucked her out of poverty to enter this new world of hope, was nowhere to be seen. She had decided to visit the country communities on behalf of Father Perussina. Where was her concern now when Olivia really needed her?

Still it seemed as if the girls were graduating just in time--the Sisters of Mercy were warned that they might have to close the *Colegio Parroquial*. Sister Carina told the older girls that Father Perussina said that the Church was losing the costly battle with the *evangelistas* and, as more people left the Church, there was less money to support the schools. He foresaw great trouble ahead. The Church itself was also deeply divided between the bishops in the big cities who wanted to win back the faithful through an expensive media campaign and the younger priests and catechists in the countryside who felt that their task was to retain the Indian and ladino support through their own self-sacrificing example. The bishops supported President Ríos Montt halfheartedly if only to keep him from attacking the Church too strongly during his Saturday afternoon sermons to the nation. The younger prelates, however, protested the formation of Civil Defense patrols from the pulpit, claiming these patrols were a form of slavery, plain and simple, since the men were not paid to serve. Sister Carina was afraid that the Church might split over this and she was sure Ríos Montt and the Pentecostals were extremely happy.

*

San Antonio del Monte was extremely silent these days. Olivia thought it might be wise to visit Brother Pedro and see if he would come to her aid. She felt that since she was not either sick or destitute, he might view her request as being frivolous though she knew he was the kind of priest that took all entreaties seriously. And besides, he had recently been beatified and was extremely powerful. Why wouldn't he respond to her now?

One Saturday she went to the San Francisco Church after morning classes. A Franciscan priest in a brown tunic was shouting at and mistreating a poor beggar who had collapsed next to his crutches.

"You can't beg here. Not on the church steps. I've told you that many times."

"I'm not bothering anyone," the man slurred back. He wasn't drunk but had some sort of speech impediment.

The priest saw Olivia in her blue skirt and jacket, and white blouse. "Let the young woman by," he said, smiling at her from ear to ear. It was a false smile.

"Over here, over here," the beggar shouted at Olivia, growing agitated.

"He's not bothering me, Father," she said, with downcast eyes.

The priest grabbed her arm, forcing her to stop. Olivia could see his long, twisted toes sticking out from his sandals beneath his skirt. "Are you coming here, for confession, my dear?"

"No, father. I am here to see Brother Pedro."

"Brother Pedro, Brother Pedro," the beggar repeated loudly.

The priest took one of the crutches and shouted—"I wasn't talking to you. Get out by the gate. Or you'll see what it's like to be beaten with your own stick."

Olivia hurried up toward the church, incense and dark motes floating out of its curtained entrance, hoping and praying the priest wouldn't follow her. No wonder the *evangelistas* had been able to win over so many new converts—like good salesmen, at least they treated their customers with respect.

"Lovely legs," she heard the priest say when she reached the Church doors. "Give my greetings to Sister Bonifacia."

Olivia resisted the temptation to tell him that Sister Carina now ran the school—she didn't want to prolong their conversation.

She made her way to Brother Pedro's wall. There was an Indian woman talking roughly to him, raising her fist to the roof. She was praying and crying at the same time, and then she kissed her *chal*, which had a small silver cross, and banged it two or three times against his crypt. What did she want from him? Did she expect him to come out of the marble, pat her head and grant her her wish?

When she had finished, she put an ear against the crypt. The only sound Olivia heard was a car horn sounding from outside.

When the woman noticed that Olivia was watching her, she smiled revealing gold teeth. She glanced back at the tomb, shrugged, and then went over to the pews where her three children were sitting quietly waiting for her to finish.

Olivia had not been back to the Church for several years. She was surprised to find so many new drawings, photographs and amulets begging Brother Pedro to intervene and dispense his healing powers. With the world in such a mess, no wonder so many people were coming to see him. What Olivia wanted from him was something less miraculous—a sign, anything that would help her decide what to do. She knew that the lecherous priest was right, that she should first go into the confessional booth—she had lots to talk about, not the least of which was how she had sneaked out of the *Colegio Parroquial* on so many nights and used Jesús's hip to satisfy herself.

Olivia knelt down in front of the wall holding Brother Pedro's bones and spread her skirt over her legs. She knocked on the crypt, as was the custom. Olivia was a good Catholic and Brother Pedro was her favorite.

Brother Pedro was different than the other monks—he prayed with a human skull in his cell and frequently lashed himself, as a way to beat the devil out of his own body. He carried the sick upon his back to the hospital he had founded and was rumored to walk around Antigua jingling a little bell hoping that the sound might echo in the hearts of sinners struggling alone with their conscience. He offered comfort and companionship.

Olivia really did need Brother Pedro. Still it wasn't easy for her to pray, to surrender herself to a holy man even though, from all accounts, he was a good listener and not in the habit of judging people.

When Olivia was in the school chapel, she would pray along with her classmates, but the words wouldn't come out whenever she was alone. Maybe Sister Bonifacia was right in claiming that because she was half-Indian, Olivia did not believe strongly enough in the Church to pray alone like a good Catholic. Or maybe she needed a saint like *San Antonio del Monte* who was dark like her and wasn't repelled by sweat or the smell of the earth.

Olivia closed her eyes and asked Brother Pedro to protect her mother, brother and her friend Meme. She also asked him to protect her father Melchior who had died in a truck accident years ago but was not a bad man—she hoped that his soul had joined God's and that he was at peace. Olivia told Brother Pedro that they were all good people who, for one reason or another, had gotten lost along the way. They hurt people without meaning to. She didn't pray for herself because though she knew she was a sinner like everyone else, her sins were not important enough for a Holy Man to worry about. She had never killed, beaten or stolen and the lies she told had not hurt others as much as herself.

Then Olivia got to the purpose of her visit—she wanted a sign, some clear indication of what she was to do.

So far she had only met up with silence. Sister Carina had told her not to worry, that she would talk to Olivia after graduation—maybe she would be a good candidate to become a nun. Olivia had listened politely because she could see that though Sister Carina cared for her. But Sister Carina was very distracted and there was nothing more ridiculous than Olivia becoming a nun..

Olivia sat on the Church stones with eyes closed waiting for Brother Pedro to either speak or knock back. She could hear the sound of a shovel being dragged along the cobblestones outside the church—every once in a while she heard a tingle, as if the shovel had run up against a hard ridge. Where was Brother Pedro's ringing bell? Maybe he wasn't in a responsive mood.

Olivia thought that maybe if she rubbed her baby Jesús medallion against the marble tomb, like the Indian woman had, he would answer back. Perhaps Brother Pedro, over the years, had become hard of hearing or deaf.

Then Olivia felt warm breath against her neck. How strange. Brother Pedro was near. Without glancing back, she raised her left hand to touch her ear and instead struck a man's chin.

Immediately she spun around. Sitting on a three-legged stool just behind her was the priest who had shooed away the cripple. He was smiling cloyingly.

"You would have more of a chance of hearing back from Brother Pedro if you joined me in the confessional," the priest said, sweeping his right arm toward the left side of the nave.

The priest's breath smelled of garlic and stale beans. He was not very old, but his teeth were yellow and his eyes were wet as if constantly leaking like a drippy faucet.

"Come," he said, grabbing her elbow.

Olivia's legs tingled when she stood up. They had fallen asleep under her. As she tried to walk, she felt her legs buckling—she was sure that she would fall. She found herself clutching the priest's arm. She was supposed to feel safe in church—why was feeling so uneasy?

The priest patted her hand and smacked his lips. Just then they were both surprised to hear the sudden tolling of bells coming from the nearby Belen Church—the space they had occupied in silence had now been breached, exposed to a thousand dagger-like eyes.

The priest turned to look around, somewhat afraid.

The feeling came back to Olivia's legs and she took his arm off of hers.

The priest held on forcefully. "Come with me, my dear."

Olivia pulled back and elbowed him away. The priest took four or five steps back and then fell to the ground, his twisted body landing awkwardly on the huge paving stones.

Brother Pedro must have heard her prayers!

"Why you little devil," the priest hissed.

Olivia ran out as fast as she could, her pounding heart outpacing the rhythm of the bells. Nothing had happened. Yet it was all so disgusting. And perhaps the priest would have hurt her if he had had the chance.

She didn't stop running until she reached the Parque Central nearly five blocks away. Indian women were selling bracelets and wall hangings to tourists and the shoeshine boys were sitting on their cases awaiting customers.

It was so calm there that Olivia felt safe. Brother Pedro had answered her prayers, given her the strength to escape the foul priest.

She realized she needed to be patient. Something would reveal itself soon. She was not running out of time. *Patience.* The patience of Princess Ixkik'.

(1982)

On a visit home a week before her high school graduation, Olivia found a blue sheet of paper on top of her mother's prayer book. The paper was torn and badly creased, and the lettering, though in pencil and awkwardly written, was clearly legible:

February 20, 1967

> *You say that the girl in the picture is my daughter, but you have no way to prove it. You're a dishonest woman to write to me after all these years. Though you claim I was, I know I wasn't the only man you were with. You are living in Sololá without me and it's only because you knew where my brother lived that you were able to find me. I don't love you. I never did. I only feel pity. I cannot send money for that poor unfortunate child who you claim is my daughter but I know is not!*

> *Melchior Xuc Padilla*

*

After reading these words, Olivia felt dizzy and terribly nauseous. To keep from falling, she stumbled over to her mother's bed and sat down. For a few seconds everything before her was black and spinning. She took deep breaths to lessen the panic. Soon she felt calm enough to think.

This letter confirmed her suspicion that her father might not be dead. Her mother had claimed that Melchior Xuc Padilla was dead: he had been driving drunk one night and had simply driven his truck over a ravine. She had been left a widow and Olivia fatherless seventeen years earlier. That's why there were alone.

But this letter proved that her father hadn't died as Lucia had claimed and that he might still be alive—

*

Her mother came home from the *cafetal* late Saturday afternoon. The shack was already in the shadows of the nearby locust trees. As soon as Lucia saw her daughter holding Melchior's letter, she grunted.

The words Olivia had rehearsed failed her. "How could you lie to me about my father, mamá?" she cried out.

Lucia half smiled. Had she left the letter out deliberately so Olivia would find it? So it seemed!

"To protect you, you fool!" Lucia hissed. "But now that you are graduating from that school, you are old enough to know the truth. It's about time that you stop thinking that your life would have been any different if that fool had been alive! Now you know that he is alive!" Lucia's once dreamy eyes were dull as obsidian behind the mere slits of her eyes. "He never loved me and he cared nothing about you. He never even bothered to come back to see you."

"He's my father. My only father!"

"He was a drunk and a womanizer," her mother raged. "Do you think I'm the only woman he deceived? I spit on him and his fountain of lies. He claimed he owned the truck he drove when it belonged to someone else. I was stupid to think he would come back for me in Solólá. The only truth he ever spoke was when he claimed he would go to his grave denying he had fathered you."

"Where is he?" Olivia's chest ached, about to explode.

"The *Mentiroso*?" Lucia asked, raising her shoulders. "Who cares?"

"Mamá, I need to know where he is."

Her mother grunted again and went to the shelf where she kept bags of rice, sugar and beans away from the field mice. She took down an envelope and threw it in Olivia's face. "Here's his last letter. Since I can't read, I had to bring this letter to a reader in Ciudad Vieja who told me what it said. For your sake, I hope you don't choke on his lying words. I only came here to tell you that I will be working till sundown. The *caporal* has promised me a few extra *quetzales* if I scrub down the *beneficio*...Why don't you make yourself useful and do the wash— if you can remember how."

Olivia was in tears. "You can't just leave me." And before she could stop herself she blurted out: "I need you, mother."

Lucia looked at her as if not understanding. All she could say was "If it hadn't been for your brother, I would be dead now," and with that, she stormed out of the hut.

Olivia felt the blow of her mother's parting words. Lucia hated her for so many reasons. All along she had thought that it was because she had been unwilling, like Guayito, to forsake schooling to remain working by her side. It was so futile to tell her that while her half-brother was the very essence of subservience, she was full of dreams. And if you can't pursue your dreams, what's the point of living?

It was clear now. Lucia hated her because Olivia reminded her of Melchior.

There was no way for her to win back her mother's love. She opened the envelope, which had a return address in Mexico City. Olivia unfolded the letter, carefully pleated into eighths. It was dated November 27th, 1981. The writing was scragglier than the letter on the Bible. Olivia had a hard time reading it because her hand was shaking.

Melchior claimed that he had been laid off from his factory job again and gotten sick. He had been bedridden for a long time. He could walk now and he thought that he would sell hardware tools around the neighborhood. He hinted that he would send money for *Navidad* if things went well. It was all so matter of fact. No cheeriness. Not a drop of emotion. But since he had written to Lucia meant he had all along stayed in contact with her.

Melchior hadn't asked after Olivia. That could be easily explained—maybe it was because he had lost all hope of ever seeing his daughter again or perhaps he knew that she had become the source of her mother's bitterness—Olivia was the one thing that connected them to each other.

She couldn't speak to her father's honesty, but Olivia knew that her mother falsified the truth. Since Sister Carina had rescued her from the drudgery of coffee picking, her mother had turned against her, become a rabid *evangelista*, claiming that the Catholic Church had lured her daughter away and reneged on its promises of compensation. "The priests steal from the collection plate," became her mother's refrain. "I was never paid for having my daughter, my right arm, taken away from me."

Even Guayito, sullen as his mother, had treated Olivia as if she had escaped from the hut with all the family's riches, as if she had no right to escape a life of servitude.

*

Olivia knew that this letter was the sign she had prayed for. About to graduate from high school, her mother wanted to destroy any illusions she might have of escaping her fate. Lucia wanted her to know that her education and socializing with "rich girls" would not free her from her destiny. She was the daughter of a coffee picker and a lazy, no-good drunk.

But Lucia had made a mistake. If she expected Olivia to feel further humiliation, the effect was the exact opposite. Instead of feeling defeat, Olivia was almost euphoric: she believed she was being *commanded* to seek out her father immediately—even if she had to leave at once for Mexico without telling anyone and foregoing her graduation.

True, Sister Carina had been waiting for months to proclaim Olivia's name along with the names of the other ten graduates, but this would not be happening. Meme, too, would surely and rightly feel betrayed by her absence. But Sister Carina had her church and Meme hankered after Paquito—what did she have?

Nothing!

There was no point for Olivia to stay in Antigua for a graduation that offered her no joy and no future—why walk dolefully to your own beheading?

She held the envelope with her father's address tightly in her hand and repeated his name over and over: *Melchior Xuc Padilla. Melchior Xuc Padilla. Melchior Xuc Padilla. He had stayed in touch with my mother because of me. My sweet and dear little father.*

She took the letter and stuffed it inside her *mochila.*

*

Two days later, Olivia woke up at the *Colegio Parroquial* before daybreak. She dressed quietly in her dorm room, putting on an innocuous flower dress and the jean jacket Meme had once given to her. She made her way unseen out of the school, carrying a cylindrical cloth bag and her *mochila* packed with clothes and the seventy-five *quetzales* she had managed to save over the years by doing favors and writing papers for her classmates.

The Antigua bus station was crowded with Indians carting their bundled wares to be sold at market. Olivia climbed aboard the 6.AM bus to the *Terminal Central* in Guatemala City and sat in a window seat toward the back of the bus. She drifted in and out of sleep as the bus staggered over the cobblestone Antigua streets toward the two-lane Pan American highway. She woke up for good half an hour later when the bus entered the capital along the cluttered *Avenida Roosevelt*. Staring out her cracked window, she saw dozens of skeletal buildings, broken down carts pulled by peasants, families risking their lives by running helter-skelter across the highway in the early morning light. These were the Indians who had been pushed off their lands in the countryside during eighteen years of armed conflict. They had streamed into the capital, taken over any abandoned patch of earth in the city, even in the ravines, and built tin and wood huts where only decades before raccoons and *chompipes*—wild turkeys—had roamed.

Olivia had wrongly imagined the capital to be clean and organized. Never tranquil, it had in recent years lost all semblance of orderliness and become a honeycomb of filth and confusion. The once broad avenues, where traffic had moved rapidly and efficiently in straight lanes, had been taken over by makeshift stands—*puestos*— where everything from flashlights and machetes to radios and used brake shoes were hawked by the *ladinos* and Indians. Every square inch of available space had been spoken for and, amid the snarled traffic and the blaring of horns, the few sellers of fresh fruits and vegetables kept wary eyes out for thieves among the shoppers and beggars.

Olivia, who wished to have everything conform to her vision of harmony, was shocked by the disorder at the edge of Guatemala City's central district. From the bus window, it seemed as if caravans of people were moving about hungrily, surging in waves, scrambling to eke out a living. And above it all, turkey vultures glided through the air, ready to touch down wherever the scent of new offal rose.

Olivia began singing Cri-Cri's *El chorrito* to herself, to somehow ease the growing anxiety. It was something she had always done, sing this song, which reminded her not of her own youth, but of an imagined world full of warmth and attainable dreams.

As soon as the bus pulled into its slot at the bus station, most of the Indian passengers scattered like potshot. A handful of predators approached the remaining passengers, dressed in their native *huipiles* and *trajes*, offering to direct them to sleeping quarters or places where they might be able to sell their wares. The wolves, most of whom looked drugged out from sniffing glue or drinking wood alcohol, preferred to prey on peddlers. Olivia was ignored, not because she didn't appear either vulnerable or fragile, but because she apparently had nothing to give, nothing to sell—she gave off the impression that contact with her would yield nothing.

At the ticket window she bought a one-way ticket to La Mesilla, the last bus stop on the Guatemalan side of the Mexican border. The bus would be leaving in an hour. Hungry now, she bought a *café con leche* and *pan dulce* at the cafeteria and waited for her bus to depart. The strong coffee and sweet pastry raised her spirits and she watched the chaos in the station from afar, as if gazing down from an outer lip on the goings-on inside a pit.

*

Her bus was nicknamed *La Consentida*. Olivia took a back row on the half–full bus, which pulled out of the terminal a little after nine. It doubled-back toward Antigua along the same route she had taken to the capital. About thirty minutes later, it stopped in San Lucas Sacatepéquez where more passengers boarded, before heading out on the highway to Chimaltenango.

It was here, in this sprawling adobe town where all sorts of car and truck parts were purchased or traded, that she had to decide whether or not to return to Antigua on a local bus. Olivia felt there was no turning back—she had decided she was going to Mexico City to look for her father.

From Chimaltenango, the road angled up into sloped and patterned green and brown fields. Here Olivia whiffed the smoky mountain air and let its succulence enter into her lungs. She could finally breathe unimpeded.

The bus continued west for another few hours before stopping at *Los Encuentros*. Here the road forked south toward Sololá, where she and her mother had supposedly once lived, and northward to

Chichicastenango and Quiché province, which according to the newspapers, was rife with guerilla activity. One day she would return, and perhaps even make her way to San Pedro La Laguna where her mother's family supposedly lived.

But her journey now was taking her further westward through more mountains and clouds toward Huehuetenango, the last large Guatemalan town before reaching *La frontera*. Just to get to the Mexican border could take twelve hours.

The highway had become very dangerous lately, especially once the larger cities were left behind. Drivers were under strict orders not to stop or travel after sunset, lest bands of thieves or guerillas— or soldiers disguised as guerillas—were to hijack the bus during a particularly deserted stretch of road and steal whatever they could from the passengers. Robberies were commonplace—silver, gold, cash, live chickens, shoes, *machetes*, anything of value. And often it didn't stop at theft, so went the rumors. Women were raped, resistors clubbed or beaten or, worse still, yanked into the guerilla or civil defense patrol ranks or hacked to death.

*

The driver had said that the bus would not be leaving *Los Encuentros* for another half an hour. Olivia did not want to disembark and chance losing her seat, so she remained on board. To pass the time, Olivia tried to imagine what her father was like. She was sure that he was a good man. For one, he had kept in touch with Lucia; two, he seemed to have sent her money from time to time; and third, he apparently was truly concerned with the fact that he had somehow reneged on his responsibilities.

Surely it was natural for her father to speak about his own hard times. It would have been cruel to brag about all his successes: *the rooster in the hen house should moderate his crows*. Not to boast of your riches had been one of the principal messages of the *Colegio Parroquial*. And her father obviously adhered to that saying.

The fortunate rich should be modest, but she knew that her father was successful. After all, he lived in Mexico City, what her many textbooks referred to as *The Paris of the Americas!*

She closed her eyes and wondered what he might look like. She tried to imagine his face: surely Melchior would be handsome, with a big thick moustache. He would be a bit fat, with a paunch, resembling most men in their forties who ate rice and beans, drank beer and failed to exercise because they were always working.

His eyes would twinkle and he would have a good sense of humor. Melchior would be, in fact, a storyteller, full of jokes and he would not be beyond teasing, but only gently, nothing acidic about him. Olivia smiled. And he would be so proud to meet his daughter, one as intelligent as Olivia—someone who had managed to escape her modest roots to graduate from a prestigious Catholic high school.

Olivia would be welcomed as Daddy's little girl. Of course he would have remarried, it would only be natural, and Olivia would do whatever she could to ensure that her relationship with her stepmother would make her father happy. She would live under his roof courteously, not demanding much, not abusing the privilege. She would set the table and wash the dishes. She would do the shopping and learn to cook.

*

When the bus was about to leave *Los Encuentros*, Olivia opened her eyes and saw that an old coppery Tzutzhil Indian dressed in his village finery was sitting next to her. He was a shrunken man, with a high forehead shading sleepy eyes. His hands stayed gripped to the seat in front of him and he stared straight ahead, never glancing out the window. Every twenty minutes or so he would let go of the seat and open a paper bag. He would chew on a tamale, close up the bag and then take a bite out of a fat quince which he kept wrapped in wax paper. Two or three times Olivia said something to him to simply make conversation, but he would shake his head or shrug his bony shoulders in response. She assumed that either he was mute or didn't speak Spanish.

At one point he went up to the driver, said something and came back smiling. His eyes were sparkling. As he sat down next to her, he said to no one in particular, but really to Olivia. "The world is big, isn't it?"

Olivia nodded. She wanted to say that she was about to discover how big it was, that she was going on a long trip to another country to meet her father, finally, but the old man was already back at his position gripping the seat and staring straight ahead...

A few minutes later the bus came to a sudden stop, and the Indian got off at the crossroads to the mountain village of San Pedro Nacta.

What the Indian man had actually meant by what he said remained a mystery to Olivia.

After he left, Olivia felt something warm beside her. She was surprised to find a couple of potato meal *paches* in her mochila. How had they gotten there? Perhaps the old man was a not a human being, but a wizard!

She ate the *paches* hungrily, savoring the small chunks of pork in the middle. Olivia closed her eyes. Yes, she was risking everything she had worked for to go see her father. Everyone, especially Sister Carina and Meme, would be disappointed that she had sacrificed the crowning glory of her education. Still, she had felt she had the right to leave *immediately*—even though it would confirm to Lucia, who had no plans to attend the graduation, that Olivia, first and foremost, was an ungrateful child.

Then Olivia held a back-and-forth conversation in her head—her departure would indicate to the nuns that another scholarship student had proved to be a disappointment to the school. Though Olivia had worked hard, clearly she, *like most Indians,* lacked discipline: *she was more interested in dreaming, or reading a book than having an intelligent conversation with another person. Hermind was constantly wandering.* In her defense, she wanted to say that she was so mistrustful of people because they were so cruel that she preferred to dream. *But you have to apply yourself and take risks.* What for? *To get ahead!* The thought of preparing for the university entrance exams depressed her. *Besides, Olivia will be one of those students to drop out after six months because she had gotten pregnant.* She knew that she would be condemned no matter what she did.

No one but Meme knew the real Olivia, the one who wanted to go to places she had read about in her history and art books—Paris, Amsterdam and London--anywhere where there would be no coffee shrubs, dirt paths, bananas, volcanoes and barefoot Indians. She wanted her past life to become simple memories so she could talk fondly about Antigua and Guatemala, the *Land of Eternal Spring,* as if she were recounting an early chapter of her life.

She wanted to escape a world that defined the perimeters of her existence.

*

In Huehuetenango more Indians climbed aboard. Boxes, suitcases, and sacks were tied to the rail on top of the bus and chickens, turkeys and pigs were huddled into a pen directly behind the driver. These new passengers had dejected faces, as if having seen the devil or a *cadeja*—an evil spirit. Olivia suspected they had probably been tortured or seen relatives murdered because they weren't talking, even among themselves. They were escaping into Mexico clutching their only possessions—animals, blankets and, for some, nothing more than a *tinaja*, a vinyl jug, or *trajes* or *chachales* or *petates* or simply a jigsaw collection of rusted tools. It was a vast, silent migration.

Olivia knew the bus would take twelve hours, but that was because the roads were so bad and the army had set up so many roadblocks to try to nab guerillas or army deserters. She hadn't realized Guatemala was such a big country, with such a varied terrain. She was taking the first step to travel the world—the Tzutzhil Indian had said it was big—and indeed, she saw mountains of all colors and shapes, tilled fields or terraced into the side of the deepest ravines in all states of growth. She saw clouds that galloped across the sky, others that dropped down softy to touch the flanks of mountains.

*

The bus reached La Mesilla around eight in the evening. Olivia waited for the Indians to spill out into the station before exiting the bus. They huddled against their belongings, for a second considering what to do or where to go. It had been market day in La Mesilla and vendors were bundling up boxes and gunnysacks to take the last local buses home.

Olivia took her bag and *mochila* and walked across the filth-strewn concrete square toward the cathedral. To her right she saw a flashing neon sign above a shoe store advertising *Hospedaje Marisol*. She took the stairs up to the second-floor reception—for five *quetzales* she was given a small room, a straw mattress bed on springs and the opportunity to share a hall bathroom with other lodgers.

Olivia wasn't ruffled at the hotel's disrepair since she understood it to be just a temporary way station.

The following morning, she was off to Mexico City. The border crossing was somewhat of a joke. There were dozens of armed soldiers lounging on both sides, but the Mexican *civiles* simply waved the bus through without checking for proper papers. Because of Guatemala's armed conflict, Mexico had simply opened up its borders to the refugees and an identity card was the only documentation Guatemalans needed to enter. But obviously, not even that.

Mexico's border towns were teeming with Indians, many of whom were herded by nuns and social workers into temporary tent camps as soon as they crossed the border. Tensions and skirmishes between the Mexican natives and the refugees were on the rise, since the latter were being helped by the authorities and given makeshift housing and food. The Mexicans who had lived there for centuries were simply ignored.

The journey through Comítan and San Cristobal de las Casas to Mexico City could take as little as a day or as much as five. Olivia kept imagining her encounter with her father, after what was sure to be that awkward first hug or kiss. *Would he welcome her gingerly or embrace her with affection, this his long-lost daughter that had been denied to him for so many years? How closely would they resemble one another? Would he be angry at her for having forsaken her high school graduation ceremony just to come and meet him? His middle name was Xuc—was he also part Maya? Would he live in a palatial house in a leafy suburb of Mexico City or would he have a simple abode, fitting to his roots?*

There were so many questions on her mind!

*

In Puebla, Olivia changed buses. She went into the ladies room and put on her best outfit—a white blouse, black sweater with the school letters *CP* emblazoned in red script and a long, black pleated skirt—to meet her father.

After crossing ice-covered mountains, the bus arrived at the *Terminal del Sur* in Coyoacán, at the southern edge of Mexico City.

It was early Sunday morning, and the tolling of dozens of church bells resounded inside the bus station, which was the hugest building she had ever been in. There were at least 40 bus stalls and thousands of people were milling about, buying tickets or waiting to get on board—more people than lived in all of Antigua!

As Olivia walked out of the Terminal, she felt her lungs gasping for air. She could tell that this was a huge gray city, with a life and pulse of its own.

She was overwhelmed to see hundreds of cars hurtling down the streets.

Olivia found a policeman and showed him her father's address. He directed her to the city bus that would take her to nearby Colonia Portales, the working-class district where her father lived. She showed this same address to the driver, who nodded and promised to tell her where to get off. He did so, at the intersection of *Eje 8* and *División del Norte*. She asked several people for directions to Melchior's until she came face to face with a squat, narrow three-story building on *Avenida Popocatépetl*—where her father lived. Her heart was thumping loudly in her chest.

The building was quite decrepit—the glass had been smashed out of the cast-iron outer door. To its left was an all-night *taquería*, which gave off the odor of scorched sunflower oil and rancid meat. On the other side of the building was a gated store, with hundreds of used tires and retreads piled high and chained together on the black tar pavement.

Olivia rang the buzzer of the downstairs apartment. A man with three-day's growth on his face answered the door. His brown robe with gold fringe was open over a pair of gray pajamas. "I don't contribute to the church, *querida*," he guffawed as soon as he saw Olivia.

He had obviously mistaken her for an *evangelista*. And she had mistaken him for her father. "Neither do I," she replied nervously, looking for the twinkle in his eyes.

The bedraggled man looked closer at her. "You're not a Seventh Day Adventist?"

"Are you Melchior Xuc Padilla?" Olivia countered with a question of her own.

"And if I were?" he asked cautiously, squinting his eyes.

"I would be his daughter."

The man shook his head. "No, no no! You certainly don't look like Melchior," he said haughtily. "My daughter? I think I would know my own handiwork. That is, my own flesh and blood."

It took all her strength to say: "Lucia's my mother. I'm Olivia—your daughter from Guatemala."

Melchior raised an eyebrow and opened his mouth to reveal yellow teeth. He might have been handsome at some point, with a firm jaw and cheekbones, but now he had huge creases—almost ravines—running down both sides of his brown face. His receding hairline exposed the prominent crown of his forehead. And because he hadn't shaved for days, his face made him look dirtier than he really was.

"I'm your daughter," Olivia insisted. He hadn't even bothered to clip the hair that grew like corn stalks from both ears and curled out of his nostrils.

"What am I supposed to do for you?" he asked her.

"Please let me in, I won't hurt you." This is not how she had imagined the reunion. Something was wrong. Where was the warmth, the humor?

"I'm not afraid of any woman," he laughed. "First of all, you should know I have no money. Secondly, I am not acknowledging having a daughter named Olivia. So why don't you tell me who you really are and what it is that you want."

Olivia took her Guatemalan identity card out of her *mochila*. "You'll see here. I use Anaya, my mother's last name."

At this Melchior smiled. "Anaya! Ha! Lucia's family name was *Tzijol. Anaya* was something she invented so she'd sound more Spanish. When I knew her, she was Josefa, Josefita, Fita—like her own mother. I don't know what any Anaya wants with me."

"You're my father. Here's the last letter you sent my mother," Olivia said, handing him the blue paper. He took the letter and started to read it over. Olivia walked by him into the apartment.

Melchior's living room was dark, full of dirty glasses, empty bottles and overflowing ashtrays. There was an odor of sewage in the air, as if the drainpipes had backed up or perhaps he shared his plumbing with the *taquería*—where they dumped the used oil down the drain.

Melchior stayed at the door, bobbing his head. He obviously recognized his own handwriting but seemed to be using the moment to consider his next move.

He sighed loudly and followed Olivia deeper into his house. He pointed to his sofa, indicating that she should sit down.

"I don't owe anyone anything," he said, acidly, looming in front of her.

"I don't want anything from you. I only want to get to know you."

"I'm a busy man. I really don't have the time."

Melchior was impenetrable. Olivia felt she was facing Rabbit 18, a Mayan stele in Copán that was in one of her history books. Rabbit 18 had been a powerful lord who ruled harshly over his great Mayan metropolis. Both the stele and her father had a frozen inscrutable expression. Rabbit 18 had been cut out of stone; but Melchior was alive. His sour breath implied it.

Olivia was beginning to feel foolish. She had hoped—no, expected—to be welcomed with open arms into her father's house. Sitting on the lumpy sofa, she felt like an intruder, an adoptee accusing the man in front of her of paternity. She had imagined something quite different: her father sitting down across from her, eyes glowing, leaking tears of joy, asking her about her childhood, her schooling, her dreams and ambitions. If she felt confident enough, she might even tell him about the magazine with Olivia Newton-John, about Ixkik'—all in her attempt to make up for all the time lost.

"Father, tell me something about yourself," she went on half-heartedly, patting the seat next to her.

Melchior sat down rigidly, his right hand rubbing his knee. He raised and lowered his right eyebrow as if he had a nervous tic. After a few seconds he took his hand off his knee and grabbed one of the dirty glasses on the table in front of him. He winced as he drank down the yellow liquid and let out a sigh, licking his lips. He then put the glass down and looked at her.

Olivia studied his face. He was not inscrutable—he had a bulbous nose like a radish: the nose of a *bolo*—that's it, he was a drunkard! Her father a drunkard.

"Do you want me to tell you about myself?" she asked, trying to raise her spirits. She wished she could remember a single one of Sister Bonifacia's adages that could serve her now—those that preached patience and forbearance—but her mind was a blank.

"Like I said, I don't know who you are so why would I want to know more about you?" There was silence for another good minute. His hand danced nervously in the air before touching his chin.

She didn't answer him because she was afraid she would start to cry.

"Are you here alone?" he finally asked. Maybe he was afraid that Lucia, nee *Josefa Tzijol*, had accompanied Olivia to Mexico. Wife and daughter to impose—that's all he needed.

"I am here alone." She felt tears forming at the edge of her eyes and she wished that the room's darkness or her father's blindness would keep him from noticing. "I don't know anyone, but you."

For a second, Melchior sat impassively and then said "Aha!" He slapped his knees, as if a light had just gone on in his head. "I can make a call for you. Help get you settled. That's what I can do. As you see, I can't be of much help to anyone," he said, sweeping one arm across his filthy living room.

"Father—"

"Please don't call me that," Melchior interrupted. He pushed himself up and walked over to the kitchen. From where she was sitting she could see him pick up a black telephone on a small table next to the refrigerator. He lifted the receiver several times—obviously he shared a party line with a neighbor—before putting it back in its crook. Finally, exasperated by waiting merely seconds, he screamed into the phone that he had been trying for fifteen minutes to make a call and *now he had to make that call*. He held the phone in his hand, inches from his face, for another half a minute, as the voice on the other end screamed. Then the noise stopped. The speaker must have hung up because suddenly Melchior began to dial a number.

He turned his back to Olivia and spoke quietly into the phone for a few minutes. Hanging up, Melchior shuffled back into the living room.

He told her that he had called Mélida Cotilla, a Oaxacan woman who rented rooms in her apartment in the Colonia Roma. "With Mélida, you'll at least be safe," he said, authoritatively. As for a job, he went on, he could be of no help. The Mexican peso had just lost 60% of its value. He had hoped to get hired as an assistant in a print shop around the corner, but the devaluation had screwed everything. In the meantime, he was buying hardware tools from a manufacturer and selling them to his neighbors house-to-house.

"Young lady, you've come to Mexico at the wrong time." He pushed down on his legs to stand up and stood looming in front of her as if about to empty his already empty robe pockets. Then he walked over to his kitchen table and wrote down Mélida's address.

He came back to Olivia and extended his hands to help pull her up from the couch. All of a sudden he seemed animated. "Do you need to use the bathroom? Can I get you a glass of water?"

"No, thank you," was all she could say.

"Well, in that case, let me put you in a *pesero*."

Dressed in his brown nubbly robe and slippers, he escorted her to the front door. Outside, the sunlight was streaming down, throwing a yellow wash over the early Mexican morning. The sun's brightness made his eyes mere slits—he couldn't get them to open very wide as he accompanied Olivia to Avenida Lázaro Cárdenas. He made no effort to carry her cloth bag and *mochila*, as if the effort to carry his own bones was work enough. Before reaching the corner, his arms were flailing in the air, hailing imaginary taxis.

Finally, a yellow Volkswagen *pesero* stopped at the corner.

Melchior quickly opened the van's door. He told Olivia that it was routed to bring her downtown, just blocks away from Mélida's apartment. As she was about to enter the van, he magically pulled out the sheet with the address and also two hundred-peso notes from his robe pocket.

"This will take care of your first day at the pensión. I can't give you more. I have seven other children to worry about."

"Father," Olivia said, swept up by emotions she could not explain. The encounter had gone wrong, but this last gesture had opened her heart. She hugged his body tightly, wishing to feel the warmth and exuberance she desperately needed.

A stiff and inert body met her clasp and her repetitions of the word "father."

"Get going. All these other passengers are waiting," was all he could say.

She wanted to say something to him—something that would right a toppled boat—but she couldn't get her tongue to click.

He slid the van door shut and waved his right hand as he walked away from her.

(1983)

Mélida Cotilla lived in a first floor back apartment in a four-story elevator building in Colonia Roma, just west of the Parque Alameda. The neighborhood was drab, dusty and noisy, but once inside the building, Olivia felt she had entered a quiet world. Perhaps it was the yellow spotlight shining on the wallpaper depicting a thin waterfall dripping honey inside a deep forest green cathedral. Or perhaps it was the sconces emitting the barest of light that created a sense of peace and serenity.

Mélida was an honest, forthright woman. The guest room was homey though the bed had a sagging mattress and a nightstand lamp whose fixture was always falling out of the socket. Born in Tlacochahuaya, a village outside of Oaxaca, she had hung colorful native cloth to decorate the walls and the one large window, which opened to a darkened courtyard. She also had placed a machine-made Santa Ana del Valle blue and white wool *tapete* on the floor. There were pictures of 1950's Mexico City—with broad tree-lined boulevards and the snowcapped volcanoes of Popocatépetl and Iztaccihuatl off in the distance—hanging on the walls.

Every evening Mélida placed a glass of fresh water on the night table by Olivia's bed.

"In case you get thirsty during the night," she explained.

A more apt explanation for her generosity was that out of force of habit, she locked the kitchen door at nine o'clock—perhaps to prevent her tenants from taking food from the refrigerator.

Ramón Figueroa, the other renter living there, worked as a salesman at a furniture store on the corner of Balderas and Juárez. Olivia rarely saw him since he would leave the apartment by seven in the morning and come home after sunset. His nightly routine was simple: he locked himself in his room and would watch television until 10 PM when he would go to bed. No one had ever seen Ramón eat anything in the apartment, which meant he ate breakfast on his way to work and had dinner at a restaurant before coming home for the evening.

Mélida's weekly rent included breakfast—two hardboiled eggs, slices of white toast and a plate of papaya and bananas, which she left on the kitchen table, covered with a paper napkin, since she left early for her real job as a porter of a nearby building on Avenida Ramos Arzipe, just north of Plaza de la República.

Mélida had strange habits, like hiding the kitchen radio in a cupboard and putting the vase with flowers in her bedroom under lock and key before she left for work. It never occurred to Olivia to make use of anything that was not hers, but then again, she felt it had more to do with some sort of weird experiences with previous tenants and nothing to do with her.

Strange habits, indeed.

And when Olivia asked her once how she knew her father, Mélida said that he had once occupied her same room when he had come from Guatemala nearly twenty years earlier.

"So you lived together?" Olivia asked, immediately realizing what she had said.

"He rented your room. That was all." Mélida laughed. "You don't really know your father."

Olivia shook her head. "But I'd like to."

"Your father is like all men, and that's why I have chosen to live alone. Men will break your heart."

*

Olivia lived out those first few days in Mexico City in a fog. If someone had asked her if it had been hot or cold, sunny or not, she wouldn't have been able to answer. She rose, she ate, and she slept as a sleepwalker would, without a sense of place or surroundings, with no awareness of those signposts that mark the passage of time. She was under glass, in a paperweight, immune to the elements, the surges of light and dark, unconscious of sights and sounds. She was aware of every little change in her own body—the start of a headache, the itch of a palm—but she was completely unaware of the world outside her body.

From the first day at Mélida's pension, she explored only one or two blocks beyond the area she already knew. It wasn't because she was afraid of the big city—she wanted to stay close to home in case her father stopped by.

She *expected* Melchior to call. He had Mélida's number—wasn't he interested in how his daughter was doing?

By the second week, Olivia was running out of money. She had to get a job. Mornings found her trudging up and down Reforma Avenue from her little room off the Parque Alameda to the *Caballito* on Insurgentes, popping her head in and out of stores and offices, trying to get any job in sales or clerking or even cleaning and sweeping.

Olivia was polite, courteous, and friendly, but the devaluation and the ensuing financial chaos in Mexico had made proprietors unwilling to hire new staff at this time. Olivia would've been happy to open boxes or file papers—anything to earn a few pesos and begin putting order in her life, not to speak of paying back the 200-peso loan she had taken from the charlatan who wouldn't admit to fathering her.

This was the call she was aching to make.

Her biggest fear was going back to Guatemala—penniless, defeated—having to beg Lucia to take her back in because she had nowhere else to go.

Finally on a Friday, at the end of an exasperating second week— after having spent five nights crying herself to sleep out of frustration and fear—, she walked into *Viajes Atlas* because it had a poster of Guatemala's Lake Atitlán on the window.

Margarita Canales, the travel agency owner, happened to be standing near the front glass door when Olivia walked in and gawked at the poster. She went over to the young girl and looked her straight in the face. In the eyes of the lost girl before her, she recognized her own ghostly teenage expression when she had decided to leave home because her father was a womanizer and her mother was, in turns, abusive and indifferent.

"Are you planning a trip?" Sra. Canales inquired.

"No, I have no money. I need a job. I will do anything," Olivia said, looking down at her feet.

Pity surged over Margarita Canales.

"I suppose you know how to use a broom and a dustpan. And polish furniture?"

Olivia nodded, not looking up.

"Please look at me when you answer. And use words!"

"Yes, ma'am," Olivia said, looking at Sra. Canales. She was a thin woman, in her late fifties, impeccably dressed. And it was clear to Olivia that she was a woman of some means.

"Good." She opened her black purse and took out some bills. "You will now work for me. Here's forty-five pesos, your daily salary, as an advance."

Olivia was about to cry. "I don't know what to say."

"Usually one says thank you. You can call me Sra. Canales. Do you come with a name?"

"Olivia Padilla. Xuc."

"What a nice name. I'll see you Monday at 9 AM sharp."

"Thank you," Olivia answered.

"Don't wear fancy clothes. You will simply be cleaning this office—that's all."

*

The Colegio Parroquial had prepared her for better, but it was being born in the coffee fields that prepared Olivia for this first job in Mexico City at forty-five pesos a day!

Olivia was grateful to be working at *Viajes Atlas,* even if all she did was sweep the floor, empty garbage cans, clean windows, polish furniture. She completed her work efficiently and then would sit on a wooden chair near the back, awaiting further instructions. After four days, Sra. Canales realized that Olivia could be dropping off tickets and invoices and bringing back checks and signed receipts to the office on Reforma Boulevard once she was done cleaning. She could well imagine Olivia typing tickets and invoices: and who knows, one day also selling tickets!

After work Olivia would hurry home, afraid to get caught in a late afternoon downpour or find herself crossing the busy Mexico City streets alone late at night. She was, after all, a small-town girl, barely nineteen, used to cobblestone streets and the warm exchanges of people who knew her; here, in this gloomy concrete and steel metropolis, she was overwhelmed dodging traffic to get home. And the crowds on the side streets, away from Reforma Boulevard,

seemed threatening—talking too loudly, hawking all sorts of things—
ready to trick her out of her few pesos.

*

The thin Mexico City air was pervasively cold and rainy, clogged by the
fumes and dust of the thousands of factories surrounding the city. Olivia
breathed deeply, but she went about almost always gasping for air.

Sundays were different. The morning air would be crisp, the sky
invariably clear and blue—and Olivia felt renewed. Miraculously,
it never seemed to rain. Sometimes she would visit the downtown
government buildings like the *Palacio Nacional, Bellas Artes* or the
Secretaría de Educación Pública festooned with large Diego Rivera
murals. She could spend hours examining the visual dramatizations of
Mexico's epic pre-colonial past and its early 20th century revolutionary
fervor. In time, she recognized Cortés, Montezuma, Benito Juárez
even La Malinche at a glance and Rivera's cartoon-like renderings of
the powerful capitalists from the North. The Mexican muralists not
only impressed her with their artistic renderings, but also managed
to educate her on Mexican history and the great social movements of
the 20th century!

But her favorite spot, the small San Ildefonso museum, was always
uncrowded, Here she would sit on a bench under an orange tree in
the patio, surrounded by a sprawling Siqueiros mural. She loved the
grand sweep of luscious colors and the crisp morning sun shining on
her face. She felt something like a religious serenity, which would give
her the strength to withstand another week of work and solitude.

Some Sundays she walked around the Zocalo. Thousands of
worshippers poured in and out of morning services at the Metropolitan
Cathedral, but she never felt tempted to go in. The Church seemed too
big, too gaudy, and she was sure that the services would lack any sense
of the intimacy of the Colegio Parroquial chapel she was accustomed
to. Yet she loved strolling here, watching parents buy trinkets for their
children from the hundreds of makeshift stands around the church
plaza. Or she would gravitate to the southern edge of the Zocalo
where speakers at political or labor rallies harangued the crowds and
tried to ignite them to protest against a government that was stealing
them blind—or so they said. She admired the speakers, peasants just

like herself, who seemed passionate about exercising their right to voice their opinions!

To speak so openly in Guatemala would have meant instant death. In Mexico you could speak and walk freely away.

Sometimes Olivia would head west through the narrow downtown streets to Alameda Park, gazing longingly at the Mexican families seeking solace in the patches of greenery. She would grow jealous of the children whose parents bought them mangoes carved like flowers on a stick, huge balloons or skeins of cotton candy. This jealousy would quickly turn into mourning as she grieved a lost childhood—never having wonderful things that other children had. She only received hand-me-downs and the Donald Duck books Sister Carina had given her.

On Sra. Canales's suggestion, she went to see Diego Rivera's *A Dream of a Sunday Afternoon in Alameda Park*, a huge mural in the lobby of the Hotel Del Prado on Avenida Juárez, flanking the southern side of the park. Among the well-dressed hotel guests and the groups of tourists that crowded the elegant second floor lobby and shopping arcade, she felt a miserable dark-skinned intruder. She identified with the Indians in the mural, many of whom were either plotting to steal from the wealthy strollers or sat armless and forlorn begging for handouts. Any moment, she imagined, a hotel detective would come up to her, question her disrespectfully and escort her out for having dared trespassed into a world to which she had not been given entree.

Sometimes, Olivia would take a bus to Chapultepec Park and wander through the zoo, gawking at animals and eating tacos and drinking *orchata*. She watched children riding in horse drawn wagons around the park shaded by towering eucalyptus trees and badly dressed old men who ducked under the black canopy of their standing box cameras to take pictures of the children. By late afternoon, Olivia would head toward the rowboat pond where lovers sought sanctuary from the hot afternoon sun in a shady nook. She'd spy them kissing one another, away from the crowds of onlookers and rowers.

Remembering Jesús made her even sadder. She would stay very quietly in the shadows, in a state of jealousy, hoping that one day she could be loved and Mexico City would stop being a city of dreams— the setting of what could be, projected on a distant movie screen.

Olivia called her father every few days during those first weeks in the capital. On the occasions he picked up the phone, he showed little interest in how she was managing to survive and, of course, never invited her back to his home. If the conversation veered toward Olivia wanting to see him, Melchior would become agitated and say that he had to get off the phone. He repeated how much he resented his wives and other children who, according to him, would only call or stop by when they needed something. They should be cooking for him, bringing him gifts and buying him new clothes.

His complaints made Olivia's heart ache. It was pointless to tell him that his stingy soul offered his offspring so little—it was ridiculous for him to expect that they would be grateful for the nothingness he had given them. For the first time she understood her mother's resentment. He only cared about himself and now that he was old, dirty and drank too much, his desire to still hold court was ridiculous.

Olivia stopped calling him when she realized that Melchior never called her. There was no point to expect love from a cold, heartless man. He didn't understand that his oldest child simply wanted his love.

*

During those first weeks at *Viajes Atlas*, Olivia admired Margarita Canales with a kind of star-struck devotion. Her employer was a sophisticated woman who exemplified elegance and style. She wore trim dark woolen skirts whose hems never strayed above the knees and she favored long sleeve silk pastel blouses that stayed perfectly no matter how she moved. And if there were a chill in the air, she would wear a matador jacket or throw on a dark *bufanda*, kept on her shoulders with an assortment of silver brooches. Her shoes, always impeccably polished, were European—she favored Charles Jourdan pumps—and her mostly gray-streaked hair was always stylishly coifed in a modified beehive or a braided bun.

But the approbation wasn't just for her looks. Sra. Canales was a sensible woman. She had inherited the travel agency from her husband Lorenzo, a notorious philanderer, who had succumbed to pancreatic cancer two years earlier at the age of 59. Ten years younger than him, she was not heartbroken by his death—she carried out all the details of the funeral and burial with her customary cold efficiency. She had been a proper wife who, after their two girls went to college, had moved into the oldest daughter's bedroom so that she simply wouldn't have to breathe the musk of sweat and cheap perfume that hovered over her husband from his other women.

Lorenzo wasn't the kind of man who required outward displays of affection from his wife. He was happy to be a good provider and father; his wife's role was to take care of the house, not to aspire to be his equal partner. He was content with his work, his afternoon and early evening trysts, his quiet evenings at home spent reading travel books or histories of Mexico's legendary heroes: Juárez, Zapata, Madero, Villa, Carranza and Cárdenas.

Lorenzo Canales had lived for the moment and spent his money carelessly. The peso devaluation sent his few stock investments to the south. Their two almost grown daughters—the eldest married and pregnant and the youngest an art major at Rice University—had no idea how destitute Margarita was.

With her husband dead, Sra. Canales could no longer be the bored housewife on the periphery of things—she had no choice but to grab, at the age of 51, the reins of her husband's floundering travel business. And she did so with passion and intelligence.

The agency was located on a prime spot of Paseo la Reforma, across from the María Isabelle Sheraton and the Polanco Suites and close to the boutiques and stylish shops of the Zona Rosa. Her husband's business had consisted of selling airline tickets and hotel packages to business clients and sightseeing tours of Mexico City to guests of the nearby hotels. But since Lorenzo lived for his dalliances, he was happy to leave Agencia Atlas in the hands of his office manager, a Monterrey accountant whose own sexual forays in the neighborhood kept him equally distracted.

When Sra. Canales took over, the business was barely breaking even. Something *was* wrong. The office never opened before noon and the agents came and went as they wished, often taking two-hour lunches. There was absolutely no sense of order. She fired the office manager immediately and within weeks, the three travel agents—all of whom she suspected had been Lorenzo's former lovers.

She hired Isabelle Bontecou, a French girl she had met at a *Club Francais* concert who had come to Mexico for an extended stay to sharpen her Spanish language skills. Isabelle was polite, thorough and organized.

Then Sra. Canales tried to expand the business. She used the *Club Francais* to quickly build up a strong client list of wealthy middle-aged women who lived in the well-to-do neighborhoods of Chapultepec, Condesa and Polanco. Margarita pointed out that instead of spending their days in boredom primping and shopping and overeating at the same old haunts in Mexico City, they could be jetting off to the United States or Europe while their husbands worked and their children were in school. They were frittering away their lives!Culture, shopping, Michelin Guide-rated restaurants: these women became the bread-and-butter of the agency.

*

At the end of Olivia's first week of work, Sra. Canales gave her five thousand pesos—$130—and told her to buy some new clothes and shoes at the Woolworth's in the Zona Rosa. She was not the kind of woman to mince words. "You may be filing or running errands, but you must always look fetching. Olivia, you never know what surprise awaits you. You've got to be prepared. Oh, and do move your spindly hair out of your face. You have a pretty face and you should let people enjoy it. And please start using face powder and lipstick. It's a simple art to make your face attractive. And Olivia, my dear, I hope you won't mind my indiscretion, but if you lost some weight, you would look so much better!"

Olivia had never been spoken to with such frankness. She wasn't offended by Margarita Canales's comments because she admired everything that rolled out of her mouth and it was clear to her that she had her best interest at heart.

Margarita Canales had said she had a pretty face. No one, not even Jesús, had ever told her that. Olivia would do far worse than to follow her advice.

Margarita Canales ran *Viajes Atlas* like her own private fiefdom. It had become a successful business, but also a laboratory for transforming the young girls in her employ into accomplished women. Her failed marriage had convinced her that women need not accept the physical, social or economic limitations life forced upon them. Talking to the girls, she referenced her own decades of marital subjection and servitude, then committed her energy to helping her staff break those same bonds. Women in Mexico were marginalized, asked to be in the shadow of their husbands and their lovers, to play their role with grudging, cheerful acceptance. Sra. Canales had sampled that diet long enough and had almost died from it: she encouraged her salesgirls to be independent, defiant and, when ready, to strike out on their own.

She took particular pride in working with the girls that God seemed to have shortchanged in some major way—the ugly, the meek, the awkward. She firmly believed that no one should accept her station in life. Though she sensed Olivia's intelligence and spunk, Margarita Canales felt she would be her greatest challenge—there was her Indian reticence, her unnatural deference and self-consciousness, her physical shortcomings, all of which could hold her back. The little spark in Olivia's eyes had fascinated Margarita Canales. She was her biggest challenge, but she knew she could elevate her.

So less than two weeks after hiring her at the *Agencia*, Sra. Canales decided to trust her instincts and train Olivia to sell travel tours.

"Do you think you can do it?"

Olivia didn't know what to answer.

"Speak up!"

"In high school I got a 92 in bookkeeping," she stuttered. "And I can type forty-five words a minute. Oh Doña Margarita, I don't want to disappoint you."

Sra. Canales concealed her misgivings. "Olivia don't worry about me. You should be concerned about disappointing yourself, the person you are in spirit! It's not your bookkeeping skills that worry me. It's the people skills—how polite you are with our clients, how successful you are in getting our customers to buy not only airline tickets, but also premier hotel and excursion packages. That's where we make our biggest commissions and I can't have someone working whose tongue falls asleep in her mouth midway through a sentence—"

"I'm so grateful for everything you've done for me. I don't want you to worry—"

"But I do, Olivia, I do worry," Sra. Canales continued. "To start, you are in Mexico City illegally and one of these days, the government might decide to send you home. And you are well, to be honest, a bit too innocent. I don't know if you have the right personality for sales. You need to be sure of yourself and have every part of your body give off confidence and desire. You can't appear confused or uncertain. This undercuts the client's trust in you, especially since you are trying to sell something that the buyer is unsure she needs. I guess what I wonder is if you are hungry enough."

. Olivia listened to Sra. Canales and saw opportunity slipping away. "I know I'm unattractive and my clothes are not stylish. Doña Margarita, my mother has worked her whole life picking coffee in a coffee plantation in Antigua. But I am not her," she said plaintively. She suddenly felt guilty for disparaging her mother. "What I mean is that my life hasn't been easy—hardship teaches you to learn fast. I'm a fast learner, especially when it's in an area that interests me. I've read articles on self-improvement in lots of magazines like *Vanidades*, *Selecciones*, *Cosmo*, *Tendencias*. If you give me a chance, I won't disappoint you."

Sra. Canales was pleased to hear the spunk in Olivia's voice. She had two full-time agents but needed a third to get through the Christmas holidays, still a few months away.

"You'll still be responsible for the filing and the deliveries."

"I can do that."

"It's a trial, Olivia, just a trial. Apprentice with Isabelle during the lunch hour, before the office becomes busy again."

Olivia felt so excited she hugged Margarita. The older woman hesitated, before finally embracing the young girl. As she tapped her shoulders, Olivia burst into tears.

*

Isabelle had been one of Sra. Canales' first successes. Born in Rouisillon in southern France, she had attended university in Orleans, majoring in languages. She spoke English, German and a bit of Italian. To improve her English, she spent her junior year at the University of Arkansas in Little Rock. And not wanting to return to France, she decided to come to Mexico to study Spanish. She lived briefly with a Mexican family and fell in love with the way of life and decided to stay and work in the capital. She had been at the agency for a little under two years.

Temperamentally, Isabelle seemed ill suited for agency work. Though curious and adventurous in her own travels, she was not sociable by nature and had a difficult time conveying to her clients her enthusiasm for a European city she herself had visited too many times. She was mousy and bookish and had a difficult time making small talk: in fact, she seemed to be slightly distracted when her clients started describing the actual details of their imagined vacations and she responded with habitual nods of her chin, when she could have offered so much more. But Margarita Canales persevered, and Isabelle became more outgoing.

Her greatest asset was that she was French. Many of the agency customers who called asked for her by name and were willing to be placed on hold for minutes at a time. The upper-class *Polanco* ladies wanted to speak to the French girl, partly to prove that they were not culturally inferior and partly to show off their language skills, honed at the *Alliance Francais* and the *Club Francais,* with an agent who spoke so many languages effortlessly. Isabelle was quite tolerant of their efforts to speak to her in the languages they were studying.

While Sra. Canales respected the other agents, it was clear that Isabelle was being groomed to take over the travel agency once Margarita retired. What Isabelle lacked in natural vitality, she more than made up by her application to details and finances. In the end, Margarita Canales had been able to convert Isabelle's natural aloofness and passivity into a valuable asset. She could be trusted and her decorous ways inspired respect and confidence.

Isabelle was happy to train an assistant. "Olivia, you can learn all the mechanical things like checking for flights, fares and seats within a few days, I'm sure. The important thing is for you to understand that our customers are nervous when they call us and it is up to us to put them at ease. We exist to serve them. We must always show confidence because with trust, we make sales. We also cannot contradict our clients—the customer is always right."

Olivia nodded her head, but she felt panic—she didn't know if she could speak to customers with a confident sense of ease.

Isabelle touched her hand. "Don't think that these are my ideas. I am only repeating what Sra. Canales has told me a thousand times. It is her litany: *the customer is always right, the customer is always right.* When I first began working here, I didn't believe that psychology played any role in selling tickets and packages. But now I know she was right, at least dealing with her clientele. The women all want to be assured that what they are planning for themselves or their husbands is perfect—a balance of culture, comfort, gastronomy and sightseeing. The Ritz Carlton in Paris; the Negresco in Nice; the Hotel Picasso in Saint-Tropez. We want them to think they are making all the decisions themselves—we just adjust their thinking in the most *sutil* of ways," Isabelle would say pronouncing certain Spanish words with a lilt.

"But I don't know how I can do that. I've never been able to change anyone's ideas. I was raised to respect everyone's opinions and to accept what I am told. I can't be what I'm not. And I can't try to figure out what people want to hear."

"The fatalistic Indian in you, Olivia," Isabelle laughed. "You can't assume that what people believe is fixed in stone. The world is in flux, always changing, and as individuals we can affect both fate and destiny through the power of choice and persuasion," Isabelle lectured. "My dear Olivia. Selling tickets is playing a character in a drama. Yes, I know I sound just like Sra. Canales, but she is right! You must always play yourself, but at a moment's notice, be ready to improvise."

*

Every afternoon during lunch, Isabelle taught Olivia how to use the multiple phone lines and the computer terminals without losing connections—how to put clients on hold with classical music or *rancheras*, depending on who the customer was; how to split computer screens to check flight availability for two clients at the same time. But most of all, she showed her how to get the customer to perceive that the tour or package you were promoting, in a charitable sleight of hand, was the result of the client's own suggestions.

Olivia recognized that Margarita Canales secret was to make the agents into masters of swift adaptation and *multi-tasking*. If she had been in the circus, she would have been the emcee as well as the juggler, acrobat and tightrope walker all at the same time—she could handle walk-in clients and phone-clients simultaneously, without having anyone feel shortchanged. All with a sense of decorum to disguise the cleverness.

Isabelle shared with her a list of those specific airline agents she had gotten to know personally over the previous two-year period. She printed out a page with personality traits and specific skills and passions, then would quiz Olivia about them. And she told her that very often the agents would offer her a fare offered to no one else—and the agency commission would be even higher!

"Inés at Mexicana de Aviación responds to questions about her teenage children, but not her husband, who is unfaithful; Jorge at Iberia is gay and likes to talk about movies and restaurants; Laura is always curt and seems interested in conducting business quickly, but you can always get her to "smile" if you ask her about her cats. And tell them how much their voices sound sweet like dessert and chocolates. And you should never confuse the voices of Lourdes and Roxanna though they are twins and both work at Continental; they hate each other's guts."

She also told her about the hotel chains that would give the agency an extra 5% commission if it steered clients to them, especially when the hotels were empty. And because Isabelle had made exploratory trips to London, Paris, Barcelona and Rome—the most popular destinations for their clients—, she was familiar with boutique hotels and established personal contact with the owners. "It is all a question of who you know and who you serve," Isabelle had nodded knowingly. "And since these little hotels are never in the travel guides, the owners are always quite generous with us."

Each night, Olivia would take three or four brochures home to study. She was awed by the Eiffel Tower, Chartres Cathedral, The Vatican, Westminster Abbey and Big Ben and the beaches of Spain's Costa Brava. She would force herself to read the descriptions of the locales, memorizing each hotel's amenities and services. It was more a game than a test, and she was surprised by how successfully she committed so many facts to memory.

Olivia realized she was quite skilled at visualizing the features of each city and each hotel. She imagined different scenarios, as she had done as a child in Ciudad Vieja, so that soon enough she saw herself walking down the very streets and entering the hotels mentioned in the brochures—she would be the one glancing up at the lobby chandelier, running her hand on the felt chair armrest or tasting the exquisite array of goat cheeses in the restaurants.

But the ultimate test was to see how others reacted to the new Olivia. She revisited the Hotel Del Prado on Juárez to see if she could blend in effortlessly with the tourist crowds. Wearing a new outfit purchased with Margarita Canales's money, she walked into the hotel lobby, ambled through the shopping arcade, visited the rooftop garden, which had a splendid view of Mexico City and the surrounding mountains with the natural grace of someone who belonged.

One Sunday, in fact, she actually penetrated the security of the María Isabel Sheraton and bathed in the heated swimming pool, pretending to be a hotel guest. No one questioned her; if she felt out of place, no one knew about it and no one looked upon her as if she were a fraud. The deception had been complete.

She called her father from Mélida's telephone to tell him about it—her transformation would be the kind of thing a parent would be proud of.

"Oh, it's you," he said, as soon as he heard her voice.

"Father, I went swimming at the María Isabel Sheraton," she blurted out. What a stupid thing to say.

"I don't understand what that means."

"I am now a travel agent. And I have new clothes. You wouldn't recognize me—"

Before she said any more, he asked if she could send him the money he had lent her a few weeks back.

"I can bring it over right now."

"No," he answered, "I'm going out to meet some friends at the park. Give the money to Mélida. She knows how to get it to me."

Olivia heard *bar* for *park.* "Father, are you even interested in knowing how I am doing?"

There was a pause on the line. "Okay, how are you?"

*

That night Olivia wrote the first of many similar letters to Sister Carina. She put down the first thoughts that came to mind and kept writing until she had nothing left to say. The letters were five or six pages long, written in hurried, terrible script. And she would sign all the letters the same—*with loving gratitude, Olivia Padilla.*

In this first letter, she asked the nun to forgive her for having left
Antigua in such a rush. She went on to tell her about the bus ride to
Mexico City to see her father, and how he had welcomed her in a way
her mother never had. She was very happy, she wrote, living in his
home and being part of his large family. She told Sister Carina about
her job, with much less embellishment. She sent this first letter with
no return address—she did not want to be found.

(1983)

As much as Olivia treasured her new life in Mexico City, there were still many dark days when she pined for her simpler life in Guatemala. She missed Antigua—the silences, the many parks and ruins where she could go and sit with a book or daydream without the urge to do anything else. She often pictured the town flanked by three volcanoes, a plume of smoke escaping from the *Volcán Pacaya*, and the quiet cobblestone streets with orange, lavender and red bougainvillea flowing over the pastel facades and crumbling walls of buildings. It was a town in which you could almost live outside of time. If there was such a thing as paradise, it was there.

Though the Mexican newspapers were full of it, Olivia could hardly remember the violence in Guatemala—the conscription of Indians into the army; the disappearance of innocent men, women and children; and President Río Montt's newly initiated scorched-earth and beans-and-rifles policies. Perhaps the violence had been the machinations of the cruel and indifferent Mayan Gods, the Lords of Xibalba, but not altogether real—a veil of terror which Olivia barely recalled.

What she did remember was her mother's house in the woods, the long rows between the coffee shrubs where she had once walked, the little stream at the bottom of ravine where she had passed so many hours listening to the water gurgle over the colorful stones of a stream. She missed Sister Carina's love and counsel. She missed being around people who knew who she was. She worried about Guayito who had just disappeared.

Most of all, Olivia missed her routine at the *Colegio Parroquial*: wakeup at 6 AM, breakfast at 6:45, prayers at 7:30, classes beginning at exactly 8. Lunch at noon and rest till 2 PM when classes would begin again till 4 PM. Volunteer school service in the library, the kitchen or with the younger students till 6 PM. Dinner at 7 PM. And more study until lights were out at 10 PM. Of course, there had always been time for a cigarette on the roof, a quick escape into town with Jimena for a coke and *canillas de leche* and later the kissing and the drinking at La Merced. She could always venture afar, knowing that the little cot in her dormitory, with the heavily starched sheets and the straw mattress, would be there awaiting her. Her routine had been a mirror of the Antigua landscape: a tranquil, frozen, timeless life inside the safety of a paperweight.

How she missed her classmates. She missed Meme's arms and lips more than she missed Chucho's and she wondered if Meme had decided to attend Marroquín College or had eloped with Paquito. Olivia even missed mole-faced Jimena; she wondered if she had adjusted to living at home again, doing the bookkeeping at Arturo Chang's store or whether she, too, had run away. Olivia's life had changed but she had a difficult time imagining how the lives of her friends had been transformed.

If she could bring herself to give Sister Carina her return address, perhaps she would find out.

Olivia felt rootless, caught somewhere between worlds, like a ship that had left port with no idea where it was going. The future frightened her. Isabelle Bontecou had become a friend of sorts, Margarita Canales at times a model and a mentor and at times an interfering, overbearing mother. But neither one would understand the terror and aloneness that Olivia felt—she looked around at vendors, merchants, and everyone seemed so foreign and uncaring.

Maybe if Olivia established similar routines in Mexico City as she had in Antigua, she would be able to quell the nervousness. Certainly that's how Mélida Cotilla ran her apartment *pensión*, as if she were still living in the village of Tlacochahuaya. The malevolent souls that hovered in and around the Zocalo were the agents of Satan, said Mélida, scheming to prey on the innocent and unaware. Olivia had great resources and had been chased by worse beggars and drunks in Guatemala than those who scrounged about in her neighborhood. All the powerful women she had met in Mexico City—Mélida, Isabelle, and especially Doña Margarita—were skilled at establishing order amid the reigning discord. They willed away solitude.

*

Olivia continued to deliver tickets, pick up payments and do the afternoon run to the bank at *Viajes Atlas*. She also carried out whatever personal errands Margarita Canales needed done: bringing her shoes for new soles and heels; dropping off fancy dresses at the *tintorería*; buying cans of hearts-of-palm and smoked oysters and croissants and brioches at *Delicias de Paris* for her evening soirees.

Isabelle continued to train Olivia during the afternoon lull when most businesses would shut down for the two-hour *comida* and *siesta* period. She learned how to attend to several clients on the phone at the same time and how to operate multiple windows on her computer screen so that she could research several itineraries simultaneously. In her spare time, she continued to read through travel brochures of cities and countries she knew she would probably never ever visit. Olivia saw all this as an initiation--a preparation for a promotion— for a better life to come.

After a month at *Viajes Atlas*, just after Olivia had returned from picking up tickets for Margarita Canales for an evening Sibelius concert at the *Palacio de Bellas Artes* and was back to studying still another brochure at the rear of the office, she heard Isabelle's thin, dyspeptic voice say aloud: "I think Olivia is ready."

Olivia raised her eyes but said nothing.

"Ready for what, my dear?" Ms. Canales was at her own desk, turning the pages of *Cosmo* in Spanish.

"Olivia is ready to be a travel agent."

Sra. Canales looked over half-moon reading glasses and raised her eyebrows as if to question Isabelle's sanity.

"It's true, Margarita, I have nothing else to teach her," Isabelle said, somewhat apologetically.

"And do you think that I have nothing else to teach her as well? The customers are my people, from my social class and rank—". Margarita Canales believed that little birds should be allowed to fly, though the actual moment of that first flight filled her with terror. What if her acolytes were unable to get into the air or worse start flying and then crash into a wall? What if they were to use their wings to escape the nest and fly away? Certainly, this had been the case with Flavia Gutiérrez and Elena Almendariz, both of whom had used the travel agency to pick up skills and then went out on their own months later.

"Margarita, I am only referring to the technical training. You will have to judge the other part."

It upset Olivia that this mousy little thing in a green corduroy jumper with a yellow cotton blouse could presume to judge whether or not she had learned enough skills to serve the ladies of Polanco or tourists from Caracas and Buenos Aires.

"Of course, Isabelle. But imagine her sitting up front," Margarita said, flicking her head back toward Olivia who pretended she was engrossed in reading her umpteenth brochure, "sitting in her chair like a hippo in a quiet pool of water, aware of nothing around her. When someone comes in the door, she lifts her large brown eyes into the air and opens her jaws if a fly had ventured too close to her... Isabelle, you know that our customers need more than that. They are putting their trust in us, in our knowledge and our imagination. They need to believe that the little hotel that we suggest on the *Rue de Bac* will be as charming and luxurious as we claim or that the grand hotel near the *Place de la Opera* will not be noisy and impersonal, but lovely as the Mouffetard Market. No, Isabelle, Olivia is **not** ready."

Olivia heard all this but said nothing. She couldn't react. She heard footsteps and when she looked up, Margarita Canales was standing over her. Olivia kept on looking down but she couldn't do anything to stop her ears from turning red. She was mortified and wounded by all she had heard.

"I want to know exactly what you eat. Every little item of every little meal and those snacks in between," she commanded, tapping Olivia on the shoulder.

"But I can't tell you, Sra. Canales—"

"Everything," she said.

Olivia lifted her eyes and began speaking almost somnambulantly. As she spoke, she visualized all the delicacies she bought her boss at *Delicias de Paris* and felt embarrassed.

"For breakfast, for example," Sra. Canales persisted.

Olivia went through a long list of items—papaya, bananas, sweet rolls, scrambled eggs and beans, coffee with lots of milk and sugar, perhaps another sweet roll to cap the meal. When she had finished, Sra. Canales insisted that from now on, she had to limit herself to a few slices of papaya, no bananas, one boiled egg, no toast, and black coffee without sugar. For lunch she could have a sliced cucumber, lettuce and tomato salad with a lemon and herb dressing. For dinner, she had to dispense with her traditional plate of rice and beans and the *molé* that Mélida occasionally prepared ("chocolate and flour, and extra sugar, my dear, are strictly speaking a dieter's venom"). For the next month she could only eat a thin *tasajo* steak or a piece of roasted chicken ("no skin") with either a salad or a cooked vegetable like string beans or *chayote*. "No beets, no corn—no vegetables with high sugar content!"

And instead of poking around the museums and parks on Sundays, trying to recreate the calm of Antigua in Mexico City, she had to go to the makeup counter of Sandborns and Woolworth's. Since Olivia had little money, she was to ask the salesgirls for samples she could take home and experiment with. "Olivia, The first thing you must realize is that poor people like you have no use for pride, which is really an impediment. You can't let it keep you from achieving your goals. I could pay for your cosmetics, but I firmly believe in personal initiative. I want you to work things out for yourself! You have to make yourself alluring."

Olivia tightened her lips. She wanted to tell Sra. Canales that she had too much confidence in a poor half-Indian, farm girl lucky enough to be discovered by a Guatemalan nun years ago.

"I don't really approve of that expression on your face. When I hired you to clean the office and to run errands, I didn't think that I could remake you even though right away I saw in you a kernel of hope for bigger and better things. You have good manners and you're polite, but that's not enough. You want to be a travel agent and work with people. That requires much more—"

Olivia dropped her eyes. She couldn't get out of her mind the image of a hippo—which is how Sra. Canales had described her to Isabelle.

"Look at me when I talk to you. I must tell you, Olivia, that the most unattractive thing in the world is to see a fat girl pouting."

Olivia felt no insult in Sra. Canales's words. To be called *a fat girl* was purely observational and to be told what to eat was simply to have a nutritionist—in this case, a *Beauty Specialist*—prescribe a regimen for her.

Sra. Canales put her hands out to Olivia and helped her stand up. "I know you can do it." She then hugged her. Olivia felt a lump in her throat—she struggled not to cry.

*

Just as Olivia had found the pluck to explore Mexican history and Mexican contemporary life through its muralists, she knew she had to find the courage to begin her own physical transformation.

Change was possible. Meme had taught her how to kiss, but what's the good of going through life and have nothing to kiss but the crook of your own elbow? Yes, she had kissed Chucho almost chastely.

> *Ashes to ashes, dust to dust,*
> *If it weren't for boys' lips, a girl would rust.*

Meme would sing to her. "Oh Olivia, you have to open your mouth to achieve ecstasy." It had everything to do with taking the initiative and not being passive.

This was *the moment*. Margarita Canales was offering her the chance to go into areas beyond her reach. It was like the awakening of passion and Olivia knew that she could not turn away from it.

*

On Saturday afternoons after the agency closed at 2 PM for the weekend, Olivia would make her way to the Woolworth's on Hamburgo and Londrés in the Zona Rosa or to the Sanborns downtown—the one known as *The House of Tiles* near the Zocalo. For the first time in her life, Olivia learned to approach cosmetic counters and allow the aproned girls to fuss about her. She would tell them she couldn't afford expensive cosmetics and, when it was proper, she would humbly ask for samples. Then the next day, on any given Sunday when Mexican families were at the zoo, in clubs, or having a wonderful *comida*, Olivia might visit three or four other cosmetic counters, accumulating dozens of samples. In time, the salesgirls began to recognize her and instead of denying her products that they knew she could never buy, they would collect free samples during the week and hold them for her visit. They could see that Olivia's face was changing--they, too, wanted to share in her transformation.

If there were few customers, the salesgirls would take pity on her. They would sit Olivia on a stool and apply new samples on her face—they would talk to her about which were the best and least expensive face grounds and mascara, lipsticks and eyeliners, nail polishes and hair dyes. But if the salesgirls were too busy to attend to her or if they feared being reprimanded by their supervisors for wasting time on an overweight half-Indian girl, they would just drop samples in Olivia's woolen Guatemalan *mochila* and continue attending to other customers. Olivia would go home, face her stained and cracked mirror and with the guidance of an anemic reading light, she would begin applying the new samples to her face, keeping in mind what Dona Margarita had told her.

"Wash your face with a good cleanser before you do anything else: the face secretes oils naturally and with the contaminated air here, your pores will stop up and your make-up will crack. You mustn't put too thick a layer of ground on your skin, Olivia, or you will never see your new face being born out of your old one. You can never be anyone other than who you are--you must learn to build on what you have—on your own foundation. By layering you can bring out the natural beauty of your face. You should think of make-up as texturing and highlighting so that the *pure you* can come out."

"But Dona Margarita, my skin is splotchy—"

"Olivia I don't want to hear excuses. I want you to work on yourself. Remember that da Vinci said that 'the eyes are the windows of the soul' and yours, my dear, are not only shuttered but also thick with vines that block the view. You need to buy yourself a good pair of scissors and a set of tweezers and pluck, pluck, pluck those long hairs!"

Again, Olivia did not take insult. It was true that she had been born with eyebrows that resembled furry caterpillars and her lashes curled into themselves like ingrown nails. As much as it hurt, Olivia plucked her eyebrows till she had the thinnest saber of hair over her eyes. As a child, she had always kept her hair full-length because this cataract of black hair covered her sideburns. Painful as it was, she began waxing and shaving the side of her face until it was smooth and then applying a special lotion said to restrict hair growth. At first the pain was unbearable, but in time she saw it as necessary steps to achieve her goals.

The hair that grew on her chin had to be plucked one hair at a time and followed by a protective, healing lotion. There were times her skin was so raw that only thin layers of grounding and powder disguised the scarring.

In time, Olivia discovered that a beige ground would mask the brown sun marks on her face, that black liner above and below the lids would brighten her sleepy eyes and make them languidly seductive. She had shapely, crescent lips; Olivia determined that purple lipstick would make the bottom lip thicker, more inviting. She began to brush her hair straight back and clip it tight against her scalp so that her face was revealed openly for the first time since she had been a child. It was not a naturally attractive face, but with care and attention, it could become amusing, perhaps alluring.

And the oddest thing was that as Olivia's body changed, so did her personality. All of a sudden she could imagine herself not simply mouthing outlandish things, but actually feeling the texture of her own words as if they were real, not acted. Whereas Sister Carina was fond of saying "The Lord does not look at the things man looks at. Man looks at the outward appearance, but the Lord looks at the heart," Olivia knew that she was now most interested in the opinions of man.

Not even Meme would recognize her.

*

Two months after Olivia had been hired to sweep and run errands, she was given the receptionist desk near the glass front doors of *Viajes Atlas*. Sra. Canales hired Concha Asturias, a thin and skinny Spaniard with a prominent nose and sweeping bangs on her forehead, to replace Olivia as the office grunt.

Olivia's new duties consisted of welcoming customers, having them fill out intake forms listing the name of the passengers, the address and the provisional dates and itinerary of the trip. As soon as either Isabelle or Sra. Canales beeped her, she was supposed to direct clients back to them with their in-take forms on clipboards. If anyone had to wait more than ten minutes, then Olivia was authorized to begin working directly with the client, but only by showing brochures and phoning airlines. She would not be given her own computer terminal for now. But in this small way, Olivia too, would begin to develop her skills of communication with new or returning clients.

In the same way that she had memorized the alphabet twelve years earlier, Olivia committed to memory the information on the hotel brochures and fact sheets. This allowed her to very rapidly upgrade itineraries by choosing slightly more expensive hotels—those that offered the agency a particularly large commission—before passing the clients on to Isabelle and Margarita who appreciated what she had done. Since she was always deferential to the wealthy, Olivia made the clients feel important—as if they were the ones deciding everything including these upgrades.

"I know you want a full-service hotel on the Il de la Cité overlooking the *Notre Dame Cathedral* or on *Trocadero* with a view of the Eiffel Tower outside your window. Such lovely views. It's too bad though that you aren't interested on this little hotel I have on the left bank near *St. Germaine des Pres*—"

"Why not?" the client might ask.

"Well you would have to walk up two flights of stairs. Besides, the concierge closes the front doors at midnight and you'd have to ring to get inside."

"No, I wouldn't want to go to Paris to climb stairs."

Olivia would smile. "But wait! Why not try this wonderful Rive Gauche luxury hotel which has an antique elevator and lace-curtained rooms overlooking the newly opened *Musee de Orsay*? This is the fashionable Left Bank. Not one of my clients has stayed there!" she would exaggerate, not really knowing what she was talking about.

This sleight-of-hand made the customers feel empowered. Olivia would simply congratulate them magnanimously for their intelligent choice, resourcefulness and great imagination, for having chosen a "new" hotel, not the same one all their Mexican friends had stayed in. And because most of her clients were women planning return trips to Europe with husbands, sisters or girlfriends, Olivia would always preface her suggestions with: "If I were going to Europe, and my wife (or sister or girlfriend) had chosen this hotel, I would be so grateful to her!"

More than seeming to use tricks or sophisticated bait-and-switch tactics, Olivia simply played into the desire of all customers to make their vacations more of a dream. It seemed altogether reasonable that if you were committing tens of thousands of pesos on a trip, it was worth spending a few thousand more and guaranteeing that the result would be truly memorable.

To Sra. Canales's surprise, some of her regular clients began calling ahead of time and asking for Olivia by name.

"How have you done this, you little sorcerer?"

Olivia would simply blush.

"Tell me your secret!" Sra. Canales could hardly contain her pleasure.

"What do you think of our Olivia now?" Isabelle would say, beaming. She didn't have a single competitive bone in her body.

In time, Olivia learned to toss her head when a compliment was paid to her, but now her eyes were wet when Margarita Canales said: "You are simply marvelous!"

She knew she had finally succeeded.

*

A month later, Olivia was promoted to full-time travel agent and Concha Asturias, no longer bony and ferret-like under Margarita's attention, became the agency's receptionist. Olivia was given a mahogany desk, her own telephone line and computer terminal away from the entrance doors. The new clothes and her freshened up looks all contributed to making Olivia feel that for the first time ever, since her childhood, she could put away her heavy and pasty tongue, the slightly sour smell her body seemed to exude, and be the woman she imagined she could be.

The old ugly image of her, which had trailed behind her like a snail's shell, didn't need to be expunged. It simply fell off on its own. And though she still felt insecure inside, her entire exterior demeanor seemed to have changed. Now that she felt more comfortable about her appearance, she felt growing confidence.

She could be whatever she wanted. Well, almost whatever. She wrote a long letter to Sister Carina, one in which she spoke frankly about her four months in Mexico. And this one she posted with a return address.

(1984)

Abraham Zadik's office was in a ten-story building that abutted *Viajes Atlas* just around the corner from Reforma Boulevard. Though he could have had his secretary purchase his airline tickets, Abraham loved walking into the glass-fronted travel office just to see the posters of Mount Fujiyama, Lake Atitlán, Angkor Wat, the Great Barrier Reef and the Twin Towers at sunset festooning the agency's white walls. Images of tourist destinations from around the world helped him to realize how far he had come from the days that he had sold staplers store to store in Caracas, Venezuela.

Abie, as his friends called him, had been booking his tickets with *Atlas* for nearly ten years and Lorenzo Canales' death didn't change that. Though he and Margarita were the same age, they were extreme opposites in manner and style. For this reason he preferred booking tickets with Isabelle whose efficiency and French lilt were the perfect antidotes for the late afternoon Mexico City rains which dampened everyone's spirits from mid-March to the end of October. And when Olivia began working at the agency, he immediately took to her, not because she was attractive or his type, but because she seemed to appreciate his off-colored jokes. He loved to tease her and see her round dark face blushing. Something about Olivia—her unwillingness to either be the butt of his jokes or be primly dismissive, as Isabelle sometimes was—pleased him. And in time, she began to answer his quips with inventive ones of her own.

Perhaps he recognized in Olivia a bit of himself—the person born to poverty in El Salvador who by sheer will power managed to transcend it. Moreover, around her, he felt no desire to conceal his modest roots. And why should he?

*

Abie's father Isaac was a Jewish salesman who had impregnated a simple salesgirl in Santa Tecla and quickly abandoned her. Abie's mother raised him in abject poverty, in a wooden hovel tottering precariously over a ravine. She kept hoping that Isaac would show up and, mindful of his obligations, acknowledge his son and take them away from this bedraggled life. But Isaac never came back. When Abie was twelve, already in sixth grade, his mother began hearing voices from other planets. Her sister offered them a room in her house in the seashore town of La Libertad. As soon as Abie felt that his mother was safe, he went off to look for work in nearby San Salvador and never looked back.

He was hired to run errands at the Swingline Staplers factory near the Ilopango Airport. When he was fifteen, he joined the assembly line and finally—as he was a quick learner and a quick talker—, he was promoted to salesman. He worked long hours, even taught himself English and when he was twenty, he jumped at the opportunity to go to Venezuela as a sole distributor of Swingline products.

In Caracas he worked hard, soberly visiting stationary stores, schools and business machine outlets during the day, but at night he rendezvoused at *La Guaira* with Bohemian artists and poets to drink and discuss politics and women with equal passion.

It was an exciting, if dangerous, era. Perez Jiménez had seized power in Venezuela in 1950. Like all good dictators, he preached self-sacrifice while stealing millions of oil dollars to build himself villas in Santa Margarita Island, Tuscany and the French Riviera.

Though dutifully working for an international corporation, Abie shared the beliefs of the swaggering young Bohemians, his friends, who saw the need for revolution. Like many of his generation, he had experienced how poverty had destroyed the peasantry—his own mother's family, for example—in El Salvador. He was captivated by Fidel Castro's successes in the mountains of Cuba's Oriente Province and his triumphant march into Havana. He saw no contradiction between making money, debauchery and socialism. "Everyone is entitled to a decent life. In the sexual field, freedom, total freedom, is necessary; capitalism enforces monogamy and obsolete social contracts such as marriage. Noah would have been a failure had marriage existed. No, we need total freedom," he liked to say, with a sparkle in his eyes, spoken like a true Existentialist.

Abraham was a bon vivant who loved to spend money, drink and laugh. He danced the *merengue* and the *guaracha* with swivel hips and knew the words to most of the popular boleros of the period. He was not attractive—much too short and barrel-shaped, with a large prominent nose and lips much too thin for his face. But his sensual eyes had the power to grip a woman in their gaze and he knew how to make the girls he danced with feel as if only they mattered. These were, of course, not high society women. Abie would hold them tight. Soon enough they had surrendered to the heat of his eyes and the press of his hips as he reeled them in closely for a kiss.

Abie began to change when he noticed he almost always picked up the tab for his friends and he was the only one trudging off to work the following morning after a late night of carousing. His buddies had the luxury to sleep off their hangovers, plan beach excursions to Cumaná. He realized that they all functioned under a temporary moral code, which allowed them to curse the capitalist hand that fed them. He had no such luxury.

Abie's dilemma was that he enjoyed his work and he became increasingly dismayed by how easily his leftist friends wriggled out of their responsibilities. He also began hungering for English cut linen suits and handmade Italian shoes and wondered why Castro never cast off his green fatigues and kepi. And when Pérez Jiménez was ousted and the patrician Rómulo Betancourt came to power, Abraham was horrified by the strikes, riots and violence instigated by his friends— all Castro sympathizers.

They were out of control—had they no respect for the law?

Abraham was a non-practicing half-Jew, yet he felt that once or twice during an evening of heavy drinking and discussion, he'd hear an anti-Semitic remark fly by him. It was always couched in language like: *Of course, Abraham, you're not like the rest of your tribe.* He never responded, aware of how difficult it was to defend a minority in an overwhelmingly Catholic country.

He nursed his bruises and, little by little, began to withdraw.

By the early sixties Abraham had developed two new heroes-- *Playboy's* Hugh Hefner and James Bond. Hef was a social libertarian who cavorted with beauties of all stripes and colors—he knew the difference between Gucci, Bally and Bruno Magali shoes, between Chivas and Vat 69, and he became a millionaire while spending his nights in trysts at the Playboy Mansion in Chicago. As for James Bond, he was handsome, sophisticated and had the skills and intelligence to triumph over the forces of darkness. He dueled spies, traitors, and megalomaniacs—all foreign enemies who were trying to overthrow legal governments who defended the rights of decent people. And, of course, James Bond always ended the evening with the most beautiful girl.

So Abraham drew the line on revolution, for now and forever. *No More Cuba Libres* became his adage—and he gave up his rum-and-cokes as easily as his unquestioning support of Fidel Castro.

By the time Abraham left Caracas and Swingline, his radical days were far behind him. His devotion to the pleasures of life and money, and his natural loquacity, prevailed over any desire to reform the existing economic order. He worked briefly in Guatemala for Pitney Bowes and was then hired as the Central American rep for *Empresa Grafica Centroamericana* headquartered in Tegucigalpa, Honduras. After years of working different territories--in El Salvador, Panama, Nicaragua—he was appointed EGC's International Sales Director and assigned to Mexico City. Abraham was the natural choice—he was happily unmarried, showing no interest in snagging a socialite wife and becoming a sober member of society. His graphic and printing services sales area included Mexico and the southwestern U.S. border market.

He spent most of his days seeing customers in Mexico City, a city he loved from the start. After having lived in shrunken Central American capitals, he treasured the teeming crowds, the noise, the wonderful European style restaurants of the Zona Rosa—the *Chalet Suizo, Humbolt's Pub* and *Vicenzo's*—where he could meet clients for an elegant, relatively inexpensive lunch. Mexico City was a real city, the perfect habitat for a naturally sociable person.

*

One day Abraham invited Olivia to one of his Saturday night soirees, which he held twice a month at his leafy home in the hills northeast of Mexico City. While most of the *Lomas de Chapultepec* mansions had metal electronic doors and cut shards on their high walls, his was a modest ranch in a wooded area off the *Ciudad Satelite* highway. In this cusp of a valley, there were maybe a dozen homes, each surrounded by high pines, feathery thorn trees and lots of brush—the whole area almost forgotten by developers. Abraham's house was tucked furthest from the dirt road, where *guajolotes*—turkeys—and wild pigs still roamed freely.

Olivia took two *peseros* and a taxi to reach Abraham's house. "Welcome to Xanadu," were the first words out of his mouth as he met her in the foyer. Clinging to his arm, just barely able to stand, was his current bed partner. Olivia recognized Zimry--she sold fragrances in a perfumery off of Balderás—where Olivia often went to pick up free samples. Zimry barely fit inside her red dress.

Abraham preferred his women to be thin and slight like Zimry, with radiant breasts pushing out to overflowing. They had to be at least two decades younger than him, compact and coltish. "Fillies," that's how he referred to them. He could never be with a naturally large woman, like Olivia, one whose sheer physical presence, buxomly frontality, would have terrified him.

"I didn't know you lived near Naucalpan--next time I'll rent a car for the weekend!" Olivia remarked, kissing Abraham on the cheek, letting him know it had taken her hours to get to his house. The lights were dim, and a dozen squat, perfumed candles burned away. *How Deep Is Your Love* was blaring on the living room stereo.

"My apologies," Abraham smiled. He was wearing an odd white toga shirt and a maroon silk scarf around his neck. "Next time I'll send my chauffeur for you. But really, Olivia, we have been waiting for you all night. Do you know Zimry Ho?"

"But of course—La *Perfumería Francesa.*"

"I didn't know you were friends," Zimry confessed, putting out a limp hand while Olivia hung her coat in the entrance way closet.

Abie pressed her tightly. "My dear Zimry. You do know that all roads lead to Abraham Zadik."

Zimry eyed Olivia suspiciously when she returned. "Where did you meet Abie?"

"I work in *Viajes Atlas* next to Abraham's building. I book his airplane tickets."

"Nothing more?" Zimry asked.

"That's not kind of you, my dear...Olivia makes my hotel reservations as well," Abraham said, enjoying the palaver of two women. He squeezed Zimry's arm. "And this young beauty I met six months ago in my yoga class. We are Yogi Banshee's most devoted students."

Abraham had found a way to achieve spiritual salvation by mixing Hef, James Bond and now yoga.

"You should come to our class," Zimry said to no one in particular. "Yoga frees your mind. After twenty minutes of practice I feel so much better about myself."

"Exercise—and breath control," Abie added, "The paths to enlightenment!"

Olivia raised an eyebrow. Isabelle, who was a bit prudish despite her emancipated French woman's acceptance of values opposed to her own, had mentioned to Olivia that Yogi Banshee's ashram was less a study center than a club where secretaries could meet wealthy businessmen. If Isabelle suspected this, then it was so. She had told Olivia that Yogi Banshee's students practiced yoga and flirted with macrobiotic regimens and a holistic approach to life, but what they most practiced was unfettered sex. Nowhere did it say that meditation limited sexuality; on the contrary, Kundalini and Tantric yoga could lead to higher sexual ecstasies. Yogi Banshee, whose girth was equal to his height, preached the value of control as a path for liberation, all with a leer in his eye.

"Olivia, let me get you a drink."

"I do need something," she replied, "after my journey to get here."

Abraham smiled broadly. He put his arm through Olivia's and walked across the foyer with Zimry clinging to his other arm. "I want you to meet a friend of mine."

Marijuana fumes came in waves toward them, clouding up the room. "Abraham, your friend would have to be directly in front of us to see him," Olivia said.

Abraham smiled. "I don't control the habits of my guests. We are all free individuals. I do want you to meet Jesús Muñoz."

"You've invited Jesús from our yoga class?" Zimry asked.

"I do find him quite good company. I didn't think I had to show you the guest list," Abraham said to her, bristling a bit.

"But Jesús is *married*."

"Was. Was. Was. He's living alone in Colonia Roma."

Zimry whispered in Olivia's ear: "Just stay away from him. He's very rich, but thin and bald like a *xoloitzcuintle*, that ugly little hairless dog."

"Thanks for the warning," Olivia said. She was wondering why she kept meeting men whose names were Jesús.

"Abraham, I don't know how you can imagine any woman would want to be with him…I need to go to the bathroom. Will you wait for me?" Zimry slurred.

Olivia put down Abraham's arm. "You stay here and wait for your girl. I'll get my own drink," she said, moving across the living room. This was not her milieu—she was already wondering when she could leave and how she would get home. She wasn't interested in meeting anyone.

*

On the console in the sunken living room sat bottles of Chivas, Gilbey's Gin, and Polish Chopin Vodka--a dozen people sprawled on the shag rug and white sofa, laughing and joking. Several doors led off from the living room, but they were all closed. Few people in the neighborhood would've guessed that a scene of sheer revelry played itself out in this quiet house on the outskirts of Mexico City.

Olivia put her bag down on a corner table and poured herself a Chivas with plenty of soda. She had only recently begun to drink alcohol. She then went out into the garden through the glass windows in the dining room to escape the smoke.

What a mistake she had made in coming--two hours to get here and now she felt untethered. She had nothing in common with the people here, she told herself, though this was not quite true. Zimry and she probably had more in common than not and she was certain that the other women here, beautiful women really, were also of modest means. The difference was that Olivia was inexperienced and the other women had surrendered their independence years ago simply to go to such parties.

Meme, with her unbridled passion, would have fit in perfectly— at the least, she would have found the parties amusing.

It wasn't that "her date" looked like a hairless dog, it was Abie's deception— Jesús was married and pretended he wasn't—that upset Olivia. So much dishonesty and duplicity: and what for? Just to get someone in bed!

But why expect Abraham to be morally enraged about anything?

Olivia felt a little calmer outside—at least the air was cool and uncontaminated. Looking northward, she saw a sky glittering with lights from the nearby *Satélite* shopping center and above, a thin layer of white clouds, which seemed to be frozen against the dark sky. Olivia tried to enjoy the moment—*to be still, present and awake even when the mind begs for sleep*, she once remembered reading, perhaps in the *Rubiyat*. She took another sip of her drink and closed her eyes. Olivia could hear the talk and laughter swilling about her--the sound of ice being crushed in a blender—but she could almost imagine she were back on the roof of the *Colegio Parroquial* or on the grounds of La Merced, a familiar world to her.

"It is a beautiful night, isn't it?"

She opened her eyes. Before her stood a man her height, with short, cropped hair. She took a sip of her drink. "It is," she said, wincing, still unused to the taste of liquor.

"May I introduce myself?"

Olivia had to smile at the man's formality.

"Horacio Quiroga," he declared, as if Olivia *should know* who he was. His skin was light brown, like a chocolate bar, and he had eyes that were faintly dreamy.

"Very glad to meet you. Are you a friend of Abraham's or a business associate?"

"That's a complicated question. I'm the manager of *La Zapatería Filogio*, off *Insurgentes Sur*, near the Hotel Chapultepec."

"A *Chilango*," Olivia demurred, using the depreciative term for a native of Mexico City.

Horacio's cheekbones formed little balls below his eyes as he smiled. "Nothing of the sort. I was born in Zirahuén, a village on a small lake not far from Pátzcuaro. Perhaps you've heard of it?"

"Well, of course. And I can tell you everything you want to know about your birthplace even though I've never been there."

Horacio smiled. The lines at the edges of his eyes also ran down his cheeks. He had a kindly look, like a satisfied bovine. When he smiled his whole face seemed to be absorbed by the effort. But he said nothing, and waited patiently for her to continue, all the while looking at her in quiet admiration.

"Why are you looking at me that way?"

"Words, really, cannot describe your beauty. You captivate me."

Olivia looked at him strangely. What strange talk: she certainly didn't consider herself a beauty. Unusual, interesting now and then, but not a beauty. Meme, yes, or skinny Angelica or brainless Zimry Ho, with her mixed Oriental and Huastec beauty—these women had features that men would find magnetic, if not tantalizing: shapely legs, teasing eyes and lips, full, welcoming breasts. What did she have to offer? She was at best a mock version of what one might call a *dark beauty*.

"Are you trying to impress me?" she asked, surprised at her own directness. It had been months since she had thought about a man or her sexuality. Maybe Horacio was the handsome frog prince who would drag her away from this stupid world.

He continued smiling his exasperating smile. "Weren't you going to tell me about Pátzcuaro?" Olivia closed her eyes. Her fantasies regarding what might be taking place—gorgeous man luring innocent, passionate beauty—made her feel foolish. Better to stick to script, to what she knew. "The center of the Purépecha town of Pátzcuaro is located approximately 4 kilometers from the lake of the same name. Originally inhabited by Tarascan Indians, Pátzcuaro is known for its woolen ponchos, ceramics and the butterfly-shaped nets of its fishermen. Today its residents earn most of their income from tourists who take the 20-minute boat trip to Isla Janitzio, visit the small villages along the lakeshore and buy textiles and souvenirs."

Horacio's eyes widened, making his cheek bones rounder. "Amazing. But you've been there."

"Never, my dear Horacio."

"How do you know these things?"

Olivia could feel the Scotch cracking her protective gear--the warmth of the alcohol radiated out toward the tips of her fingers, curved down into her womb. She sidled up to Horacio, who was slightly shorter than she, and whispered: "I have many secrets." The words simply escaped from her mouth and then she belched.

"How enchanting," he answered, innocently.

"I'm so sorry." Olivia shook her head at his response and almost laughed. He seemed to be a small-town boy lost in a large city. "What is someone like you doing at this party?"

"I'm wondering that as well," he said, scratching his head. "Abraham said I should come. But I have spent the whole evening here in the yard admiring trees, the breeze, and the sky. It doesn't seem as if we are in Mexico City, but in a small town somewhere... But to be honest, from the moment you walked out here, I have forgotten all about nature. I am only curious to know you better."

"Perhaps some other night, Horacio. Tonight, I need to find a way back home," she said bluntly. Olivia was a novice at small talk in Guatemala and here she felt totally inexperienced. Most of what she knew had come from books or been gleaned from the experience of others—Margarita, Meme, even Jimena—and from her ability to memorize travel brochures!

"I have a car. Let me take you. This is not my kind of party." He offered Olivia his arm.

"My purse is by the console in the living room."

They went back into the smoke-filled house, where bodies were melting into one another on chairs and sofas and corners of the living room. Huge pillows had been placed on the rug to serve as ramparts and protective cornices.

"My pensión is in *Colonia Roma*," Olivia said.

"That's perfect. I live with my mother in *Narvarte*, on *Avenida Dr. Vertiz* almost across from the *Parque de los Venados*. It would be my pleasure to take you home."

The fact that Horacio lived with his mother put Olivia at ease.

She went inside to get her purse. She opened it, pulled out her lipstick and dragged it across her lips, using the protective glass of a Tamayo print above the console as a mirror. When she was ready, she glanced around the living room to bid goodbye to Abraham, but he was nowhere to be seen.

Neither was Zimry.

"Let's go," she said to Horacio. He nodded and walked straight out of the house, with Olivia a few steps behind him. Head spinning, she ran up to him and grabbed his arm—she needed his support.

Outside it was now raining, and the air had turned cold and clammy.

Olivia felt dampness soaking through her blouse and shivered. "I forgot my umbrella."

"Here, take my coat," Horacio said handing it to her. "Put it on your head. Give me your hand."

Horacio's red Golfo was parked down the hill from the house. As they walked toward it, Olivia asked: "How well do you know Abraham? You seem so unlike him." Horacio laughed mawkishly. "It's a secret I'll share only with you. We are not friends. Abraham comes to the *zapatería* because he has a problem—he cannot wear ordinary shoes. His right foot is a centimeter longer and wider than his left. I measure his feet and have shoes made to order in Leon, Guanajuato. They fit him to a tee. He is so vain, he would never admit this to anyone. I am intimate with his feet and through these encounters, we have become acquaintenances."

When they reached Horacio's car, he rushed over to the passenger's side and gallantly opened the door for Olivia to get in. His face was splattered with rain.

Olivia was tired. It had been a long week. As she sat down in the passenger seat with Horacio's coat still around her shoulders, she felt the depths of her exhaustion.

Horacio started the engine and drove slowly, moving the gears with hardly a pause. The wheels glided softly over the pine needles on the dirt road. Olivia closed her eyes. She heard the tires crushing gravel as the car climbed onto the asphalt. Horacio put on the windshield wipers; they made a muffled, swishing sound that seemed to further lull her to sleep. Her chin dropped down to her chest and she started to snore evenly.

Horacio eased his car into the *periférico* that circled the northern part of Mexico City before angling downtown. As he drove he glanced at her from time to time; her mouth was ajar and he saw a bead of saliva running down the left side of her mouth. He took his handkerchief out but decided not to disturb her. His handkerchief dropped to his lap and he drove slowly as if her sleep and comfort depended fully on his measured driving.

When he reached Colonia Roma, he stopped the car and dabbed her mouth.

Olivia, woke up, startled, and threw her head back. "Where am I? Where am I?" She repeated, dazed.

"You're almost home, *mi princesa*," Horacio said gently. "But to get you there, I need your exact address."

She swallowed with difficulty, not sure how much time had passed. She remembered getting into the car, hearing the falling rain, and that was all. Her thoughts had been jostled by deep dreams, one in which her father was chasing her through the woods trying to get her to drink from a glass. She could not, would not stop running, because she was certain he was trying to poison her. But then she ran into a man who started kissing her in the woods, pressing his body up against hers--

"Your address, Olivia," Horacio repeated. He had pulled in front of the Hotel Cortés on Avenida Hidalgo, just across the northern flank of a wet and empty Alameda Park.

She looked at him. He was sitting hunched, with one hand on the steering wheel and the other on the shift, smiling again. It was at once a knowing and vapid smile. No one would ever say that Horacio was handsome, but there was something extremely attractive about him, the comfort he seemed to give to people as he looked at them with his dreamy, if slightly inert, eyes.

Olivia's mouth was dry and she felt hot inside the car. She was consumed by what she would characterize as a sinful thought—she wanted to spend the night with Horacio. To preserve her own sense of decency, she told herself that she would only be interested in sharing a bed with him like brother and sister, not have sex.

But the fact was that she wanted to make love.

Even if she were willing to risk her reputation by inviting Horacio to stay with her, her landlady Mélida Cotilla would not tolerate overnight guests. And Olivia was not about to suggest he take her home to his apartment, especially since he had volunteered that he lived with his mother. It would have been too forward of her. Nonetheless, she ached to feel the warmth of another body next to hers.

She said nothing about this, but instead gave him her address.

He drove slowly the three blocks to her *pensión*.

"Sealed and delivered. Safely, I might add."

Olivia leaned toward him and kissed him. He seemed startled.

Olivia liked his glabrous lips. She took his handkerchief from his lap and wiped her lipstick off his lips. He allowed her to draw his head toward her and she kissed him again, slipping her tongue between his lips, as Meme had taught her long ago. She curled her tongue around his and felt her small breasts heaving. She was surprised to feel an ache in her chest and the surge of warmth coursing through her body.

She pressed against him, pushing him toward the driver's door and window, pinning him down. She felt she was back at La Merced, with Jesús.

She moved Horacio's right hand to her breast and whispered. "Please touch it."

He was unaccustomed to such forward behavior. Still he did as he was told and timidly stroked the cup of her bra.

"Pinch it, pinch it," she whispered, as she rolled her tongue deeper into the vortex of his mouth. She moved her hand to her blouse and forced his fingers to softly rub the nipple of her right breast. "I'm not made of porcelain," she added.

Olivia directed Horacio's fingers. She felt her body come alive as it hadn't for so many months. She pushed his hands over her nipples, arching her back toward him. Her body loosened its grip on her chest like a hand. She was floating in air and nothing could stop her. And then she felt herself bubbling and a soft gurgle came out of her mouth. She sighed quietly and fell limp against his chest.

When she looked up at his face a minute later, he smiled automatically, as if he had handed a customer a shoehorn to fit a recalcitrant foot inside a tight shoe. She tried to read his expression to understand what had just happened, but his bracketed face revealed nothing to her. He was a small-town boy and felt nervous doing this, in a car, on a street in Mexico City.

"Olivia." he said, "I would like to see you again." He kissed her on her forehead several times. She kept her eyes closed and raised, instead, her hand and covered his mouth.

"Shush, shush. No words, please." She seemed to be flying through the most peaceful of dreams. "Isn't it beautiful to hear the sound of rain?" she murmured.

They stayed quietly like this for a few minutes until he said to her: "I need to get home. My mother worries. She might be waiting up for me."

Olivia took the house keys out of her purse. "Could you wait until I am inside?" she asked him.

Horacio nodded. Olivia opened the car door. The sidewalk was wet and black. She walked slowly to the front of her building, unlocked the door, turned around and blew him a kiss.

When he was sure Olivia was safely in the building, Horacio drove away. He was somewhat confused over what had just happened.

Olivia was the kind of girl with whom he could share his life. Had he been asked to define what he felt, he wouldn't have been able to describe it though he could have characterized his mood as being in a state of nervous infatuation. *Olivia was mysterious and unpredictable* and that pleased him.

As Olivia undressed and brushed her teeth, she felt a lead apron had been taken off of her—she had been released into pleasure with no need to make amends.

Because the party had taken place on the weekend before the Easter holidays, Abraham didn't stop by the travel agency to talk to Olivia until more than a week had passed. At the door of *Viajes Atlas*, he bumped into Margarita Canales, who was just leaving to meet a friend for lunch at the *Chalet Suizo*.

"How were your holidays, Abraham?"

"Splendid. Absolutely splendid. I hardly went out of my house."

"Of that I'm sure," she smiled, her tongue barely grazing her finely etched lips.

Abraham crinkled his nose. "Oh, I know you don't think very much of me."

Margarita touched his shoulders. "Abraham, I do find you very amusing—like a child. I say that affectionately. You could almost be my son though we are the same age."

Abraham smiled—Margarita's hair was speckled gray and she saw no need to disguise it—his was still black.

"You must take a magic potion to keep you young."

"Not at all, I simply surround myself—"

Margarita interrupted him by putting a finger on his chest. She felt dryness in her throat. "I don't need to hear the details, Abraham. Let's leave it at that. I'm happy, though, that you've become such a regular visitor with us. Maybe I should set you up with a table and chair—next to Olivia," she suggested above the roar of midday Monday traffic on *Reforma Boulevard*.

Abraham was nonplussed. He waited till a car stopped honking. "You might say that Olivia and I, well, we've become friends."

Margarita arched an eyebrow. "Abraham, as long as you remember that she is under my employ. She isn't one of your typical girls—"

Abie laughed. He pulled down on the sleeves of his blue striped gabardine jacket. "Of course not, my dear Margarita. Our friendship is quite Platonic. Olivia is innocent, like the women from Santa Tecla, my hometown in El Salvador, with none of the false sophistication that permeates this otherwise lovely city. I find her quite refreshing. But to calm your fears, she is not my type. Friendship is the extent of our relationship."

"She's very unfamiliar with your kind of life, Abraham. She's not worldly. I don't want to see her get hurt. You know she is here alone, with no one to watch over her. You can't treat her--"

Abraham had heard enough. "Margarita, I'm sure you're late for your lunch," he said, feeling accused, about to tell her that it was none of her business. "Would you like me to get you a taxi?"

Margarita was frustrated by the course of the conversation. Always wanting to get the last word in, she quipped: "I was born here in Colonia del Valle and I can certainly take care of myself, Abraham. I will repeat—Olivia is not to be toyed with. She is quite fragile." She went through the door, not looking back. "Good afternoon."

Abraham was about to say something but shrugged his shoulders instead.

As he walked across the office, Isabelle tilted her head up. He went by her desk and dropped a hand to graze her shoulder. She lifted her mousy eyes and smiled. Abraham closed his own, rounded his lips and blew her a kiss.

Isabelle snorted and went back to her typing.

Olivia was on the phone with a client. She gestured for Abraham to sit down and raised a finger in the air to ask him to wait.

As soon as she hung up, Abraham said: "Olivia, I barely saw you at my party."

"Yes, I know. I tried to say goodbye, but you and Zimry had vanished--"

"Nonsense. I was in the kitchen making a *taboule* salad. Jesús came and we looked for you all over, but you had simply vanished— unless, of course, you were hiding in one of my bedrooms!"

"My dear Abraham, you have a very keen imagination. While you were with your Zimry, I was outside admiring nature—"

"How romantic of you."

"Well, it was quite nice. Do you every go outside to enjoy the night air or are you simply a house mouse?" Olivia asked provocatively. Abraham was tickled by the spunkiness of Olivia's response—it was what he loved about her—sharp but never crude remarks. "Well, you should come another night then. I want you to meet Jesús."

"I don't think so, Abraham."

"You're not going to let Zimry's comment about his being married deter you? Jesús is getting a divorce, but you know how conservative this Catholic mausoleum of a country is. He and his wife have not slept together for years—they have separate bedrooms—why they don't even eat together…You disappoint me, Olivia. I didn't figure you to be judgmental. You give off the sense of being a modern-thinking woman. What happened to you, anyway?"

"Horacio Quiroga was kind enough to give me a ride home."

"Ah, now I understand," Abie said, as if he hadn't known this all along and simply wanted Olivia to admit it. "You've been smitten by my little shoemaker."

"I don't know if I would characterize it like that."

Abraham reached for Olivia's hand and stroked her fingers.

"You better not!" she said.

"Better not what?" he countered licking his lips.

"You know exactly what!"

Abraham smiled broadly—he was old enough to be her father. She was really like a daughter to him. He leaned his head down and kissed Olivia on the forehead. "We Central Americans need to watch out for one another. I want you to know that I like Horacio very much, but if things don't work out, well, there's always Jesús."

Olivia raised her left eyebrow.

*

Horacio Quiroga and Olivia started seeing one another.

There was a kind of modesty to their relationship that somehow managed to keep both of them happy. In the bright daylight glare and in the clearing of sobriety, the vagaries of that first night had disappeared—it was as if the wrestling in the car ride after Abraham's party had never taken place. It was more Horacio's approach, and Olivia was content to take his cue.

Before meeting Olivia, Horacio had been a man ruled by habit. He'd wake up each morning at 6:45 AM and make breakfast for his mother. He would listen to the 8 AM radio news and by 8:20 would be in his Golfo driving to the *Zapatería* in the *Polanco* district so he could open up promptly by 9 AM, Monday through Saturday. Luis Porrua, his assistant, would be there with *pan dulce* and coffee, his morning breakfast, and Horacio would read the *Excelsior* for the next forty-five minutes before opening the shop to the public precisely at 10 AM. He would work through lunch and at 7 PM pull down the gates of the store and head for home. He would watch some TV and then share a light supper with his mother before going to bed at ten o'clock with a magazine.

His mother, Doña Amalia, was not a demanding woman. She was accustomed to the devotion of her only son and felt no need to express it. She didn't mind spending her days alone in the apartment, sometimes going shopping with a neighbor at the supermarket, but mostly staying in to watch her favorite *telenovelas* and game shows throughout the afternoon, as long as her son spent the evening hours with her. It had been this way now for so many years.

After meeting Olivia, Horacio would sometimes leave Luis Porrua in charge of the shoe store. He would take his car out of the parking lot below *Fenoglio's Shoe Store* and dash over to *Reforma Boulevard* to meet Olivia for an executive lunch at *VIPS* or *Sanborns*, but never for no more than an hour. Sometimes he would kiss her on the cheek when he dropped her back off, sometimes not.

He had no plans to be entangled by emotions. Habit or courteous decorum informed his thirty-one-year-old life, Olivia didn't know which. She would have preferred a bit more interest from him, but the lack of calamity in his life appealed to her, at least initially, because it made no demands of her. But as the weeks passed, Olivia wanted more out of their relationship—candlelight, wine, the seduction of perfume. She felt she was constantly dropping hints— *Wouldn't it be nice to have dinner at the Torre Latinoamericana or go hear the mariachis at the Plaza Garibaldi?*—but he would respond with a kind of nervous shudder and she would remain wanting, with a lingering wetness in her mouth.

He was pleasant and handsome, dressed stylishly—was almost dashing, one might say—but it was as if he were incapable of providing heat beyond the proper limits of say, warming leftovers on a hotplate or on a stove.

Doña Amalia must dominate Horacio, Olivia thought. Perhaps he was incapable of challenging her authority. How had he ever been allowed to go Abraham's party? Had it been a monumental act of defiance? She knew she had to meet this woman to know.

But after almost eighteen months of loneliness in Mexico City, Olivia had a man who sought her out at least during the daylight hours. And he would call her religiously every day at work and offer to help her in any way he could—drive her to see clients or drop off tickets. He often drove to *Viajes Atlas* so he could bring Olivia to her *pensión* on his way home. It was so odd—during the day he would be attentive, but at night, he would leave her forlorned.

*

When Olivia turned twenty-one, she felt on the cusp of something. She had been seeing Horacio now for nearly six months and though she enjoyed his company, she felt completely sexless or unsexed in his presence. Now her body was experiencing new sensations as if the percolating of hormones, so common to a girl of twelve, was finally happening to her nine years later. Oh yes, she had had experiences at the *Colegio Parroquial* where her bubbling her sexuality had led her to lose control momentarily, but she felt that these were isolated moments, surprising flashes and sudden spikes, which once they had passed, allowed her to resume her tranquil life. In fact, she could dismiss these responses as her attempt to become part of a defiant group of girls at school.

What she was feeling now was different. Her body wanted something more than a casual brush with passion. She felt a deepening pull inside of her—sudden warming of her breasts, the nipples becoming erect and tender, a kind of twitching between her legs. Horacio was the logical person with whom to explore, cull out or quench, these desires. But every time she was with him, and he took her hand or chastely kissed her, she sensed she was with her brother. She wanted to grab his hands and put them on her breasts again or better yet, to have them touch the curve between her legs.

Horacio is nice, very nice, a gentleman, sweet and attentive. But Olivia needed something more. It made her feel self-conscious, even a bit guilty, to tell herself that she wanted a sizzling affair! She wished she could simply pick up the phone and call Meme, an authority on desire, who would tell her how to quench her thirst even if she had to go to a bar and pick up any man!

One night Olivia woke up with a start. Without thinking, she parted her legs and began touching herself. Her breasts were full and warm, her mouth thirsty, almost parched. She wished she had three hands, to touch between her legs and stroke her breasts as well. She heard church bells ringing, it was two in the morning, and she was sure her body was lifting off from her bed in pleasure.

But then without warning, Brother Pedro de Betancourt's face came into her mind and she was not alone. He seemed to smirk at her. All of a sudden she moved her hand away from between her legs. She felt burdened by guilt, the sense that what she had been doing was not only wrong, but also ridiculous.

*

One Wednesday night after work, Olivia insisted that Isabelle join her for a drink at the *Carrousel Internacional* on Niza and Hamburgo in the Zona Rosa, a short walk from *Viajes Atlas*.

"I can't, Olivia," I need to read three chapters of Mexican history— from the end of Benito Juarez's rule to the Revolution. Porfirio Diaz. I have a test tomorrow night at the UNAM."

"Just one drink—" Olivia pleaded.

"One drink," Isabelle said, rolling her eyes.

It was a hot March night in Mexico City, packed with dust and fumes, before the cooling rains of May. The air tasted stale, the streets crowded with shoppers in a hurry, kids hawking newspapers, old men sitting on the sidewalks selling cigarettes, cashews, gum. The sky was thick and unforgiving.

The girls decided to sit at the bar. A mariachi quartet was going around taking requests from the few tables that were occupied, playing loudly to try and attract more customers. The air-conditioning felt refreshing at first, though the cold air reached them in draughts.

"What will it be, young ladies?" the bartender asked.

"I'll take a Coca-Cola," Isabelle said.

"Bring her a *Cuba Libre.*"

"I've told you I'm studying tonight."

"It will make you study better."

Isabelle shook her head. "And for you?" the bartender asked, turning to Olivia.

"Make it a frozen margarita—with salt around the edge, please."

"*Herradura* or *Don Julio*?"

"The cheapest," Olivia answered. It pained her that she had to be so thrifty—maybe it was time to ask Margarita Canales for a raise.

When the bartender left, Isabelle asked: "So what is it that can't wait?"

"Well, I just thought it would be nice to get together with my friend and colleague."

"How nice," said Isabelle. "But I think you have something on your mind."

"I don't know how to talk about this."

The bartender brought them their drinks and a small bowl of mixed nuts. Olivia's margarita was in a large goblet, so big it had to be balanced in two hands.

"*Salud, amor y pesetas*," said Isabelle.

"I would settle for *amor*," said Olivia.

"Is it about Horacio?"

"Sort of."

"You seem to make a nice couple. He's always so solicitous of you when he comes by the office."

"That's the problem. I want more from him, but I don't know how to get it."

"Why not ask," the practical Isabelle answered, "or simply grab it."

"It's not so easy."

"Oh, Olivia, I am sure he would marry you."

"That's not what I want. I don't want to get married!"

"What is it, then?"

Olivia was disheartened. What had she been thinking? *Isabelle was not Meme.* She felt ridiculous, utterly ridiculous, bringing up the issue of sex with Isabelle. Wasn't she twenty-six and *French*? She couldn't possibly be a virgin, but Olivia sensed that sex for her friend had to be automatic or rational—the first or final chapter of a courtship, what happens at a certain moment, casual, but not passionate.

"Sex," Olivia said, with certain embarrassment.

Isabelle picked up her drink and took the most deliberate of sips even though she was only drinking Coke.

"You're a woman. Horacio is a man. It would be natural for you to want each other."

Olivia shook her head. "That's not the issue."

"Is it about contraception?"

Olivia laughed heartily. Isabelle was altogether clueless. What had Olivia been thinking? That she could talk to her about the passionate rushes that were flooding her ten years too late? About the desire to touch herself at the oddest moments, even in restaurant bathrooms? How Horacio seemed to be uninterested in her body? She was sure he wasn't gay, but maybe he had some sort of sexual dysfunction which prevented him from feeling the natural impulses that all men have.

Olivia said that the problem was Horacio's mother, Doña Amalia, and his unwillingness to challenge her. Isabelle thought hard, but she offered her most direct advice—Horacio should simply invite Olivia for dinner at home. That would break the ice, she posited.

When Olivia finished her *margarita*, she and Isabelle parted ways.

Olivia was a little drunk. She decided to walk home to her *pensión*. Strolling down the broad sidewalks of Reforma Boulevard, she ignored the noise, the lights and the throngs of people around her. After the air-conditioning in the bar, the Mexico City air seemed pleasurably warm.

Live for today because you don't know what crap tomorrow might bring, her mother had once said to her when Olivia had asked her about the future. It was one of those typical outbursts that came out of her mother's cynical mouth— not exactly elegant, certainly not edifying or instructive—especially from a person who was shackled to her habits. Not the kind of comment Sister Carina would have approved of for the students of the *Colegio Parroquial*.

The body is a cauldron of sin, Sister Bonifacia was fond of saying.

Olivia wished she could be a good Catholic girl. Since arriving in Mexico, she had barely stepped inside a church. She couldn't imagine conversing with a priest or a nun, much less hearing a sermon. There seemed to be too much pageantry, gold and filigree, too many paintings and statues with pained saints and Biblical figures for her to feel comfortable in Mexican churches. And she would never, ever submit herself to confession in an ornately carved box with a priest that had none of the simplicity and earnestness of Brother Pedro. She needed direction and instruction, but not religion.

Without looking, Olivia had stepped off the curb on the corner of Calle Roma against the light. A car took the corner, sounded his horn and the driver called her *bruta ciega*. Olivia got back on the curb and waited for the traffic to clear and the light to turn.

Salud, amor y pesetas y el tiempo para gozarlos. Olivia loved this toast of the Spanish—health, love and money and enough time to enjoy them.

There was nothing wrong with that.

She seemed to have health.

She could always use more money, but at least she had enough to support herself.

Amor—that was the rub. She had companionship, but no *amor*.

No *amor* and certainly no *pasión*. Maybe there was something physically wrong with Horacio and she would have to try and find another man, a real man.

She thought of Jesús, saw the image of a soapy, hairless dog and felt the urge to vomit.

There had to be a solution.

(1986)

A few days before Christmas Isabelle suggested that she and Olivia go together to Havana, bridging the New Year's holiday with that of the Three King's. Olivia had not left Mexico since arriving from Guatemala and she was aching to travel; she wondered what life could be like in an island country in the Caribbean.

"I would love to, Isabelle, but you know I can't afford it."

In her years of working with Margarita Canales, Isabelle had taken long weekend trips to Queretaro, Pátzcuaro, Valle de Bravo, Puebla in Mexico and had also managed to visit Monterrey, Guadalajara and Oaxaca. And, of course, she had been back to Europe five times. She could have given French and English lessons while she took night courses at the UNAM to get her master's degree in Spanish, but the discount travel offers were why she remained at *Viajes Atlas*.

"Olivia, we've just been offered a special package to Havana. Normally the trip, which includes airfare and hotel, costs $800 per person, but this promotional offer is for $650. I know I can get it for about half that," said Isabelle.

"But I don't have even that kind of money."

"What about asking Horacio? I'm sure he would give his sweetheart the money." Olivia shook her head. She knew she couldn't ask him.

"Then let me invite you," Isabelle said. "Please? It would make me so happy. It would be my Christmas gift to you—and to me! I'll pay for the package—you'll only have to pay your share of meals and entertainment."

Olivia needed little convincing. Horacio had decided to take his mother home to Pátzcuaro, to spend the long holiday with her two brothers and their families, as they had done so for the last twenty years.

The last thing Olivia wanted was to stay alone in Mexico City, which had turned unseasonably cold and miserable. She hadn't spoken to her surly father in months. When she had called him in September, he had complained of the gout and about barely being able to walk. And when she last telephoned him a few weeks later to see if his knees were doing better, his phone line had been cut. She could have taken the subway or a *pesero* to see him, but to what end? To come up against Rabbit 18?

She was fed up with his complaints. He was dead to her now and she had decided that she could no longer grieve.

*

Olivia had also considered flying back to Guatemala to visit her mother in Antigua, but the airfare was too expensive, even with the travel agency discount. And if she could afford it, she would not be going back in the style which she wanted.

Isabelle's offer meant she could get away, not only from Mexico City, but from the sameness of her life. For months now, she had felt that her relationship with Horacio was stale—they would meet for lunch twice weekly, occasionally she would join him and Doña Amalia for Friday night dinner and once a month they would go to an early evening movie. Perhaps after ten days of taking care of *mamá*, he might return to Mexico City with renewed infatuation or the semblance of desire for Olivia. Any desire.

Isabelle booked their tickets and on New Year's Day, they boarded an Air Cubana flight to Havana.

Olivia had of course never been on an airplane. She had been unprepared for its rapid ascent from the tarmac, the way it seemed to glide gracefully into the air and then push onward into, and beyond, a bank of clouds. It made her realize how small her world had been, still was, and how when seen from above, it all seemed so shrunken and insignificant. Even snowcapped Popocatepetl—Smoking Mountain—which rose majestically above the Valley of Mexico to the south seemed toy-like and unreal.

The only real thing was her, here, held in by the seatbelt and looking out the window. Even Isabelle who was sitting next to her engrossed in reading the Christmas issue of *Elle*, seemed completely unaware of this momentous occasion. Perhaps for Isabelle air travel had become routine, unexciting—to use a French word, *blasé.*

The flight to Havana simply overwhelmed Olivia. For the first time in her life she saw white sand, blue water, brown and green coral formations, liners and fishing boats, thin gauzy clouds, a world she couldn't have ever imagined from her days at the coffee plantation. It was a forever expanding world, beyond the confines of what her mind might have visualized through her own readings.

And if her mother could see her now, drinking a Cuba Libre that had just been served by a flight attendant dressed in a blue and white uniform!

Olivia's eyes welled up. There was no point of writing; her mother was illiterate. Worse than that, she wouldn't even care, would end up harboring resentment for having had to go again to Ciudad Vieja to have a reader unknown to her tell her what her daughter had written. She would do better to write to Sister Carina who, though she was sure had never been on anything higher than a third-floor landing, would appreciate the description of what she had just seen.

"You're crying," Isabelle said to her. "This trip is making you sad."

"No," Olivia said, drying off her tears with her cocktail napkin. "I am not sad. It's so beautiful."

Isabelle leaned over the arm rest and looked out the window. She saw blue sky, water and clouds, nothing out of the ordinary. She glanced back at Olivia, put down her magazine, and squeezed her shoulders with her bony hands.

*

After the bustle and chaos of Mexico City's airport, Havana's largely empty José Martí airfield seemed quaint with its rundown brown leather chairs and sofas and an aspect of oblivion, as if time had somehow passed it by. On the way to *the Hotel Nacional* in the *Vedado* area of Havana, their sputtering 1952 Chevy Bel Air taxi passed billboards festooned with revolutionary slogans and with portraits of Che and Fidel smiling in their fatigues. Olivia suspected that these signs could not mean much to the average Cuban—slogans were best for the people who had the leisure to invent them or who could draw benefit from these quotes.

Antigua and Guatemala City were no modern metropolises, but they seemed so much more developed than Havana where time had stopped—the old American cars and slightly newer Russian Ladas wheezed in slow motion down the mostly empty city streets. Crowds lined the sidewalks, where they patiently awaited *camellos*—huge ungainly tractors with camel humps on the central axis that served as buses. These buses were the only way for them to get home or to places of work many miles away.

*

The *Nacional* was almost story-book in appearance, perched on a sloped hill overlooking the Malecón, with a perfect view of Havana harbor. In pre-Castro days it had been the pinnacle of luxury—Winston Churchill, Meyer Lansky, Marlon Brando had all bedded down there. Isabelle, who had tasted the luxury of the *Quinta Real, Meridien* and *Intercontinental hotels* found the *Nacional*, with its lumpy mattresses and cigarette burned furniture, severely lacking. The hotel didn't even offer room service! But Olivia, who had never spent a night in a hotel, could not believe that the Nacional had two swimming pools and several bars scattered along the grounds. And each day, Isabelle said, maids would come in and change the bed sheets, pockmarked as they were, and give them each a new set of towels!

Isabelle wanted to spend the week sunbathing by the pools, but Olivia insisted that they use discounted coupons for guided tours of Habana Vieja, the marina where Hemingway had anchored his fishing boat *Pilar*, and the Morro fortress on the peninsula across the harbor. Instead of eating every night in the hotel, Olivia suggested that they have dinner at the Ambos Mundo Hotel rooftop restaurant and the Bodeguita del Medio in Habana Vieja, where the faded elegance more than made up for the blandness of the food. One night they went to the *Yara* to see *Missing*, a film about a lost young American boy and the U.S. complicity in overthrowing Chile's President Allende. The movie theater was stiflingly hot without air-conditioning, and so after the movie they stood in line at Coppelia Park for ice cream. Another night they heard jazz at *El Gato Tuerto*, a glitzy, smoky bar near their hotel, filled with Italian and Spanish men and their teenage Cuban consorts.

Olivia liked the people that they met at the hotel and the tourist stops though she felt that somehow they were failing to find the places where real Cubans congregated. She realized that Isabelle would be happy with a week of loitering around the hotel that required nothing of her—being a tourist in a foreign country was a recognizable experience for her even if their hotel, so beautiful from the outside, was ghastly inside—but Olvia wanted so much more. She had in a sense lived her whole life on an island—an island prison—but she wanted to know what it was like to live on *this* island, where the people dressed lightly and the music and aromas were so seductive...

The warm Caribbean air and the lighthearted smoothness of the Cuban people, especially the men, made her curious to meet them. With their boisterous laughs and unnerving directness, they seemed infinitely more attractive to her than their Mexican counterparts. And somehow, her physical abundance—certainly a liability in Mexico City—seemed to attract flirty stares from the Cuban men. When she and Isabelle walked down the street, the men would turn around to look at the sway of their hips—*her* hips!

By the fourth night, Olivia insisted that they be more adventurous. She convinced Isabelle to eat at an illegal *paladar* in Centro Habana that offered twelve different pork dishes. The waiter, a thin, talkative Cuban from Cienfuegos whose hair was black and thin, suggested that they go afterwards to the *Herón Azul* bar on the veranda of the UNEAC building in the Vedado district.

"It's where the young people go—artists, writers and musicians. And it's not far from the Nacional—you can even walk home from the club. You'll like the music—and you will understand the ingredients of the Cuban soul."

*

Olivia felt giddy when the taxi let them off in front of a gated mansion on a leafy tree-lined street of El Vedado, a wealthy neighborhood in pre-Castro days. There were blue lights in the garden and the sound of live music flowed over the building to neighboring rooftops.

Isabelle had not wanted to go—and as they walked toward the veranda, a bored expression seemed glued to her face. As soon as they sat down at a table, she began criticizing the club as being a pickup joint.

As the trio of musicians in their early twenties played a song, she dismissed them as amateur crooners and the club as a hangout for lonely, penniless Cuban men trying to snag free drinks from the bevy of young European and American girls sitting at the bar.

"Oh, Olivia, this place is so fake. Don't you know why the waiter suggested that we come here?"

"So we would enjoy ourselves."

Isabelle shook her head. "He thinks we are two fools attracted to Cuba by the romance of revolution and socialism. Have you been listening to the lyrics?"

"I like the music," Olivia answered defiantly, swaying her shoulders to the bolero being played by the musicians.

"What does the singer know about these things?" Isabelle asked.

"You are in a very bad mood, my dear," was all Olivia could say. She was tiring of Isabelle's constant criticisms. Yes, she was European, had visited dozens of countries, but this was Olivia's first vacation and she liked the songs that nostalgically recalled distant lovers, the simple pleasures of farm workers and cane pickers and the glorious triumphant days of the Revolution when all seemed possible.

As a waiter approached their table to take their order, Isabelle pointed to one end of the bar. "I'm sure that our waiter friend is perched right there on his nights off from the restaurant."

Olivia ordered a *mojito* for herself and Isabelle, upon being told that there was no French white wine, ordered a coke with lemon.

The drinks came quickly. Olivia loved the combination of mint, lemon, sugar and rum and downed her *mojito* in three sips. Right away she ordered another one. The rum was going right to her head and she could feel herself relaxing to the music.

When the trio began playing Silvio Rodríguez's anthem to Comandante Che, a muscular mulatto in a light blue *guayabera*, white slacks and sandals who had been standing at the bar came up to their table. "*Compañeras!* Why are you sitting alone?"

Isabelle shrugged with obvious indifference.

"You're from Colombia?"

Olivia's eyes widened as she surveyed his dark, confident features. "No, my darling," she responded, surprised at her own forwardness.

"Of course!" he persevered, snapping his fingers. "Lima, Peru! Caracas!"

Isabelle looked down to the floor and shifted uncomfortably on her chair. She found this sort of flirting venal. "Let's go back to the hotel, Olivia," she whispered.

"Why is it so important to know where we're from? *How boring!* We're not objects from a *pinché* travel brochure," Olivia said, using a very Mexican word and putting both hands squarely on her hips. Their guidebook had warned them that Cuban men were fond of trying to pick up foreign women by first guessing their country of origin, but Olivia found this exchange charming. He would never guess that she was from Guatemala.

"Let's go, Olivia." Isabelle said more forcefully. She wanted to go back to the safety of the *Nacional.*

"Let's see how long it takes him to figure out where we are from," she whispered back.

The mulatto went through a dozen countries in Latin America until he finally lifted both arms in the air, thumbs up and forefingers out as if he his hands were pistols. "Mexico. Mariachis. Tequila. I knew it as soon as I saw you. Eduardo Estrada, expert travel guide and auto mechanic at your service!"

Olivia invited Eduardo to sit next to her and ordered him a *mojito.*

"Isn't Cuba wonderful? Rum. Music. Socialism." He had the habit of always mentioning three things at a time.

"Don't get me started," Isabelle fidgeted on her stool.

"What's wrong with your friend?" Eduardo asked.

Olivia turned to Isabelle and kissed her on the cheek: "Why are you in such a bad, bad mood?"

Isabelle raised her thin eyebrows and looked down at her watch. "It's late, Olivia. And frankly, you are drunk and you don't know what you are doing. This guy isn't Horacio."

"Precisely."

"--I know the type."

"He's just being friendly."

"This is going to lead to trouble." Isabelle stood up.

"Don't go, please. Tell me your names," said Eduardo, seeing opportunity slip through his fingers. "Tell me all about Mexico. Benito Juarez. Diego Rivera. Tamales," Eduardo said desperately.

Olivia pulled Isabelle back down.

At this point, the singer quieted the musicians and sat down on a stool he pulled over from the bar and brought the standing microphone level with his chest. He wanted to perform a solo. "I wrote this bolero last week," he said, amid puffs of a cigarette he kept in an ashtray next to him. "I want to dedicate this song to all the dreamers of this world who have pursued beauty, only to have it vanish in front of their eyes." He blew out a few circular puffs and threw his cigarette to the floor, quashing it with the toe of his left shoe.

He began strumming softly on his acoustic guitar and the lights were lowered. Eduardo, without asking, took Olivia's hand and escorted her to the small dance floor on the edge of the veranda. He was a bit taller than she was. Their cheeks touched and he inhaled deeply, enthralled by the sample of *Paloma* perfume that Olivia had dabbed on before leaving the hotel.

The song was slow and very sentimental—another ballad about unrequited love. Olivia looked over at Isabelle who was motioning with her head that she was leaving. She widened her eyes to inquire if Olivia would join her.

When Olivia shook her head no, Isabelle shrugged, smiled and waved goodbye with her bending fingers. She walked down the steps to the walkway through the garden and disappeared in the shadows leading to the street.

Unchained, Olivia was now happy.

The singer played a few more bars, and another six or seven couples joined Olivia and Eduardo on the dance floor. Eduardo felt her breasts heaving against his chest and he edged her toward the middle of the dance floor, into the press of the other dancers. When he was sure no one sitting at the tables or stools or on the dance floor could see, he slid his hands down just below the small of her back and rested them on her buttocks.

Olivia pressed her lips together and looked Eduardo in the face. He had closed his eyes. Who did he imagine he was dancing with? An Afro-Cuban sorceress? A voluptuous Diego Rivera woman? She smiled at his unseeing face and placed her left hand below his back. She moved her hands back and forth along the surface of his muscular buttocks.

Eduardo pulled away.

Olivia looked at him. "Is something wrong?"

"No, I wasn't sure—"

Olivia laughed. "You were sure all right, at least your hands were!"

"Oh yes," he said awkwardly.

Olivia felt emboldened, as if the rum were doing the talking for her. "And don't I also have the right to explore? I don't want to be dragged down a one-way street all by myself!"

Eduardo smiled, pulled Olivia back to him and they continued dancing awkwardly. He seemed hesitant, outmaneuvered. To reassure him, Olivia simply relaxed her body into his, giving him permission to move her around the dance floor. This pleased him and he held her firmly like the steering wheel of a car.

Olivia had never been so happy, as she now was, secure in his muscular arms.

When the bolero ended, he led her by the hand back to the table. Eduardo looked around the club. "And your friend? Is she in the ladies room?"

"She's gone back to the hotel," Olivia said. She took out a fuchsia lipstick and touched up her lips.

"By herself? Havana is a very safe city, but full of *jineteros* at night."

"Don't worry about Isabelle. She's physically tiny, but she's really a very big and experienced girl. She's traveled all over the world. I am the inexperienced one. I don't know if you know what I mean."

Eduardo took another sip of her *mojito*, extracting the last drops from a swamp of mint at the bottom of her glass. Olivia signaled for the bartender to bring two more drinks. She might be on a strict budget, but she knew that Eduardo had no money and to expect him to order another round was futile. She sensed that he was a frequent visitor to the *Herón Azul* and was used to having foreign women buy him drinks.

It was a familiar ritual. He amused them with stories, jokes and lots of praise—and beyond free drinks, maybe he could squeeze out a meal *y quien sabe que más?*

So many of Havana's men played the same game, the guidebook said.

"Olivia, you're unlike any woman I've ever known."

She raised an eyebrow. She was truly gratified to learn that he considered her a woman, not a girl—girls in Cuba matured quickly, were women at fourteen or fifteen—not like in Guatemala where you

were considered a girl until you married. "Each one of us is different…
But what makes you say that about me?"

"Well, let me quote to you an Arsenio Rodríguez *son* I like a lot:

Me gustas porque eres zalamera.
Me gustas porque eres vanidosa.
Me gustas porque eres paluchera
Me gustas porque tienes muchas cosas.

"You think that I'm a flirt?"

"A very subtle kind."

"And coy?"

"Just a bit," he smiled, flashing his bright white teeth.

"Okay, if you say so, Eduardo," Olivia said, surprised at this view of
her. She took another sip of her *mojito*—the blue lights of the veranda
were twinkling. "But what's a *paluchera*? I don't like the sound of the word."

"It's the same as a *farolera*."

"Please—no more Cuban words! What does it mean in Spanish?"

"A showoff," he said smiling, and touching her hand.

Olivia straightened up, raising both eyes. "You think I'm like that?"

"Oh, yes," he giggled.

"No one has ever said I was a showoff. I didn't know you were a
gypsy. Tell me more!"

He was embarrassed. "Well the song goes on like this:

Me gustas por lo suave que caminas.
Me gusta como mueves tu cintura.
Me gustas porque andas con dulzura.
Tú tienes muchas cosas que me gustan.

"Hmmm. First I'm a flirt, then coy and last of all, a showoff. And now
it's all about how I walk and move my hips. Next you're going to tell
me that you would go anywhere with me. That you fell in love the
moment you saw me and that you want to marry me."

"I do love you and would marry you—"

"Oh, Eduardo. If I could make you mine, I would. I suppose it
would be better if I could buy you a house, a new car and help get you
out of Cuba, too!"

"It's not like that, Olivia."

She could see that she had hurt him.

*

They finished their drinks, and Olivia made no effort to order more. Her head was spinning enough, and the musicians were putting their instruments away.

"What would you like to do now?"

"You tell me." Olivia felt a bit nervous. She wasn't about to propose the next move.

"I have a motorbike—" he said, and he leaned over, kissed her in the mouth, wedging her lips open with his tongue.

Olivia thought of Meme and smiled. She would have known exactly what to do. Why she would have driven the motorcycle herself and had Eduardo hopping on the back, grinding into her as they drove off to a secluded spot at the beach!

"What's so funny?"

"Take me anywhere," she laughed, not sure what she meant. Olivia wanted to spend the night in Eduardo's arms, but she had no idea how this could be pulled off in Cuba. She couldn't bring Eduardo to the *Nacional*—first, there was Isabelle, and secondly, Cubans weren't allowed beyond the lobbies of the hotels. Eduardo was embarrassed to confess that he shared a room with his uncle and two brothers in an apartment in Centro Habana. Besides, he was afraid to sneak her into his building and risk being denounced by the local Committee for the Defense of the Revolution and be imprisoned for having relations with tourists.

"So much for your socialism—" Olivia teased, relieved by the news. The idea of making love to Eduardo, with his uncle and brothers listening in through a cloth curtain, hardly seemed romantic.

Eduardo's bike had little gas and would never make it to Boca Ciega or any of the other *Playa del Este* beaches where they might find a bit of privacy. In the end, he settled for taking her to a seafront strip of the *Malecón* toward Miramar.

Olivia enjoyed the ride along the waterfront, her hair flapping in her face, pressing her body into his, the salt air warm and moist. Eduardo drove his bike up on the sidewalk and they sat dangling their legs over the seawall facing the water, with their backs toward the roadway and the darkened leafy houses. It was quiet, except for the sea gently lapping the rocks jutting out of the water. Men fished from these rocks, from the few rowboats that floated along the shore. The full moon, off to the left, was bigger than anything Olivia had ever seen and it hung like a pendant about to sink into the darkened waters to the west.

Olivia and Eduardo were not alone. Dozens of couples were sitting on the walls, drinking rum from unmarked bottles and openly exploring one another's bodies. No one cared if anyone was watching—all the couples were enveloped in a kind of communal privacy—together but alone.

Olivia had been fondled in the dark corners of Antigua, and with Horacio she had explored the limits of proper sexual conduct, always safe in the knowledge that nothing would happen to compromise her reputation. But here she was with a man who truly wanted her. *Her. No one else. At least at that moment.*

She liked the way his tongue had explored her mouth at the *Heron Azul*—it hadn't fallen asleep in her mouth, as Horacio's did, or shoot in like a lance as she imagined an impatient lover's would, but it gently cajoled its way beyond her lips, deep into her mouth.

It made her feel precious and adored, wanting to be possessed by a man for whom lovemaking seemed natural more than deliberate.

If he were using her, she also was using him.

"I love you, Olivia," he said tenderly.

Eduardo had climbed down from the seawall and was pushing his waist against hers and she could feel his bulge. There was something wonderful, almost adolescent, about him. It reminded Olivia of the awkward nights she had spent on the second floor of La Merced with Chucho. But after an hour of kissing and whispering against the seawall, Eduardo took Olivia back to the *Nacional*—all she and Eduardo had to show for an evening of flirting and gentle lovemaking was damp briny clothes and wet underwear.

The following night after Isabelle and Olivia had had dinner and lots of wine on the rooftop restaurant of the Seville Hotel, Eduardo picked her up at the Nacional on his motorbike and took her to Victor Hugo Park near the UNEAC building. Other couples were there, distantly spaced. He unrolled a blanket underneath an unclaimed banyan tree and snuggled next to her.

"I love you, Olivia," Eduardo said, with determination.

They began kissing and touching. Eduardo pressed insistently into her against the darkened trunk under the cover of night. Olivia had never been entered before, but she took him in without pain or discomfort, meeting the steady thrusts of his hips compliantly. She didn't climax, as she had with Horacio that night in the car after Abraham Zadik's party. Yet she felt a sense of fullness after having Eduardo inside of her, accommodating him the way a sponge absorbs water.

"I love you, too, Eduardo," Olivia said.

"*Eres pechona, culona y muy sabrosona,*" Eduardo had replied, with a sadness that almost muffled his voice.

He held her tightly, as if nothing, no one would ever separate them. *Pechona, culona y muy sabrosona*—words in triplicate from another song, she supposed.

"Do you have to go to Pinar del Río tomorrow?" Eduardo asked.

"Yes. It's been planned," Olivia said sadly. "For two days. But I will see you when I get back."

*

The next morning Olivia and Isabelle began their bus tour to villages outside of Havana. They visited the tobacco fields of Pinar del Río in the morning, before circling back to the coast to see the beautiful classical theater in Matanzas and spend the night at a luxury resort hotel on Varadero Beach. The following morning as they strolled barefoot along the beach, a policeman asked them for their identity cards. He demanded to see Olivia's passport—he suspected she was a Cuban trying to pick up Isabelle, a pale-skinned foreigner. The whole time Isabelle kept screaming--"She's my friend! She's from Guatemala. We came here together from Mexico. Can't you see? We are not lovers!"

The policeman looked over their passports and finally let them go.

*

They returned to Havana late that night. Olivia called Eduardo the following morning at his uncle's apartment, but he had already left for work. Olivia and Isabelle spent the day exploring Havana—visiting the small Chinese neighborhood and then going on a tour of a tobacco factory just behind the Capitolio. They stopped by all the state memorials—*Lenin Park, La Plaza de La Revolución*, and the *Granma Memorial*, a huge glass-encased monument, which displayed the boat that had brought Castro and Che Guevara back to Cuba to start the revolution. They walked all around Old Havana, meandering through the narrow streets near the Cathedral and the open-air bookstalls in the Plaza de Armas.

Isabelle sensed Olivia's distraction. "All along I thought you were having an affair with Eduardo and I have been very happy for you. Now I know I'm wrong. You've fallen in love."

"You're crazy, Isabelle. A French woman like you should know better than to confuse sex with love. We have been having fun. Eduardo is a man. And I am a woman, who he finds attractive."

"Precisely, my point."

Olivia felt a need to explain to Isabelle something about her life. "In Guatemala, all I ever met were boys wanting to be men and in Mexico I have only met men who are afraid of being men. Something's always wrong with them—they are either married, engaged, gay or simply liars. When I look at Eduardo, I know what and who he is. Yes, there is a dance and a courtship, but I know what he can give me."

"That's not what I am saying. You more than like him."

"I won't be fooled."

"You already have been!"

Olivia shook her head. "This is only a Cuban romance! Eduardo is a *campesino* from Holguín. He has a wife and two daughters there, living with his own mother. I didn't even have to force that out of him—he simply volunteered it. He sees his wife twice a year and can't afford to bring her to Havana. He says he no longer loves her, and I believe him. And I believe him when he says he truly loves me. But do you think I could live with myself knowing he had abandoned his wife and children because of me? Besides, where and how would we live?"

"You couldn't stay in Cuba," Isabelle went on.

"Of course not!"

"There's nothing you can do. He can't leave Cuba."

"Isabelle, I know all that. Please, don't destroy my dream. Let me enjoy it. I'm going to get back on the airplane to Mexico with you," Olivia answered, with tears in her eyes.

Isabelle looked carefully at her friend and said nothing. *Olivia was in love. Anyone could see it. The pain of it was written all over her face.*

*

That evening Olivia took Eduardo to a chicken, rice and black bean dinner at *El Aljibe* Restaurant in Miramar. There was a quartet of musicians playing Cuban boleros and trovas under a huge, thatched roof and plenty of rum. It was a noisy place, full of tourists, but it was the only place Eduardo could recommend. Though he would not be paying, he felt he was the host.

Eduardo was in a jovial mood and his tongue flapped eagerly. She learned from him how hopeless life was for the ordinary Cuban. He had dreams, plenty of dreams. He didn't want to work construction but be a car mechanic or actually run his own car shop or even sell new automobiles. He wished for more than the obligatory allotment of clothes from the state store and the meager amounts of sugar, meat and rice to which he was entitled. Cuba was not a country for a man with ambitions or dreams, no matter how realistic they were. He would one day have to leave.

Olivia realized that Eduardo could telescopically see his future life in Cuba—simple pleasures and simple needs and no chance for advancement. The state would help take care of him when he got sick and old: the problem was that this wasn't what he wanted.

Eduardo worked in southwest Havana. He was on a building crew converting an old cardboard factory into *El Coco*, an AIDS hospice. The work was hard, dirty and dangerous and Eduardo was paid $15 per month. There was a chance he could become the foreman of his work crew, though that was uncertain, since he hadn't joined the Cuban Youth Group as a boy in Holguín, which was the surest way for him to join the Communist Party. His only way to advance was to give the present foreman part of his salary and, in this way, have him sponsor him for membership.

"And all your praise of Socialism?"

"That's for the tourists! I love this country, but there's no future for me here," he said, with his eyes darkening.

*

Since their arrival, Olivia and Isabelle had been making small talk at the hotel restaurant with a waitress, Carmelita, who served them breakfast every day. Despite the required silly starched white dress, which made her look like a Swiss farmgirl, Carmelita was no plastic doll. She had come to Havana from Cienfuegos, with dreams of becoming a nurse. She could draw blood and connect IVs, but because she hadn't finished her course work for her degree, she ended up waiting tables—and making more money.

Carmelita knew nothing about Olivia and Eduardo, but one morning when Olivia had overslept and was having breakfast alone, she said to her: "Miss Olivia, you look so unhappy. You don't know what to do. You need someone to advise you."

Olivia shook her head. "I know what I would like to do and also what I must do—and that doesn't make me very happy."

"Sometimes we need help. I know someone who can help you."

"A palm reader?"

"You need to consult with a powerful spirit."

"Oh yes," Olivia laughed. "Go visit a very old and black gypsy surrounded by candles and incense and have her read my palm or throw black beans on a piece of glass and read my future in the pattern! I don't think so."

Carmelita touched Olivia's shoulders. "I don't believe in *santería*, either. But you should visit the grave of Amalia, *La Milagrosa*, in the cemetery. She is powerful because she is good. She's the protector of children and has helped me many times."

Olivia shook her head.

"Please, go visit her."

Olivia promised Carmelita she would visit Amalia if she found the time.

*

That afternoon Olivia let Isabelle go alone on a tour of Finca Vigía where Hemingway had lived for the last 20 years of his life. She took a taxi to the Cementerio Colón. Compared to the graveyard outside of Antigua, with its helter-skelter rows of painted elevated tombs and crosses and piles of flowers, this cemetery was truly a city of the dead with broad, well laid out streets in the form of a grid and lots of vegetation. The mausoleums, the size of Ciudad Vieja shacks, were brightly painted and clearly numbered.

There was more order in this cemetery than in all Havana!

A groundskeeper directed Olivia to the flower-festooned statue of *La Milagrosa*. Amalia, as she was known before beatification, had died giving birth in 1901. A child had been buried at her feet, but when her casket had been exhumed several years later, the baby was found folded in her mother's arms as if they had never been parted. From then on, a cult of worship had developed around her.

In the stark blue, clear Havana sky, the statue was remarkably pure. Carved out of the whitest marble, Amalia stood with one arm raised around a cross towering over her while the other arm cradled a life-like baby whose chin rested against her breasts, eyes closed. Amalia stared lovingly out across the cemetery into the Havana streets like a benevolent and protective spirit. Her eyes were kind and just a hint of a smile was on her lips.

Olivia followed the other worshippers to the edge of the statue, whose base was strewn with gladiolas. She couldn't remember any of the *Colegio Parroquial* prayers and this was not the place for Hail Mary's. All she could say was "*I am a little lamb lost from my flock. Miss Amelia please help me find my way home.*"

Olivia stood in front of the statue, trying her best to empty her mind of confusion and focus all her energy on her wish. When she was done praying, she walked away from Amalia as all the other pilgrims had done--without turning her back to the statue.

The whole ritual seemed a bit over-dramatic, yet Olivia felt oddly purged of anxiety. She walked down the wide palm-lined avenues as if floating on air, having banished her normally doubtful and questioning nature. She had been pleased by the purity of her request and by the conviction that Amalia could actually help her. *I have only asked for guidance.* She walked out through the back of the cemetery and paused briefly in the small Chinese cemetery across the street before grabbing a taxi back to the *Nacional*.

*

On their last night together, Eduardo and Olivia found themselves again in Victor Hugo Park. A cold front had moved in across the Florida straits and gale winds were blowing. Though Eduardo had brought several blankets, they were both overwhelmed by the cold air, especially after making love.

"Olivia," Eduardo shivered, "I would go anywhere with you." He wrapped one of the blankets about both of them. "You know that don't you?"

Olivia hugged him tighter. She had never imagined that a man would say that to her. "I wish I could just stay with you in Cuba..."

Eduardo took a deep breath. His expression was so serious that his thin eyebrows formed a straight line across his forehead. "Marry me."

"You know I can't."

"Take me with you to Mexico."

Olivia smiled. "I could marry you and stay here in Havana." If they were truly in love, they could surely live together anywhere.

"You know that wouldn't work. I couldn't support you. In Mexico we would have a chance. You will see that I'm a very hard worker."

She rocked him gently. "Do you love me that much?"

"I do."

Olivia laughed. "Lover boy, don't you think I look at myself in the mirror? I know what I am: a dark, overweight woman with a heart full of love."

"That's not true. You're beautiful, not only to my eyes, but to the world. You shouldn't say those things about yourself. You have such a special beauty—"

Olivia put her cold finger to his mouth. "I could almost believe you. But when I look deep into your eyes, Eduardo, I don't see love reflected in them. I see a man who desperately wants to leave Cuba. I wish I could believe you. I wish I could help you even if you were to leave me two months later."

"That's not true," Eduardo said kissing her fingers, "I wouldn't leave you."

She shushed him a second time.

"If I could let you out of your, cage, within months you would find another woman and I would be the one left all alone."

"How can you say that?"

"Because I can and because I know what I am talking about. You are a sweet, sweet man. Please take me home now."

Eduardo, himself confused and unable to stop shivering, obliged her. As he dropped her in front of the hotel, she embraced him forcefully and kissed him in the mouth where their tongues danced together.

"You'll be back to see me, won't you Olivia?"

"I'll try."

"You won't forget me, will you?"

Olivia smiled, pained. "I will never forget you, my handsome man."

He smiled and kissed her on the cheeks. "We will see each other again. As a Yoruba, I believe that kisses on both cheeks mean you will be back. I know I'll see you again."

Olivia hugged Eduardo.

*

Olivia and Isabelle's flight was to leave Havana the next day at three in the afternoon. Eduardo had promised to take time off from work and come to see her at the airport.

For the first hour of their two-hour wait for the flight, Olivia kept craning her neck over the worn sofas, hoping to catch a glimpse of Eduardo walking into the airport through the glass doors.

All her waiting seemed futile.

"His motorcycle probably broke down, Olivia." Isabelle said, touching her friend's hand. Cuba was not her kind of country and she was grateful to be going back to Mexico. "He'll be here soon."

Olivia shook her head. She had suspected that Eduardo wouldn't come. Taking time off from work would cost him too much, and his absence would arouse suspicion among his fellow workers. She knew he had believed in his own words when he had said them—and that's all that really mattered. Or maybe he, too, had a hole in his heart so deep that seeing her would only make it worse.

Or perhaps he was convinced that she would return at the first opportunity—for him, all because he had fulfilled the Yoruba proverb by kissing her on both cheeks.

Cuba, was a poor country that, after all, produced many beautiful and valuable things. But most of all, it fabricated dreams—the dreams of those thousands who believed there was a better world beyond the shores of the island.

Olivia and Isabelle paid their exit tax at the last possible moment and made their way to immigration. There was no turning back.

She fought back the urge to cry as she went through the tinted glass double doors into the waiting room for their flight. Isabelle was already there, sitting, reading a French novel. Olivia couldn't calm herself—she knew she had experienced something altogether new and powerful with Eduardo, something that she would never be able to duplicate—a first love.

All of a sudden she laughed aloud.

Isabelle put down her book and said: "What's so funny?"

"Everything in threes," Olivia said. *Handsome, passionate and attentive.*

"I don't understand."

"Eduardo. Everything he said was in threes," Olivia said, laughing again, knowing that her friend would not understand.

When Olivia returned to Mexico City, she didn't want to see Horacio. She was in a terribly mood, feeling at times rage and at others humiliation. For days she kept avoiding his calls at work until he insisted on speaking to her. He wanted to pick her up that very afternoon at the travel agency and go to a *VIPS* to talk, but she told him that she wasn't feeling well and managed to put him off till the next day. She agreed to meet him after work at *La Fonda del Refugio* in the *Zona Rosa*.

When Olivia arrived at the restaurant, she saw that Horacio had gotten there first and was sitting at a corner table near the back reading a newspaper. She didn't know why, but she suddenly felt anger boiling up inside of her. She went straight to her seat and sat down, barely acknowledging his presence. When he saw her, he put down his paper and made a gesture to stand up and kiss her on the cheek, but she turned her face away. She hated his sense of measure. *He always knows what will come next.*

A waiter came immediately to the table with a pitcher and filled their glasses with purified water. He asked them for their drink orders.

"Bring us a bottle of the red house wine," Horacio said, knowing it was French and would be expensive enough.

Without skipping a beat, Olivia said "Please bring me a vodka tonic. Make it a double. And could you bring us some *taquitos al pastor* and *sopes* with the drinks and take our dinner order?"

"Are you in such a rush, Olivia?"

"I am," she answered sharply.

Horacio scratched his head and asked her if she wanted the chicken molé.

"Anything you want."

Horacio gave the order to the waiter. His calm, slightly elevated, tone of voice grated in her ears. All the things she had found so endearing about him—his calmness and gallantry—now struck her as pathetic. Why was she seeing this person? His sweetness was cloying, his attentiveness repulsed her. Who was he to decide what she would drink or eat? All this acting like he was "the man in charge."

After the waiter left, Horacio started talking about his trip to Patzcuaro with his mother, the boat trips they took, the visit to a butterfly park near Morelia. She wasn't even listening to what he was saying, she was just disgusted with the drone of his voice. When he mentioned that his mother had told him that she was happy to be with him, Olivia suddenly shouted: "Please be quiet."

He leaned over to grab her hand.

"Don't touch me!"

"Olivia, what is happening to you? I don't understand."

Her face was red, her lips twitching. "You're controlled by your mother—"

"I thought you liked her."

"You're like a lap dog. Why can't you be more of a man?"

There, she had said it!

Horacio looked at her with thick, wounded eyes. "What happened to you in Cuba?"

"I met a man in Havana, a real man—"

"I forgive you."

"For what? You know nothing about it and already you want to forgive me. Eduardo knows how to treat a woman." Olivia's voice was rising to a hysterical pitch. It was as if she were drunk, completely unaware of the fact that she was making a spectacle of herself in public.

"Just please lower your voice. We are in public." She accused him of not being a man, of being completely under the control of his mother. She told him about her affair with Eduardo, blurting out details Horacio considered almost sordid.

"He knows how to make love to a woman. He could teach you a few things!"

"For decency's sake, Olivia, please spare me the details," he said leaning toward her.

Olivia was addled by his words. She pulled away and shouted in a trembling voice—*"tengo la impresión que te faltan cojones"*—that he lacked balls.

Horacio just sat there blinking his eyes and picking at his fingernails.

Of course in the middle of this tirade, Olivia had forgotten that Eduardo had not had the courage to see her off at the José Martí Airport—this after all the whispered sweet words of how much he loved her and the sacrifices that he would be willing to make to be with her.

The musicians that normally played romantic tunes had switched to playing more boisterous *rancheras*, in the hopes of diverting attention from the unhappy couple. Still, some of the restaurant guests turned to stare at Horacio and Olivia. The waiter then appeared with the drinks, put them down and waited for his assistant to bring the *taquitos* and hot sauces to the table.

"I don't want to be with you when you're like this, Olivia," Horacio said standing up. His hand was shaking as he took out his wallet and put down a large handful of pesos on the table.

"You're going to leave me like this?"

Horacio looked at the waiter and shrugged, as if apologizing for this mad woman.

This infuriated Olivia. She took a huge drink from her cocktail and hissed "Go back to your mother!"

He looked at her for a few seconds, his eyes tearing. "Who are you?" he said to her. "Who are you?" he repeated and then he walked out of the restaurant.

Olivia hung her head for a few seconds, took her bag and left. She couldn't understand why she felt so much venom and hatred.

*

Horacio had been so upset by the confrontation that he stayed home from work for a few days, claiming he was sick. Finally he called Abraham Zadik and told him about it.

Abie was shocked by what Horacio had told him—clearly Olivia had lost her mind. He waited another day and then came into the *Viajes Atlas* office just before lunch, hoping he could get Olivia alone and find out what had happened. He also hoped that he might be able to mend things between his two friends.

"Horacio called me and told me everything," Abraham declared, when he was sure that he and Olivia were alone.

"Please, Abie. You know nothing about this," Olivia said, surprised at her growing directness with him. Abraham's concern was surprising: at fifty-five was he tiring of the bachelor life and developing something that could be called a conscience?

"Horacio doesn't have much experience with women, but he isn't a bad sort of person. Besides, I think you could make each other happy."

"Horacio is not what I want. I'm not looking for companionship. I'm too young to live with him and his mother in an old age home."

"I know Horacio cares for you very much."

"But it isn't only about him—is it? Horacio is almost *beside* the point. Maybe you think that someone like me should be grateful to have the affections of *any* man. I know I'm not sexy or beautiful—"

"Olivia, please, no one is talking about—"

"No, Abie. I'm not blind to who and what I am." She thought about Lucia and Melchior—Olivia had had enough courage to leave them both or rather not accept the meager crumbs they were willing to give her. All of a sudden she realized what bothered her most. "Do I hate myself so much that I'll take anything not to be alone?"

"Zimry and I, well—"

"You may love Zimry, but please don't compare me to her."

Abraham put a finger up in the air. "Olivia, if you would let me speak. Yes, I know you had an affair in Havana. Congratulations! I hope you have many more. But all I want to say is that the two of you might be able to work something out. You have to at least give Horacio another chance!"

Olivia walked Abie to the door. She smiled and said thank you, *pero no gracias*—but no thank you. She knew she needed many, many things, but at the moment words were not enough. "I understand what you're trying to do but..." she stopped herself, not knowing exactly what she wanted to say. As a child, she had been sustained by her dreams—the blonde on the *Vanidades* cover, who surely was middle-aged by now, the Mayan princess, the fantasy of being embraced by her father—and all she could do was smile.

At the agency door, Abie kissed her on the forehead.

"You know that like Isabelle and Margarita, I am on your side."

Olivia breathed out deeply and gave Abie a hug. "Yes, I know. But I need time to think—to think of what I need to do."

She patted him on the back and he walked out, a bit confused. Abraham had seen something in her face—some deeper resolve—that made him understand that at least for now, it was useless to try and bring Horacio and Olivia together again.

*

After the fiasco of their dinner at *El Refugio*, Olivia did not see Horacio again for many months. From Abie, she found out that his mother had died and that he had moved into a smaller apartment to be closer to the shoe store. After her death, he had begun filling up his nights and weekends by taking photography classes and making frequent trips back to Pátzcuaro to spend time with his relatives. At home, he took pictures of Pátzcuaro's buildings, focusing on the angles of the rooftops and the texture of their pockmarked yellow walls. Abie said that Horacio had developed an artist's eye. She had wanted to send him a condolence card but feared that somehow it would provoke his rage—almost as if she were congratulating him on his new life after the death of his mother.

Sorry your mother got sick and died. She never showed much interest in me, on the few evenings you invited me over. I know you cared deeply for her. I hope her death has freed you. Maybe one day you will give up fitting shoes and become a full-time photographer. I miss not seeing you, but you never understood that I wasn't just a simple decorative ornament...

Olivia couldn't write—there would be no way for her to keep bitterness from slipping into her words.

(1987)

From the time Olivia had begun working at *Viajes Atlas*, she had dreamed of going to Italy. Margarita Canales had placed new-framed posters of Milan's *Duomo* and Siena's *Il Campo* filled with pageantry and horses when she had redecorated the agency walls in March. Italy seemed like such a Romantic country, with ancient museums, crumbling edifices, a startling landscape and such delicious cuisine. And so many of the women who visited the travel agency booked first class excursions to Rome, Florence and Milan, with maybe a short trip down the Amalfi Coast or visiting either Sicily, Capri or Sardinia, even before visiting Paris.

In April, a bomb was found at the Bologna train station; there was fear that the Red Guard were once again rising up and would terrorize Italy with kidnappings and murders as they had done in 1980. Students at many Italian universities were protesting against the United States for supporting the Contra forces in Nicaragua and for arming the Salvadoran army to continue their carnage against the peasant population.

The U.S. government warned American tourists to avoid Italy and the Mexican government followed suit. Once again the Polanco ladies were going to Paris.

But whatever is bad for tourism is usually good for travel agents and the intrepid traveler. In mid-June, travel agency employees were offered special round trip fares from Mexico City to Milan, with almost free hotels to boot.

Olivia had not taken a trip since her return from Cuba. She had let her work at the agency consume her, and she had refused Isabelle's offers to go with her to Acapulco and Puerto Vallarta for extended beach weekends. She also stopped primping herself up. It was as if she had given up on herself or were preparing to enter a nunnery.

"I don't like your new look one bit," Margarita Canales remarked to her.

Isabelle piped in, in her defense: "The natural look is in."

Margarita quickly added: "That is all well and good if you are endowed at birth with natural beauty, but most of us are not so fortunate. Olivia, you are regressing—have you developed an allergy to lipstick and rouge?"

Olivia felt she could say nothing in her defense. She had lost all drive. If she could have found solace in food, she would have gained weight, too, but eating itself seemed too much of an effort.

*

If there was a good thing to Olivia's withdrawal, it was that she had managed to save up money for the first time in her life. She could afford to go to Italy on her own—stay in inexpensive albergos or pensioni, lunch on bread, cheese and apples, have supper and house wine at select restaurants. She could pay to listen to religious music in the churches, experience the yellow light slanting down on the poplars and over the endless sunflower fields, seemingly not having a care in the world.

She mentioned her interest in Italy to Margarita, who seemed to be growing increasingly bored with the travel agency.

"Maybe I'll go with you!" she said, her green eyes lighting up.

Without checking herself, Olivia lowered her head.

Margarita caught the gesture. "You are an ingrate! For that look, you will be spared a luxurious trip to Italy with an ideal travel companion, my dear Olivia!"

"I don't want to be ungrateful, but maybe I should visit Europe on my own."

Margarita clucked: "In truth, I should visit my daughter in Texas or go to Paris—"

"Maybe you can meet me in Rome," Olivia said softly.

"Nonsense, my girl. You've made your desires very clear to me. I haven't trained you here so that you will do everything I suggest--there's really nothing wrong with experiencing Italy on your own. But let me help you pay for the trip. Hotels are expensive and so are museums—I don't want to hear of you going to Florence and not seeing those marvelous Titians and Raphael's at the Uffizi and the

David at the Accademia because you don't want to buy tickets. This would be foolish. You must promise me something!"

Olivia nodded.

"I will give you five hundred dollars. And I want you to bring me receipts of every church and museum you go to—I want to be sure you have visited the true Italy!"

Isabelle, who overheard the conversation, walked up to Olivia's desk and put her arm around her. "I wish I could go with you."

"This first trip to Europe, I should do alone," Olivia answered bravely. Somehow she would survive the loneliness of the single traveler. She certainly didn't want to be dragging Isabelle around with her—their experience in Havana was all too fresh in her mind. And who knows? Maybe there would be opportunities to meet a new friend, to act irresponsibly, as she had in Havana.

"Of course," Isabelle replied.

"You'll have a marvelous time," Margarita said. "Write all this down."

Olivia opened her notebook and waited for her to speak again.

And speak she did! Despite her disavowals, she got so caught up in her own memories of Italy that she virtually began planning Olivia's every move. Restaurants, museums, concerts, opera, yes, but most of her suggestions focused on fashion, leather and cosmetic shops on Rome's Via Veneto or near the Spanish Steps (*Everyone goes there! And you must make a wish and toss a coin into the Trevi Fountain and have dark chocolate ice cream—I forget the name, something like tartufo con panna at the Piazza Navona with the three Bernini fountains. The Terme di Caracalla and the Piazzi de Spagna! And oh, the Villa Borghese—see the Canovas and how the rich Romans lived. But don't go to the Coliseum and the Roman Forum—they are foul places full of smelly beggars and cat feces. And the Vatican—the Pieta and the Sistine Chapel! You will understand the true glory of the Pope and the Catholic Church! And the little chapel—I can't recall its name—where Michelangelo's Moses can be found—no tourists go there, believe me! Why I don't know!*), Via del Corso, around the fancy Florence shops near Santa Croce and the Pitti Palace, the cobblestone walkways of Siena.

Isabelle had to keep reminding Margarita that Olivia would be going for only ten days, and on a limited budget—that she should be free to discover the marvels of Italy on her own and not have everything pre-planned for her.

"It's not right, Margarita."

"I know, I know. But Italy is special. You must do everything there is to do and give up on sleep."

Olivia took notes, but after thirty minutes of jotting down all the breathless advice, she couldn't hold off a yawn.

"That's enough for today, my dear."

"With what Sra. Canales has told you, all you need is a good travel guide for everything else," Isabelle demurred.

Margarita nodded at her. "You're so practical, my girl. You were born so, I would think." And she put her arm around her. "Practical, and always so right. My darling!"

Isabelle shrugged her shoulders. She was indifferent to Margarita's sarcasm.

*

That afternoon Margarita Canales joined some of her English friends at Anderson's for lunch.

"No matter what else you do," Isabelle said, once Margarita was out the door, "you should visit the Italian Rivera. The Ligurian coast is very special. My parents took me there once when we were staying in Nice. Take the train to Vernazza, one of the five villages in the *Cinqueterre* region south of Genoa. You won't regret it."

"I never even heard of it," Olivia replied. She knew little about Italy—what she remembered from school—Columbus was originally from Genoa, Michelangelo and Leonardo de Vinci lived and worked in Florence and Siena. She remembered the black and white images of handsome stars and starlets in the teen magazines she had read at the Colegio Parroquial and here were the travel brochures and the posters of tourist sites on the agency walls. "What's so special about the coast?"

Isabelle smiled. "Vernazza is like a perfect emerald surrounded by golden rocky cliffs! Just imagine hiking over hills that wind their way from village to village through tiered olive groves and vineyards overlooking the sea. And on one part of the path, you'll see the land jutting out like a stone ship pointing its prow into the blue Mediterranean—that's Vernazza."

"Paradise on earth," answered Olivia, growing animated.

"Paradise, to be sure," Isabelle said, with a tinge of nostalgia. "At least from what I remember."

*

Olivia flew into Milan and stayed in the Palazzo delle Stelline, a small hotel on the Via del Corso that Margarita Canales had booked and paid for her. The Palazzo had been an orphanage up until the seventies when it was restored as a hotel, a block away from the Church of La Carmina and Leonardo's Last Supper. But Milan was not the Italy Olivia had imagined—in June she found a hot city, humid and formal, without the kind of easy intimacy that she had imagined Italian cities should exude. She went to the Duomo with dozens of European visitors and scaled the hundreds of steps up the bell tower. Later she had a raspberry ice cream on the Piazza. She gawked at the expensive shops in the glass enclosed Galeria and ambled by the yellow walls of La Scala, imagining what it might be like to be wearing silk and listening to *Madame Butterfly* on plush velvet seating. She wore a light dress that day and lunched on bread, cheese and tomatoes leaning against the *Castello Sforzesco* walls on the edge of Parco Sempione. By the time she made it back to see the *Last Supper*, the museum had closed—the painting would be undergoing restoration for the whole next year! She took a card saying that the church was *chiuso*—so Margarita would know she hadn't forgotten to go.

Olivia also found Milan terribly expensive—she felt she would be charged just for looking at shoes or blouses through plate glass windows—and so after two days of strolling through the city all alone, she took the train to Venice.

How could anyone visit Italy without going to Venice, Margarita had asked?

The train left Milan at eight in the morning and trundled slowly out of the station and the endless train yards. Olivia initially had her cabin all to herself, but by the time the train had left Milan's city center, three American backpackers had joined her in the berth. They smiled sleepily at her and then huddled against each other like mice and ate sausage and cheese out of brown paper bags. They drank water from huge plastic bottles that they passed back and forth to one another and which had obviously been filled and refilled countless times. Less than an hour out of Milan, as the train barreled through the northern Italian landscape, they fell asleep against each other.

Olivia nestled against the window. She had never seen such beautiful landscape, pristine and orderly, and yet full of life. She really hadn't traveled through much of Guatemala, but she always felt overwhelmed by the high mountains, the densely patterned fields and the press of clouds that seemed to settle into the arms of the valleys. It was so difficult for her to breathe in Guatemala with so much landscape rising up around her. For her, the trek up the Agua Volcano exemplified her feelings about the Guatemalan landscape—it was a compressing terrain that could turn dangerous. Her classmates had talked to her about the beauty and serenity of Lago Atitlán, and how the desert vistas around Zacapa made you aware of how large the sky could be. But these were only second-hand accounts, not places she had experienced.

The Italian landscape opened out and seemed always on the verge of unfolding like a tapestry before her eyes. Everywhere there were little treasures to be seen: a church steeple; a windmill; gorgeous fields of yellow sunflowers bending toward the sunlight; majestic wheat swaying in the breeze; the beautiful, red-tiled farmhouses off in the distance; the oxcarts and the hay wagons by a brown barn; a stone bridge rising to a narrow point to cross a green river. The fields were patterned and zigzagged, but they let you breathe. She could imagine herself walking through meadows full of flowers, inhaling the lavender air blowing through the grass stalks, seeing huge bumblebees and dragonflies darting around. The air would be warm and billowy, almost like a pillow, and Olivia would feel the weightlessness of her legs.

The train rumbled on and she closed her lids. Soon she was sleeping.

When Olivia awoke, the train was halfway over the trestle bridge from Mestre to Venice. The backpackers were busily organizing their things. Olivia, traveling with one cloth suitcase, simply smiled at them.

Out of the train station, Olivia stood on the edge of the Grand Canal and looked about. The sun was shining brightly through mist, and a light film of smoke was in the air. Though the canal waters smelled slightly putrid, Olivia breathed in its majesty.

Olivia now felt she was in Italy! The coffee picker's daughter (she would never forget what she did as an eight-year-old) was in Venice, the most romantic and charming of Europe's cities. She had made it to Italy, and it would never be taken away. She asked a policeman to take a picture of her—the proof that she had been there—as she smiled into the camera and basked in this moment of pure pleasure— gondolas in the water, domed buildings behind her, and the musical Italian language popping through the air. As the policeman signaled for Olivia to put down her suitcase and then he adjusted the lenses, she thought of her mother sticking pieces of wood into the cooking fire and a shadow crossed her face.

The policeman snapped and Olivia blinked—the snapshot would be of an Olivia momentarily saddened by a hostile memory.

Why had she allowed her mother to negate, once again, her happiness?

*

Olivia took a boat to the Piazza San Marco. She strolled through the square, avoiding the pigeons, astonished by the grandeur of the gold-domed buildings around her. She made her way through a narrow street passing two outrageously expensive cafés—six dollars for a café latte!—and looked for a reasonably priced hotel. She went into two or three *albergos*, before she found a *locanda* near the *Accademia* Bridge, one which she could afford thanks to Margarita Canales's contribution: bathroom down the hall, but clean room for 60,000 lire—the cost of a comfortable suite in Mexico City. But this was *Venezia*, she had to remind herself—dreamland of the entire world, the center of 14th century seafaring Europe.

Olivia walked the Venice streets almost as if it were a desert mirage. She visited museums, the glass blowing on Murano Island, the lovely colorful buildings of the isle of Burano where the daintiest silk embroidery could be found. She went into the Jewish ghetto in the Dorsoduro and walked into a synagogue for the first time. It was wooden and tiny, the size of a little church chapel. She thought that the people working inside might be Jewish. She wanted to tell them that she had a Jewish friend, Abraham Zadik—but what would this mean to them?

To Olivia, Abraham was simply a man whose eyes twinkled and who seemed to have no prohibitions. He was a friend who teased her all the time, but actually was quite kind. Zimry was his girlfriend. Horacio made his shoes, or rather: he fit and ordered them, with an elevated sole and heels so that Abraham could stand higher than he really was. She had no idea what made a person a Jew, but according to the brochure, this was the area where they had been rounded up and imprisoned in the 14th century for simply being Jewish.

She spent three nights in Venice, eating overcooked fusilli and spaghetti, tough veal, and vegetables drowning in water in cheap cafeterias. One night she walked into Harry's, a loud bar filled with Americans and English tourists, wearing funny hats and brightly colored shirts. She drank sour-tasting beer and sat on a stool at the far end of the bar. No one spoke to her—was she so unattractive? She tried to relax with the crowd, to appear lighthearted, but she was neither confident nor witty enough in English to join the rapid-fire conversations about her. She finished her beer and went back to her room, feeling somewhat defeated.

*

The next morning Olivia left Venice and went by train to Florence. She was lucky enough to find a cheap room in the Piazza Santo Spirito, not far from the Boboli Gardens. Olivia tried visiting all the required sites with religious piety, as one goes to church, the church of high culture, but she found the Arno and the Ponte Vicchio disappointing, and the massive crowds throughout Florence disorienting. The lines, the endless lines into all the tourist venues were so overwhelming, that Olivia did not even try to go into the Uffizi, the Palazzo Bargello, the Pitti Palace or the Medici Chapel. She thought she would tell Margarita that they were all closed due to bomb scares—what would she know of these things back in Mexico City?

Less crowded was a small church near her hotel, which became her favorite—the Chiesa di Santa Maria del Carmine. In the Brancacci chapel, Masaccio frescoes depicted Adam and Eve being driven out of the Garden of Eden and becoming aware of their own nakedness as a result of Eve's original sin of eating the apple that a serpent offered her. Their faces captured the terror of their predicament. Whatever the Church said they had done—eating from the Tree of Knowledge, for example—to Olivia, Eve had only eaten an apple and shared it with her husband.

What was so wrong with that?

*

There were times during the trip that Olivia felt so alone. How much better it would have been to travel with Margarita and have her picking up the tab at truly great restaurants or having someone to talk to at dinner or in her hotel room. Olivia found solace in little parks where she wrote postcards to Isabelle, Margarita, Abraham, and even Eduardo working construction in hot Havana. She wondered if any of them thought of her—if they so much as missed her. She sent Sister Carina a card that had a picture of the Duomo in Florence and told her how she had prayed in the pews, thinking of all the wonderful nuns at the school. And though she debated it for days, she sent a postcard to Horacio, apologizing for the first time for her public outburst at *the Fondo del Refugio* and sending her condolences for his mother's death so many months earlier.

Olivia believed that she should be happy in Italy, but she couldn't cast off the blanket of depression—this funk of not only being all alone, but also being untethered, at loose ends. She smiled at the other breakfast guests in her albergo, tried out her Italian with the waiters and porters, but when the required words had come to an end, she couldn't speak any further. *She felt that she had nothing else to say.*

And as much as Olivia tried to be upbeat, she was pulled down by the thought that this trip was a mistake—*she was not ready to travel alone. Like Eve, she had been expelled from Paradise and she hadn't prepared for the obstacles that awaited her.*

It didn't matter to Olivia that her comparison with Eve was faulty—she had done nothing to transgress, nothing to deserve this feeling of emptiness. After all, Eve had Adam, and they would somehow manage together because neither of them was alone. But she was alone in this world.

Coming to Europe by herself had been a huge mistake. What on earth had she been thinking?

*

Her trip was barely half over, and all she wanted was to go to Milan and board the plane at Malpensa back to Mexico City. She was tired of Italy, at least the Italy she was seeing. She decided to skip side-trips to Siena, Perugia and Assisi—Margarita would not forgive her—and what about Rome? What excuses would she give? A torrid heat wave? A strike by railroad workers? More bomb threats?

She wanted to be back in her rented room at the pensión in the Colonia Roma, visit the chimpanzees at the Chapultepec Park Zoo, spend a boring lunch with Isabelle, if she wanted to, or sit leafing through a travel magazine at *Viajes Atlas*. She wanted to call Horacio and apologize to him for her irrational outburst.

Something tugged on her, telling her that she should go back to Mexico City—now that Sister Carina had her address, perhaps she had written to her with some sort of bad, urgent news—that her mother or Meme had passed away. She was so indecisive, but she knew that if she returned prematurely to Mexico, she would die, actually die, of embarrassment.

So from Florence she went to Pisa. She couldn't miss the Leaning Tower. But what a stupid town, Olivia thought, and so many stupid people. Tens of thousands of them gawking at a crooked bell tower that, frankly, was not as nice as the one in Milan or Florence and stuck out of the grass like a broken thumb.

As she was about to buy her ticket to Rome and Naples, she remembered Isabelle's suggestion to visit Vernazza. Could it be so near? At the Pisa train station, she checked her guidebook and the train board—she was thrilled to discover that she was no more than a half hour train ride away from La Spezia, the southern terminus of the coastal train to Genoa that went through *Cinqueterre* and Vernazza.

But the detour to Vernazza meant she wouldn't have time to make it to Rome. Did she really need to go there? Why did she need to go sit on something called the Spanish Steps?

She boarded the train to La Spezia, deciding that she was tired of tourists and would deal with Margarita's disapproval when she returned to Mexico.

*

When Olivia got to La Spezia, she waited two hours for the next local train up the coast toward Genoa. She walked outside—it was market day in the park immediately facing the train station, and farmers were selling artichokes, eggplants, squash flowers from their stands. Olivia bought two fat tomatoes, a chunk of asiago and a hard roll; she found a shaded bench in the park and ate looking out to the many boats anchored in the harbor. She could smell the brackish seawater, mixed in with the odor of burnt oil from the nearby factories that lined one end of the half-moon bay.

La Spezia was not Havana, but at least here Olivia felt at ease, something she had not felt in Milan, Venice or Florence.

Maybe it was the proximity to the water.

After eating, Olivia dashed off a second set of postcards and sent them from the nearby post office. She was lightheaded, almost giddy from the warm sea air.

The train left for Vernazza at three. The berths were crowded with Italian tourists dressed in short shorts and ridiculous straw hats, carrying cameras, plastic beach bags and towels on their shoulders. Olivia decided to stand at the rear end of one of the cars, her travel bag under her legs. The train burrowed through tunnels, skirted stone mountainsides, crossed trestles that spanned small inlets. Within fifteen minutes it stopped at Ríomaggiore, the first of the Cinqueterre villages, and about half the passengers filed out. Ten minutes later it pulled into the center of Manarola and then into the Corniglia station, which was in an inlet below the cliffside town. Eight minutes later, she was in Vernazza.

She followed the crowd out of the station and went down the only main street in town, toward the harbor. The street was no more than six arm lengths wide and no cars, except for small delivery trucks, were allowed in the village. The buildings were brightly colored—peeling green, yellow, umber, salmon and orange—like the buildings she had seen on the island of Burano near Venice. She walked by bread stores, vegetable stands, and several clothing stores that were just opening for the afternoon. A couple and a small family sat under umbrellas of one restaurant, the *Grotta Blu*. A waiter wearing brown skimpy shorts and a red cotton tee shirt leaned against one of the tables, with his arms crossed in front of his chest—he was swarthy, with a black mustache, and two days growth on his face. He seemed to be posing, awfully proud of himself. Olivia couldn't keep herself from looking at him he seemed so ludicrous. And then she smiled. He caught her smile and winked leeringly.

His boldness intimidated her and she turned away. She thought she heard him snicker as she passed him with her bag, and she kept going down the stone path toward the harbor not looking back. Eduardo had been proud, but ultimately shy—how could she explain it?—but this man seemed to be mocking her with his arrogance.

Olivia knew that there were no hotels in Vernazza. Her guidebook said there would be signs advertising rooms to let on the dozen twisted footpaths that led off from the main road and angled up to the sheer cliff face on both sides of the village. Vernazza was just as Isabelle had described it: a stone ship with a massive prow jutting into the water. A green emerald perched inside a setting of golden rocks.

Olivia followed the main street until it ended at a crescent-shaped plaza at the foot of the harbor. There was a small gray beach here where several dozen people lay on towels or played ball or splashed with their children in the knee-high water. Beyond the inlet was a protective stone jetty that curved like a scimitar, where boats tied up and sunbathers lay on the massive outcroppings of blue-gray stones. Further out, there were half a dozen larger wooden boats anchored in the bay, still as a blue sheet with the slightest curling at the surface whenever a breeze blew landward. All around the plaza were restaurants, some with linen others without, and brightly colored umbrellas and folded metal chairs. It was beautiful, picture postcard beautiful.

Olivia had worked up a sweat. She wanted to change from her brown cotton dress to something lighter, skimpier, but first she needed to find a place to stay. She went into Gianni Franzi, a restaurant on the left side of the plaza which had a hand-painted sign offering rooms. A big-boned lady stood at the coffee counter washing dishes. In her broken Italian, Olivia asked for a room. The woman wiped her forehead with the back of her hand, asked for Olivia's passport and gave her a card to fill out. When she asked her how long she was staying, Olivia answered a couple of nights. She decided that she would stay here for the remaining nights in Italy without even asking to see a room. She would figure out a way to go directly to Malpensa to take her airplane home. This village would be the end of her trip to Italy.

The woman gave her a wooden triangle with two keys—Olivia was told to take the path up the side of the restaurant until she couldn't go up any further.

Her room was at the top of a very narrow staircase. It was a cramped little space with bed, chair, sink and a window that looked down into an alleyway filled with laundry lines. From her tiny bathroom—such luxury—she had a sidelong view of the huge slabs of rock beyond the little harbor, which opened to a bay in the Mediterranean. From this window, she could see how the coast ran northward, with promontories and knolls jutting out along the way. Gray green olive fields terraced down the helmet-shaped hills, all the way to the blue water's edge.

Olivia changed quickly into a one-piece lavender bathing suit. She looked into the mirror clasped on the back of her room door—her body bulged here and there through the swimsuit, which stretched to fit the fullness of her hips. In Mexico, it seemed as if her skin had lightened, but now she was dark again, like a carob seed. She could modify her appearance, but she couldn't undo what she was, despite Margarita Canales's insistence that looks could be modified. Olivia pulled her black hair back, tying it with a ribbon. She grabbed the shredded towel in the bathroom and went out.

She walked along the stone pier until she found a large flat rock at the point where the seawater flowed into the bay. Olivia sat down on her towel and felt the sun penetrating into her skin. If only her mother could see her now, sunbathing on the Italian Riviera—she would realize how far from her roots her daughter had traveled. The world was a big, complicated place and Olivia could safely say that she was a part of it because people would miss her if she were to disappear, something she had never felt in Guatemala. Since coming to Mexico she had remade her life—actually, *made her life*—no thanks to her mother or her father who if anything had placed obstacle after obstacle in her path. She didn't want to minimize the help that Margarita,

Abraham or even Isabelle had given her, but practically speaking, her transformation had been mostly her doing.

Olivia lay down and closed her eyes. She saw in her mind's eye her poor mother working in the coffee fields with the basket of coffee beans around her waist or tending to saplings in the nursery. Olivia closed her hands and almost felt the beans and the smooth leaves of the coffee plants—she took a deep breath and beyond the salty tang of seawater, she could smell the damp, rich earth of Antigua.

Ay mamá!

Did Lucia still dream of one day being put in charge of the *beneficio*, of drying the coffee beans on the slab of cement? And where was Guayito? Whenever Olivia saw a headline in Mexico that mentioned Guatemala, she turned the page quickly—she knew there was carnage in her homeland. What would be the point of reading about the grisly details of murders and amputations, massacres and shootings, mass burials—if her brother were to die, no one would ever know. He would end up another dead Indian in an unmarked grave. What could reading articles change what was going on there?

Olivia took deep breaths, letting the squeals of children playing on the sand lull her to sleep.

*

That evening, after showering, Olivia put on a rayon yellow dress, which revealed the top of her bodice, and walked back into town toward the *Grotta Blu*. She wasn't sure she would eat there, but she wanted to prove to the skimpily clad waiter that she was not afraid of him, that his taunting snicker, perhaps commenting on her large behind, could be answered. Olivia walked up and down the road twice before she realized that she kept missing the restaurant because it had been closed for the night. She felt disappointed, almost cheated, and even dawdled at one of the metal tables that had been left out in situ, should the waiter decide to open up the restaurant. Finally, after a few minutes, Olivia went back to the harbor and took a table at *Al Gambero Rossi* on the far side of the square. Olivia sat alone at her blue-clothed table. Her meal was expensive and horrid—frutti di mare, a stew of rubbery calamari, octopus and shrimp, bathed in a sweet tomato sauce over a bed of slippery spaghetti. But she enjoyed the half-liter of wine, which allowed her to congratulate herself for having had the boldness to attempt to confront the preening waiter earlier that evening even if the encounter hadn't happened.

The next day, Olivia put on a short-sleeved jersey, shorts, and thongs to hike to the neighboring village of Monterroso. The ascent north out of the village was extremely steep, and by the time she reached the edge of the village, she was bathed in sweat and huffing up a storm. It was a one-kilometer hike through olive groves and pine forests—even eight-year-olds had made the trek—but she was unable to get beyond the ramparts of the city that hung four hundred feet above the harbor. She had worn the wrong shoes and kept slipping on the damp stones on the path. Her calves already hurt. She paused to rest, but her skin was on fire and flies kept landing on her face. What was the point in torturing herself?

She went back down to Vernazza, changed in her room and set up camp on her familiar rock beyond the harbor. She spent the rest of the morning tanning and dipping in the cool blue water whenever she felt hot.

For lunch, Olivia went back into town—if the *Blu Grotta* were to be closed again, she would buy some sausage and bread at the little grocery next door. But the restaurant was open. Olivia sat down at an outside table waiting for a waiter to take her order, but no one came. A wild saxophone solo reached out to her from inside. She went to the coffee bar and waited, though her heart was racing. Finally, she grabbed a glass and started tapping it with a spoon she found on the counter. Getting no response, she tapped louder and louder and louder.

"Basta, basta," came the voice from behind a curtain. The waiter appeared, doused in sweat and hefting a crate of cucumbers in his arms. When he saw Olivia, he mumbled something to himself—obviously funny because he laughed—and he put the crate down behind the bar. He grabbed a towel from the counter and let his eyes drift up and down Olivia's body as if appraising her.

His gaze made her feet tingle. "And what's so funny?" she asked him in Spanish.

"Ah, a pretty little *española*—just like my wife. Question after question after question, followed by a barrage of curses and accusations!" He went over and kissed Olivia on the cheek. "What took you so long to come back to see me, *cara bella*?" He grabbed a glass from under the counter, filled it with water and poured it on his neck.

She was about to tell him, foolishly, that she *had* come back, but his restaurant had been boarded up.

"I'm sorry, but you must be confusing me with someone else."

He lowered the music, a Dexter Gordon solo. "No, no no. I don't think so. Weren't you here two years ago with two beautiful girls from Andalusia?" he asked, stretching the "th" with his tongue to his teeth when he pronounced the "c." "You were backpacking through Italy. I made you all a special insalata caprese. Your friends ignored me, but you liked my cooking and my music. You flirted with me!"

"Not me. I'm sorry," she whispered. He was so sure of himself and seemed unconcerned that he reeked of sweat. Something about his insolence reminded her of what Abraham Zadik must have been like as a young man in Caracas.

"So it was you," he said happily, grabbing her wrist.

She wrenched her hand away. "I have never been to Italy!" You must be confusing me with one of your other mistresses," Olivia said, turning to leave.

"Please, please, I meant no insult. Many, many people pass through Vernazza. Please, sit down. Let Máximo wait upon you," he said, gesturing to one of the tables inside the restaurant.

"Máximo? Is that your real name?"

"Of course it is," he said sharply, somewhat aggrieved. Then he smiled: "I could tell you that my mother named me for a famous Roman gladiator, but the truth is she named me Máximo at birth, for the most obvious of reasons!"

Olivia arched her brows. Men: why do I always meet men who are enchanted with themselves? Not all of them, certainly not Horacio. But even Eduardo was not beyond parading himself as if he were the most precious gift a woman would want!

"Oh, now, now. It's not what you think," his eyes were shining, and he let his tongue poke out of his mouth as part of his smile.

"How do you know what I think?"

"Touché," he said, grabbing the towel and wiping his face. He opened a small refrigerator under the bar and took a cold bottle of *acgua frissante* and poured it over his neck, letting it roll into the sink. "Please sit down." He pointed to a chair.

As she sat down, he flicked the fan on and sat next to her.

"I was nameless for a month until my mother decided on Máximo—because she felt that everything I did that first month was in extremes—crying, screaming, shaking. And it's true. I am passionate about everything—wine, literature, music, politics, sailing, horseback riding—and other things, too."

"Other things?" Olivia repeated. She found Máximo's boldness intriguing and more than a bit challenging.

"Well you know," he said confidently, "women, too. Even my wife says I'm a snake. Not a little friendly green snake, but one of those cobras that wiggles and dances out of a basket in India." He illustrated this by raising and twisting an arm in the air. "And I guess there's no point disputing that she knows what she's talking about. She has a sixth sense for these things."

"Does she?" Olivia blurted out. His constant mentioning of his wife infuriated her. Why be so open about it? Why mention her at every turn when it was unnecessary? Was it to push her away or simply to let her know what the stakes were? This man! He seemed to say aloud whatever thought came to his mind.

If she could say aloud what she was thinking it would have been: *If you play with this fire you might get burned. On the other hand, if you do nothing, everything remains as before. You get to take nothing with you, but memories and ashes.*

*

So Olivia stayed for lunch. He told her that she was the last customer before shutting down for the afternoon though it was barely 1 and he closed the outside door, pulled across a white curtain and put the air conditioner on.

Máximo went behind the counter and made her a huge spinach salad with grilled asparagus and eggplant, cucumber slices and moist flakes of tuna. He opened a bottle of Prosecco, even when she said she didn't want any, and poured out two frosted glasses.

After having kissed her cheek when he had first seen her, he kept his distance, though he made sure to brush up against her when he refilled her glass or brought her more bread. To avoid a long-convoluted explanation of her past, she told him she was Mexican.

He was surprised because the only Mexican women he had ever met had bleached blond hair and had disembarked from gigantic yachts that had been anchored far out in the Vernazza harbor.

"Real or frosted, I couldn't tell," he said, shrugging his broad shoulders.

"And why was that?"

He giggled like a boy. "Well, they came with their husbands. You know, those swarthy men with gold chains and big rings and wavy hair. Big money. They acted as if they owned not only the women, but also this little village!"

"And you are not like that, I suppose?"

"My dear Olivia, you with the precious olive skin. So beautiful and alluring. Let me tell you about myself: I am the son of a poor Genovese fisherman who one day washed up on the shores of Monterroso and married my mother. About twelve years ago I came here to Vernazza and opened up my little grotto. I'm a man who has had no schooling, but I have learned about the world by reading books, looking at pictures, listening to music. Since I have had no formal education I, therefore, have no ambition. Everything I want is here. I'm a lazy fisherman: I throw out my net and catch whatever washes ashore to me. And all of it happens to taste good—like olives in winter and fresh peaches and pears in the fall."

"You're a poet," Olivia said, charmed by his way of speaking.

He leaned back and twirled his mustache. "I take pleasure in life since as far as I can tell, that's all I have. We have a little saying here in Italy—*La dolce far niente*. It means *the sweetness of doing nothing*. I have made a virtue out of laziness. To let the pleasures of life wash over me, like the waves—not to argue, not to struggle, not to possess. I give that all over to Mr. Ferrari or Mr. Ferramino who want to build empires and spend their old age in castles counting money. We all end up in the same place—in a little wooden box, underground, a delectable meal for worms who, by the way, don't care much what they eat and certainly have no use for fancy clothes or jewelry..."

Three glasses of Prosecco, and Olivia's head was swimming. She liked Máximo, she really did. But it was three in the afternoon and the combination of sun, food and alcohol made her fell full and hot, like a sun roasted tomato about to burst.

"Máximo, what do I owe you?"

"Must you go?" he asked casually.

"Yes—for now."

His eyes brightened. "I told you that this meal was on me."

"Please, Máximo, I wish to pay."

He threw up his hands. "In that case, give me two thousand *lira*— for the salad."

Olivia pointed to the empty bottle.

"This is my treat. It's been a pleasure to wait upon you and feel the caress of your lovely eyes and the pout of your lips."

Olivia smiled. She paid him and stood up. He grabbed her wrist.

"I'm a lonely man." His eyes were hungry. "Will you come back to see me?"

"What about your wife?"

"Marcela?" he asked aloud, to no one in particular. He tightened his lids, wincing. "She stays at the restaurant till ten at night and then goes home to her sick mother. I close up alone. Will you come back to see me, Olivia? It would be my pleasure to serve you again." He moved toward her and kissed her lips. It was a short kiss, as if he were simply tasting her. "I would like that very much."

Olivia rolled her tongue. "We'll see, Mr. Máximo," she said coyly. But she knew—as he knew—that she would be back. She had felt his kiss deep down inside of her, and it made her throat feel dry and parched again.

*

Olivia took a long nap, showered for the second time and sat wondering if she should go back to the *Blu Grotta*. Her mind said no, her body yes and she could feel the tug of war, with her heart pulsing. She went outside to the small patio above her room and looked out over the water, watching the sun go down behind a film of clouds. The soft evening breezes cooled her down.

When it was dark, she went back to her room and spent an hour making up her face. She was happy.

She showed up at the *Blu Grotta* at ten-thirty, when there were just a handful of customers sitting outside under the restaurant's blue umbrellas. When Máximo saw her, he signaled for her to come in and sit at the table they had sat earlier in the afternoon.

Máximo looked clean: he had gone home, showered and shaved. A green silk shirt had replaced his see-through net jersey and he was wearing a brown pair of pressed slacks and those ever-constant sandals.

It was a hot night. She breathed in his spray of cologne—was it Vetiver?—as he moved efficiently around her. Within half an hour he had emptied the tables by telling his customers that he needed to close up early and, besides, they would find cooler restaurants by the harbor.

*

After closing the restaurant, Máximo took Olivia downstairs where he had jerry-rigged a bed by throwing two tablecloths over a foam cushion, which rested on crates of fresh vegetables. A ceiling fan sputtered overhead, drawing the heat out of the restaurant through an open window that faced an alleyway.

"You plan ahead," Olivia said.

"I try to be ready though I know everything is determined by chance."

"I see. And what about my dinner?"

"Are you hungry?" he asked apologetically.

"Not really." She had never met anyone like him. Despite his bluster, Máximo was attentive to details—this she had noticed as he had cut the vegetables, prepared the salad for her—and not one to rush things.

He undressed her gently, putting her dress on a hanger and her shoes on a chair. He took off his clothes with equal care. And when they were both naked, he laid her down on his improvised bed and began exploring her body with his hands. It was as if he were caressing an undiscovered cave painting, with great care, admiration and wonder. He glided over the ridges and crevices of her body with a delicacy of stroke, as if exploring something altogether new, but with the confidence of someone who had been here before.

He entered Olivia only when she was ready to receive him, so as not to hurt her. And though she could feel the corners of the crates pinching her legs, back and buttocks through the mattress, she was lost in the steady thrusts of his hips, the soft graze of his hands.

She liked the way he had penetrated her and how he now made her feel as if pleasure, her pleasure, was what he most sought. He led her on, coaxing little cries out of her with increasing intensity, building into her and then he paused. He remained hard, barely moving, until she asked him if something was wrong. Once again, he would start thrusting into her, rocking from side to side, and when he sensed she could not hold herself off any longer, he moved into her again and again as deep as he could until she tightened her arms around him and shuddered. And when Olivia felt the expanding of waves in her own body, it was then that he pushed further into her until he gave off a strange goat-like cry that startled the quiet of the night.

For a while they stayed intertwined, in a sea of sweat. Then slowly, he moved off of Olivia. He curled beside her as she lay flat and placed his right arm across her belly. He gently turned her to her side and pressed into her body from behind. She could feel his penis stirring, against her buttocks. She heard him whispering words in Italian into her ear and then Máximo fell asleep.

*

They made love two more times that night, and each time they finished, Máximo would doze while Olivia stayed wide awake, in tranquil bliss. Before the sun came up, while Máximo lay under one of the tablecloths over a box of lettuce, Olivia got up and gathered her things. She walked gingerly up the stairs from the basement and went to the bathroom behind the counter to wash her face and put on fresh makeup. There she slipped her dress over her head. As she was about to open the locked glass door to let herself out, she turned and went back into the restaurant. She took a cream-colored *Blu Grotta* card from the pile on the ledge by the cash register, with the address and phone number of the restaurant and with the words *Máximo Colibri, Proprietario* in script at the bottom.

Outside, the village was still dark. She could hear the stirring of birds in their nests, the ruffle of feathers, the early morning chirping. Olivia couldn't help herself. She was crying softly, the way ice sometimes gurgles when it melts in warm air.

It was all so appropriate. Bold first name, but nothing ironic about his last name—he wasn't a buzzard or scavenger just the lightest of birds, a *colibri*. A hummingbird—drawing sweetness where it could, in mid-flight, never lingering inside a flower for more than the briefest of moments, colorful and shapely in its stark nakedness, a mad fluttering of wings that hardly created a stir, and a glorious, curved beak.

Always thirsty!

Olivia walked swiftly down the main street towards the footpath that would lead her up to her room. She had done well to leave when she had. She knew that Máximo would be waking up soon and wonder why she had gone off without saying goodbye. Perhaps he would be relieved, not having to say obligatory words that would somehow make what had occurred between them something more and something less than it really had been—two lonely souls exploring each other in the depths of night.

Maybe he was already anticipating how to explain his absence to Marcela who, Olivia was sure, was accustomed to his infidelities. He would go home and have breakfast with her and her ailing mother and tell them that a drinking party had stayed late and he had fallen asleep in the basement. Marcela would not create a scene as she had the first times Máximo had come back to her, smelling of other women's perfumes.

If she still thought of him as a snake, she had developed enough foresight not to disturb him.

Perhaps he would go through the day expecting to have Olivia coming back to him after she had rested—surely she would come down to see him, wanting to share another meal, some teasing and laughter, and then another night of intimacy. The game rules had been clearly defined and both had enjoyed the game.

Or perhaps Olivia, the dark girl, would leave, and he would never see her again. He was used to it—taking as much as he could, savoring the moments and knowing that since there were no obligations, it would be easy to let go.

Or maybe, Olivia thought, the scenario between Máximo and Marcela would be more complex:

I worked late, sweetheart. The customers didn't want to leave. Francesco stopped by. We started drinking grappa. I drank too much. I decided to sleep on the mattress in the cellar. You know the one. Why is this upsetting you, Marcela? You not only have your mother—you have me.

Olivia dabbed her eyes as she climbed the footpath to her room. Instead of going directly into it, she took a detour to the small sitting area that had been carved out of the stone cliff overlooking the Mediterranean where she had sat the night before.

In daylight the view seemed so different, less mournful. The sunlight danced orange on the tips of the waves that moved steadily toward the shore. Two or three boats were already out fishing. Gazing straight to the west, Olivia saw the distant island of Sardinia in the morning light, like a blue humpback whale. There was movement, but everything seemed still, full of promise.

She felt elated, enormously satisfied, for the first time in years. She let the view steady her breathing.

Could she stay here with him? How long would it last? Unlike Eduardo, Máximo had never said that he loved her, not even in his garbled words in Italian. He knew better than to spoil the moment with words that the next instant would be insincere.

He had shared with her his philosophy: he believed completely in *la dolce far niente. The sweetness of doing nothing.* She would never get more from him, this *colibri.*

Olivia knew that she had to leave immediately. She went back to her room. It wouldn't take long to pack her bags—so what if she wouldn't get back the deposit for her room? She had plenty of money, Margarita Canales had made sure of that. Her flight out of Malpensa connected in Paris for the plane to Mexico City.

Olivia fluffed out her hair and combed out the knots. She could smell Máximo's cologne mixed with her perfume. It wasn't only in her hair, and on her skin, but deep inside her body.

Olivia started down the stairs, with her bag across her chest. She would take the eight AM local going north along the Ligurian coast, switch in Genoa for the train to Milan. She would spend the last two nights there, at the Palazzo delle Stelline, maybe pay a guard to let her sneak a peek at the Last Supper. She would go to no museums or shops, simply walk the quiet back streets where tourists wouldn't go.

*

The side trip to Vernazza had done her a world of good. She felt sated.

Máximo was a hummingbird.

Good for him.

(1987)

Long before Olivia had begun attending the *Colegio Parroquial*, she had had a fantasy in which she visualized her ideal childhood. She never considered how it would happen given her humble roots, but she imagined living with her mother in Antigua, in a modest colonial house with cast-iron bars on the windows on one of the many cobble-stoned streets, a brick fireplace in a cozy sitting room, an open courtyard hung with orchids, wandering Jews, spider plants in clay pots and half a dozen kinds of bougainvillea. She would spend mornings dressing and undressing her dolls in her own private bedroom and afternoons she would shoot marbles or play *capiruchos* with Guayito in the courtyard—if it was very hot, Lucia would spray cold water on their naked bodies. And later, after the sun had set, she, her mother and her little brother would have dinner at home, served of course by a maid named La Nena who had been with the family for twenty-five years and who was really part of the family.

Her childhood would unravel the way it should: school, friends and lots of pleasure and adventures. There would be laughter and lots of tears—wasn't that what life was about?—but the outcome would be, in balance, good.

Olivia imagined her betrothal taking place at the age of twenty. It would occur after many months of courtship, with a nice-looking boy, who was polite, attentive and with decent financial prospects— she even came up with a name: David Figueroa. He was a bit plump like her and dark skinned, with thick charcoal hair and black eyes that were kind and without any mischief—a man she could trust. He would come and visit every evening after dinner, sit on the large living room sofa and talk of his future working side by side in his father's appliance store. His first contribution to the family business would be to modernize the existing stock and sales tracking system to eliminate the need for renting a warehouse to store the extra merchandise. David's moon-like face would reflect the love Olivia felt for him, and it was already determined that one day he would ask her mother for her hand in matrimony.

David would leave Lucia's home promptly at nine o'clock, and Olivia would walk him to the door and allow him to kiss her on the cheek. When she went to bed later that night, the bed sheets and blankets enfolding her, she would feel full of love and have more sweet dreams. She would be sitting on a cliff watching the most exquisite of sunsets, the dropping away of the sun, the explosion of orange and yellow streaks in the sky, the arrival of the first evening stars almost like beacons to dispel any swirls of dark confusion.

Nothing like this had happened or would happen. Whatever life she had, whatever life she would have, had nothing to do with this kind of fanciful dream. She knew it was a farce, really, but it was hers to hold.

*

Olivia remembered this reverie as she looked out her window on the flight back to Mexico City from Paris. The feeling of satisfaction she had felt with Máximo had all but dissipated—she felt unsettled now, unsure what the next step would be.

If only she could stop thinking about the future!

She wished she could rise above her emotions in the same way that the jet she was flying on flew above the clouds, above the mass of confused thoughts that kept pulling her back down. The one night with Máximo had been so intense that now that she was away from him, all she felt was the gaping wound of his absence. Their lovemaking had been magical precisely because it had been so natural; Olivia feared she would never find again that kind of happiness, certainly not with a man.

She began reviewing all the men she had ever cared for.

Jesús. The less said, the better. A short teenage romance that she barely remembered. Lots of panting and grinding, mostly hers, against the walls of La Merced Church. *Horacio* had offered real possibilities. Handsome with soulful eyes, attentive, with his own business. But after that first initial excitement, more Mama's boy than man. Still she had to admit there was something about him that attracted her, but she had treated him miserably. Ah, *Eduardo*. He had been chocolatey and wonderful, but the situation totally impossible—too much distance, more than an ocean, between his life and hers. And she could never trust his motives. And the latest: *Máximo*. Like Eduardo, irrefutably and unquestionably, a man. Despite the pain she felt in her chest just thinking about him, wasn't he also a tethered child? It was all so convenient: the absent Spanish wife, mysterious Marcela. Yes, the lovemaking had been wonderful, but it had all happened in one, brief night and it was absurd to imagine her staying in Vernazza. To expect more, to think that more had happened, was to deny a reality that was hitting Olivia like a ton of bricks. How could she even imagine there was something enduring between them?

She realized that there had been a deep failing in every single one of them—they all had been big boys, but boys, nonetheless.

The flight attendant came by offering drinks. Olivia ordered two whiskeys, which she poured in one glass without ice and gulped down like water. If only Melchior had been a real father—perhaps he would have been able to offer her some advice on how to deal with men— but he not only had disowned her, but also belonged to the fraternity of errant, irresponsible children.

Olivia didn't know what she had expected from the whiskey— kernels of wisdom?—but all she got was a headache that drummed against her temples. The best she could do was stretch out across the empty seat next to hers and burrow her head in a sea of pillows to block out the light.

*

It was nine o'clock when Olivia's airplane touched down in Mexico City. There was a lot of confusion at the airport—too many flights arriving simultaneously, not enough gates, baggage handlers or carrousels—so by the time her taxi reached her apartment in Colonia Roma it was well past midnight. Her key had barely turned in the lock, when Mélida herself opened the door and assailed her.

"Where have you been? I was so worried. Weren't you supposed to arrive this afternoon? I even called *Viajes Atlas* this afternoon and spoke to the French girl there!"

"Is something wrong?" was all Olivia could say. Her head was still pounding. She went into the apartment and closed the door behind her.

"This letter came the day you left," Mélida went on, pulling an envelope out of her apron pocket and handing it to Olivia. The landlady's dark brown face was worried. Had she been sitting up each and every night these past ten days waiting for Olivia's return?

Olivia put down her bag at the same time that she glanced quickly, with squinty eyes, at the envelope. It had no return address, but she saw a quetzal on the cancelled stamp, and knew that the letter was from Guatemala. From her mother? That was a laugh. Olivia had written to her at the coffee plantation during her first few months in Mexico, to explain why she had left and to let her know how she was doing. Surely one of the other pickers would have read the letters to her and offered to send a few words back. But Olivia's letters went unanswered and she finally stopped writing.

"I thought you might not come back from Italy—maybe you met someone, fell in love and decided not to come back to us." Melida's voice was reaching her as if traveling through glass. "I'm talking to you, young lady."

Olivia blushed. Her landlady was off the mark, but not by much— Olivia gave her a kiss and said that she would tell her all about it in the morning.

*

When she was alone in her room and certain that Mélida was in hers, Olivia put on the light by her bed and ripped open the envelope. It was from Sister Carina, as she had imagined.

Sister Carina was never prompt in answering her letters, but when she did they would be quite long, with lots of gossipy news about the school and the teachers and always with lots of questions, about her father, her job, Mexico City, her religious habits anything that qualified as news. In her first letter to Olivia, she had been very upset with her for having left the *Colegio Parroquial* before graduating—she was very clear in letting her know how annoyed she was, especially since Olivia had been *her* special scholarship student. In time she had accepted Olivia's explanation, if for no other reason than there was no point in continuing to beat a dead horse.

Olivia had been gone now for almost five years. When a powerful earthquake shook Mexico City in 1986 leveling hundreds of buildings, including tourist hotels and historical landmarks, Sister Carina had sent Olivia a telegram, worried that her prize pupil might have been injured, asking her to get in touch.

Once the telephone lines were back in service, Olivia called Sister Carina at the school though the call had cost her almost a day's salary. The conversation had been short, less than five minutes, and each time one of them spoke, the other would interrupt; then there would be silence on the line until one of them started up again, and the same old pattern began. But at least they had heard each other's voice.

Apparently, Lucia had come to see Sister Carina a few days earlier to find out if she knew how to get in touch with Olivia. Her mother had written to Melchior in Mexico through a scribe, but he had moved again and the letter came back unopened. She then called him from one of the public telephones at the Antigua post office, but the woman who answered started screaming when she heard Melchior's name.

The letter, in Sister Carina's typically elliptical style, went like this:

My beautiful and very special Olivia,

I hope you will forgive me for not having answered your recent letter (not so recent anymore, since you wrote to me a year ago to let me know how you had survived the earthquake. I have to tell you again, before I go on, how wonderful it was to hear your voice, so strong and confident, when we talked that day on the telephone).

I have no legitimate excuse for not writing other than to tell you that the troubles in Guatemala have depressed me more and more and have not only kept me from writing to you and others but has also kept me away from my hours of prayer and meditation. Guatemala has become a very dangerous place— thousands more people have left—some to the Mexican border and beyond, others to temporary camps, still others have disappeared and I fear are buried in mass graves. How can this have happened in this Land of Eternal Spring? I believe that God is punishing us for not having cared strongly enough for all His little lambs to speak up when they were being slaughtered.

Gone is Ríos Montt, the evangelist president who invoked the name of our Savior every time he spoke, and then attacked our Mother Church. He dismissed our protests against the army for killing Indians simply because they did not want to be conscripted into his service. He said that the government, the military and the Church must work together as if they were branches of the same tree. Our great Bishop Gerardi answered him strongly that we in Guatemala were not living in the 12th century needing another Holy Crusade. Thank God that monster is finally gone.

So our new President Cerezo should be better. He has a beautiful wife, but there are already rumors of infidelity and there have been reports that his army is responsible for new massacres in Santiago de Atitlán and El Aguacate.

What homily can I give you that puts all this violence in context and would help you understand how awful all this is? To be honest, my little one, I am a simple nun too old to make sense of what has occurred.

Oh, Olivia you should be grateful you are living in a civilized country so far away from this. Your heart would break, as mine does every day, to see soldiers bayoneting Indians for not moving quickly enough or for not understanding their questions. The abuse of others has become commonplace—even the taking of human life is no longer in the purview of our Creator…I know that what I am about to say is a sin, but I wish I were not here on Earth to bear witness to all this horror. I don't want to take my life, but if something were to happen, I would feel relieved to join my God.

I won't try to soften it, but I have some very bad news for you. Your mother has asked me to write to tell you that your brother Guayo is dead. I still don't know how it happened or why. Your mother blurted out two or three conflicting accounts of how he was killed. I suspect that the reason for this is that she doesn't really know what happened, and she is consumed by grief. The death certificate says he was shot four times—twice in the chest, and once in the stomach and through the neck, she says. We don't know if he was killed by his fellow kaibiles or if he was shot by guerillas. Only pieces of his body were found—

apparently his killers chopped him up to try to obscure his real identity. But you cannot fool a mother, even one as silent and as hardhearted as yours.

The burial happened last month. Of this you can be sure: all our prayers have commended his holy soul to our Creator.

I know that I am asking much of you, but I think that it would please your mother if you were to come to visit. She is very weak and her mind is not operating all that well. She has stopped working in the fields and wants to go back to San Pedro La Laguna and try and make amends with her family. This is not a good idea, because the army is fighting with the Indians there as well. Your mother also has no money.

I wish I could help her. Each time I see her she is more confused. She has begun to talk to the walls and the mirrors. I am seventy-six and have no money either. My joints hurt and I now walk with a cane.

I know she has been harsh with you and I bear some of the responsibility because I took you away from her. You were such a sweet child. I still can hear your voice reading aloud by the stream…

I cannot tell you what you should do—you should pray and let your heart give you counsel..

I should tell you pleasant things as well. I know you like receiving news about your friends or maybe I just like conveying happier stories. I see Jimena almost every week when I go to her father's store. You remember that she married her cousin José Chang Liu, and she has just given birth to twin girls. José works with her father (his uncle) at the La Fe store. Jimena is always there with the girls. She has changed so much, Olivia. She is a quiet, thoughtful woman.

I know you would want to know what has happened to Meme. She is involved in street theater in Guatemala City, has had a child, but did not marry the father. I worry about her because this is not a good moment to make fun of the government.

Olivia, you will do what you can do. But as you mourn your brother, remember the words our Savior said to Martha:

He that believeth in me, though he were dead, yet shall he live. And whosoever liveth and believeth in me shall never die.

May the Lord continue to keep and protect you. We used to
have so much to be grateful for. You were always such a sweet girl.
*   Though I find life very difficult for me, your memory keeps*
me alive.

Yours,
Sister Carina

After reading the letter, Olivia started crying, but the tears got caught
in her throat. She didn't know what to do. One part of her wanted
to turn around, go back to the airport and take the next flight to
Guatemala City. But it was well after midnight and her head hurt so
much that she could barely keep her eyes open.

*

She spent a fitful, restless night. The passing hours brought only more
exhaustion. She was incapable of calming herself and at the same
time unable to pour out her grief. Guayito was dead. Shouldn't she
feel sorrow? She tried to force herself to cry—to feel something—but
she had long ago stopped loving him. At the very least, she should feel
regret, disappointment or pain.

Sister Carina was wrong. Olivia was not sweet. She was a selfish
girl preoccupied by her own issues. She felt nothing, absolutely
nothing over the death of her brother. Still, she had an ache behind
her eyes, which had been aggravated by the whiskies on the airplane..

In the morning, Olivia couldn't eat the breakfast Mélida had left
out for her. She was only able to drink the warm pot of coffee, hoping
the caffeine would help. But as she walked to work, she felt nauseous.
She had used no protection with Máximo; maybe she was, curses,
pregnant! She was hoping that Margarita Canales would fold her into
her arms and simply hold her so that she could finally cry.

The first words out of Isabelle's mouth as soon as she saw her was:
"You look miserable, Olivia."

Concha, the receptionist, shook her head and gave Olivia a kiss.
"Don't listen to her. She's been in a bad mood all week--"

"We've had eight days of cold and rain," Isabelle complained, not
taking her eyes off her computer terminal. "How was Italy?"

Olivia looked dazed. "Where is Margarita?"

"Lucky for you, she decided to visit her daughter in Texas."

"She can't be gone!"

"She is. And I'm surprised you're not grateful."

The one person she wanted to see was not there. Olivia looked around the travel agency and felt thousands of eyes glaring at her. "When I got back last night, Mélida gave me a letter from Sister Carina, the nun who always took care of me," she mumbled. "She wrote to tell me that Guayito, my brother, is dead."

Isabelle looked up from her computer screen. "What happened to him?"

When Olivia looked at her it was now through the thinnest layer of tears. "—It's a bit confusing. He died God knows when and where, but his body was found a few weeks ago." Her voice was flat.

"You poor thing!" Concha hugged her.

"Oh, Olivia. I'm sorry," said Isabelle, finally coming over to comfort her friend. "Is there anything we can do for you? What will you do?"

"I don't know. I feel so lost, so completely lost. I want to cry, but I can't. I wish someone would tell me what to do."

The phone started ringing and Isabelle answered it. Within ten seconds, another phone line rang and Concha was on to it. The day had begun, in full throttle. There was no time to weep or console— the office was short-staffed, with Margarita gone.

Olivia had no choice but to work at her desk at the back of the travel agency.

As luck would have it, Abraham stopped by a few minutes later. He was in his typically garrulous mood, wanting to buy a ticket from Olivia to Guadalajara and Monterrey, but when he walked in, Isabelle shook her head at him.

Olivia was on the phone with a longtime client, trying to be friendly and pleasant, holding her head, with closed eyes. She was utilizing her job voice, a couple of registers above normal: gayness over anything, even if her eyes were red and bleary, her heart in the darkest closet.

Abraham walked through the office and sat down next to her desk. Seeing she was busy, he started leafing through a travel brochure touting the pleasures of Bali and the South Pacific. Once Olivia had finished her call, she stood up and asked him if he would hold her.

Abraham was surprised. He stood up and raised her with his hands. As he put his arms around her, Olivia started crying and talking all at the same time. She told him about everything—Venice, Florence, Milan; Máximo; and finally, about her brother's death—all in a breathless voice as if she were afraid she would be sucked down into a vortex before she got the whole story out.

Abraham simply listened, without his usual banter to lighten the mood. When she stopped, he said: "You know, Olivia, you're young enough to be my daughter—"

"Please Abraham."

He stepped away from her, holding her hands. "No, I mean it. I fear I've been a bad friend to you. You're here all alone. I could have done so much more for you. Taken better care of you—offered you fatherly advice."

Olivia thought of Melchior and started to cry again, imbedding her head into his shoulder.

Abraham continued to hold her, patting her shoulder every so often to console her. He had never been close to a woman, in this way, and it made him feel awkward.

Olivia felt him rocking her gently. She never would have imagined Abraham as the comforting sort. "You wouldn't make such a bad father," she said to him.

"What nonsense," he said, embarrassed by her words.

"No, really. You've got such nice strong arms," Olivia said laughing.

She had been cheated out of her childhood. How nice it would have been to have a father to love her unconditionally, to buy her cotton candy on a stick or a pinwheel in Alameda Park or to take her for tea at the Hotel Regis. Someone who would not be judgmental or curt with her, but embracing and supportive.

Abraham was no taller than Olivia. Though they were well away from earshot, he spoke softly into her ear so only she could hear his words. "We come from the same world, Olivia. We both grew up scraping our feet against dirt floors. It's something we're not likely to forget. But it makes us feel unworthy, as if someone is going to find out that we are imposters."

"I feel so rotten inside. I want something to take this empty feeling away."

"I don't think anything can."

"There has to be something!"

Olivia felt Abraham shaking his head and pulling away from her. "I wish I knew what it was. I've substituted many things, but nothing seems to work. Maybe at this point in my life I should give love a chance," he said.

Something in the way he said this made Olivia giggle. It was all a bit absurd. Leave it to her to finally find a fatherly figure in someone like Abraham—a womanizing playboy—and then discover, all of a sudden, that he ends up turning sentimental on her!

It was too funny for words. "What do you know of love, Abraham? You with your parties, your drinks—"

"And all my women?" he asked.

"Yes—and all your *bosomy* women."

"My dear Olivia, I'm beginning to understand that my dalliances were momentary distractions, entertainment, nothing more. Booze, sex, possessions can go a long way to fill a void. That's what happened in my life. I'm not proud of it, but it's how I've lived. Always for the moment, for what I could get quickly and easily. So you're right— what do I know of love? Absolutely nothing. But this might be a good enough reason to try it out. Don't you think?"

Olivia looked at Abraham. She felt she had gone too far in mocking him. His thick-lidded eyes were red and veined.

"I have no right to judge you," was all she could say.

"I never feel judged by you." Abraham shrugged and sat back down. "Sometimes I think that I do too good a job to cover up my weaknesses."

"What do you mean?" Olivia asked.

He touched her cheek. "It doesn't really matter…I know you're going to laugh at this, but I read somewhere, maybe in the *Advisor* column of what you would call my "disgusting *Playboy*'s," that Plato once said that we're whole in our mother's womb, but once we are born, the wholeness—like a ball—is cut in half. We spend the rest of our lives trying to get the two halves back together again. It's never so simple. No matter what we do, one of the halves is always miles ahead of the other or one step behind and the two parts can never quite come together. Maybe it doesn't happen until we're dead. Certainly once we are dead, we don't have to worry about the stupid halves coming together anymore, do we?"

Olivia sat back down, trying to figure out a way to get the old bravado back in Abie's eyes—to get things on the usual track. Somehow her news about Guayito had sparked his desire to tell her something important.

"And so how does Zimry fit into this?"

Abraham pulled his chair closer to hers. "Well, I know you think she's a silly little thing. She sells perfumes, says stupid things and sometimes drinks too much..." As he talked, Olivia looked down at Abie's hands—they were dark like hers, but thickly veined and splotched with age marks. Though old and tired looking, suddenly they became quite animated. She glanced back at his head—his hair flecked with gray, more age marks on both temples, and at the vortex of his forehead, a widow's peak.

Abraham had aged rapidly. He knew that his days as a so-called playboy were numbered. He wasn't fabulously rich or cultured. He had never been that good-looking, but he had lively, seductive eyes. They were his trademarks—and they had never aged until now.

"Actually, Zimry is not as dumb and frivolous as she sometimes acts. You might not believe this, Olivia, but I think there are lots of things she can do. She knows quite a bit about jewelry and clothes. And she is a natural designer." He said this with almost boyish charm. And then he looked around the agency to make sure neither Concha nor Isabelle could hear him. "You might as well be the first to know, Olivia—Zimry has no idea about this—but I'm going to ask her to marry me."

"No way!" she answered, happy that he had confided in her, but thrown by the confession—too much for an aching head.

"Yes, I know, I know. I'm twice her age, maybe a good deal more. But look—we happen to have a good time together. We enjoy each other's company. I at least enjoy hers and I think the feeling is mutual."

Olivia raised an eyebrow. "You decided to marry her just like that?"

"Yes," he said, knowingly, "just like that! But also not just like that—we share this yoga thing, the macrobiotic diet—and she gets so excited when I buy her things. With me she can stop selling perfume and if she wants, she can open a boutique or art gallery—maybe even sell Horacio's photographs. Zimry is quite versatile. I don't know if I told you that she has become a serious student of Tarot. She has been studying it for some time now—"

Olivia felt her dark mood lifting and she wasn't at all upset that Abraham had forgotten completely about her news. It was sweet, the way he was talking, with a bold, spirited voice.

Now that he was "grown up," Abraham might end up being a generous husband, loving and attentive. Olivia suddenly understood why Zimry might love him back and she felt envious, but not in a hurtful, spiteful sort of way. Simple jealousy.

"And you're sure that Zimry loves you."

She half-expected him to be shaken, thrown into doubt by the question—as she would've been—but he was as bubbly as ever. "My dear Olivia, to be honest, I really don't know a thing about her feelings or her motives. Maybe Zimry has been scheming to marry me all along and take me for all I'm worth—which isn't much. I suppose I could come up with some sort of a nuptial agreement where if we divorce, we both come out of the marriage just as we went in. But I can't live that way. I never have. Life's a crapshoot. I'm in the habit of throwing the dice and waiting to see how they come up. Seven come eleven. In the meantime, life should be fun—"

"Well, congratulations!" Olivia said, hugging him.

"Thank you," he replied, with twinkling eyes. "But please keep it a secret between us."

"My lips are sealed," she answered.

*

Olivia did not fly back to Guatemala. She felt the moment of her return had passed—all that she'd see of her brother would be a cross on a dirt mound, a handful of flowers, some squiggly words written in cheap, grainy paint on a piece of plywood. And though Sister Carina had said that her mother was not doing well, Olivia didn't want to see her. Not yet. She couldn't imagine embracing a woman who when her mind was right, hardly "remembered" her.

Perhaps it was cruel of her not to go back. Her mother had made her own decisions in life and Olivia felt that she hadn't existed to be the ideal daughter to a mother who had been substantially less than ideal. And yes, she was sick—maybe Guayito's death had somehow accelerated her dementia. But why go back now, just when she was beginning to put her life together?

She would only end up sinking deeper into a depressing swamp.

In the end, she suspected that her mother wasn't as sick as she acted. It was simply a ruse to get Olivia to come back and once there, she would begin heaping abuse upon her again. Lucia was skilled at finding ways to ridicule her accomplishments over so many years. Wasn't this their personal dance? The kindest words her mother had ever said to her was when Olivia had asked, begged her really, for words of support, for the words a mother would offer an ugly child who asked her mother for assurance. Lucia had answered quite cynically and mechanically: In *My* Eyes, You Are Beautiful.

What was that worth? Was it enough? Would that ever be enough?

*

Abraham's confession jarred her, made her re-exam her own situation. Within the week, Olivia decided to call Horacio at the shoe store. He was surprised to hear from her. To her questions, he could only mumble one-syllable answers and twice mistakenly called her Alma, his mother's name.

"Abraham told me about your mother dying. I'm so sorry. Did you get my postcard from Italy?"

"Yes. It arrived at our old apartment in Narvarte. After she died, I decided to move to Condesa, much closer to the shoe store. I enjoyed the photo of the Sistine Chapel."

Olivia laughed. "You know, Horacio—I never even made it there. One day in Florence, I went to a tobacco shop and bought all these pretty postcards from the places I should have visited in Italy, but never did—"

"Same Olivia," he said, and she could imagine him shaking his head and smiling.

"Same Olivia, but different," she answered him.

"Same Horacio, only different," he said back to her, not pausing.

"Touché."

Horacio was silent at the other end. If Olivia was different, so was he: more reserved, less solicitous. Once burned, twice shy, and he was monumentally injured, less willing to be drawn in. And after all his mother, the only person with whom he had ever lived, had died.

"I know I said some awful things last time we were together. I don't know what got into me. I can only apologize for that. You deserve better."

He waited for her to continue speaking. "Can I ask you a question, Horacio?"

"Sure, anything you'd like," he said, barely able to get the words out of his mouth, "but I can't stay on too long. I have to get back to a client."

"Do you think if I called you next week, perhaps we could get together and talk?"

All the ugly things that Olivia had said had hurt him deeply, but Horacio was not a vengeful man, one who carried a grudge. With a flick of the wrist, insults could be easily forgotten. Surely, words were not blows, and there were no broken chairs or jagged pieces of porcelain to speak of. Just a broken, sullen heart.

And he was quite lonely living alone.

"The things you said to me were not only unnecessary, but quite mean."

His directness surprised her. "They were," she answered him.

"I don't want to be treated like that," he said sharply into the phone receiver. "I won't let you talk to me that way. I deserve to be treated with respect—the same respect you would give to someone or something you care for."

Horacio had change, and it had nothing to do with being reserved. On the contrary, he seemed sure of himself, almost self-confident, without really coming across smug. This was new—it was as if he finally valued himself, instead of being so willing to accept any kindness with utter gratefulness.

Olivia liked that change. It was something that she hoped would last.

"I'm so sorry, Horacio. Really I am."

"I hope you really are."

"I would like to see your face," Olivia said to him.

And he surprised her by saying. "We'll see, Oli—give me a call next week."

*

He had called her Oli. She felt pleased after she hung up, as if the dark clouds that had been barely parted by Abraham's confession had been completely dissipated by Horacio's words.

She sat quietly at her desk, smiling at the posters of Italy on the wall.

Horacio was no Máximo, but he was pleasant looking and she liked kissing his lips, which were soft like Meme's.

His way of speaking had always been measured, but now he pronounced his words with varying emphasis, as if he had understood that not all things in life were equal. And he had a nice voice. The scene at the restaurant, his mother's death, the solitude that followed had changed him.

Olivia felt excited about the thought of seeing him. They hadn't seen each other for well over a year.

He is nice-looking, Olivia repeated to herself. And though his eyes were not lively like Máximo's or Abraham's, for example, they had the kind of warmth that could please her, give her a sense of calm.

These were such odd thoughts for Olivia to have, when in fact Horacio had spent much of the phone conversation scolding her for the way she had mistreated him.

You used to love me, Horacio. Will you give me a second chance?

To love and be loved in return, she remembered this verse from a song.

It was after six in the evening. It was raining once again. Concha and Isabelle had left together sharing an umbrella, locking the front door so no one else could come in.

The lights from the streetlamps were dancing and the tree branches, shuffled by the wind, swayed.

She wasn't bothered by the searing, horizontal rain. The way he had shortened her name—Oli—was to her a kind of hope, at that moment, made of pure gold.

(1990)

Olivia couldn't believe it--the Aviateca flight from Mexico to
Guatemala was taking less than two hours when the long overland trip
of eight years ago had taken more than two days! Traveling by land,
she had been so aware of how slowly things had changed—mountains
to jungle, colorful costumes to sober outfits, thatched roof and adobe
houses to concrete homes, thick billowy, funnel clouds to wispy white
cotton threads! She half-expected the airplane to alight on a runway on
the border, forcing her and the other passengers to disembark to show
their identification papers to customs officials brandishing rifles and
machine guns.

What a world of difference, she thought, as her flight swooped over
the lush mountains and volcanoes rimming Guatemala City—she felt
her sense of hope, which she identified with Mexico City—dissipate
and be replaced by all the doubts and memories of Guatemala, woven to
form a gloomy, indecipherable tapestry, as soon as the airplane dropped
its wheels for the final approach to the runway. And after the airplane
had pulled into the gate, and Olivia had walked off the moveable
bridge into the Aurora Airport concourse, it struck her that she was
not returning home as much as revisiting the scene of a horrid crime.
She was not a returning witness or wrongly accused defendant—
she was the victim, and the panic, the tightening of her throat, the
syncopated beat of her eye twitching was the simple proof. Yes, the
inviting smells of Pollo Campero and the stalls of Indian fabrics could
distract the other arriving passengers—such innocents!—but the
groups of armed soldiers in green fatigue packing machine guns by
the baggage area and the second-floor balcony or the blue-uniformed
police hovering nervously in groups of two by the cab stands aroused
in her sheer terror.

For a brief moment, she considered going back upstairs to the
Aviateca ticket office and simply buying her return to Mexico,

*but then her sense of mission overcame her fears. She had things
to do.*

*

*Olivia got into a taxi to take the forty-minute ride from the airport to
Antigua and Ciudad Vieja.*

*"First time in Guatemala?" the gray-haired diminutive driver asked
her, once he had placed her bag in the oversized trunk of his 50s black
Packard. He wore dark slacks and a Momostenango sweater over his
white shirt and tie. Sitting in the back seat, Olivia could see that his
collar was wrinkled, badly frayed. She could smell his sweat and the
cheap cologne which attempted to disguise it.*

*"No, I was born in San Pedro La Laguna," Olivia answered,
surprised that the driver hadn't recognized a fellow Chapín. "Well, my
mother's from there. I was actually born in Sololá."*

*"Aha. Of course," he replied, taciturnly, having realized his error.
He was so typically Guatemalan: Curious enough to be polite but
reserved enough not to ask any more questions. And certainly incapable
of admitting to a mistake.*

*He drove cautiously with both hands on the steering wheel as if his
grip kept the car from barreling off the road.*

*

*It was nearly five o'clock when the Packard climbed out of the city
plateau. Olivia saw off to the left, as the cab struggled over the mountains
encircling the capital, a red sun gamely trying to provide some light
above the yellow blanket of smog that hung over the huge buildings
that stuck out from the surface of flatlands. Many single-level homes
in the center of Guatemala City had been knocked down and replaced
by modern high rises since she had left five years earlier and the result
was a jagged, confusing skyline. Slums had grown like a cancer in all
directions around the city center, smothering the plateau, climbing up
the precipitous hills, drawing down into the steepest ravines.*

*Decades of Civil War and mass killings had had their effect on the
edges of the capital, converting woodland and birdsong into wretched
slums. The garbage dumps, which had once been hidden from sight*

east and south of the airport, sprouted everywhere—they were now home to hundreds of Indians who had been forced off their lands by the government Civil Defense patrols and had taken residence in putrid shantytowns. And beyond the Roosevelt Hospital, along the road leading into the mountains toward Sacatepequez, which half a dozen years ago had been a fragrant forest of pine and eucalyptus, fires now smoldered and birds of ash danced to the sky.

Olivia closed her eyes. Twenty minutes of the tug-of-war between memory and reality had exhausted her. And what would it be like to see her mother, with whom she had shared the most painful years of her youth? What physical changes had she endured? Would she be gray and thin, or black haired and big bellied?

Olivia had waited for two years to pass after Guayito had died and had only decided to return because Sister Carina had called her insisting that this was the time for her to return. Somehow the kind nun had managed to place Doña Lucia in a "asilo de ancianos" on the road to Los Aposentos; Sister Carina had described it to Olivia as a Church-sponsored nursing home for its fervent, but nearly indigent, congregants.

Sister Carina herself would be leaving the next day, to join a younger brother who had moved to Toronto ten years earlier. He had married a Canadian woman there and had two children. As the violence increased and the church was becoming more vulnerable—hadn't Father Gerardi been forced to close the Santa Cruz del Quiché diocese under the threat of murder?—he pleaded for her to join them. Sister Carina was too old and too frail to remain in the convent with the other nuns. "It's not that my faith has failed me, Olivia, it's that the cries of my family have been heard. And I wanted you to know where you could find your mother before I left. Do you remember when Sister Bonifacia would say over and over again to you girls: Be not overcome with evil—"

"—but overcome evil with good," Olivia rejoined, almost shouting into the telephone, pleased at herself for having remembered.

"Well, yes, my dearest Olivia, that's what she used to say. But there's no reason for me to stay here anymore. I can't see what role to play. Satan has been crowned king. Murder and dismemberment are the orders of the day. And there are few places to find good."

"You're frightening me, Sister Carina," Olivia had whispered.

"We are all scared. The sadness of each day is about to stop my heart."

*

Olivia checked into the Hotel Aurora a few short blocks from where the crumbling San José Cathedral kept silent vigil over the tree-filled parque central. The Aurora was a charming hotel in an old colonial building; it had two iron filigree gates, by a bakery that was now closed for the night, and a vast grassy courtyard surrounded by guestrooms. In the center of the courtyard was a lighted celestial blue fountain, whose softly gurgling water melded into the last cricket sounds of the night.

The night clerk gave Olivia a room with a queen-sized bed and a private bath. Olivia had stayed in hotels much more luxurious, but never in Guatemala. When she had picked coffee less than two miles away from the Hotel Aurora—or later when she walked by the hotel on her way to see Hermano Pedro de Betancourt at the San Francisco Church—she never ever would have imagined that one day she would be staying there, a guest in a room with a four-poster bed, mahogany dressers, an antique carved mirror, a bathroom with a porcelain tub and a ceramic jug of water to wash her face before going to sleep.

After so much traveling, Olivia was hungry. She went upstairs to eat at Doña Luisa's, a restaurant on the second story of the hotel. She took a table overlooking the 4ta Calle. Her window opened onto a balcony, beyond which she could see the dark outline of the Volcán de Agua above the red roofed houses. Lights flickered along the slopes of the volcano, except near the top, which was enveloped in a black beard of darkness—she remembered when she had climbed it with her schoolmates and slept snugly in the cone, after the terrifying ash spewed by the Pacaya Volcano.

It was all so serene now, in the moonlight.

A young waitress in a wrap-around Indian skirt and an embroidered red blouse brought her the menu. Instrumental Carlos Antonio Jobim music was playing. The restaurant was empty except for a middle-aged American couple talking softly to each other. The man was holding the woman's hands and looking into her eyes as she spoke to him: they seemed to be very much in love. Olivia thought of Horacio and *felt reassured. She ordered a hamburgesa, which she ate with a tall glass of horchata.*

Olivia was dead tired when she crawled into her bed. She wanted to sleep deeply but instead found herself waking up almost every hour with unquenchable thirst. She would drink a glass of water and get back into bed. Then around 4 AM she developed a blistering headache. She tried resting quietly on her back but the early morning passing of buses awakened her. She stayed open-eyed, listening to a little ringing bell announcing the garbage truck as it moved down the block. She glanced at her watch. It was six o'clock. Someone put on a radio; scratchy marimba music, El Rancho Grande, came on.

Olivia's head throbbed with each skip of the needle. It was time to get up.

After showering and dressing, she ate a continental breakfast at one of the small tables around the courtyard. The sun was climbing over the rooftops and sending a spray of light over the fountain into her eyes. She drank her coffee black, hoping it would calm her pulsing temples.

The coffee failed her; Olivia was resigned to having a headache badger her for the rest of the day.

*

She wished she could have seen Meme, but Sister Carina had lost contact with her. Right-wing death squads had threatened her after she left the theater company in Guatemala City to perform on her own. They were not pleased by her first performance piece, in which she walked barefoot around Guatemala City dressed in black like a nun, with her painted face issuing out of a hood and a noose around her head. She wasn't a stupid girl—when she was asked by reporters who she was, she said her name was Malinche, a Mexican Indian girl who had been Hernán Cortés' translator, and her mother was La Llorona—the Weeping Woman.

Every morning Meme could be seen by the Cathedral or at the entrance to the National Palace or in the park across sitting stone-faced on a bench, with her roped neck hanging down. She was a nuisance, frightening away commerce and tourists, and responsible for why business had plummeted in the little stores by the Portal. And when the Prensa Libre *reported that she had given up her only child for adoption*

(Sister Carina had sent Olivia the article), she had declared that Guatemala was a country of orphans and bastards, a death pit. To bring up children in this sort of environment without acknowledging this truth was a sin, a deadly sin, like rape and murder. In fact, she announced that she had donated her daughter to one of the orphanages that had been accused of trafficking in children—stealing them from their poor parents in Mixco or Zunil—and selling them to rich Americans in the United States who could not have children.

"One less bastard in this country won't hurt," she had said. And she donated the five hundred quetzales that she had received for her daughter from the orphanage to the Guatemalan chapter of the Red Cross...

One day, Meme simply had disappeared—the Cerezo government said she was living safely in Houston, but Human Rights Groups claimed she had been kidnapped, dismembered and her limbs and trunk thrown like the pieces of a puzzle into any of a number of recently discovered mass graves.

*

Olivia decided to walk to her mother's nursing home, just across the town square on the edge of the outdoor market. A waitress at the hotel had laughed when Olivia mentioned the Asilo Aposentos, saying it was more a lunatic asylum than a nursing home.

"No matter what the Church says," the waitress had added, "all the people in there are crazy."

Olivia walked by Almacén La Fe. She saw a woman, with straight hair and thick lensed-glasses who might have been Jimena, leaning against a display case. Should she go in? What would she say? Olivia kept on walking—what would have been the point of reuniting, admitting that she had been a coffee picker's daughter all along and finally exchanging tales of how their lives had changed?

At the Asilo entrance, a woman in a nurse's outfit greeted her. She warned Olivia that her mother was now refusing to get out of bed. "Miss Olivia," said the diminutive woman in a starched light blue uniform and white cap, "there is nothing wrong with your mother's legs. The doctors have examined her. She could easily get by with a cane. She simply does not want to walk anymore."

"What about her mind?"

The nurse hesitated in answering. *"That's another matter. Her mind walks where few feet have gone."*

On the way to her mother's room, Olivia passed a woman sitting on a cast iron chair in the courtyard, surrounded by large ceramic planters filled with geraniums. She was talking to an imaginary person sitting on a chair across from her: *"Bring me my black shoes. Bring me my black shoes. I want them now. For the love of God, bring me my black shiny shoes."*

She would wait a few seconds and the litany would begin again.

When the woman saw Olivia she looked up at her and said, *"You look like an honest soul: will you bring me my black shoes?"*

Olivia smiled back nervously.

The woman reached out to her: *"They say all my shoes are brown. But I know they're not. If you see my black shoes, please bring them to me."*

Her mother's room was on the second floor. As Olivia reached the stairs, she ran into a pregnant young girl of about sixteen who stopped her and said that her name was Ruth Ortiz. She told Olivia that she didn't want to bother her, but that she looked as if she lived outside the Nursing Home and maybe she could help her. She was from Mazatenango and all her life she had wanted to be an honest to goodness clown, a she-clown, though it might sound crazy. She knew that in Guatemala there were no clown schools, but maybe Olivia knew where she could get a book about make up and clown costumes and stunts and tricks. She said that she was here because she was an orphan, and that the nuns had taken pity on her, but that she knew that there was a big future in circus work, especially in a country like Guatemala that was so sad and where laughs were in short demand...

Before Olivia could answer her, a nurse came up and said: *"There you are, Zoila."*

"My name is Ruth. I've told you that several times. And I have a sister named Marcela."

The nurse took her gently by the elbow. *"Yes, Ruth, I've been looking for you in the library to give you your medicine. Let's go upstairs."*

The nurse winked at Olivia, indicating that she should go up the stairs first.

*

Olivia found her mother's room in the middle of the western corridor. Lucia was sitting up in her bed, leaning against two straw pillows, motionless under her white sheets. She had aged terribly in five years, and she was more wizened than ever. A nurse had propped her up in bed, as if this would make her more presentable. Her eyes were wide, as if jacked open with little wires. She seemed to be looking out toward the façade of the Church and Convent of La Merced through the room's one window. Lucia turned in Olivia's direction when she heard her enter the room.

"Mami."

Her mother smiled at her and said: "Rake. Rake."

"It's me. Olivia."

Her mother kept smiling and then closed her eyes. "Olivia," she whispered. "Did I tell you that I am now a dryer and soon I'll be working in the beneficio?"

The nurse who had escorted Ruth to her room called out from the lintel. "Her eyes are open but I don't think that Lucia can see you. Her brain doesn't register what her eyes might see. Think of it as a movie camera projecting out the wrong picture…In fact, she seems more alert when she closes her eyes."

"Rake. Rake." Her mother repeated.

Olivia came and caressed her mother's crinkled forehead. Lucia took her hand and started rubbing it against her cheek. She began singing a little nursery song:

"Allá en la fuente habia un chorrito
Se hacia grandote, se hacia chiquito
Estaba de mal humor,
Pobre chorrito tenía calor."

She repeated this verse several times and then said "Rake, Rake."

"I'll leave the two of you alone," the nurse said, "so you can talk in privacy."

Olivia glared back at her. What privacy, what talk? She could feel anger percolating inside of her. "Mamí, I love you so much. I'm sorry, I'm so sorry. What have they done to you?"

Olivia held her mother who stiffened at her embrace. "Rake, rake," she repeated. "Everybody loves me especially when I am raking the coffee beans."

Olivia kissed her creased face. "Mami, I didn't mean to leave you, but I had to go away. Can you understand that? I couldn't stay here. I couldn't. I would've ended up pregnant and unhappy—"

"Rake. Rake."

"—Mami, I'm glad you don't have to pick coffee anymore. Soon you won't even have to rake. You'll be able to relax. Take it easy. Olivia will be with you. I'll rake. I'll take care of you. You can stay home and rest."

Olivia stayed with her mother throughout the morning. For brief moments it seemed as if her mere presence relaxed Lucia, and she would close her eyes, but then she would go back to her open-eyed repetitions, which grew steadily more anxious. At mid-morning, a nurse came back and changed her soiled diaper and rubbed down her bony body with alcohol. Olivia saw the purple bruises forming blood masses on her legs and the way her bones nearly pierced the skin.

It was more than Olivia could bear. She told the nurse that she would return in the afternoon, though she wasn't sure that she would.

Olivia walked out of the nursing home across from the San Merced Church plaza. She felt hungry. She walked down the Calle de la Recolección, which skirted Antigua's oldest ruins. She remembered that one day during her first year at the Colegio Parroquial, she had skipped classes to chase the lizards among the huge fallen stones. There had been lots of crickets, and a bright cardinal that seemed to be sleeping on a eucalyptus branch.

At the Alameda de Santa Lucia, Olivia turned left and walked another two blocks until she reached the market in front of the new bus station. She was hungry and thirsty. She stopped at a puesto next to a spice shop and ordered a batido of platano and papaya, and two pork tacos with red sauce and grated cheese. As she ate, she listened to an old cassette of Agustín Lara singing Solamente una vez. She felt melancholy, listening to this song about how long ago, a woman had submitted her soul to a lover and the bells of happiness had rung in her heart.

If the woman was truly happy, why was Lara singing the verses so sadly?

Olivia felt dazed. Her childhood had been spent in a finca less than a mile away; her adolescence in a school just five blocks away; and less than three minute's from here, her mother was dying, slipping in and out of dementia, projecting a film that made no sense.

Tears began threading their way down Olivia's face.

The woman who had brought her food and drink asked: "What's wrong, my angel?"

Olivia looked up at her and shook her head. Augustín Lara was now singing María Bonita *from the record shop right behind her. Olivia wanted to get off her stool and ask the shop owner please, for the love of God, couldn't he put on something more festive? This song of love and betrayal was piercing her heart.*

"Your boyfriend has tricked you, hasn't he?" The woman asked, with her large yellow teeth shining back at her. "They use words as easily as we women shuck corn."

"It's nothing like that," Olivia said, wiping her tears. If anything, she had found peace with Horacio. In the year apart, he had become a man; and in the two years that they had been together, his quiet strength—reflected in his lovemaking as well—had managed to calm her. They had found a way to love one another—to make the act of lovemaking the finding of peace.

"La Locha knows everything about betrayal and heartbreak."

Olivia laughed out loud, opened her purse and pulled out five quetzales. "Thank you, but I must get back to my mother."

"You have change coming," the woman said. "The winds are blowing away the flying snakes—"

But by then Olivia was back on the streets.

Outside, people were rushing towards the buses. The sky had opened up and the rain was beginning to fall in huge cold pellets. The Volcán de Agua to the south was enveloped in menacing clouds that seemed twisted and gnarled.

Olivia hurried back to her mother's Asilo, clinging to building walls and eaves to keep from getting wet.

Her mother was curled up toward her bedroom wall when Olivia walked in. Lucia turned to the door and smiled, opening her eyes.

"Rake, rake."

Olivia tried to make cheerful conversation with her mother, despite the sense that Lucia's mind was quite gone. Why had Olivia come back? She would have done better to live with the memory of never seeing her mother again, to simply learn about her death by telephone and come back to Guatemala to bury her in a plain coffin. Anything but seeing her mother distraught, so much the victim, so pitiful that Olivia could forget the lack of love she received.

Olivia felt she was a child again, lonely, lost, powerless, cast out and searching everywhere for a pair of loving arms to embrace her.

Olivia went to her mother's side and sat her up in the bed. "Mommy, it's me, your daughter, Olivia. Your only daughter, remember? I want you to close your eyes and listen to me." Olivia took a Kleenex and wiped the drool from the corners of Lucia's mouth.

Her mother repeated "rake" twice before she closed her eyes.

As Olivia stroked Lucia's hair, she told her mother all about Horacio. She told her how they had been living together for the last year in an apartment in the Colonia del Valle, off Insurgentes, not far from Chapultepec Park in Mexico City. As the months passed, Horacio was spending less time at his shoe store and devoting more of his energy to his photography—in fact, he had converted one of the bedrooms into a dark room. He was a good man, sensible and loving, with traditional values—perfect for the small-town girl she was. His quiet strength meant a lot to her—next year they would get married, not in a church but at the Club Francés.

Margarita and Abraham had offered to pay for the wedding—Margarita giving away the bride and Abraham having a duel role as best man and "father" of the groom. Isabelle the bride's maid, Concha the flower girl.

And soon, they would have a child of their own.

"I don't know if you would like Mexico City, but I'm sure you would love Horacio."

*

Olivia had, for so long, believed that the life she lived was unreal—that one day, through the intervention of San Antonio del Monte or a miracle of Hermano Pedro, her suffering would lift and her true destiny revealed. It was the dream of her riding the sun-powered oxcart like a chariot up through the sky into the vault of heaven.

But so much had happened since then.

What she had learned in the past year was that this was her life and if she could learn to savor it, it was sweet. Maybe this was some sort of variation of Máximo's saying la dolce far niente. *What she had come to discover was that every morning life, like the daylight, was born anew. No matter what happened, what tragedies befell individuals or families* or even nations, life would continue as surely as the sun would rise up. It didn't matter if a bank of clouds prevented it from streaming through a window. It was always there. Life was not a dream but something real and palpable—it was a deep ocean crawling with grouper, tiger fish, smelt, minnows, needlefish, bass, bream and more than a few barracudas, moray eels and sharks. And it went on and on, constantly changing, slippery to grasp—but it was something to marvel at—until it came to an end.

Olivia knew that her mother was near that end. There was nothing she could do or say that would ease, delay or prevent her death. Lucia's life was slipping through her own hands. Olivia held her in her arms, stroking her, and talked to her for a good while longer that afternoon. And as she was about to leave, she kissed her on the forehead and sang to her the verses that Sister Carina used to sing to her:

Oh, had I the wings of the dove
I would fly away and join my love